COFFEE   JONATHAN
MYSTERIOUS   HOUSE
MABERRY   GALAXY   SUPPORTING
WRITERS   THANKS
.

The Faith Machine

Tone Milazzo

The Faith Machine text copyright © Tone Milazzo
Edited by Benjamin White

Published in North America and Europe by Running Wild Press. Visit Running Wild Press at www.runningwildpress.com Educators, librarians, book clubs (as well as the eternally curious), go to www.runningwildpress.com for teaching tools.

ISBN (pbk) 978-1-947041-47-9
ISBN (ebook) 978-1-947041-48-6

Printed in the United States of America.

Chapter 1

To say the Colonial Motel was past its prime assumed it ever had one. Run-down, infested by a dozen kinds of vermin, and stuck between cities off I-94's run through Indiana, the motor lodge was a good place to make a drug deal and a likely place to get robbed.

Which summed up Park and Ainia's evening.

Dr. Ken Park sat, back against the bed, and stared at the lamp's torn shade. He was no stranger to hallucinogens, but the woman's psychic attack had sucker-punched him in the prefrontal cortex. His pistol lay on the stained carpet, empty and out of reach. Colors still pulsed and shadows twitched, but he'd straightened out for the most part. The trip felt like hours. The clock said fifteen minutes.

Sweat ran into his eyes as he crawled toward the open door after Ainia, his best agent. She'd chased after the psychic and her boyfriend. No telling what would happen out there if the woman's card — jargon for psychic power — had set Ainia tripping too. The mission might be a wash. What mattered now though was her safety.

Ainia dropped into the doorway, curled in a squat, like a cat ready to pounce. She was dressed in a sports bra and shorts, hair cut short like a boy's, body a tight coil of muscle, her life written across it in scars. Park knew most of the stories. None were pretty.

"Ainia," he mumbled, "it's fading. Just another ten—"

She closed her eyes and hissed.

He rose to his heels, hands up. "Stay calm, wait this out, and you'll be fine." An aggravated, hallucinating Ainia scared him more than the unexpected trip did.

She caught him looking at his gun. "Don't bother. I'm fine." She rolled inside, leaned against the bed, and covered her eyes. "Wouldn't do you any good, even if it was loaded."

He waited on the floor with her for a few more minutes, until the shadows stopped flowing. "I'm good now. How about you?"

She nodded. "Why'd you unload your gun? You should've been firing it."

He gathered the pistol and empty magazine. "Those two were gone before I could draw. I didn't want to risk shooting you." He picked bullets out of the worn carpet, loading the pistol magazine with sweaty, shaking fingers. A round slipped out of his grip, arcing through the air.

She caught it and handed it back. "How sweet."

He slid the magazine back into his pistol. "What happened to your shirt?"

"I tore it off, thought it was filled with bugs, hundreds of biters. In this place it might have been. Still, maybe the cops were right. Could that be some kind of aerosol weapon?"

He shook his head, stood, and jammed the pistol back into its underarm holster. "The cops didn't know what they were dealing with. It sure wasn't like any drug I've ever tried. I think the woman was the psychic we're looking for. Everything went weird after she hit that snuff bullet."

"Snuff bullet? I thought that was some kind of asthma medicine. What if she's not psychic? What if it's in the drug itself?"

"Then we'd be in a lot of trouble. Fortunately, cards are in people, not chemicals. It's psychosomatic. Ingesting the drug just activates her card."

The empty spot on the floor between their bags reminded Park of his failure. The bait had been too good. A ten-pound bag of sugar pills, pressed to look like Sudafed. The tweaker and her boyfriend had snatched it and run. "Shit. Have we ever had a mission go south so fast before?"

She stood and loosened up her neck. "Doesn't matter. We fall, we learn, we get up, and try again."

He checked himself in the bathroom mirror. His hair was stuck to his forehead with sweat. "I look like crap."

She pulled a yellow lacrosse ball out of her gym bag and idly began rolling it back and forth between her hands with hypnotic grace. "At least we identified the target. I bet you're glad we didn't have the real stuff with us."

He washed his face. "That'd be great if we were here to flood the market with dummy meth. But our mission was to evaluate the psychic. Now they're gone, and I didn't even get a chance to talk to her."

"You think an addict is Project Dead Blind material?" She took her turn at the sink.

He peeled off his sweaty coat and shirt. "They deserve a chance, like everyone else. The new girl, Agent Gabby, she's in recovery and has a lot of potential."

The hotel phone rang. She stopped the ball, balancing it on the back on one finger. "Is that who I think it is?"

He shrugged and went to pick up the phone. "We won't know until we answer will we?" He lifted the receiver. "Hello?"

"Hi, Dr. Park. It's Exposition Joe." He nodded at Ainia. She threw her hands up and stepped back. The chipper-voiced teen continued, "You ever heard of urban decay?"

"I'm…" Park sighed, bracing himself for another asymmetric conversation with Project Dead Blind's precognate. "I'm aware cities aren't exempt from the force of entropy. If that's what you mean, Joe."

"Kinda. More like the people who are all about it. They take pictures of ruined old buildings and post them online. Sometimes they break into places, like this water park in Indiana, Splash Down Dunes. It used to be an amusement park called Enchanted Forest. I guess it's still amusing, if you think about it —"

"Are you saying our target robbed us, then ran off to an abandoned water park?"

"Something like that. When you go there, you'll see what you need to see. Hey, I gotta go. Say hi to Ainia for me." Joe hung up.

He put the phone back in its cradle. "Joe says hi."

"Yeah. Great." She rocked the lacrosse ball on the back of her hand. "What else did he say?"

"He told me about an abandoned water park near here." Park powered up his satphone and called up the map.

Ainia flipped the ball over, snatching it in the palm of her hand. "'Near here'? How does he know where 'here' is? He's not on this mission. I don't trust Joe."

"The same way he knew the phone number to this room."

"That doesn't answer my question."

He didn't have an answer that would satisfy her. "But he's never wrong. Let's see this abandoned water park."

She dropped the ball back into her bag. "If you're lucky, the balloon animal guy will still be around."

"I can make my own balloon animals," he said, a note of defensiveness in his voice.

She cast a skeptical look in his direction, but reconsidered. "You probably can, too. Dork."

Real Name: Ken Park or Park Hyun-Ki
Born: 1985 Centreville, VA
Lives: Washington DC
Appearance: Asian (Korean), black hair, black eyes, 5'7", thin build

A spy before he graduated from sixth grade, Agent Park self-trained in sleight of hand, lock picking, information gathering, technology, and surveillance.

He came to Project Dead Blind's attention after exposing his eighth grade math teacher for selling grades in an elaborate sting operation, which started with statistical analysis of data, and ended with Park averting a violent confrontation with the teacher and his three sons. He sealed them in their car with fast-drying epoxy.

Since then, I've groomed Park to be the field leader for the Office of Intergovernmental and External Affairs, as my knees weren't going to be up to the job forever. I guided his education through a BA in Cognitive Psychology, a PhD in Abnormal Psychology as well as the best training the private sector has to offer.

Park is skilled and capable, but soft, maybe too soft for this work. I intended for him to be my successor, but I'm starting to wonder if his leadership has hit its limit in the field.

   -James Ensign

Chapter 2

They cleaned up and changed—Ainia into blue coveralls and ball cap, Park into a black suit with clipboard in hand. The agents climbed into her pickup, orange in the yellow light of the parking lot. According to the GPS, the remains of Splash Down Dunes were an hour's drive away. Night gave way to dawn as they pulled off the highway and parked by the gate.

A man on a dark green-and-black sport motorcycle in matching racing suit and helmet pulled into the parking lot, a hard-shell backpack strapped to his back. He circled around the lot, leaving the way he came. Ainia watched him go. "Didn't expect to see a rice-burner here in Harley country."

Park slid a pair of lock picks out of his belt buckle. "Maybe he's looking for a way out?"

"Just cruising on by, that look suspicious to you?"

"Like he wants to be seen?" The padlock on the gate popped open in Park's capable hands. "Sounds like every guy on a motorcycle."

The agents wandered the park together, looking for what Exposition Joe said they needed to see. Weeds burst through seams in the concrete and asphalt. Despite their abandonment, the tangle of fiberglass tubes and water slides retained their cheery disposition. Bright primary colors retained their vibrancy; a touch sun-bleached on the edges. Marred by spray paint and scuff marks, the park showed telltale signs of skateboarder appropriation.

Ainia fished her lacrosse ball out of the coverall's pocket and bounced it off a concession stand. "Sun's up. Sure no one's going to notice us out here like this?"

"They'll notice. They won't care. With a suit, clipboard, and the right attitude you can go anywhere. Watch." He demonstrated by glaring at the horizon like it was late. "You'd be surprised where this expression has taken me. Having you along as a contractor— that seals the deal. Let's point in case someone is looking."

"Point where?"

"There." He pointed.

"At what?"

"Nothing. It doesn't matter, just point with me."

She aimed her finger halfheartedly with him.

"See? We look like professionals." He grinned.

She rolled her eyes and wandered between a pair of concrete dolphin statues, one of which had "Suck your own dick" spray-painted on its side. She sized up one of the park's taller slides. "How about I take a look from higher ground?"

Park nodded. "But be careful, this place is condemned."

"Don't worry. I'm a professional." She jumped up on the side of a tubular water slide and scaled its twenty feet, swinging hand over hand as if she were on a set of monkey bars. "You know, because I'm wearing coveralls."

She got to the top of the slide, outlined against the early morning light. "Here, let me point at something."

Ainia pointed in the distance for a second before dropping her arm and squinting, then dropping to her belly, hiding.

Park watched her from ground level. "What's up?"

"I hate to admit it, but I see a light. In the shelter on the top of those long red slides. Toss me the binos."

He threw a small pair of binoculars up to her. "Sounds like a good place for a lab. Above the rest of the buildings for ventilation, no neighbors to see anything suspicious, pour the waste down the slide. I bet the pool at the bottom is disgusting."

"Doesn't look like a lab to me. The psychic, her boyfriend, and a lot of five-gallon jugs. He's shaking one and its insides are burning."

"That's not good. They're using the 'shake and bake' method to cook meth—throw everything in a bottle and—"

A series of loud pops interrupted him.

The distant lab erupted in a ball of smoke and fire.

Ainia dropped the binoculars down to Park. "I think our problem just solved itself."

"Shit." Park's shoulders sank as he watched the ball of black smoke rise. "What a damn, pointless waste."

3 of Diamonds

Codename: Ainia

Real name: Guadalupe Gutierrez

Born: 1993 Dallas, TX

Lives: Brooklyn, NY

Appearance: Latina (Mexican), brown hair, brown eyes, 4'10", athletic build, numerous scars

Card: Acquired Savant Syndrome (Reflexes), Synesthesia, Migraines, Poor Impulse Control, Fidgety

Agent Ainia had an active, angry, and violent youth. As Guadalupe she had been a capable fighter, but something happened after a bender of destruction. Her third fight in as many hours sent her into a coma. Three days later, she awoke a different person.

This agent is convinced she's the reincarnation of the Amazon warrior Ainia, from the Achilles myth. Ainia's post-trauma fighting techniques follow no known martial art. Rather, she says Amazons simply "follow the music."

Post-injury, Ainia exhibits the symptoms of mild brain damage. In addition to the aforementioned synesthesia, she is fidgety and carries a lacrosse ball to bounce off nearby surfaces in creative and challenging ways to keep her body busy.

-James Ensign

Chapter 3

Floating in their tank on the other side of the world, at the bottom of the installation designated CIG-1, the Collective watched Caseman Seven sitting on the green-and-black motorcycle.

When Ainia's truck pulled onto the highway going east, he zipped down the hill from the west, through the water park, and parked outside the burning remains of the meth lab. Pulling a short crowbar from his saddlebag, he raced up the stairs, through the flames.

The tweakers' burnt corpses lay where they'd died. Last month, the Collective had watched Caseman Seven teach them a cheap and easy method to make the drug they craved and help set up their operation, neglecting to warn them of the danger.

Ducking under a plume of smoke, he attacked a loose floorboard with the crowbar, breaking it in two. Jamming his arm into the hole, he came out with a cash box. It was a flimsy thing — the Caseman could have pried it open with the crowbar in a minute, but he didn't have to. The Collective told him the combination.

The box held three ounces of crystal meth and roughly two thousand dollars in loose bills. Caseman Seven stuffed both the drugs and the money in his jacket and left the box to burn.

Despite Park's feelings, the tweakers' deaths weren't a waste, the Collective mused. In fact, their deaths served the highest purpose.

Chapter 4

The white marble fountain rose out of Dupont Circle in Washington, DC's Old City. Carvings of classical nudes on the column symbolized the sea, stars, and wind. The previous night's heavy wind had filled the Circle with autumn leaves.

Droplets fell on Park's overcoat as he sorted leaves with the toe of his loafer. He formed an integrated pattern along the rise of the fountain's edge. Curved rows organized by color: red, yellow, and brown. An occasional breeze set him back, but Park persisted, imposing order on what nature handed him while checking his six.

Ainia kept her distance. Marching the perimeter of the Circle, hood pulled up, and hands stuffed in her pockets to keep her from fussing and drawing attention.

Someone stumbled along the hedge. The man looked to be in his fifties—forties in street years—white, bearded, and bundled in dirty layers of torn clothes. He shambled into the Circle, mumbling a rhythm to himself while swinging an old telephone receiver by its cord. Park flinched with every loop as the receiver flew closer to the man's face. The doctor abandoned his leaves to intercept.

"Good morning, sir. How are you doing?" Park closed into the man's space. "Do you have someplace to go when it gets cold?" Park caught the phone receiver on its downward spin, popped the jack with his thumb, disengaging the curly cord, and slipped the receiver into his coat pocket.

The man continued to spin his cord, oblivious to the missing weight, but no longer in danger of braining himself. "Sometimes. Sometimes I gotta make do on my own. But God provides."

"I'm sure He does." Park pulled a bill and a card from his wallet. "Look, here's a twenty on the condition that you head over to the Department of Mental Health on E Street, South East. This is their card." He pressed the papers into the man's palm.

A leaf slapped against the man's unflinching face and hung there a couple of seconds before peeling off.

"Will you promise you'll go there now? I'd take you there but I have an appointment I can't miss."

The homeless man's gaze drifted up over Park's shoulder. "I'm sorry I killed your people back in 'Nam."

"You're not old enough to be a Vietnam vet. Besides, I'm Korean." The guy tried to apologize again but Park interrupted him. "You weren't in the Korean War either. Are you going to go to Mental Health on E for me?"

The man stopped swinging his cord and swayed. "God wants you to know something. The suffering's about to start." Park held his breath when the man leaned in to whisper, "And it ain't gonna get better. It's gonna get a lot worse. You'll watch helpless as the world burns."

"Okay, well, thanks for the warning. Don't forget, the hospital on E." He watched the vagrant head roughly in the direction of the hospital, spinning his cord. Park ran his fingers through his hair and returned to the fountain. The wind had undone most of his work with the leaves.

The old man who'd trained him was almost on top of Park before he noticed. In his trademark round glasses and navy blue trench coat, James Ensign walked across Park's remaining leaves. "Been waiting long?"

"I had company." Park tried to hand the receiver to Ensign. "It's for you. I think it's God."

Ensign dismissed the offered phone. "How did it go in Indiana?"

"Not well. Not well at all. The psychic died in a self-inflicted accident shortly after contact. We didn't get anything, not even any data on her card. Here's the full report." They shook hands and Park slipped Ensign a strip of microfiche. Project Dead Blind lacked the resources to keep digital information secure, so they still used analog media.

Ensign nodded, blandly acknowledging Park's report of failure and death. "Just as well. Cards with addictions are difficult to manage. The one we have should be enough to keep you busy."

Ensign's indifference to the Indiana tragedy didn't make Park feel any better.

Ensign started walking around the fountain, indicating Park should follow. "A game was dealt, international rules."

The white noise of the rushing water engulfed their conversation. "This is a big one, Park. We may have found a Faith Machine, a good old-fashioned Soviet psychotronic super-weapon. They harness the power of prayer."

"The communists weaponized religion? Did they invent cars that ran on irony as well?"

Ensign ignored Park's questions. "We believe the Jonestown suicides back in '78 were a test run of an installation. One of a series built across the globe. We know the project ran until the end of the Cold War. What happened in between is a mystery. It's possible they refined the technology over the years. The question is how." Ensign lowered his voice and fished in his coat pocket. "One thing we know for sure, the machine has a tell. When it's in operation, religious icons resonate violently. In Liberia, crosses fell off the walls by the hundreds, a real rain-of-frogs style phenomena."

"Just crosses? What about other religious icons?"

"Any religion should do, but just in case—" Ensign pulled a silver charm bracelet out of his pocket and tossed it to Park. A cross, a Dharmachakra wheel, and the word "Allah" written in Arabic hung from the chain. "Those three should cover it."

Park pocketed the charms.

"You don't have to wear it out in the open, but wear it. Use the charms to locate the Faith Machine and arrange its extraction to the US. You'll need as many eyes as you can get. So there's one in here for everyone." Ensign held out his briefcase.

Park stared at the case without taking it. "James, I've never taken more than three of them on a mission. How am I going to manage six?"

"You'll order them, that's how." Ensign pushed the briefcase into Park's arms. "They're not your patients. They're your agents."

Ensign left Park at the fountain without saying goodbye. The last of Park's leaves blew off in the wind.

Once Ensign left, Ainia joined Park by the fountain. He gave her a satphone and passport from his briefcase. "You're not going to like this." He tossed the bracelet of icons to her.

She glared at it lying in her palm like he'd tossed her a rotten fish. "My god may be dead, but I'm not taking up with any of these."

"You won't have to. But keep it on you."

"Where are we going?"

"Liberia. And not just us, we're bringing everyone."

Ainia raised an eyebrow. "That's a lot of cats to herd. You up to it?"

"Nope. That's why I have you to kick their asses back in line. Ready to go to the airport?"

She stuffed the phone into her hoodie pocket. "Have I ever stalled in the execution of my orders, Commander?"

"Not once." Park's Prius unlocked with a chirp. "You'll inspire the others with your example."

She dropped into the passenger seat. "I wish it was that easy.

5 of Spades

Codename: Isaac Deal

Real name: Dennis Osbey

Born: 1975 Atlanta, GA

Lives: Same

Appearance: Black, 6' 2" athletic build but gaining middle-age weight

Card: Telepathic reflection of learned abilities, Bipolar disorder

I used to think Isaac's passive telepathy had an abrasive effect on the people he was in contact with, a consequence of mimicking their skills. But over the years as I've built up my poker face (my psychic defense) until I've become immune to his ability (I beat him at chess, confirming this).

Even with this resistance to his ability, my opinion of his character remains low. That said, his ability to parrot the skills of everyone in his proximity is astoundingly useful.

Isaac is easily motivated to stay with the Project. The missions provide him with a sense of purpose. His presence on the team irritates Park. With his inflated sense of confidence, Isaac can use Park's skills, without training, better than Park. This keeps Park on his toes, forcing him to compete with himself.

-James Ensign

Chapter 5

An LCD touchscreen played a video animation of the elevator car ascending through the floors of the Atlanta high-rise apartment. Park and Ainia felt no sensation of movement and the crystal chandelier hung motionless from the car's ceiling. He caught her eyeballing it, ready to jump. "Please don't."

"Only because you asked so nicely. What does Isaac Deal do between missions?"

"He sells cars," Park said. "Mercedes-Benz."

"How does Mr. Unreliable hold down a job like that?"

"They have an arrangement. Isaac shows up when he feels like it, sells a whole lot of cars, makes his quota, then disappears until the next quarter."

"I see. He's consistently inconsistent."

The doors opened into a lavish hallway furnished with fine wood cabinets that would never hold anything, fine chairs no one would ever sit in, and the faint sound of a stringed instrument playing Indian music.

Park stepped into the hall and stopped. "That's strange. When did they start pumping in world Muzak? Wait...it's coming from this way." He followed the sound.

Ainia held her ground. "Are we here to activate Agent Deal, or to solve the mystery of the hallway hippie?"

The music flowed from a door left ajar. Park pushed it open into Isaac Deal's apartment. "Looks like we're doing both."

The apartment was far larger than one man needed. The living area was packed with two couches, two love seats, a bronze statue of a giraffe, and an impressive throw pillow collection, as if to hide this embarrassment of space.

They saw Isaac Deal through the open kitchen. His back to the intruders, the African-American sat on the granite-top kitchen island in a lime green silk robe playing a red stringed instrument.

"Hello, Isaac," Park said. "When did you take up the sitar?"

Isaac continued playing. Their arrival left him unmoved. "About an hour ago. My downstairs neighbor was in an early-eighties prog-rock band."

"And he lent that to you?" asked Park.

"Nope. My upstairs neighbor used to burgle houses. Put the two together—" Isaac ended the piece with a guitar trill straight out of a country music bar band "—and I'm borrowing this here sitar." He slipped off the counter. "Now what can I do ya' for?"

Park set his briefcase on the counter. "We came to get your input. A game was dealt."

Isaac put the sitar aside. "What's the story?"

Park told Isaac about the Faith Machine and its tell manifesting in Monrovia.

"And that's all you have?" Isaac asked. "You might as well be going in blind. Park, you're going to have to be ready for anything."

Ainia kicked a chair off the wall, jumped on it on the rebound, balancing on it at an angle like an acrobat. "Between Park and me, we already are."

"You're good at breaking things, Ainia, but how good are you at finding them? This is a safari. You're going to need some extra help, someone dynamic. I'm going with you."

"Really?" Park was relieved.

"I'm the only black guy in the project. How are you going to Africa without me?"

"Glad to have you on board, Isaac." Park smiled and reached into his coat pocket. "Here's your—" The pocket was empty.

Isaac smiled and held up the satphone. "Gotcha. See you kids in Monrovia."

When they were back in the hallway, Ainia asked, "Why do you put up with him? He couldn't have picked your pocket without your help and we all know it."

"He's handy to have around. It's like having a backup me, but not a backup you. Someday we need to figure out why his card doesn't work on you." Park pushed the elevator button.

"He couldn't handle my skills. You two go through this act every time. He's your subordinate. Order him to go, don't act like it's his call to make."

The elevator doors opened. "I would love to, but Isaac never does what he's told."

7 of Spades

Codename: Gabby

Real name: Molly White

Born: 1998 Danville, KY

Lives: Same

Appearance: White/American Indian, brown hair, brown eyes, 5'4" normal build, small tattoos

Card: Speech-induced paralysis effective over digital signals, history of addiction

If it weren't for the power of Gabby's card, I would have passed over this agent. She's undisciplined and dangerously so, as her criminal record and history of substance abuse will attest. But Park is convinced she can be salvaged and we're an agent short.

Her ability to freeze an audience's motor skills is powerful and effective. Gabby had been using her card without even realizing it. It wasn't until she served some time in jail and detox that her card drew our attention. Park recruited her and took responsibility for her training.

In the hands of a more intelligent agent, Gabby's card would be devastating. I suppose I should be grateful we have her in the fold where we can keep an eye on her. Her rural upbringing might prove an asset on domestic missions. Perhaps Park can *My Fair Lady* her into a more useful agent.

-James Ensign

Chapter 6

The road cut through the lush Kentucky woods, past abandoned farmhouses and occupied trailers, both overgrown by kudzu vine. Park drove while Ainia navigated, reading the map on Park's phone in one hand, spinning her lacrosse ball in the other.

"It's coming up on the left, far left. Are you sure this is right, Commander? The map marker is about a quarter mile off the road."

"Her driveway's not on the map. It's the first turn after the burned-out blue house. I'm counting on that landmark. I hope no one's cleaned it up."

They passed an overturned camper with a tree growing through it. "I don't think we have to worry about that." Ainia shook her head. "Never mind, let's talk about Agent Gabby. What should I expect?"

"You know the cliché from the show *Cops?* Jobless, shirtless, trucker-cap-wearing guy, pulled over for a DUI? Imagine that guy as a woman—usually with a shirt."

"So she's a redneck."

"No…well, maybe." He fidgeted. "I wouldn't say that out loud around here."

"The gas station sold 'Redneck Drinking Team' baby jumpers, Park. They're in on the secret."

"There's the burnt blue house," he said, turning off the road and parking in the shade of the blue remains. "We'd better walk from here. The last time I drove up to the trailer her mother took a shot at the car."

"Good thing this is a rental." Ainia stepped out of the car, tossed Park his phone, and stretched out in a handstand, walking around the car on her hands, balancing the lacrosse ball on one foot. "What's Gabby's card?"

Park collected his briefcase from the backseat and headed up the dirt drive through the woods. "She can override voluntary nervous systems through the Brocha's area of the brain. When she talks, she can make you stop and listen."

"Do they speak hillbilly in Liberia?" Ainia flipped onto her feet. "She hasn't been with the program long. Are you sure she's up for a mission?"

"Ensign says so. Besides, she's holding a Seven of Spades. The most powerful agent the project's ever had."

"A Seven?" Ainia stopped her juggling.

Park smirked. "Feeling outclassed?"

"Please." She rolled her eyes. "Ensign decided I was a Three, that's fine." She bounced her ball off two trees, catching it without looking. "I think I've shown more than once what this Three can do. So Gabby's powerful, but is she disciplined?"

"Ahh…well, we're working on that. Here she comes now."

A dusky young woman in an AC/DC belly shirt came running down the drive, swinging an ax after a man in a dirty T-shirt and boxers. "Jacob! I told you I didn't wanna be on the internet!" Her unkempt brown hair bounced with her wild gait as she closed in.

Gabby stopped trying to kill Jacob when she saw Park and Ainia. "Oh, hi, Park! What are you doin' here?" She let the ax head hit the ground. Hoping for relative safety of any available witnesses, Jacob stopped running and hid behind Park and Ainia.

"We have a job for you. That is, if you're not planning on getting arrested today. What's going on here?"

"This jerkwad," she jabbed the ax at Jacob, "took a bunch of motorcycle parts from the guys at the racetrack. When I was sleepin' he'd put them in bed next to me and took a picture to put on the Craigslist.

Now there's a dozen naked pictures of me out there." She took a halfhearted swing at Jacob, who ducked behind Park.

"That bothers you more than the stealing?"

Gabby stared at Park in dawning comprehension. "Yeaaah, that too." She hoisted the ax onto her shoulder. "So why didn't you call me?"

The way Gabby said "call me" made Ainia ask, "You've been calling her?"

"This guy's been calling you?" shouted Jacob, determined to change the course of the argument. "Who is he?"

Gabby said, "What's it to you, *ex*-boyfriend?"

Jacob liked his odds against the unarmed Park better than Gabby's ax. He came at Park, fists balled. "I'll kill him!"

"No. You won't." Ainia stepped into the action, tossing her lacrosse ball back and forth.

"You want some too?" Jacob went to push Ainia. With one hand she grabbed his wrist, twisted, flipped, and Jacob was facedown in the dirt with her foot on his neck. "Shh," she cautioned.

Park led Gabby away from the scene. "I didn't call because we have a mission. E-mail, texts, even phone calls can be spoofed." He considered Jacob, squirming under Ainia's foot. "At least you used the ax and kept your card close to your vest."

Gabby scratched her face with the ax, leaving a smudge of dirt and rust on her cheek. "When I'm angry I forget I can do that."

"Good enough. We're calling up everyone. That means you too. Anything keeping you here?"

She glanced back at Jacob, still pinned to the ground by Ainia. "Not at all."

Park tossed her an envelope with a passport, plane tickets, and satphone. "Then pack your things. I'll see you in Africa.

5 of Clubs

Codename: 97:4

Real name: Jannete Burke

Born: 1992 Cincinnati, OH

Lives: Same

Appearance: White, blonde hair, blue eyes, 5'5" slender build, Lichtenberg scars on arms

Card: Electrokinesis, pica, religious delusions

When I want the wrong kind of person killed for the right reasons, 97:4's my woman.

The religious child of secular parents, 97:4 is dedicated to serving her spiritual ideals of an objective good. She wastes most of her time dwelling on whatever that means. Her morality is an obstacle to her effectiveness, more so than Park's. 97:4 can only be put in play if the narrative is spun as a tale of good over evil.

Her other uses are marginal, and her uncompromising attitude makes her exceptionally poor at infiltration. Judgmental, she rubs the other agents the wrong way if kept in close quarters for too long. We keep her family Bible as a means of control. The activation of her card depends on her consumption of its pages.

-James Ensign

Chapter 7

By 8:00 p.m. the Cincinnati soup kitchen was closed. 97:4 stood elbows deep in the sink with the pots and pans. Her golden hair contrasted with her gray knit cap like the golden crosses hanging from her neck, wrists and ears against her flannel shirt.

The rushing water proved too loud to hear him cough twice, so Park called, "97:4." She remained facing the sink and dishes.

Ainia bounced her lacrosse ball off a pot hanging from the drying rack with a crash. 97:4 turned, ready to fight. Park scowled at Ainia, who shrugged. "Don't give me that look. I got results." She left to play handball on the other side of the kitchen.

"No." 97:4 turned back to the sink. "And lock the door on your way out. It should have been locked before."

"It was. Don't worry, Ainia didn't kick it in. Don't you want to hear the mission briefing before you refuse?"

She rinsed the last pan, turned off the water, and faced him. She pulled her sleeves down over her scars, which were jagged and splitting, like the electricity that had branded her. "I need to sweep up."

"I'm not asking you to go right now."

"And I have to be here in the morning to let the handyman in. Heater's busted."

"Or even tomorrow. You can have a day or two—"

"I'm doing more good here."

"I'm not saying you're not doing good here, but this is special. You're special."

She gave an exasperated sigh and grabbed a broom.

"What?" asked Park.

97:4 ignored him and started sweeping.

"Oh, this is about Detroit, isn't it? Look, that was a mistake, even a tragedy. But we did what we could. Sometimes the intelligence is incomplete. But if we only bet on sure things we'd never make a play. Dead Blind isn't perfect, but it's the best we have. You have to think of the greater good."

"The greater good?" 97:4 swept out a corner. "The greater good makes our government get in bed with dictators. These missions of yours are all about power. Power is corruption waiting to happen."

"What if faith itself is being corrupted?" Park placed his briefcase on the table.

97:4's broom slowed to a halt. The case had her attention more than he did. He told her about the Soviet tool for exploiting belief. "Does that sound right to you? We can put a stop to it. Isn't this the reason God gave you this card?"

She stared at his briefcase. "Is my Bible in there?"

"Does that matter?" Park asked, knowing the answer.

She turned her head, closed her eyes. "I'm in."

"Great, great," Park opened the case. "Here's your phone and the paperwork. And you'll need this." Park handed her a chain with the cross, wheel and word, and explained the Faith Machine's tell. 97:4 handed it back to him, tapping at the crosses around her neck and hanging from her ears.

When Park and Ainia got back to the car, Ainia stared at him until he asked, "Okay. What is it?"

"I'm trying to figure out if you told 97:4 a lie."

"I told her everything that was in the briefing." Park started the engine.

"None of that mattered. She'd have her Bible back in her hands. That's why she agreed to come along, and you know it."

"I told her we're going to right a wrong," Park said, backing out of the parking spot. "That's no lie."

Ace of Hearts

Codename: Pollyanna

Real name: Shirley Vian

Born: 1988 Beaver Falls, PA

Lives: Same

Appearance: 5'6" Caucasian, overweight, brown curly hair, brown eyes

Card: Extreme probability distortion through personal conviction, post-traumatic stress disorder, depression

Before 2000 Shirley had the perfect life—good grades, lots of friends, loving professional parents, a brother and sister, temple on Saturdays, a safe /comfortable suburban home. A brutal home invasion-turned-mass murder took it all away—her parents and her siblings, her safety—and left her with a darker perspective on life.

That perspective allows Codename Pollyanna to manipulate fortune. Her bad attitude lets her store up every stroke of bad luck—blown-out tires, fried hairdos, fires, and frosts. It all goes in the probability bank, manifesting as an ache below her sternum, a pool of bad luck waiting to be cashed in for good, and a lot of it. This reversal of fortune is difficult for Pollyanna as it requires a positive attitude. With training, we've had some success channeling this through cognitive behavioral techniques— the power of positive thinking.

-James Ensign

Chapter 8

They found Pollyanna outside a 7-Eleven in Beaver Falls, PA. The convenience store stood between an apartment building and a family restaurant, both at quarter capacity. Park recognized the thirty-something white woman's brown tousled hair, heavy, hourglass figure, and green hoodie with the five-leaf clover logo for a bar long out of business. She squatted, repeatedly rolling a die on the ground, slapping herself five times out of six.

Park and Ainia watched from the rental car parked across the street. In the passenger seat, Ainia rubbed her eyes and shook her head. "Looks like she's getting worse."

"There's a method to her madness," said Park. "If she doesn't roll a six, she gets a slap. All those slaps add up. A little bad luck every time. It all goes in her karma bank."

"Can't she slap herself at home?"

"Exposure raises the stakes. Out here a loss isn't just painful, it's embarrassing too."

"She might have a better grip on her card if she wasn't so superstitious. And she's outside a convenience store because…she's building up luck for a lotto ticket. Got it."

"But it won't work for her, not when she has selfish ends in mind. This luck she's storing up, she could use to help someone else win, someone who really needed it. But she's too broke to think of someone else right now. So she keeps on trying." Park finished writing something in his notebook and put it away.

"Isn't that the definition of insanity?" Ainia sat up and slapped the dashboard. "Let's wish her luck and leave her to it."

"You don't like the Aces, do you? Pollyanna and Exposition Joe?" Park checked the dashboard for cracks.

"I don't like loose cannons. The Aces are too erratic in the field." Ainia shook her head. "Take Pollyanna: Luck, even good luck, is unreliable. Who decides what good luck is? Not her and not us."

"I see your point. She swings wide and often whiffs, but when she hits, she hits hard. Besides, orders are orders. Everyone is coming." Park stepped out of the car. "Come on, Ainia. Let's bring her a little luck."

She didn't budge. "I'm going to stay here. Pollyanna's card isn't the only thing I don't like about her."

Park smiled at her through the window. "Look at the big bad Amazon warrior, scared of a little social interaction." He shrugged. "Suit yourself."

Pollyanna had stopped rolling the die and now paced in front of the store, mumbling, an insincere smile on her face.

"What are you gambling for, Pollyanna?" Park asked as he walked up.

Her fake smile faded a bit when she saw him. She winced and rubbed at the bottom of her sternum. "Oh, the very best of causes, Dr. Park. A needy orphan."

"Scratchers or lottery?"

"Scratchers." She twisted her fingers together. "I live in the moment."

"Then let's go." Park tapped the 7-Eleven door frame three times. They bellied up to the counter. Park ordered two scratchers: Mega Scrabble and Atlantic City High. Pollyanna threw down the two dollars before Park could reach for his wallet. "The stakes are mine, Dr. Park."

He offered her a dime and a quarter. "Choose your weapon."

She took the dime and attacked the gray latex concealing the scratcher's potential. Park was still halfway through his when she punched the Slim Jims and Swisher Sweets off the counter. "Fuck! What the fuck is wrong with me? What's the fucking point of having this fucking card if it can't even pay my fucking bills?" She made a grab for his ticket. "I bet you won, didn't you?"

Park hid the scratcher in his coat pocket. "I don't know what you mean."

"The hell you don't. Hand it over, asshole. That's mine, I paid for it."

"It's only five dollars."

"It's *my* five dollars!" She yanked the ticket from Park's pocket and badgered the clerk until he cashed her out.

Park apologized to the clerk and led Pollyanna back outside. "Now, ready to make some real money?"

"Why now?" Her anger gave way, slightly, to insecurity. "You never bring me on missions."

"That's not true. We bring you on every mission your card—"

"It's been six months, Park. Ten grand, six months ago. How am I supposed to live on that? And with this card—fucking disability is more like it—I can barely scrape by as a hairdresser. No one will rent me a booth. I have to work out of my house and the power and water keep going out...I'm a twenty-first-century Miss fucking Havisham." Pollyanna drifted, staring at the cracks in the concrete. "What have you got?"

Park gave her the basic briefing.

"Everyone? All seven? Nothing lucky about that." She covered her eyes with the losing scratcher still in her hand, seemingly about to cry.

"So you're not coming?" Park asked.

"Of course I'm coming." Pollyanna crumpled her failed scratcher in her fist. "I'm fucking broke, aren't I?"

Park gave Pollyanna the envelope with her papers and phone, bid her farewell, and joined Ainia back in his car.

Ainia watched Pollyanna kick over a sign advertising cartons of Lucky Strikes. "She seems happy."

Park pulled out into traffic. "One of her better days. That's almost everybody. Now we wait for Exposition Joe."

"Shouldn't we have a better way of contacting him?"

"Ensign does. He says Joe's in."

"It's not like we could stop him. Is he even on this team?"

"He's erratic by nature, but he's been a powerful asset." Park turned the car onto the main thoroughfare and into traffic.

"You don't even know where he lives. How do you know where his allegiance lies?"

"I profiled him and Ensign…did his cryptic vetting process, too." They pulled up behind a truck delivering cases of beer to the Shop N' Save. Park hit his signal, looked over his shoulder, and waited for someone to let him into the next lane.

"What does Joe want? Where did he come from? Why is he here?" She gave an exaggerated shrug, shaking her head in a way that told Park no answer he gave would be satisfactory.

The rear passenger side door opened and someone got in. Ainia whipped around, ready to punch. She relaxed as quickly. "Well, speak of the devil."

Exposition Joe's young blond head popped up between the two. "Hi guys. Africa this time? Cool."

"See? Who's feeding him this information?" Ainia turned to Joe. "How'd you know we're going to Africa?"

"Because you told me, just now," said Joe. "Okay, Dr. Park, your turn."

"What?" Park had forgotten what he was about to say. "Oh, right. See, Ainia, Joe can see the future, but not far, only a few seconds. He's not *in* our heads he's *a*head-ahead of the rest of us." He handed Joe his envelope.

Ainia wasn't having it. "And he happened to be in this part of Pennsylvania when we're stuck behind a truck?"

"What if I said it was all part of God's plan?" Joe said, trying to tease a smile out of Ainia.

She glared at the teenager. "Don't start. I'll be getting enough of that from 97:4."

Joe flipped through his folder. "Or maybe I make the future."

Park turned off the blinker. No one was letting him out into traffic anyway. "I doubt it, Joe."

"Could be. Who's to decide? You?" Joe stopped abruptly, shot a glance at the empty seat next to him, and started again. "What else do you decide? What's right? What's wrong?" Joe emptied the envelope into his backpack.

"Ah, here we go." The traffic had started moving again and Park checked for an opening, using that as an excuse to dodge Joe's question.

"Don't worry about it, Doctor. I'm just messing with you. See you two in Africa." Joe popped out of the car and walked through traffic without looking.

"What did he mean by all that?" asked Ainia.

Park concentrated on the merging traffic. "Who knows with Joe?"

Ace of Spades

Codename: Exposition Joe

Real name: Joseph [last name unknown]

Born: 2002, Kansas City, KS

Lives: Transient

Appearance: Blond hair, hazel eyes, white 5'3"
regular build

Card: Precognition, schizophrenia

A teenage runaway we can't get rid of.

Exposition Joe has one of the most powerful
cards I've ever encountered. He literally sees the
future. Unfortunately, he can't do anything to
change it. But for those of us with less
foresight, his influence has proved a valuable, if
uncontrollable, asset. Never officially recruited
into Project Dead Blind, Joe isn't so much an
agent as a tolerated, recurring, positive
interference.

-James Ensign

Chapter 9

Park had given up on finding the US Embassy's driveway and parked across the street, outside the Masonic Lodge. The warm Liberian rain hit the Lodge's roof, ran down a cracked gutter, and streamed to the ground, washing mud off a pile of corroded machine gun shell casings. The Lodge was a fine example of both Palladian architecture and structural decay.

He stepped out of the rented BMW sedan and into a pothole. Leather shoes sank up to the laces. Sighing away the misfortune, he tapped the roof of the car three times and grabbed his briefcase and umbrella.

As he locked the car, a preteen boy in a dirty Cardinals Super Bowl XLIII Champions T-shirt ran up, calling, "Chinaman! Hey, Chinaman!"

An understandable mistake—between the suit, car, briefcase, and his ethnicity, Park could pass for one of the many Chinese businessmen representing their communist government in Liberia.

"Dry your car for you?" The kid waved a dirty towel. "No water spots!"

Park caught a few raindrops in his open palm. "Do you know something about the weather I don't?"

Undeterred, the kid pitched again. "Clean your shoes?"

"Now *that* I need." He fished some change from his pocket. "How's fifty cents?"

The kid had already started cleaning off the mud. "You need a guide too? A bodyguard? Jimmy's tough, I come from West Point. Protect you from pickpockets!"

Park knew about West Point from the travel guide. It was Monrovia's most dangerous slum. Park double-checked his back pocket, though he'd been sitting on it since he left the hotel.

"Thanks, Jimmy, but I can take care of myself. If I ever head to West Point I'll give you a call." Park grabbed the kid around his cheap plastic watchband and folded the boy's fingers over the coins. "Here's your money."

Another boy of Jimmy's age crashed into Park from behind, his attention on Jimmy's payday. The new boy asked, "How much did you get, Jimmy?"

"Fifty cents, Thomas. American!"

Jimmy and Thomas ran off together. Park walked down the street to the embassy to establish his cover and gather intelligence. He checked his back pocket, unsurprised and unconcerned to discover it empty. He waited for a motorcycle carrying one adult and seven children clenched together to pass before crossing the street.

The embassy had been recently restaffed after years of civil war and the bloody reign of Charles Taylor. Park patiently navigated the bureaucracy until he found what he wanted.

When he left the building, the storm had broken. His satphone vibrated in its underarm holster. This was the first time he'd gotten a signal since arriving in Liberia that morning, so he called Ainia while he could.

She greeted him with, "There you are. There's a guy in the hotel who looks like you. Suit, haircut, the works. His briefcase is metal though. Did you find something, Commander?"

"Looks like it. An abandoned facility out in the bush, no record of ownership. It's been there since the eighties. There's no known link to the Soviet Union, but everything else lines up. It's way out there. I'll text you the coordinates. Has everyone checked in?"

"Pollyanna's plane is late, and I haven't seen Joe yet. Isaac's been in the casino for hours. 97:4 went straight up to her room. Gabby's with me, in the lobby. Can I leave Isaac here and take Gabby to the facility instead? I want a chance to get to know the new girl."

"Good idea. We can assume Isaac's going to stay in the casino until we need him."

After a moment of dead air, Ainia asked, "Park?"

"Hi. Yes, I'm still on. Did you hear any of that?"

"You cut out after 'assume'."

"Great," Park said dryly. "This storm hasn't hit land and it's already tearing up our communications." The agents went back and forth with the plan in fragments until they were both on the same page. "I'm going to see a preacher who calls himself The Baptist. He should have something to say about the fallen crosses. 97:4 might be an asset."

"You're not worried she'll ditch our mission and join his?" Ainia asked.

"Funny. Can you tell her to get ready? I have one last thing to take care of here."

Jimmy and Thomas waited by his rental car. Jimmy held a mangled magazine in his angry fist. "What is this?"

Park smiled. "Jimmy, just the man I wanted to see. And Thomas, was it?"

"You made us look like fools." Jimmy threw the magazine at the man's feet.

Park picked it up and evened out the creases. "This is the latest issue of *Business Liberia*, complimentary with my hotel room. A little thin, but there was a good article in there about the future of private education in Monrovia. Do you want to read it?" He offered the magazine back to the boys.

Thomas smacked it out of his hand. "You put that in your pocket to mock us."

"My pocket? Folded up in my back pocket to look like a wallet? And that made you look like fools? I'm sorry, that wasn't my intention. Though I lose a lot of magazines this way when I travel."

"You owe us." Thomas and Jimmy gave determined nods.

"How about I give your watch back and we call it even?" Park popped back his sleeve, revealing Jimmy's cheap plastic watch wrapped around his wrist. He tossed it back to the boy. "Thanks, Jimmy. That came in handy in the embassy. My phone is still on East Coast time."

Jimmy held the watch in his open palm, stunned.

"Nabbed that while your friend picked my pocket." Nonchalantly, Park tapped the car door three times and tossed his things into the car. "Now let's talk business. I'm going to West Point to see The Baptist. I need a guide and a bodyguard. You kids want to make an honest buck?"

Chapter 10

Five men sat at the poker table in The Oceano, Mamba Point Hotel's casino: two well-to-do Liberians dressed in slick embroidered shirts, two Chinese businessmen, collars and ties loosened, and Isaac Deal. His African-American complexion looked pale among the darker Africans but didn't stand out as much as his purple-and-gold-trimmed silk dashiki with the FUBU logo across the back.

Isaac raised seventy thousand dollars. The first Liberian folded right away. The second Liberian thought about it for a moment, and then folded as well. They were casual players with nothing to prove, smiling as they lost. But the Chinese were serious. After losing so many hands to the graceless American, the older businessman had begun to push back. The younger one watched his compatriot for a cue as he glared at Isaac, trying to intimidate.

Isaac shot the older man a wink and a smile. "Back in the States, everyone plays Texas Hold 'Em, but here it's Oasis. Doesn't matter to me though. Whatever the game, I'm always the best player in the room. What do you play back in China? Shanghai Surprise? Hong Kong Ding Dong? Something like that?"

The older man growled as he considered his bet, mumbling under his breath in Mandarin.

"What's that you say?" Isaac smiled, cupping his hand to his ear. "That for everyone at the table or just your boy?" He let the moment hang for a beat. "I'm messing with you. Go on then. Do what you got to do. You need all the help you can get."

Isaac smiled at the dealer. Then leaned in to look at the man's ear. "You ought to get that lump looked at. You might be starting a skin tumor up on your helix."

The dealer stood, dumbfounded.

"Right up there." Isaac tapped the top of his own ear. The dealer ran worried fingers over the rough and discolored spot. "It's pretty dark, man, even on you. Could be melanoma."

One of the Liberian players said, "I thought the same thing. Are you a doctor too?"

"Naw, man, that's something I learned from you. Dropped out of college in my second year. I made too much money in sales." Isaac tapped the table in front of the Chinese. "What's up, Shanghai? You gonna play?"

The older man sneered, threw out his hand, and bought a new one from the dealer. He looked at the cards, bragged to his associate in Mandarin, and went all in. The younger businessman, under unspoken pressure from his superior, fumbled his chips forward as if it was his idea.

Isaac did the same. "Now we're talking." He put in more than the other two combined.

"You don't have to do that," the dealer cautioned.

"Just deal the cards." Isaac's eyes locked on the senior Chinese man.

The older man had nothing, jack high. His coworker had a pair of threes. Isaac had a pair of tens. He leaned in to collect the pot and said in perfect Mandarin, "I don't need a poker face. Because I always have the right cards, Shanghai. If you're not convinced, I'd be happy to prove it to you next hand."

Isaac mocked the rest of the players as he collected the pot. "And to you. And you, and you." By the time Isaac finished collecting his chips in trays, the others had left the table. "Almost four hundred grand. Not that it's real money. Just this African-edition Monopoly stuff."

He flipped a ten-thousand-dollar chip back and forth along his knuckles, eyed the motion curiously, asking himself, "Now who around here can do that?"

Through the oscillating chip, he saw four young men, dirty and rough, step up to the table. The oldest one was half Isaac's age. The dealer left. Their dangerous air drew stares from the staff and gamblers.

"Baby badasses!" Isaac smiled and took a quick glance at the TV behind him. "What? Did someone leave *Sesame Street* on?"

They gathered around the table and aimed cold glares at the American. Isaac grinned back at their leader— the one in a torn, red mesh shirt sharpening a large, nasty-looking, red-enameled knife. He leaned across the table, considered Isaac's dashiki, and sneered, "We heard you are special. But you look like a clown."

"You came looking for a clown? Sorry, kiddies, I'm all out of balloons." He caught one of them looking at the chip flipping across his knuckles and smiled. "But I can do a trick or two."

The leader looked around the casino. "Shouldn't you be by the riverside?" he mocked. The others laughed at his private joke.

Isaac dropped the chip into his palm, "Now why would you ask that? Nothing you've said has made any kind of sense, boy." He sat with his pile of winnings, waiting for an answer until their confidence drifted and the men started to squirm. The leader stuck his red knife in his belt. A defiant gesture, but Isaac knew he had them beat.

"You're not after my money, 'cause I didn't have any, not until now. The way the staff is whispering, security's about to bum rush you out of here any minute. You know you don't have much time. So I wonder, what are you here for?"

A blond teenage boy plopped down next to Isaac and said, "Hey Isaac, I need ten thousand dollars."

Isaac kept his eyes on the toughs, but smiled. "Exposition Joe! Just the boy I wanted to see. I got your ten grand right here, but I want to know something fir—"

"They're General Mamba's men, here to kidnap you," Exposition Joe pocketed a Mamba Point Hotel matchbook.

"Mamba? The guy this hotel's named after?"

"No, they're both named after the snake. They know who you are. More than you do. Later tonight—"

Isaac stopped him with a raised hand. "That's enough. Don't take the fun out of it. Here." Isaac flipped the ten-thousand-dollar chip into Joe's hands. "Do yourself a favor and spend that all in one place."

"Thanks." Joe took off as quickly as he'd come.

Isaac stood up, shaking a handful of chips. "Cards on the table now, huh, kids? You fools think you're gonna walk up in here and snatch me?"

The four advanced on Isaac but he stepped back and tossed the trays of chips into the air. The patrons watching the showdown rushed forward, dropping on their knees. They grabbed up the discarded chips, blocking the young toughs.

"See you bitches tonight." Isaac blew them a kiss and slipped away. One of the thugs bent over to grab a chip. His leader kicked it out of his reach and pulled him up by his neck.

Chapter 11

The building was big, boxy, and abandoned. Ainia pulled the truck up to a dark hole in the wall big enough to let a semi inside. Broken chunks of cinder block littered the ground. They'd spent an hour on the highway, another on a dirt road, and twenty minutes weaving through the jungle. It had rained the whole way.

Gabby leaned over the dash and squinted. "Let me take her inside, Ainia. When else am I going to get a chance to spin some donuts inside a commie army base? I'm sure there's room."

Ainia cut the engine. "This building has thirty years of jungle rot, and you want to drive three tons of pickup into it? I'm tempted to let you learn from that mistake."

"I prolly wouldn't." Gabby grinned under her tangled mop of hair.

Ainia climbed out of the truck and up the debris that used to be the wall. Gabby followed, slipping on the wet bricks and cursing. The hole opened into a room that could hold a basketball court. Jungle pushed in through every crevice, blocking the light with leaves. Not that there was much to see. The room was empty save for trash and a stack of wooden benches at the far end.

"I think this is a dead end. But we're here. Might as well take a look around." Ainia started around the perimeter of the room.

Gabby wandered, kicking at anything that looked untethered. "Hey, Ainia, can you tell me about the guy I'm replacing?"

"Agent Chaney? He was a great infiltration specialist. The man was amazing. He'd run a comb through his hair and change his face. Or at least, he'd convinced you he had."

"What happened to him?"

"He fell in love with a screwdriver and they eloped." Ainia smiled. "Welcome to Project Dead Blind, kid. Did Ensign teach you a poker face yet?"

"Yeah. I mean I think so. I haven't gotten a chance to try it out." Gabby jumped on top of a pile of fallen ceiling tiles, shook her fists to the sky to a beat and sang, "'Ah eh ah yeh-ah ah ah-ya, thunder!'" She waited for Ainia to join in on the chorus.

Ainia stopped searching and stared at Gabby. "What the hell was that?"

"It's AC/DC. Come on." Gabby's fist shook again, harder. "'Ah eh ah yeh-ah ah ah-ya, thunder!'"

"Yeah, I know the song. I've been to a football game before. A poker face is supposed to be a poem in a language you don't know. Speech without comprehension interferes with telepathy."

Gabby squirmed. "I can't remember any foreign words. Ensign said I could get by with a song I don't understand for now."

Ainia scratched her forehead and resumed the search. "He's the expert."

"You ever seen Bigfoot on one of these missions? The real one or the drone? Though I guess they're hard to tell apart."

"You're way off."

"See, the government made a drone copy of Bigfoot to spy on folks out in the country. When people see it, they're too amazed to be suspicious."

"Is that a fact?" Ania kicked over a ruined crate.

"What's the facts got to do with it?" Gabby flipped a coil of dirty rope and backed away from a snake that slithered free. "How about aliens? Any of that UFO, Roswell stuff on this job?"

"You're not serious?"

"Yeah, I am. I mean, look at what we can do. We got superpowers. What's the limit? Maybe we're the product of alien cross-breeding. Mom said my dad's supposed to be Shawnee Indian, but she was pretty drunk at the time. Who's to say it was *Jim* Beam she was under the influence of, maybe it was *laser* beam instead?" She pointed finger-guns at her ovaries, "Pew! Pew!"

"No. I haven't seen any little green men, little gray men, or Bigfeet of any kind. No Loch Ness monsters either, before you ask. The world is stranger than you know, but not the kind of strange you believe. As for the cards, I don't know about the rest of you, but I'm the product of the Amazon nation."

"Where's that? Arizona or some place?"

The wind kicked up, howling through the open wall. Ainia waited for it to die down. "More like *when* than where. Three thousand years ago."

"Ainia? How old are you?"

"Old enough to know that seeing is believing. And fairy tales are for fools." Ainia pointed around the room with a branch. "Looks like a small armed force used this place as a camp—there's spent rifle shells all over the place. Those stacks of cardboard and grass mats were their bedding. I figure about fifty of them. But nothing that looks like this 'Faith Machine' we're supposed to find."

"How do you know? They didn't tell us what it looks like."

"It's Soviet-made. You can count on it being big and clunky. All I see here is trash. But, no point in driving all the way out here for nothing. Let's fight."

"Yeah. Wait. What?"

"Let's see what you're made of, new girl." Ainia feinted a jab at Gabby's face. "I hear you can stop me in my tracks by talking."

"I ca—"

Ainia slapped her across the mouth. "What if I don't let you?"

"You crazy, Mexican bitch! I'll—ow!" Ainia punched her in the stomach.

"I'm not Mexican. I told you, I'm an Amazon. If you can't stop me with your card." Ainia kicked Gabby's foot out from under her, dropping her face-first on the coil of rope. "—then you better stop me with your fists."

Gabby roared and tried to tackle her, but Ainia stepped aside, and she spilled onto the floor. "You're not going to do it that way, hillbilly. I need to practice my poker face. Get up." And Ainia began to drone, "'*Τραγουδήστε, θεά, η οργή του γιου του Πηλέα »Αχιλλέας.*'"

"That's how you wanna go at it, huh?" Gabby pushed herself up and threw a handful of dirt at Ainia's face. The Amazon stepped back and smirked. The cloud of dirt came up short.

"'*και την καταστροφή της, η οποία έβαλε πόνους χιλιάδες κατά των Αχαιών.*'" Ainia circled her opponent and teammate, fists up.

Gabby looked around for something to use as a weapon, but the only thing in reach was the old rope. "I can tell these magic poems are going to be a real pain."

Ainia shook her head, still smirking. "'*εκσφενδόνισε σε πλήθη τους στο σπίτι του Άδη ισχυρές ψυχές.*'"

"What's the point in having me around if Ensign's gonna teach everyone how to cut me off? And what's the point in rhyming if you're not putting it to music?" Gabby came at her with a haymaker. Ainia raised her guard, stepped into the punch and twisted. Gabby's momentum carried her around to the other side. Ainia jabbed the back of her head.

"You futhin' bith! You mae me bie my tongue!"

Ainia kicked Gabby on the hip, knocking her down again. "'*των ηρώων, αλλά έδωσε τα σώματά τους να είναι η λεπτή γλέντι.*'"

Gabby pounded the ground with her fists. "Cut it out with the Mexican talk!"

"This isn't Spanish, it's Greek."

"*Let me bend your ear.*" Gabby's words raced down Ainia's spine and streamed out to her fingers and toes. Ainia's body, so quick, was now locked up stiff as a board, her gifted reflexes now useless. Now she understood why Gabby rated a Seven.

"AC/DC's Thunderstruck. Best rock song ever recorded." Gabby picked herself up, smiled, and kept talking. The fight was over. "But the lyrics always had me wondering, and Ensign said that would do for a poker face."

Gabby pushed Ainia and she dropped on her side like a mannequin, still in her fighting stance. "Look at the first couple of lines. He's stuck on the railroad track and someone's not gonna help him because they've been 'thunderstruck.' I wanna know why he was messing 'round with trains during a storm."

While Gabby lectured Ainia on the riddle of AC/DC's 1990 hit she collected the rope from the ground. She tied one end around Ainia's ankles and wrapped the rest around her in disorganized loops. "Lightning, trains. But at the end, it sounds like he's fine. I mean, what the hell is that about? That guitar riff still makes me wet though." Gabby was out of rope. "There. I should hang you from the ceiling like a psycho piñata."

When Gabby stopped talking, Ainia snapped back into motion and rolled onto her back. "Well done, kid. Now untie me."

"No way." Gabby turned and headed back to the truck. "I'm gonna leave you there to think about your sins."

"I'm not joking, Gabby, untie me." Ainia started to struggle free.

"I ain't jokin' either." Gabby climbed into the truck and drove over the pile of broken cinder blocks, right into the building.

Gabby pulled up next to Ainia and leaned out the window. "Now I'm gonna do a dozen donuts. And maybe a dozen more."

Ainia cursed and twisted in Gabby's sloppy bonds.

Gabby peeled out toward the stack of broken benches and pulled the handbrake. The truck spun around 180 degrees, but the wet tile floor was a smoother surface than asphalt. The truck kept sliding and smashed tailgate first into the stack of furniture as the last loop of rope fell from

Ainia's body. On impact with the truck, the benches accordioned up against the far wall. Broken boards flew everywhere. The truck nested in the wooden remains. Gabby's expression of shock flashed through the windshield before the floor gave way. The truck dropped out of sight, and a wave of green foamy water rose up. Dirty water and chunks of broken wood spilled across the floor.

Ainia raced over to the hole. Down below, the truck was hood deep in the filthy water. Gabby had climbed out the driver's side window and was sitting cross-legged on the roof. Decrepit connections, electrical and otherwise, cluttered the basement. A large machine once stood in the space the pickup now occupied. "I got good news and bad news. I think I found where they kept the Faith Machine, but it ain't here no more."

"Is that what you think?" Ainia crouched at the edge of the hole. "While you're down there thinking, how about thinking up a way to get back to Monrovia without wheels."

"What's that sound?" Gabby asked from below.

Engine straining, a large truck approached, crashing through the jungle. "Wheels."

Chapter 12

From the darkness of its tank, the Collective looked through the eyes of men and saw the world.

From a hotel hallway, Dr. Park explained to 97:4 why he'd hired children to be their guides.

Over his newspaper, Isaac watched General Mamba's men where they waited across the street, watching back.

Ainia and Gabby peered over the broken wall of the abandoned Soviet installation, preparing for a fight with the unknown approaching driver.

And through the taxi cab window, Pollyanna fought with a goat for possession of her suitcase, cursing when the handle snapped.

The Collective watched, satisfied that everything was going according to plan. The agents of Project Dead Blind would suffer greatly before the world would end.

Chapter 13

Through the window of Park's rental car, 97:4 stared into the eyes of a woman with one arm withered from atrophy. A thick knotted scar ran deep down her shoulder. Her other arm held a child wrapped in rags. This tragic family wasn't the worst they'd seen, and they were barely into West Point. "Let me out. I need to help."

Driving the only working car in West Point, Park navigated through crowds of locals turning out to see foreigners who'd strayed too far from luxury. "How are you going to help, 97?"

"I'll think of something. And it'll be better than tracking down some Russian mad scientist's superweapon."

"Are you two fighting?" Thomas asked from the backseat.

"No, not really. We're having a difference of opinion." Park scowled at 97:4. "One I thought we'd resolved back in Cincinnati."

"The fighting comes later. Right, Park?" She turned to face the kids. "Hey, guys. What would you do for a machine that makes sacrilege?"

Park tried to say, "Don't drag them into this." But the kids shouted over him with more questions.

"What does the machine look like?" Jimmy asked.

"Can't say. We haven't found it, but it's probably big."

"Is it a tank?" asked Thomas, hopefully.

"I doubt it. Maybe. I don't know. Like I said, we haven't found it yet."

Jimmy shook his head. "I'm not buying anything without seeing it first."

"We're not buying it either. We're Americans, we're taking it."

Thomas said to Jimmy, "They don't have it. Maybe we should grab it first."

"Then we can trade it for a tank!"

"I told you— What's with you and tanks? You know what? Never mind. Discussion over." She turned back around and studied the dashboard to avoid looking out the window.

The kids leaned forward into the front seat, pleading for a chance to continue negotiations.

"Now you worked them up." Park blew the horn at a thickening crowd blocking their way. "And this isn't an oil field we're after, 97:4. It's a weapon."

"So you keep saying." 97:4 caught another glance of the misery surrounding them and covered her eyes.

"We're here!" Jimmy announced. Up ahead stood a scene reminiscent of an old-time Christian revival meeting. A dozen or so smaller tents of varying styles and stability surrounded a large white tent that dominated the field. Some men were trying to repair a cluster of makeshift shelters, blue tarps flapping in the storm. The signage conveyed the spirit of the Southern U.S. Peeling paint and rain left the Bible verses unreadable. Paintings depicted Jesus radiating light and accompanied by an African man in matching white linen robes.

The site had seen better days.

"It sure looks like the right place." 97:4 stepped out of the car. Park and the kids followed. The Americans flinched when they stepped out of the air-conditioning and into the heat, humidity, and stench of West Point. The tall blonde woman drew stares from all directions. 97:4's golden crosses were worth more money than this entire community would see in a year. From the way she folded in on herself, she was keenly aware of that.

Desperate people watched the agents with both curiosity and varying levels of malice.

"It's been a long time since I've been in a church, but I remember them being…welcoming." Ignoring the daggers glared his way, Park reached into the car trunk for 97:4's Bible. "And more organized."

"You saw the conditions these people are living in. Were you expecting Kumbaya and arts-n-crafts? These people are suffer-oh!" The crosses at her wrists, neck, and ears jumped. She grabbed at her necklace. "Park, did you feel that?"

Park nodded, his hand over his pants pocket where he kept Ensign's charm bracelet. "I saw it first. The tent's so covered in crosses, the whole thing shook to the west. But the wind's blowing to the east." Park whipped his phone out to take notes.

She watched him work. "What are you doing?"

"Logging the time, place and direction. The tent is…" he checked the map on his phone "…east of where I'm standing. I saw the tent move a half second before I felt the charm, roughly ten feet away. Twenty feet a second…that's about fourteen miles an hour."

"Are you calculating the speed of faith?" She tensed with distaste.

"You could say that." Park finished typing. Under 97:4's scrutiny, he holstered the phone under his arm. "97, the Faith Machine is the source of this phenomena. There's no reason to believe it's anything more."

"Everything has led us to this church. When we get here, this… phenomenon happens. And you're calling it coincidence?" She reached for the entrance flap and stepped inside. "We'll see about that."

"Mr. Park?" Jimmy tugged at his coat, worried. "She shouldn't go in there."

Park tapped the tent flap three times, rushed into the darkness after her, and collided with someone standing inside. "Is that you, 97?"

"Yes."

The two stood still and silent, waiting for their eyes to adjust. Silhouettes moved in the light of candles or stoves. It stank of old incense and neglected humanity.

Park put his hand on her shoulder. "I don't think this is a church."

"This is the right place though, or at least it was. We wanted to find The Baptist and you hired the guides who brought us here. Now we're here. But why?"

"Why? Because I made a mistake, that's why. I asked the wrong kids to bring us to The Baptist."

"No, you didn't." Jimmy, Thomas, or both, had followed them inside. "You wanted to see The Baptist's mission. This was it."

"*Was* it? Why didn't you tell me he's pulled out of West Point?"

"Because then you wouldn't have hired us to bring you here." Jimmy said, matter-of-factly.

Park sighed.

Someone approached from the gloom. "Beers?"

97:4 and Park said, "Um?" and "What?"

The stranger said, "Would you like some beers while you consider?"

Park declined.

"Consider what?" 97:4 asked, guarded.

"The options. Can you see?"

They were starting to, a little. Blankets hanging from ropes partitioned the tent. A few scarred and hungry-looking men stood about. A few worn women sat on benches, waiting for their next go. A young girl in a tube top and nothing else staggered toward them. The sound of selfish rutting came from the other side of the blankets. Park understood. This was far from a house of God.

"You turned His church into a whorehouse?" 97:4 gritted her teeth.

"Let's get out of here. Calm down and think this through."

"I won't be calm, Park. Not until I've cleaned God's house."

"We're outnumbered, and I'm unarmed." Park tried to guide her back outside.

She remained unmoved. "Then you'd better give me my Bible."

Outside, an intense hissing sound faded fast.

"What was that?" asked 97:4.

Another hiss followed in short order. Inside, one of the men pulled a long knife from where it had been stuck in the bar. Something cracked.

"Those were our tires. Okay, here's your—" Someone pushed past him. Park stumbled. His hands flew up, launching the Bible into the darkness of the tent.

Chapter 14

Sheets of water poured down the awning in front of the Mamba Point Hotel. Isaac leaned against a pilaster, pretending to read a newspaper, squinting through the rain at four silhouettes across the street.

"Isaac!" a woman called from a cab. Pollyanna fell out of the backseat, a piece of luggage flailing in each hand. The cab driver tried to help her stand. That earned him a swing. He ducked under her carry-on.

"Fuck you! Fuck you! And fuck you! Here!" She pulled a few bills from her breast pocket, letting them fall to the ground. "Don't lose it at the goddamn goat races, you son of a bitch."

She kicked at him as he scooped up his money and dove back into his cab. She spit after it and trudged over to Isaac, her luggage in tow. A wheel stuck on her roller, leaving a long, black scuff behind her. Mud caked her shoes, knees, hands, and some of her face.

"I hate…" Exhausted, she was unable to decide what she hated most at the moment.

Isaac folded the newspaper under his arm, making no effort to help. "You smell like a farm."

"Good to see you too, asshole. My connecting flight died on the tarmac. I took that cab from Roberts International. Then we got stuck in a herd of goats halfway from the middle of nowhere. Instead of pushing through like a professional, my driver stopped to bet on some kind of goat fight." She held up a carry-on with a side torn open. "Then the goats turned on me. What are you doing out here, anyway?"

"Me?" Isaac straightened up. "Some local hooligans are set to try and snatch me tonight. But they're scared to do it here in the hotel lights. I've been standing here for hours, watching them watching me until they do something stupid. Then I got 'em."

Pollyanna sat on her luggage. "You're playing Dirty Harry when you should be playing James Bond. How about you save it for the mission?"

"Some guys come at me out of the blue like that? Believe me, it's connected to our mission. I bet I'll have found this Faith Machine tonight. The rest of you could have stayed at home. Besides, it's out of my hands. Exposition Joe told me what they're about, when I gave him ten grand. When Joe says it'll happen, it'll happen." Isaac winked.

Pollyanna considered Isaac for a second. "You gave Joe ten grand?"

Isaac gave her body a slow once-over, and broke into a slimy smile when he reached her eyes.

"Ugh." Pollyanna retched and dragged her bags into the hotel. "Good luck with that, Dirty Harry."

Isaac watched her from waist to ankle until she turned out of sight. "Ought to be illegal." He smiled and was about to check on his would-be kidnappers when he felt his phone vibrate. Reaching into his pocket, his fingers wrapped around his charm bracelet. His phone was in his other pocket.

Isaac stared at the loop of religious icons, expecting them to shake again, casting a suspicious glance back into the lobby. "Okay, that definitely happened. Now what do I do about it?" He started composing a text message to Park, *My bling went off. What now?* but deleted it. "That doesn't matter. I already got my lead on this case."

A brown station wagon filled with oranges cleared the street. The thugs were gone from their station. Isaac almost dropped the phone while stuffing it back in his pocket. Checking up and down the street, he saw no sign of the four. He dropped his paper and walked, quick and nervous, through the lobby, the restaurants, the café, the pool area, and the casino, looking for his would-be attackers at every entrance.

"This'll go a lot easier if I see them coming," he said to himself, standing outside the gift shop. "It's cool. This is cool. I still have the upper hand. They still have to come to me, right? Maybe they snuck around back when they saw me talking to Polly. Polly! Oh no!"

Isaac ran for the rooms. Skipping the elevators, he flew up the first two floors, jogged up the third, and trotted up the fourth. He was not a young man anymore. He burst into the hall on Pollyanna's floor and caught sight of her at the far end. He slowed down and caught his breath, relieved he wasn't too late.

"Pollyanna!" he gasped, relieved. "Hold up, girl. I think those guys saw me talking to you—Look out!" A service cart came up behind her, stacked high with rolls of toilet paper. One of the thugs jumped out from behind it. Pollyanna screamed and whirled on the man with extraordinary speed, knocking him over with her carry-on.

Isaac closed in, but the stairs had taken it out of him. His foot caught on something, spilling him chin-first on to the ground. Someone was on his back: a red-enameled knife was at his throat. Isaac recognized the voice speaking to Pollyanna from the casino, "Come, come now, missy. You wouldn't want me to ruin this fine carpet with the blood of such a foul savior, would you?"

Chapter 15

The air rushed out of another slashed tire. Inside the danger and darkness of the tent, 97:4 said, "Jimmy? Thomas? I need that Bible."

The man with the beers had withdrawn into the dark. Park reached for his phone. "Just a second."

"How many seconds do you think we have?" She groped the ground with the kids.

Park activated the flashlight on his satphone. The uncertain horrors they'd imagined in the darkness became real ones in the harsh white LED light. All eyes were on the Americans and their guides. Harsh eyes of the men, angry at the exposure. Cold, dead eyes of the women and girls, beaten and drugged beyond caring. The girl in the tube top opened her arms, silently pleading for help.

"Park!" 97:4 said. "Down here! I need the light—" The sight of the women stopped her mid-sentence. "I'm going to kill every man in this tent." Her voice thick with emotion, she pushed his arm down, pointing the light in time to catch the bartender scooping up her Bible.

She screamed, "No!" and grabbed the book. He pulled back and tried to fight her off. Jimmy and Thomas assaulted him from behind, their punches landing in his kidneys. He dropped the Bible and fell to the ground. 97:4 tore out a page of scripture, bit off a corner, and chewed.

The tent flap opened, letting in wind, sunlight, and three hard men holding machetes and knives.

Park stepped between them and his team. "I know what you're thinking. And it's a bad idea."

The three watched 97:4 take another bite out of the page, while Jimmy and Thomas hid behind her. The men laughed. "Really?" one of them asked as he pulled back his shirtsleeve, revealing a snake branded on his upper arm. "You see that?" The other two revealed identical brands. "That's the mark of General Mamba. We're master thieves. For us, thieving is never a bad idea."

"And if we don't hand over our money, dignity, car keys, whatever, then you'll hack us to pieces? You're robbers, not thieves. A thief takes by stealth, not threat of force."

The leader shook his machete in Park's face. "Keep talking, Chinaman. Every word from your lips buys you another cut."

Park pushed the blade aside with two fingers. "So you're killers too?"

They laughed again. "Oh yes, Chinaman. We are killers. We've killed many men, women, and children. Today will be your end. For us, it is just another day."

97:4 stuffed the rest of the page into her mouth and washed it down with the remains of a beer the bartender had dropped.

Park scratched his nose and considered a second. "You're wrong on two counts. One, I'm not Chinese, despite appearances. That's a minor point. A Koreaman can die too. We're not immune to machetes after all. And count two—I don't have to tell you about count two, do I?"

The men were confused. Their anger grew.

"Maybe I do. Count two is…There is no count two. I've been stalling." Over his shoulder, he asked, "97:4, are you ready?"

"*His lightnings lit up the world. The earth saw and trembled.*" An unnatural buzz in her voice, her hair engorged with static charge, she stepped around Park. The book she'd fought so hard for a moment ago passed to Park without a care.

The men laughed again, unimpressed. "We're not just thieves and killers, Chinaman, or whatever you are," said their leader. "Let us show you." He stepped up to 97:4.

Park threw himself over the boys.

Mamba's man placed a hand on 97:4's shoulder. His arm exploded in a zap of light, the flesh destroyed from his sleeve on down, bone destroyed from the elbow. The rest of him flew back through the open tent flap. His hand hung at 97:4's shoulder, slid to the ground, and crumbled into black ash.

The sudden smell of ozone overwhelmed the stench of the tent. Electrical sparks ran up and down 97:4's body, shot from her eyes, and lit the tent. The rest of Mamba's men threw arms over their faces, openmouthed and covered in liquefied parts of their leader. Someone screamed.

"Killers?" 97:4's voice buzzed.

The second man came to his senses and swung his machete at 97:4. Electricity arced from her skin to the blade, raced down his body and into the ground, obliterating his leg. The charred remains of his body hung stiff for a second before falling like a tree after a lightning strike.

The last one dropped his machete and sank to his knees, pleading before the woman. 97:4 asked again, "Do you repent?"

"Yes! Yes! Please! I will repent! Oh, please." He buried his face in the dirt.

"You expect me to believe that? Thief, killer, and liar too." She took her time with this one, grabbing the back of his neck. He shook, arms flailing. Then he smoldered. When she was done, the tent reeked like burnt roast. 97:4 turned to the pimps.

Park pulled Jimmy and Thomas to their feet and dragged them out into the rain, giving 97:4 wide berth. They passed the remains of the first of General Mamba's men, tattered strands of smoking skin where his shoulder used to be. The three took shelter behind the rental car with its slashed tires. The streets were clear. The people of West Point were no strangers to sudden and explosive violence. Inside, 97:4 shouted an order. Women and girls poured out from the sides of the tent in all directions. Lightning arced. Men screamed. What remained of The

Baptist's mission in West Point burst into flames.

97:4 trudged out of the burning tent. Her spark had gone. Park stood. The boys stayed hidden behind the car. He was about to say something, but she cut him off. "Don't you dare talk to me about your mission or keeping a low profile. I don't regret a single thing I've done here, only that I can't do more."

"I handed you the Bible, 97:4. I can't be your judge." He popped the trunk of the sabotaged car and removed his briefcase. "Roadside assistance won't show, I'm sure. We're going to have to find a quick way out of here. You boys have any suggestions?"

"Don't look anyone in the eye and walk fast," Jimmy said from the other side of the car. "And give the woman her Bible."

97:4 grimaced and turned away.

"That's not an option. Not for another couple of hours." Park finished gathering his things and checked his phone. "The signal's not getting through the storm. Jimmy's right, 97:4. We're going to have to hope trouble stays out of the rain."

A full-sized dark blue Chevy Blazer with a jacked-up suspension turned the corner, headed their way. The huge knobby tires, too large for the streets of West Point, carelessly sheared or crushed the tents and whatever else passed for buildings. Pedestrians scattered before it, to escape the slow-moving menace.

The monstrous vehicle pulled up to the burning remains of The Baptist's mission, paused, revved its engine, and made for Park's rental. Park, 97:4, and the boys ran for cover. The truck crushed the sedan beneath its wheels.

The truck perched on top of the ruined car. The driver's side window rolled down, and Exposition Joe's head popped out. "You guys need a ride?"

Gabby leaned her torso out the window behind him. "Park! What happened to your car? Don't you Asians know how to drive?"

Park held his briefcase over his head, sheltering himself from the rain. "I need so many explanations right now."

Ainia dropped out of the passenger side and trotted up to Park. "I'm sorry, Commander. I should have stopped him. I didn't think they were serious about crushing your car."

Gabby slapped the side of the truck. "It ain't her fault. It was my idea. But I don't regret that he did. That was awesome. Let's go rent another car!"

Joe dropped out of the truck. "I did it. No point in playing the blame game."

Park pretended the car didn't matter. "Let's head back to the hotel, find Isaac and Pollyanna, and compare notes."

Joe rolled his shoulders, stretching after a long drive. "They're not there. Isaac and Pollyanna were kidnapped around noon. They're in the hands of General Mamba."

Chapter 16

The Blazer had no trouble crossing the beaten, muddy roads. For the past hour, its headlights illuminated grass fields, homesteads in garish colors, and looming patches of jungle. Park sat between Joe and Ainia in the front. Gabby, 97:4, and the kids sat in the back. Jimmy and Thomas told and retold the story of 97:4's rampage to each other, Gabby, and anyone else who would pay attention. 97:4 stared into the rain.

"So, where'd this truck come from?" Park questioned Joe. He pieced together the events that put most of his team on this road and sent Isaac and Pollyanna into the hands of General Mamba.

Joe fiddled with the climate control, turned down the temperature, and set the air to recirculate. "I bought it with money Isaac won in the casino. When he ran into his kidnappers the first time."

Ainia's interest in their captured teammates seemed almost academic. "You knew hours in advance and didn't warn your leaders?"

"Sorry, but you weren't due to know until now." Joe nodded, eyes on the road. "But now we're all heading in the right direction. And we got this sweet ride. It's a trade-off, right? Kind of?"

She looked into Park's eyes and mouthed the words, *See what I mean?*

Park turned back to Joe. "How did you find the rest of us? You can see through time, not space."

"The storm was going to clear and Ainia was going to get a signal through to me."

"Eventually. But not now."

"Nope."

Park shifted uncomfortably in the seat. "Isn't that a paradox?"

Joe turned the AC on full blast and channeled it through the floor vents. "You'd think so, wouldn't you?"

"Did you find Park and 97:4 the same way?" Ainia asked, knowing the answer.

Joe leaned forward and placed both hands on the steering wheel, eyes straight ahead. "No. They were going to die. We would have figured it out the next day. Would you like to know how?"

Park glanced back at 97:4, who had turned away from the window. "I'm sure it wasn't pretty."

Joe nodded and reached for the climate controls. Ainia grabbed his wrist and put his hand back on the steering wheel. "Leave it."

Park turned back to Joe. "What's next, Joe? I'll come out and ask; will Isaac and Pollyanna make it out okay?"

"I wish I could tell you, Dr. Park," said Joe. The Blazer crested a hill. "We're here."

The headlights fell on another revival-style compound sprawled out before them. A large new church dominated the site. The only building in the area, it was a white postmodern structure composed of dozens of acute-triangle-shaped facings. Signs and tents covered the area, like the remains of the camp in West Point, but bigger and in far better condition. More paintings of Jesus side by side with the African man in matching white robes peppered the landscape.

Joe pulled the Blazer up to the church. A crowd of men, women, and children gathered to receive the Americans as they spilled out of the truck. Joe tossed the keys to his commander. "Tomorrow, it won't matter how we got here." He indicated the church. "Just that we got here."

"We'll see about that." Park slid the keys into his pocket and turned to the crowd. "All right! Hello! Can anyone point us to The Baptist?"

The gathering Liberians wanted to know all about the unexpected foreigners. After some confusing back and forth questions and interruptions, they led the team into the church and asked them to wait for The Baptist to receive them. As they were rushed inside, Park's hand shot out to knock three times on the doorway.

The interior matched the exterior. Between three-sided beams, stained glass windows, unspectacular in the night, depicted a dozen scenes from the Old Testament. Inside the doorway, a plaque thanked The Samaritans, an American religious organization, for their generous donation.

A white sheet hung behind the altar, concealing whatever display was built into the wall. Another rough painting of The Baptist in his white robes was projected onto the sheet acting as a movie screen. In this instance, The Baptist being baptized by another, fairer, African man. The painting was crude by comparison to the architect's intention for the rest of the interior.

Park's team lingered in the empty hall. Jimmy and Thomas had glommed on to Gabby, the three sharing stories of home. Gabby told the kids about all the stuff she and her brother had to steal because they were poor. The kids told her good-humored stories of true poverty. She giggled with them like a third child, oblivious to their developing crushes. Exposition Joe sat against the far wall and stared at the ceiling, away from the others.

Ainia stuck to Park's side, bouncing her lacrosse ball. "I don't like this. You're counting on a lot of help from a man you haven't met. And given what we know about him, he's not a man we can count on."

"I don't like this either." Park confided. "But I hate losing Isaac and Pollyanna to General Mamba, and I'm desperate for support and intelligence. We experienced the Faith Machine's tell when we arrived in West Point. I'm guesstimating the source, but it could be here. If he has the Machine maybe he'll offer to us it for us. So to The Baptist we must go."

"Go? More like get dragged, which is our other problem—Joe. He could have prevented this mess, but he chose not to." Ainia watched Joe through the reflection in a polished brass lighting fixture. "He let Isaac and Pollyanna get snatched. Do you accept that?"

"Ainia, ignore the words and see the actions. While Isaac and Pollyanna were kidnapped, Joe was rescuing you and Gabby from the jungle, and 97:4 and me from West Point. Would the team be better off scattered and stranded? You and Gabby could have worked your way back to Monrovia. But I doubt 97:4 and I would have gotten out of West Point alive."

97:4 glared at Ainia and her bouncing lacrosse ball. The Amazon bounced it a few more times before switching over to contact juggling. "My gut still says he's not on our side."

"Ask your gut again, whose side is he on? When did a teenage runaway from Pennsylvania throw in with a Liberian warlord?"

"Who says General Mamba's the only force we're up against?"

"Fair point." Park looked over his shoulder as if he might catch an unseen threat.

The church doors flew open, and the robed man from the paintings with Jesus entered. The Baptist wasn't alone. An entourage of men, women, and children followed in his wake. Two dozen of them, maybe three, singing a Southern Gospel hymn with an African flair.

The agents of Project Dead Blind broke off from what they were doing and gathered in the center like circling wagons. The congregation spilled in, surrounding the Americans with a joyful noise, until The Baptist raised his hands and they gracefully wrapped at the end of the verse.

"Welcome, Americans and Chinaman!" The Baptist boomed.

Gabby whispered to Park, "I think he means you."

Park dismissed her with a "not now" wave of the hand. "Thank you, Mister Baptist. I'm Dr. Park. I admire your church and the intensity of your flock. Clearly, you are doing good work here."

"Please, call me John."

"Of course," Ainia muttered.

"I do what I can to make the world a better place for my fellow man." The Baptist stood on the steps leading up to the altar. The congregation gathered, kneeling to either side. He looked down at Park. "But the question is, what is the Office of Intergovernmental and External Affairs doing here in Liberia?"

Park straightened his tie. "Right now I'm wondering how you know who we are, John."

"With his many voices, God told me you were coming. God guides my every step." The Baptist stepped forward and paused, waiting for his line to land. "I see you don't believe that, Dr. Park. Perhaps you will believe this. I understand the value of knowledge. Even a preacher needs to know the devil's work. I have more eyes and ears than the pairs God has granted me. I have answered your question. Now will you answer mine? Why are you here?"

"I apologize. I didn't mean to dodge." Park straightened up. "Back during the Cold War, the Soviet Union stashed a cache of chemical weapons here. We're here to locate that cache and extract it safely. But General Mamba kidnapped two of my people, and I want them back."

"A rough-looking bunch for government bureaucrats." The Baptist let the implication hang for a moment, and then broke into a smile. "I know of the white woman and half-white man taken from the heart of Monrovia's high end. Such boldness could not go unnoticed."

"I can't wait to tell Isaac he's half-white over here." Gabby chuckled. Ainia's glare cut her off.

"I know of General Mamba, one of the last warlords still in the business of war." The Baptist continued. "You understand that means he has an army, and you have—what, exactly? A handful of *bureaucrats*? Better you call your government for help. When your Marines come, I will tell them what I know. I fear, to tell you would be to kill you." Park felt the man's mood alternate between overt distrust and genuine concern.

"We can't wait, John." Park barely prevented himself from pleading. "They'll be dead within days if they stay in Mamba's hands."

The Baptist leaned forward, studying Park. "How well do you trust your sources?"

Park avoided looking at Exposition Joe, looking at Ainia instead. "They haven't failed me before."

"Dr. Park? Doctor of what?"

"Psychiatry."

The Baptist shook his head. "I don't understand how that qualifies you to lead a chemical weapons extraction. Tell me, which of your team is the chemist?"

"Two of them. The two General Mamba took," Park lied.

"Hmm. Then they are truly out of their depth. For General Mamba is at war with their kind, the materialists. He's taking them to a special place to bring them to a special end. I could tell you more, but I don't think you're prepared. Your...cultural limitations might prevent you from accepting the truth."

"Try me. I assure you my experiences have left me with an open mind."

"I'm not convinced that there is a place on this battlefield for the secular." The Baptist brushed his chin and considered. "The civil war transcended the corporeal. Some generals made an alliance with the great beyond. Not just guns, but gods. Not just soldiers, but spirits. But these alliances came with consequences. General Mamba's allies need to feed. Perhaps your friends have the qualities they seek?"

"Do you know a lot about these spiritual allies, John?"

"Indeed. They used to be my allies as well." He turned and lifted his hands to the cross behind the altar. "Until I found the strongest ally of all."

The congregation broke out into cheers of "Hallelujah" and "Amen."

Park lost his patience. He shouted over the crowd, "John! John, can you tell me where General Mamba's 'special place' is? My team and I will do the rest."

His congregation grew more excited, The Baptist also had to shout, "I can't let you go to General Mamba's camp, Dr. Park. He has an army. It's too dangerous."

"We can be dangerous too," answered Park over the crowd.

"My man Charles will help you." The Baptist shouted over his congregation. "That is the best I can do. But I made a promise to God never to allow a child to go to war. You must leave the boys behind, even the white one."

Park flinched and looked at Joe. Exposition Joe shrugged, like he'd lost a penny bet.

Chapter 17

Exposition Joe, Jimmy, and Thomas watched from the church steps as the Blazer went over the crest with the rest of Project Dead Blind.

The Baptist put his hand on the boy's shoulder, "Do not worry, Joseph, this is meant to be."

"Don't tell me. This is all part of God's plan. He's whispering in your ear at this very moment."

"Not at this very moment, but He has before." The Baptist led Joe back inside the church.

"There's a lot of that going around."

"But of course. We are approaching the end times. The savior returns, and as before, the savior needs a Baptist. It's only logical."

"Sure it is. That why you gave Dr. Park that whole 'child soldier' talk? The truth would have been harder to sell."

"You took the words right out of my mouth, child. He is not a man of faith. But we are, aren't we, Joseph? That's why I have to keep you here, and safe."

"And the rest of my team? What's your plan for them?"

The Baptist's smile dropped. "Well, that's between them and God." He turned and led the boys back inside the church. The choir had filtered outside and returned to their tents. Joe, Jimmy, Thomas, and The Baptist were escorted by two of the men; men who hadn't been singing and didn't smile. The six walked toward an entrance at the back of the hall.

"Do the Samaritans come around much?" Joe asked, as they passed the commemorative plaque.

"No, they've never been here. So generous they are. They built this church for us, fully funded, fully planned, asking nothing in return. They haven't even visited to receive their thanks." He led them through a corridor to the last office on the left. "Shamefully, we've never had a reason to set their office right." The door opened into a room with the contents of an office without any of the order. Unopened boxes of office supplies stacked were against the far wall. A desk stood on end like a monolith in the center of the room.

The Baptist held out his hand. "May I have your mobile phone, please?"

Joe looked him up and down and then glanced over at his men. While The Baptist still seemed as friendly now as when he'd entered the church, his men had only crossed arms and scowls for the boys.

Exposition Joe handed the phone over. "It was nice of you to act like I had a choice."

The Baptist pocketed the phone. "We always have choices, Joseph. If we couldn't choose wrong, then what would be the worth of choosing right?"

The Baptist and his men locked the door behind them, leaving the three boys in the dark office alone.

"Right…"

"What happens now?" asked Jimmy.

"What I usually do in situations like this is sit back and wait for God to help me out."

"Does that ever work?" asked Thomas, skeptical.

God stepped into Joe's field of view with no fanfare. Appearing as a skinny old man with a wild mop of hair, he sported the same white woolly beard and worn, ill-fitting, hemp suit as He'd worn on His first manifestation three years ago. A rolled document held in one hand.

Whenever the Almighty appeared to him, Joe surveyed the room to see if anyone else noticed. No one ever did. "Hello, Joseph. Ready to get to work?"

"Yes." Exposition Joe circled around the sideways desk. "Everything happens for a reason."

"You're standing on top of it." God pointed to the floor with the document.

Joe looked at the linoleum tile floor between his feet and grunted. "Guys, let's put this desk right."

As the three eased the desk into place, something slid and clanged inside one of the drawers. Joe shot the others a "how about that?" look, searched the desk, and found a keypad remote.

"What's that for?" asked Jimmy.

"I've never seen a remote like this before. I could start at one and enter all the numbers until I find the right one. But I don't have to, because I know I'll stop at—"

"53787," said God.

Joe entered 53787. A section of the floor under Thomas's feet popped open and rose with a hiss. Thomas laughed and started to dance.

Joe pulled the boy off as the riser picked up speed, almost crushing Thomas flat against the ceiling. "Today's not your day to die."

Hydraulic jacks had lifted an elevator cart up through the floor. The roof of the cart was the piece of floor. There was a simple two-button interface inside the contraption at waist level.

God stepped between Joe and the cart. "Grab one of those." He jabbed a thumb at a stack of document boxes. Joe shrugged and did as he was told, carrying the box into the elevator. The boys made to follow, but Joe stopped them.

Joe said, "I better check it out first."

"Are you sure you want to go alone?"

"Who says I'll be alone?" Joe asked Jimmy, as God joined him in the cart.

Hands full, Joe pushed the button down with his hip. The elevator hissed and descended. It was a short ride to the level below. The deity was radiant in the dark, without giving off light.

Cut off from the boys above, Joe turned to God. "Back in Pennsylvania, Dr. Park said I either see the future, or I make the future. I was going to suggest that I hear the person who makes the future. But you stopped me. Why?"

God stepped backward, out of the elevator. "Tell Dr. Park you're a prophet of God? That doesn't go over so well these days. Follow me."

Joe stepped into the black without hesitation, following a few steps farther until the deity held out his palm, open and facing Joe at chest level. "Right here you'll find a switch."

Joe flipped it with a corner of the box. A single bulb illuminated a small plain white room with a single door by the switch.

And God said, "Let there be light."

"That's an old joke." Joe set the box down.

"They're all old jokes to me."

Joe reached for the doorknob as God pointed back at the control panel. "Aren't you forgetting somebody? It's not their day to die."

Joe sent the elevator back up. As it ascended, God wagged the rolled document at Joe. "Your little test was meaningless."

Joe kept his back to God. "I don't follow."

"You pretended to forget about Jimmy and Thomas. What if I hadn't reminded you? What if I had let those boys die? I've let many children die. The universe seems cold and unjust. But I'm the ultimate judge of right and wrong—My every action is holy."

The elevator stopped. Joe listened to the muffled voices and footsteps above as Jimmy and Thomas stepped into the car. The car began its descent.

Joe turned to God. "If God isn't good then what is?"

Jimmy jumped out of the car when it was halfway down. "Candy" he answered, thinking the question was for him.

God leaned against the wall and smiled at Jimmy. "From the mouths of babes."

Jimmy and Joe waited for Thomas, who wouldn't let go of the handrail until the car came to a full stop.

Joe opened the door into a larger room covered, floor to ceiling, in small teal tiles. Even the other side of the door was tiled, and missing a doorknob. They entered opposite another door, a sturdy one with a half-dozen deadbolts.

Thomas was the first to step into the room. "This place looks like a government shower."

"You know what?" said Joe. "It does."

"What is that?" Thomas pointed at the center of the room. "That" was an open clamshell tub made of cedar, large enough to hold a full-grown man lying on his back and spread-eagled with room to spare. Iron bolts held it together. The bolts were covered in fresh scratches, evidence of recent reassembly. The base was warped and gray with water damage, now dry. Dozens of gold wires, in a deliberate tangle of angled bends, mounted like a halo at the joint of the shell. The stem of the golden wires ran down a series of electrode pads along the operator's spine.

Joe ran his hand along the inside, still damp from the last use. "It's a Faith Machine, a weapon of God, from the last century."

Jimmy said, "Funny-looking weapon."

God huffed. "It's not My weapon. It's an abomination. A Tower of Babel built by science."

"Is this what the number lady was talking about?" asked Thomas.

"I don't know," said Joe.

God consulted the document. "Yes."

"Probably," said Joe.

Thomas stepped closer to his friend. "Jimmy, we should leave. Maybe there's a way out of here. Then we can tell the number lady where we found the thing she was looking for and she'll pay us. How do we get out of here, Joseph?"

"We don't. Not yet." Joe spilled the contents of the document box under the Faith Machine. Loose papers spread across the floor. He opened two bottles of correction fluid and poured them on top.

Jimmy asked, "Joseph, what are you doing?"

God didn't look up from the pages. "What he came here to do."

"It has to burn." Joe opened the official Mamba Point Hotel matchbook and struck a match. "They all have to burn."

Chapter 18

Being kidnapped and held prisoner brought the kid out in Isaac. "You so fat, the back of your neck looks like a pack of hot dogs." Isaac sat on the floor of an empty underground office, hands tied behind his back.

Two of his kidnappers stood guard. One of the guards was a little overweight.

"You so fat, you walked by the TV and I missed three episodes. It must take you two trips to haul ass. Your blood type is probably butter."

The heavier guard cursed and lunged for Isaac. The other guard held him back. "Stop! You know this one is to remain unharmed."

Isaac popped to his feet. "That's right, Chunky Style. Touch this and see how the Mamba-man likes it."

The bigger guard lunged again. His comrade intervened, pushing him out into the hall, warning him to calm down. He sneered at Isaac and cracked his knuckles. "You laugh now. But when the General finishes with you, he'll hand you over to us. Will you be laughing then?"

"Buddy." Isaac sneered, casting deliberate eyes around the empty room. "I don't know much about warlords, but they don't hole up in brand new buildings. So why don't you tell me what's going on here?"

The guard shifted from foot to foot and took his eyes off Isaac.

"Ah. See, I didn't know for sure, now you told me. You wanna know what else I know?" Isaac leaned in like he was telling the guard a secret. "There's more to this General Mamba cat than meets the eye. Or maybe less."

Fat Stuff opened the door and targeted Isaac with a cocky glare. Two more guards and a man in a white linen robes, closer to Isaac's age, followed Fat Stuff. The robed man smiled, his guards didn't.

Isaac braced himself. "Looks like I'm gonna get my ass beat."

The robed man dropped to his knees and proclaimed to the heavens, "*I was sent forth from the power, and I have come to those who reflect upon me, and I have been found among those who seek after me!*" His eyes closed, grin raised wide.

Isaac didn't have a clue how to react to this. Neither did the guards.

"You're getting to the crazy part early, General."

"Calm yourself, Isaac Deal." The robed man stood slowly, with signs of a bad knee. "I am not the general. I am The Baptist, and one of God's Baptists would never inflict harm on another."

"I…" Isaac looked back and forth at the dangerous men in the room. While they weren't happy to be in Isaac's company, they also weren't beating him. "Are you calling me a Baptist?"

"I will explain, Isaac. My name is John." The Baptist stepped aside and gestured toward the open door.

"So, General Mamba…"

"Is who I used to be. Before I found God I made war. Mamba's name still has its uses."

Isaac dropped his guard with one more cautious look at his jailers and followed The Baptist's lead. "I'm sure it does."

The man in robes was giddy with excitement. He walked fast, threatening to break into a run. "Can you feel the vibrations in the air? The quaking in the ground?"

"No, can't say I d—"

The Baptist interrupted him with another proclamation. "*Look upon me, you who reflect upon me, and you hearers, hear me! You who are waiting for me, take me to yourselves!*"

Again the moment lingered. Isaac broke the silence. "You do that a lot?"

"I find myself taken in the moment, my friend. We stand at the threshold of a great juncture."

Isaac shrugged. A guard reminded him to watch his manners with a shove. Isaac remained belligerent. "Where did you take Pollyanna, my lady friend?"

"Your friend is at another location. You know what the Bible says, 'Don't put all your eggs in one basket.'"

"It surely does." Isaac found neither the man's honesty nor his knowledge of scripture convincing. "What does the Bible say about kidnapping?"

The Baptist laughed, as if Isaac had made a joke. "Oh, you know it doesn't matter. Or won't matter soon enough."

Isaac stopped. "I don't like the sound of that."

The Baptist turned, concerned about Isaac's ignorance. "Brother. Didn't God speak to you as He has to me?" The Baptist took Isaac's shoulders, eyes arched with sad compassion. "I assumed you had access to the American machine. When you arrived as He said...well, I assumed too much."

The Baptist fell against the wall, one hand stretched upward. "*And do not banish me from your sight. And do not make your voice hate me, nor your hearing. Do not be ignorant of me anywhere or any time. Be on your guard!*"

He continued as if he hadn't interrupted himself. "I used to be a very evil man. I would carve up a woman, stake her to the ground, and flay her open. If I could remove her heart, still beating, from her chest, and take a bite, then we were sure to win in battle that day." The Baptist licked his lips, realized he was enjoying his reminiscences, and composed himself.

Isaac tried to pull away, but the guards grabbed him, holding tight. "What the fuck did that have to do with the civil war?"

"Nothing, the war was an excuse."

Isaac leaned as far back as he could. "People like you give Africa a bad name."

The Baptist fell to the ground. "*For I am the first and the last! I am the honored one and the scorned one! I am the whore and the holy one!*" He crept back to standing and resumed his story. "One day a preacher washed away my sins. But I am still sinning, Isaac. Every day I atone for the sins I commit, and every day I sin even more. God told me He sent you, Isaac Deal, to bring about the second coming. So if you baptize me as God's son on earth then I become God, and nothing I do will be a sin."

"And you'll stop killing people?"

"Of course not." The Baptist gave away a sinister grin. "Haven't you read the Bible?"

"Yeah. I'm guessing you didn't get to the second half." Isaac stopped struggling. "You say God sent me here to turn you into Jesus 2-point-0? And sending your baby badasses to snatch me up from the hotel, and holding my friend hostage, is all part of God's plan?"

The Baptist's eyes rolled back in his head, but before he shuddered, Isaac interrupted him, impatient. "You can quote the Bible, or whatever, all day long. It's not going to impress me."

The Baptist sneered, a con man who'd been called on his con. He straightened up in body and speech. "This isn't God's plan. It's mine. I'm going to steal the great transubstantiation. And you're going to help me." He reached into the pocket of his rough cotton robe and pulled out three state-of-the-art satellite phones. "One was yours, one was Pollyanna's, and one was the tow-headed Joseph's. The rest of your team is on their way to an ambush. If you do this willingly, I'll let you warn them. If there's still time." The Baptist grinned. "Now come!"

The guards pushed Isaac down the hall after The Baptist.

They stopped at the end of the hall and waited for John to unlock a series of deadbolts on the sturdy door.

"Perhaps, Isaac, if you had the American machine, I would be the one baptizing you." His hands trembled with anticipation as they turned the first lock without a click.

"Open?" The Baptist tried the next. The deadbolt was also unlocked. He skipped the others and turned the doorknob halfway before letting go with a yelp.

"Hot?" The Baptist held his open palm out to the door.

A faint trail of yellow smoke oozed out from under the door.

The Baptist turned to his guards. "One of you, give me your shirt." The Baptist wrapped his hand and reached for the door.

Isaac dropped to the ground, taking one of the guards with him.

The Baptist opened the door.

The heat inside the room hit the oxygen in the hall and exploded in a ball of flame.

Chapter 19

97:4 stared out the passenger window of the Blazer into the rainy night and tucked a stray strand of her blonde hair back under her cap.

Their guide, Charles, an impressive slab of a man in a linen coat and raw cotton pants, had convinced Park he would find General Mamba in under an hour. That had been two hours ago.

"This! This is it! Pull over here!" Charles said.

"This *time* this is it," Park corrected. "I want you to say it again with confidence."

"You were pretty sure of yourself the last two times, Charlie," Gabby said. "Make this one count. I could have stayed back at the church with the kids and got more done."

"Show of hands," 97:4 said. "Who here has found a campsite, in the dark, in the rain, in the African jungle?" Ainia raised her hand from the front seat. "How about that? The only one not casting stones."

Park pulled the Blazer into a patch of grass, cut the engine, and opened the door. "Well, at least it's warm." He stepped into the wilderness in his coat and tie.

Ainia dropped out of the passenger seat into the grass. "The temperature's the one thing out here that won't try to kill us."

97:4 climbed into the front seat. "You and Ainia went the last two times. If you want, Gabby and I could take a turn."

Park shook his head. "We're keeping you big guns in reserve. If you hear gunshots, come in blazing."

97:4 watched Park and Ainia follow Charles into the darkness.

Gabby dropped 97:4's Bible into the front seat and climbed after it. She was going to say something, but caught 97:4 staring at the book. Gabby scooped it up and put it out of sight between her hip and the door. She smiled at 97:4 as if nothing had happened, and turned on the stereo. "Let's see what's on African radio. If I was back home, I might be doing exactly what we're doing right now." Gabby tried to find a strong signal, landing on talk radio for a moment before dialing on. "Parked in a truck out in the woods, listening to the radio. Except back in Kentucky I could find a decent classic rock station. And out here I ain't worried about killing the battery, 'cause you could give it a jump."

Gabby smiled but 97:4 turned back to the darkness and the rain, pretending she hadn't heard.

"Hey, 97, what's wrong?"

"You heard what Park and I went through in West Point? He left out a few things. I killed six men today."

Gabby left the dial on dead air and let 97:4 continue.

"Bad men. Men who deserved to die. The way they treated women, children…. But tomorrow, next week, sometime soon, another six bad men will step up and take their places." She looked Gabby in the eye. "So tell me, what's the point?"

Gabby left the dial alone. "What do you wanna do? Save the world?"

"What's wrong with that?"

"There's a whole lotta world out there, and only one you."

97:4 held her hands up, fingers arched, and imagined electricity racing back and forth between them before she shoved them away. "Then what else is this good for? Why should we bother with Project Dead Blind and Park's pointless missions?" Venom lined her voice when she said Park's name.

"You don't like Park, do you?" asked Gabby.

97:4 sighed. "It's not that. Every mission, I say it's my last. Every time he talks me into another one. I keep forgetting he's as lost as the rest of us. He only acts like he knows what he's doing."

"Well, I know what I could be doing." Gabby grinned. "I could be doing Park."

97:4 snorted and choked down a wave of appalled laughter. "Stop right there. That's wrong on so many levels, I don't know where to start."

"All those shots they gave us before we flew over here? They forgot to give me the one for Yellow Fever."

97:4 held up a finger and licked her lips, restraining herself. "Okay, that was pretty funny. But that doesn't make it right."

"Of course it ain't right. What would be the fun in that?"

"Boundaries, Gabby, boundaries. Learn them and don't cross them. They're there for a reason. Park's your boss *and* your sponsor."

Gabby's smile dropped. She turned back to fiddle with the radio.

"I'm sorry." 97:4 nervously tried to recover. "Park didn't tell me. I figured it out. I can tell you're in a program. I work with addicts every day. I know the signs, and this is one of them. It's natural to develop feelings for your sponsor."

"Oh, yeah? Well, from the way you keep looking at this Bible, I'm not the only addict on this team." Gabby opened the door to get out.

"I didn't mean—"

"Forget it." Gabby dropped out of the truck and turned back. 97:4 braced herself for an earful of hate, but Gabby kept her eyes down, grabbed the Bible, and closed the door.

"Don't go," 97:4 called after her.

"Seriously, forget it." Gabby said through the gap in the glass. "I ain't mad. I gotta drain the lizard."

97:4 climbed into the front seat. "What lizard?"

"You know what I mean." Gabby snapped, and disappeared into the darkness.

For a long moment, it was 97:4 alone with her stomach. The organ growled with hunger and anxiety. They weren't prepared. True, Isaac and Pollyanna were in trouble, but they should have picked up some raincoats and food.

She opened the glove compartment, and out spilled a half dozen empty pistol magazines. "Well isn't that perfect? Where did Exposition Joe buy this thing?"

The magazines were slippery, and for every handful 97:4 stuffed back in the glove compartment, half of them poured back out. The last one had a white piece of paper stuffed into the spring. 97:4 unfolded the mysterious note while Gabby returned and sat behind the wheel. The note read, *97:4, Duck! E.J.*

"Gabby!"

"I said forget—"

97:4 threw herself over Gabby. Automatic gunfire shattered the windshield and sprayed the front seat.

Chapter 20

The LED lights from Park's and Ainia's phones outshone the cheap D cell flashlight Charles carried. The blue-tinted light tickled the falling rain and gave the jungle a sterile sheen. Another gust of wind knocked Park off balance. He landed on one knee, cursing under his breath.

Ainia passed him with ease. She slipped a little, but flowed with the motion and stayed on her feet. "Better to have wind than bugs. Believe me."

Park was ankle deep in mud. "This country hates my shoes. I should have geared up. I don't know what I was thinking, coming out here like this."

Ainia lingered while Park got back on his feet. "You were thinking that time might be running out. You were thinking about your people. No shame in that."

Charles kept walking. He was a dozen steps ahead before he realized they'd fallen behind. "This time I have the right place. This is it. Come! Come!"

Park lowered his voice. "I don't think this is the right place."

"It's the right place for an ambush," Ainia agreed. "But then the whole countryside is when you're following a stranger into the jungle."

"He's carrying a gun," whispered Park. "It's in a holster under his arm."

"And for someone who's been lost, he's pretty sure where he's going. Want me to take care of him?"

"No. I'll do it." Park straightened up. "We need him to be able to answer questions."

Park trudged up the hill after Charles, breathing heavily. "How much farther?"

"Over the next hill," Charles assured them. His tone could have been one of amusement at the Westerner struggling through the jungle. It also could have been one of smugness at leading him into an ambush.

"Wait up, Charles." Park stopped the man as he was about to turn back up the hill.

"Let me ask you something about that." Park pointed to a tangle of trees up ahead and rested his phone hand on Charles's shoulder.

Charles looked where Park pointed. Park kept pointing and said nothing. Charles turned back to ask what he was pointing at. Park turned the light from his phone into the man's eyes and reached into his coat. Charles pulled away from the light, and Park pulled Charles's gun from its holster.

Park put the pistol barrel in Charles's face. "How many men do you have waiting for us up ahead?"

Charles reached for his empty holster, paused, and raised his hands, smiling. "Not up ahead."

The sound of automatic gunfire erupted from back where they'd left the truck, 97:4, and Gabby.

Park instinctively faced the sound.

Ainia shouted, "He's getting away!"

Park spun around to see Charles's cheap flashlight bouncing through the jungle. He took aim with two hands but couldn't pull the trigger.

Ainia ran up next to him. "What the hell, Park?"

"I'm not going to shoot a man in the back."

"Back or not, some people need to be shot." She set her fists on her hips. "So much for your questions."

Chapter 21

General Mamba's kidnappers had moved Pollyanna from the pickup into a camper on their first stop. After the second stop, the camper had gone its own way. This was the third stop. The two thugs had parked and left her alone without saying a word. Tied up and alone in the back of a Winnebago, she played the Positive Game.

"What a wonderful opportunity this is!" Pollyanna forced herself to say in a childish and cheerful voice. "Perhaps my kidnappers will stumble across a lion out there. That wouldn't be a bad thing, in the big picture. Lions need to eat too, after all." She waited, forcing a smile until her cheeks burned like the spot under her solar plexus where her bad luck collected.

The pain remained, telling Pollyanna nothing had happened. "Goddamn it. Help me out here!" she screamed at the universe. "I'm stuck in a rape-mobile in the middle of Africa. What the fuck does a bitch gotta do to catch a break?"

The driver's door opened. In crept two black kids Pollyanna didn't know, and one white kid she did. "Joe?"

"Hi, Pollyanna. Save your luck. You're going to need it to save the others. Jimmy, go back there and unlock Pollyanna's handcuffs. Here's the key." Joe pulled down the visor, catching the handcuff key as it fell out. "Everyone, keep your heads down. They're going to start shooting." Joe started the Winnebago, threw it into gear, and gunned it straight ahead.

Pollyanna's former kidnappers yelled from behind the vehicle, firing their guns. Bullets pierced the fiberglass and splintered through the cabinets. Joe hunched over the steering wheel. Thomas dropped down into the foot well. Jimmy and Pollyanna pressed themselves to the floor.

Joe dodged trees in the front and gunfire from the back. He shouted over his shoulder, "They were taking a leak, left the keys in the ignition and everything. Guess no one expects their car to get stolen out in the jungle."

Pollyanna said, "Yeah? Well that's what they get for '*entering the camp of Red Chief, the terror of the plains.*'"

Jimmy unlocked her handcuffs. "That's not all we stole. We lifted a Jeep and burned down a church. This has been most exciting."

The camper hit a ditch. Everyone flew up a few inches and came back down, hard.

"It was a bad church." Joe pulled the Winnebago onto what passed for a road in these parts. The last of the gunfire was far behind them.

"Whatever you say, Joe. You, kid in the front, get in the back." She and Thomas switched places. The kids started searching the cupboards and drawers in the back. "Did Park send you to spring me, or are you off on your own again?"

"Park thinks he's rescuing you and Isaac, but he led the rest of the team into a trap. Isaac's on his own, but the fire I set will help him escape. One way or another they'll all be in deep trouble soon, and we're going to have to help."

"It's up to you and me to save the day? Joe, we're fucked. I couldn't even save myself."

"Don't blame yourself, Pollyanna. It wasn't time. It's a good thing you haven't been able to play your card, because we have a big round coming up. The stakes are high, but don't worry. The game is rigged in our favor."

"As long as no one dies." Pollyanna settled into the front seat.

"Oh yes. People are going to die. People are dying right now."

Chapter 22

97:4 held still in the ruined truck cab. The weight of broken glass pulled at her hair. Rain knocked cubes of glass from the shattered windshield.

Gabby whispered. "Who the heck is that?" into 97:4's stomach.

"Doesn't matter. They're going to make sure the job's finished." As her adrenaline eased, 97:4 took stock of herself. "I wasn't hit. Were you?"

"No." Gabby twisted under her. "Crap, I got glass in my ear."

97:4 rolled off her teammate but kept her head down. "Give me my Bible. I'll take care of this."

"What are you going to do, electrocute them from here? No way. You'll fry me, or they'll plug you if you step into the open. 'Sides, Park said you only get this in an emergency."

97:4 locked unbelieving eyes onto Gabby's. "What do you think this is?"

Cautious footsteps approached, hushing the women.

97:4 broke the silence. "I know what I'm doing, Gabby." She pried under Gabby for her Bible.

Gabby rolled over, trying to put the leather-bound book out of 97:4's reach. "97, I got this."

The footsteps came around to Gabby's open door.

"Gimme the Bible, you redneck junkie bitch," 97:4 spit through gritted teeth.

"Tweaker bitch, actually." Gabby sneered, raising her voice, "*Let me bend your ear.*"

97:4 stopped. The footsteps stopped. Gabby kept talking. She left the Bible in 97:4's frozen grip, slid out of the truck, and shook off the fragments of glass. "You know I saw a UFO once. Not back home, not at first. It followed me home."

She stepped out of 97:4's field of view. "My boyfriend and I had been driving for forty-eight hours, like you do under that particular influence."

Gabby strained and pulled something away, "Let's say—" there was a hard crack, followed by the sound of a body falling in the mud, "it was in our best interest not to be pulled over at the time. There'd be questions about the bags in the backseat." 97:4 couldn't care less about Gabby's story, couldn't move, and couldn't stop listening as Gabby stepped through the brush.

"Anyway, I'd catch the spaceship in the rearview mirror, round, white, and all aglow."

Another grunt, knock, and another body fell to the ground.

"Being spaceman technology and all, I could only see it in the mirror. When I turned around to take a look, the damned thing disappeared."

Another thud.

"I must have tried to catch a straight look at that thing ten thousand times over that ride. The next day, my neck hurt something awful for all the whipping around and turning."

And another.

"Funny thing, it was the dome light all along, reflected in the window." Gabby leaned the rifle up against the truck and lifted the Bible out of 97:4's frozen fingers. "I knocked out all four of them gunmen, and didn't spill a drop of blood doing it. Not bad for a redneck tweaker bitch?"

97:4's control over her body was restored when the story ended. She turned over. "Gabby, I'm sorry."

Gabby slammed the truck door in 97:4's face.

Chapter 23

On the floor of the smoke-filled hall, Isaac used the rope around his wrists to choke the guard he'd taken down with him. The guard had managed a few weak stabs at Isaac's arms before slumping lifeless.

"That's what I need. Thanks." Isaac used the dead man's knife to cut himself free and crawled down the hall, over the bodies of the unconscious guards. Keeping to the floor, where the air was breathable, up the stairs and out of the building into the late evening. In The Baptist's compound again—without a hood over his head this time.

A handful of worshipers were up and about, performing evening chores, unaware their church's basement was on fire.

"Now this is unexpected." Isaac hid the knife under his shirt. Smoke poured from the doorway, drawing attention. Isaac shut the door, straightened up, waved at the witnesses, and strolled down the slope toward a tent surrounded by a dozen trucks, cars, and motorcycles.

Snoring boomed from the tent in waves. Isaac ducked behind an '87 El Dorado converted into a pickup truck via chainsaw. Surveying the array of beaten, decrepit, and jury-rigged vehicles, he crawled the lot, dismissing one after the other. "Smells bad. No doors. Notorious electrical problems." He came upon a minibike on the far side of the lot, small enough for a child. Isaac scratched his nose, considering. "What the hell. Looks like fun."

Isaac squatted down on the bike, reached for the ignition, and found it empty. He pushed the bike around the lot, toward the tent, and ran over a hubcap. The cap flipped into the air, clattering in the dark. Isaac stopped and clenched, waiting for the snoring to resume.

Isaac stopped outside the tent and reassessed the ignition. He pulled the knife from his waistband, jammed it in the ignition, and turned. The bike started. "Should have thought of that on my own."

The tent flap flew open and a wide-eyed, potbellied man burst forth, wielding a wrench like a club.

"Thank God you're awake!" Isaac grabbed whatever was in reach—a quart of oil—and pushed them into the man's arms.

"Here. Take these up to the church. The backup generator has been leaking, and it's almost dry."

The mechanic looked at the stranger on his minibike. "But—"

"No time, man! Move!" Isaac peeled out of the lot and away from the compound.

Downshifting to make it over the hill, when he hit the crest, Isaac forgot how the gears worked and made the rest of his escape in first gear.

Chapter 23

In the jungle, Park squatted by one of Gabby's four prisoners. Ainia, 97:4, and Gabby held AK-47s on their would-be killers. They had tied the four men to trees while Ainia found their Suzuki Samurai hidden in the copse. The men were barely conscious from the wallops Gabby had delivered.

Park stood. "They don't know anything. Or at least we're not getting it out of them anytime soon." He shouldered his rifle and turned to his team. "We're going back to The Baptist and getting some hard answers this time. First question is going to be, 'Why are you pretending to be a preacher, General Mamba?'" The ambush had Park thinking the General and the Baptist were one and the same. The prisoners weren't shocked by his accusation, confirming his suspicion.

The most coherent of the former gunmen said, "Cannot...leave us here like this. What of mercy?"

Park raised an eyebrow. "Mercy? What do you think this is? Mercy is giving you a chance. Mercy is keeping us from killing you four in cold blood. And if you're lucky, mercy will keep us safe long enough to send authorities to pick you up." He climbed into the driver's seat. "Before the jungle eats you. It's a better chance than you gave us."

The women joined Park in the Samurai and he pulled off, back the way they came.

Ainia rode shotgun, watching the prisoners fade away in the rearview mirror. "You keep leaving loose ends. You're going to wake up with one tied around your neck."

"I'm not going to kill those men because they're an inconvenience."

"They're killers, Commander."

"And I'm not. They're no longer a threat." Park started the windshield wipers.

"Don't be so sure."

Park slowed the car. "The storm is still screwing with the GPS. We're already lost."

"We're not lost," Ainia said with confidence. "Go down this hill, cross the field to the left, then follow the embankment for three miles."

Gabby asked, "How do you know all that?"

97:4 said, "She led Amazon warriors back and forth across terrain like this before they invented maps."

"I wasn't asking you," Gabby snapped.

97:4 shrugged and rolled her eyes.

Ainia turned on the women in the backseat. "I don't know what happened between the two of you, but put it aside until the mission is over. You keep acting like children and you're going to get someone killed. When we get Isaac and Pollyanna back, you can have it out in the ring. Hell, I'll even ref. Until then, take your frustrations out on the enemy."

97:4 and Gabby looked away from each other.

She faced front and said to Park, "Because when we find The Baptist, things are going to get bloody."

Chapter 24

The RV parked over the crossroads in the rain, surrounded by grassland and patches of trees. Jimmy and Thomas were asleep in the back. Pollyanna stretched. "Between the Benadryl coma on the flight, the jet lag, and the regular attempts on my life, it's been real easy to keep up all night. How are you staying awake, Joe?"

Joe drummed his fingers on the steering wheel.

"Joe?" Pollyanna leaned forward to look at the teenager. "I asked you a question."

"You did? Sorry, I was distracted. What was it?"

"Were you seeing the future again?"

"Yeah."

"What did you see?"

"Isaac, riding up this road toward us." Joe pointed without taking his hand off the wheel.

"That's good, right?" Pollyanna lit a cigarette and took a drag.

"Good or bad, it is."

Pollyanna huffed. "I suppose. Wait. Riding? Riding what?"

"A small motorcycle."

"Oh. Okay, I can buy that. For some reason I pictured him riding a horse. I thought you might be joking."

"I never joke."

"I know. You're kinda boring that way." She ashed into the cup holder. "You don't joke either."

"I'm kinda morose that way." She blew smoke into Joe's face. "Ain't we a ton of fun?"

"There's no time for fun, Pollyanna." Joe waved the smoke clear.

"No shit, kid. What's that sound?" A buzzing noise approached, stopped, came back with a surge, then grew louder, as a single headlamp broke through the rain, cresting the road ahead. "That Isaac?"

"Yeah." Joe started the RV. In the back, Jimmy and Thomas asked what was happening. Joe ignored their questions. "Hang tight, guys!" He threw the RV into drive.

Pollyanna clipped her seatbelt. "What are you doing? Turn your headlights on!"

Joe drove at the oncoming minibike. "Not yet."

"You're going to run him over?"

"No, I'm just going to try. He won't recognize us in the dark and won't stop any other way. Trust me." The vehicles were closing fast. Joe hit the headlights. Pollyanna made out Isaac's dashiki, teeth, and eyes, the last open wide with terror. The man fell off his bike to their left. Joe pulled hard to the right and barely missed Isaac.

The RV skidded to a stop in the mud. Joe threw it in park and turned to Pollyanna. "It was the only way."

"The fuck?" Pollyanna shouted. Joe had already jumped out of the RV to help Isaac up out of the mud. Pollyanna took a stunned moment to recover, then heaved herself after him.

The minibike lay sideways in the mud, engine still running, back wheel spinning freely. Its headlamp lit the scene. Isaac's purple silk was covered in brown mud. As Joe helped him stand, Isaac said, "Exposition Joe, just the man I wanted to see. Ha! How'd that ten grand do ya?"

Jimmy and Thomas popped out of the back of the RV. Isaac pointed a nervous finger at the children and asked Joe, "You didn't buy yourself a pair of…. Those days are over, Joe."

Isaac let his joke land, laughed, and elbowed Joe in the ribs. "Oh man, when am I ever going to be able to make that joke again, huh?

Pollyanna! Come here, girl! Give me a hug!"

Pollyanna stepped back. "You keep your filthy body to yourself. That goes for when you're clean too."

Isaac made to chase after her with open arms. "You weren't the one who tried to run over me, were you?"

Pollyanna stood her ground, blocking Isaac with the cherry on her cigarette. "No. That was Joe. And I don't have any business telling Joe how to drive." Joe smiled and winked like they were co-conspirators. "Also, fuck you. You can't talk about driving." She pointed at the minibike, bent cigarette cocked in her fingers. "You know that thing has more than one gear, right?"

Isaac walked toward the RV, dismissing the bike with a backward wave. "I don't even want to look at that thing. Let's go back to the hotel. Where are Park and the rest?"

Joe walked over to the bike and cut the engine. "They're heading back to The Baptist's compound."

"Oh, no. That dude's nuts." Isaac shook mud off his dashiki. "He had this whole plan for me to turn him into God. We have to stop them."

"We'll be too late to stop them, but we'll be in time to free them. We have to get moving—me and Pollyanna in the RV, and you on the minibike."

Isaac choked. "Are you out of your mind? You've seen me on that thing. I don't know how to ride for shit."

"But you *can* ride it, Isaac. They'll need it and you to get something, when everything's over."

Chapter 25

Park had a plan worked out halfway back to the compound. That plan went up in flames with The Baptist's church. The plume of smoke rose through the early morning light a mile away. As the smell hit them, the four ditched the Suzuki and crept forward on foot, with rifles at the ready.

When they reached the first tent, Park held up his hand and took a knee. The three women followed suit. "We're getting into black ops territory here, so I'm giving tactical command to Ainia. Let's be careful with the trigger fingers."

Ainia nodded. "First things first, let's make sure the area's clear of hostiles. We'll head clockwise around the perimeter, spiraling inward. Marching order goes me, 97:4, Gabby, and Park in the rear."

Gabby smiled. "This feels like a war movie."

Ainia glared at her. "You think this is a movie? If you don't get right, Gabby, I'll leave you here."

"I'm right, I'm right. I was just saying what was on my mind."

"Get any thought of movies, video games, or any other make-believe horseshit out of your head. This could get very real very quickly." Ainia looked over her shoulder and around the side of the tent. "Looks like there was some action out front of the church. We won't be able to tell until we get closer."

"I can tell you now. Hand me your phone." Park reached for his own, called up the camera apps, tapped the phones together, and handed

Ainia's back to her. Park's camera fed onto her display. He stood, set his phone on night-vision, zoomed all the way in, and held it around the corner. Everyone else gathered around Ainia's screen.

97:4 asked, "Why can't my phone do that?"

Park had difficulty pointing his phone while watching Ainia's. "It can. All the phones have the same capabilities. Haven't you read the manual?"

"No one ever reads the manual, Park," said Gabby, shooting a brief glance at 97:4.

"When we get back to the States we'll spend a day doing hands-on phone training."

97:4 cracked her knuckles. "Are you suggesting we aren't tech savvy because we're women?"

"You just admitted you... Don't turn this around on me, 97."

Ainia interrupted, growling, "Everyone needs to shut up. Park, you need to hold that thing still. All you're giving me is seasickness."

Once Park focused on his camerawork, Ainia was able to confirm. "A pickup truck and bodies, lots of bodies." Ainia looked up from the screen. Everyone else had turned away. She powered off her phone and shouldered her rifle. "The plan remains the same. We circle in, low and slow."

Ainia led the team from tent to tent, around the cindering ruin of the church, and back around to the front, on the edge of the clearing. Fourteen hours ago they'd pulled up to this exact spot in Exposition Joe's Blazer. The Baptist's congregation had welcomed them with open arms. Now that congregation lay dead at their feet. Necks sliced open, their blood soaking the earth.

The pickup truck was parked in the center of the massacre, driver's door open and the engine running.

Gabby cried silently.

Ainia stepped back. "There's something wrong here. Who left this truck running?"

A hand reached up from the carnage and grabbed Gabby's ankle before Park could warn her. She screamed and pointed her rifle around toward the face of a dying woman.

Through bloody lips, the woman said, "The General…is back."

Gabby asked, "Back from where?" as a rifle barrel jabbed her in the spine. Among the dead and dying, men turned over, drawing the rifles their bodies had concealed. Project Dead Blind was outgunned six to one.

A burned man in a scorched white robe staggered up and sneered. "Dr. Park! Didn't find your chemical weapons, I see."

Park squinted at the wreck before him. "John? What happened?"

"You happened!" the Baptist screamed in disjointed mania. "You. With your lies and distractions. You came here to destroy me. First my whores in West Point." His arm swung back to the burning wreck. "Then my baptismal. I was going to become God. Now there's no moving forward, so I moved back. Back to the old days." He stepped on the corpse of a woman holding the corpse of a child. "Without my Faith Machine, I don't need the congregation anymore. So we had some fun with them."

His men, covered in the blood and gore of their victims, stood and disarmed the agents.

Tears running down her face, Gabby resisted. The gunman, a handprint of blood smeared across his face, spit at her, but she held tight. He brought his own rifle up to her face. He froze when Gabby said, "*Let me bend your ear.*"

She twisted her rifle out of the man's grip. "Back home, I had a neighbor with a pack of mean old dogs." She wound between the soldier and spies to her target, The Baptist. "They were a real pain in the ass. Barking, biting, and crapping all over the place. Till one day my Uncle Lou got an idea to do something about it." She eased the rifle to her shoulder, bringing the barrel up to the man's face. "He figured you don't have to shoot every dog, just the top dog."

The Baptist snatched the barrel and pulled it aside. He cracked Gabby across the temple with his pistol and wrapped an arm around her before she hit the ground. "I hear too many voices to hear yours, little girl. The rest of you disarm, now."

Ainia readily gave over her rifle. So did Park, after considering his options and discovering none.

97:4 hesitated and looked to Park.

The Baptist shot her in the arm.

She cried out, fell to her knees, and dropped her rifle. He put the gun to Gabby's temple. "Hesitate again and this won't be a flesh wound."

Ainia still looked like she wanted to fight, but Park shook his head and disarmed, raising his hands above his head. The Baptist's soldiers took their guns, pushed them onto their knees, and bound their hands behind their backs.

"Yes, tie them up," The Baptist said, throwing Gabby to the ground. "And gag this one. I'll sell their brains to my Chinaman. All except you, Dr. Park. You've cost me great losses. I intend to take them out on you."

Park looked around, scanning the area for tactical options. His eyes fell on a blond figure on the edge of the compound, standing on top of an RV. Joe waved his arms wildly at Park. "You won't get the chance, John. Exposition Joe's going to get us out of here."

The Baptist laughed. "Joseph? The boy? And how is he going to do that?"

"Who knows with Joe?"

The Baptist took deliberate aim between Park's eyes. "Wherever Joseph is, he cannot help you now."

Chapter 26

From the roof of the RV, Exposition Joe and Pollyanna watched Ainia lead the others through the ruined compound. Pollyanna took a sip from the warm can of orange pop she'd found inside the RV, and winced with distaste. She pointed the can at Park as he trotted to the next piece of cover. "For once, I'm not getting the shit end of the stick. I hate all that G.I. Joe shit. It's better up here with the Exposition Joe shit. Wondering what the fuck is going on while you call all the shots."

"It doesn't bother you that I see the future? It bothers Ainia."

"Fuck Ainia. I like having someone around who knows what's going on. When we get back to the States, you should come to the track with me. We could pull some serious *Rain Man* shit. Matching suits and all. I can do drag for a day."

"Sure. If it's in the Script."

Pollyanna lit another cigarette. "It's not in the Script, is it?"

"Nope. We're all going to be real busy when this is over."

"I won't make any appointments then." She took a drag and poked Joe in the arm. "How come we don't contradict each other? You keep saying the future's been written, 'the Script.' But I make luck. How can there be both luck and destiny? I call bullshit."

"There's something special about you, Pollyanna. I see when you play your card, but not how it plays. You leave a blank spot in the Script. A crate could fall out of the sky and crush The Baptist, or there'll be a freak earthquake and he'll fall into an open crack in the earth." Joe watched

Ainia's team disappear behind a tent. "Probably not one of those, but whatever it ends up being, it saves the day."

Pollyanna snorted into her can. She wiped her mouth on the back of her wrist. "Oh well. We're fucked."

"Seriously," Joe said. "To do your thing, you have to care. Under all that bitterness, you care about Park, 97:4, even Ainia. You care about the innocents too."

"Fat load of good caring does. Innocents get steamrolled. What innocents are you talking about, anyway?"

Joe pointed toward the burning church. "While I freed you, The Baptist had his soldiers kill his congregation, children, women, and the men."

The pop can trembled in Pollyanna's hand. "W-why? Why did he do that?"

"Because there was no one there to stop him. Like before, when he was a warlord. But you're going to stop him from doing it again. When the time comes, in a few seconds actually, you'll step up and do what's needed. It's because you care. I've seen it."

"What if you're wrong?"

"I'm never wrong. Get ready." Sunlight graced the tops of the higher tents. Joe twisted back to face the rising sun.

Ainia's squad broke into view again when she led them into the clearing in front of the church.

"This is where they get ambushed," Joe said, like he was calling a predictable movie.

"Wait. What?" was all Pollyanna could say before The Baptist's men sat up, pointing their rifles.

Joe turned to Pollyanna. "You're ready."

She waved him off. "Shit. I don't—no, I'm not ready."

"Pollyanna. Listen to me. You're ready." He looked back at Ainia's team.

Pollyanna asked, "Why isn't anybody moving? Except…is that the new girl?"

"Yeah. Gabby is almost going to wrap things up. Unfortunately, The Baptist is schizophrenic." Joe and Pollyanna saw him pistol-whip Gabby. "Her power doesn't work on people like us. You're ready."

"Stop saying that!" Pollyanna's cigarette burned her fingers. She cursed and dropped it. "Look at that. I can't even get cancer without fucking up."

A shot. 97:4 fell.

"But—" Pollyanna's voice quivered like a nervous child's. Her hands went to her lower sternum. "But this simply can't be. We didn't…97:4 didn't come all this way to die in the dirt. It's so absurd as to be out of the question."

Joe smiled. "Told you you're ready. Park's going to look this way." He stood, waved his arms a few times, and sat back down. "Keep going, Pollyanna, keep caring."

Pollyanna spoke in the inflections of a proper schoolgirl from the turn of the previous century. "Project Dead Blind is an elite team of psychic agents. The seven of us are some of the most powerful individuals on the planet. We're demigods among men. A force such as this is more than a match for this self-proclaimed Baptist, be he madman, warlord, or killer. More importantly, we're the good guys."

Pollyanna stood, hands still clenched to her chest as if in prayer. "Let luck reign."

Chapter 27

The pistol pointed between his eyes. Park said, "Ainia, if he pulls that trigger, kill every one of these bastards."

"Now you're talking."

"Last order indeed, Dr. Park." The Baptist pulled the trigger. Park flinched. The pistol hammer clicked, but didn't fire.

Annoyed, The Baptist drew the gun away from Park's head, turned it sideways and reached to eject the misfired round. The powder ignited. The round hit the gut of the soldier standing over Park's left shoulder.

The man dropped his rifle, stumbled back, and fell into the cab of the running pickup truck. Flailing in pain, he pushed the stick shift into first gear. The truck bucked into motion, running down six of The Baptist's men.

Park grabbed The Baptist's pistol arm with both hands and dragged him to the ground.

Ainia pulled a red-enameled knife off of a soldier and stabbed him in the neck. Moving through the rest, she flowed with grace, an exotic dance, ending the soldiers' lives.

The dying man in the truck cab tugged on the steering wheel, trying to right himself, sending the vehicle in a tight circle around the agents of Project Dead Blind and through The Baptist's soldiers. Two soldiers tried to stop the truck, grabbing its grille. They went under the wheels. Another tried to climb into the cab and fell under the back tire.

Gabby ripped off her gag and used it as a compress on 97:4's bullet wound. 97:4 reached into Gabby's satchel, tore a page from the Bible within, and ate it. The last two of The Baptist's men turned their rifles on Ainia. 97:4 drove her fingers into the mud and sent everything she had through the wet ground. With an electric crack, the gunmen launched into the sky.

Park and The Baptist wrestled over the pistol. Park was losing.

Ainia wrapped a hand around The Baptist's forehead. With the knife, now red twice over, she slit the man's throat, spraying Park with the African's blood.

Bleeding out, The Baptist collapsed onto Park. The pistol, slick with blood, slipped out of Park's grip. "Christ, Ainia."

She shrugged, "Just following your orders, Commander. Not that I'm complaining. It's about time you got blood on your hands…"

Park pushed himself free of The Baptist's corpse. The last one of the day.

Chapter 28

While the freed agents checked on each other in the distance, Joe turned to Pollyanna and smiled. "See? I knew you cared."

Pollyanna unbuttoned her blouse and gave her sternum one last rub through her T-shirt. The pain was gone. "That wasn't all me."

Joe started down the ladder mounted on the back of the RV. "They're good, but not that good. They couldn't have done it without you."

Pollyanna drew a cigarette, but thought twice and slipped it back into the pack. "Yeah, but you're the one who put this all together. You're not fooling me, Joe. We're all pawns in whatever game you're playing."

He paused with only his head still above the RV roof.

"Game? I wish. I miss games." Joe dropped out of sight.

She didn't hear the minibike until Isaac rode over the crest. He pulled up below her, next to the RV, and cut the engine. "Sounds like you're learning how to ride that thing."

Isaac pointed a thumb over his back at the medic's kit. "Back and forth from the aid station, I had a lot of time to practice. Did I miss all the excitement?"

"97:4's been shot." She pointed toward the burned-out church. "You'd better head over there."

Isaac nodded and turned the bike around. "Sounds like she's having a bad day."

Pollyanna faced the sun rising in a smokeless patch of sky and sighed.

"Everyone on the team lived and the bad guys died. No, today was a good day."

Isaac started the engine and pulled away.

Chapter 29

Dr. Park sat at an old steel and linoleum table, signing the last of the admissions paperwork at Harry Moniba Primary School. It had taken some bureaucratic maneuvering to get Jimmy and Thomas enrolled. A donation from the Office of Intergovernmental and External Affairs was the hammer that had taken care of most of the nails that needed pounding.

The boys sat on a bench in the hall. Thomas pretended to read a poster about the food pyramid. Jimmy slouched on the bench, staring at the floor.

Park folded his hands. "Okay. Put it back."

The boys looked up and gave Park their puppy dog-eyes. Before they could start with their excuses, he commanded, "Do it."

The boys looked at each other for last minute ideas. Finding none, Jimmy leaned forward and an electric stapler slipped out from behind him.

Thomas caught it. "What was that doing there?"

"I'm sure." Park took the stapler. "I can't imagine what you were planning on doing with that. You kids don't need to steal anymore. You'll be set here at the school. Doesn't that sound better than picking pockets on the street?"

Jimmy and Thomas each waited for the other to answer Park's question.

"It'll be less dramatic. You'll get used to it. Stop stealing for a couple of years. Give it a shot, will you? For me?" Park's voice strayed into the tones of a pleading parent at the end.

He sighed. "I'm trying to do some good here by you kids. I'm probably not going to have a job when I get back. My mission was a failure. We destroyed the machine we were sent here to collect."

He knelt to look the kids in the eye. "But if I can take you two off the streets and into an education, then that'll be the one good thing I've done in Liberia."

He'd taken the boys from guilty to confused.

Jimmy said, "Dr. Park, we know a lot of people who are just people, a few good people and a whole lot of bad people. You're one of the good ones, and you don't even have a reason to be."

Thomas added, "The Baptist was a bad, bad man before you came. He had an army. That didn't stop you and your friends from stopping him. No matter how things ended, you stood up for what's right."

Park gave them both a hug.

Chapter 30

General Wu surveyed the ashen ruins of The Baptist's church in the morning light. Her dark green suit and sensible black flats weren't her uniform, but might as well have been.

An official from the Chinese embassy, in safari shorts and a khaki shirt, locked the car and caught up with her. "This is the church. Or was."

General Wu looked over her sunglasses at him.

He lowered his eyes. "Of course, you know that."

Charles followed up the slope. Charles carried himself with the bored air of one waiting to get paid until he noticed Wu looking in his direction. The weight of the tragedy suddenly fell upon the man's shoulders. He sniffed and wiped an invisible tear from his eye.

"Right this way. Dozens of victims all through this area. Be careful, there's still blood on the ground." The embassy official scurried to the patch of ground where The Baptist had made his last stand. "The authorities were called, anonymously, of course."

Wu followed, minding her steps. "How were they killed?"

"Machete and small arms fire, for the most part. Over a dozen showed signs of vehicular damage. Here's the interesting part." The embassy official hopped over to a jagged patch of darkened earth. "Electrical burns on the ground and on two of the casualties."

General Wu knelt to inspect the burnt grass. Without being asked, the official dropped to his knees and pushed the ash and dirt away, excavating a rough but solid piece of mineral. The earth was fused into a crust and branching out in a spiked V shape.

"Was there any physical evidence like this in the West Point slum?" General Wu stood and brushed off her knees.

"No, ma'am. Not like this, just the burnt remains of a tent. The corpses were removed by whatever unsavory means they use in the slum. But we did find a witness who saw a blonde woman enter before the tent burst into sparks."

"It's safe to assume there was only one blonde electrokinetic in country. Right? Russian? American? Even Dutch? You said there were four of them, including the blonde?"

Charles nodded. "Two short brown women, led by a Chinaman. They said they were from America."

"I know what they said. People say a lot of things in this trade. How do you know their leader is Chinese?"

Charles had no answer.

"You don't. You can't tell a Japanese man from Korean from the Chinese, can you, Charles?"

"No, but I know witches when I see them. Like the one who trapped my men with her words."

"Mmm. That's the other interesting part, isn't it?" She headed for the ruin. "Charles, is this a regional custom? To place a church far from the populated areas, with a surrounding shanty town?"

"No. The Baptist was a great and good man. We are less for having lost him. The Chinaman came here to kill him and end his mission for God. The devil sent him. I'm sure."

"If he was so evil, why'd he let your men live? He even reported their location to the government, while you ran home, leaving them behind. Does that seem evil?"

"He shot at me."

"No doubt."

The embassy official spoke up. "There are many oddities about this institution, which was, in fact, built by American Christian philanthropists. Well, they claim to be philanthropists. There aren't many records of them making charitable donations; mostly political ones.

"And then there's this." The official led them to the edge of the burned-out basement and the ruined Faith Machine below, now ash and wiring.

General Wu stood at the edge of the pit. "Charles, what was down there, in that basement?"

"That's where The Baptist kept his private baptismal, where he communed with God."

Wu raised an eyebrow. "Did he now? Did it look something like a clamshell? Made of cedar? A host of golden wiring at the joint?"

"Yes, yes, yes. How did you know? You've been here before?" Charles seemed genuinely surprised.

"No, but I wish I had." She slung her purse over her shoulder. "This was something I've been seeking for decades, ever since I helped destroy another machine like it in Hong Kong. That was a mistake, and this," she pointed to the ruin below, "was a waste. I'm done here. Pay this man and take me to the airport."

Chapter 31

General Wu sat at the coffee bar of the Roberts International Airport, drinking tea and watching people queue up for their flights. The airport was simple and showing its age. It reminded her of the airports of China's provincial capitals back in the eighties. That blonde woman and her friends had been here days ago. Wu would know who they were and where they were going if the embassy official had a spy in the airport.

But he didn't. *Incompetence.* Probably why he'd been assigned to a backwater like Liberia.

Collecting the three coins she'd received in change, Wu threw the I Ching. *How should I find the saboteurs who destroyed the Faith Machine?* Six tosses—dark, dark, light, dark, light, dark. *Hexagram Thirty-Nine, Chein. Limping difficulties. Progress is impeded. Stop, and reassess the situation.*

Returning to China would be a mistake. Maybe she wasn't done in Liberia.

While she watched passengers shed watches, wallets, and keys into plastic tubs before passing through metal detectors, a message came over the PA system warning that unattended bags would be destroyed.

If the saboteurs had been through here, Wu thought, maybe they had left something behind. Finishing her tea, she found the airport's lost and found, claiming she'd left something at the bar when she'd arrived. The clerk brought out a plastic tub like the ones at the metal detector, filled with leftovers, cell phones, handbags, and keys.

Pushing through the refuse, Wu spied a blue folder at the bottom and dragged it out of the tub. The cover read, *Pollyanna Whittier: The Office of Intergovernmental and External Affairs.*

The general twitched with delight, quickly composing herself. Thanking the clerk, she absconded with the file.

If the "Office of Intergovernmental and External Affairs" cover was active, that meant James Ensign's little enterprise was still in business. This looked like the Hong Kong incident all over again, but this time no mistakes.

Wu canceled her flight to Beijing and booked the first flight to the US.

Chapter 32

Caseman Twenty-Two folded his coat on top of his aluminum briefcase, loosened his tie, rolled up his sleeves, and unplugged the refrigerator containing the liquid nitrogen.

Caseman Four came stumbling into the abandoned hospital ward, clutching his doctor's bag in both hands. He'd been sleeping in his dark blue suit. Four straightened his glasses. "What are you doing?"

"What does it look like?" Caseman Twenty-Two unlocked the wheels on the cart and pushed the tank down the hall toward the OR. "No point in delaying the inevitable, is there?"

Even living in this foreign squalor, Twenty-Two looked like he'd stepped out of the background of a propaganda poster. Four, stooped and disheveled, clearly played toadie to the taller man.

Four followed Twenty-Two. He shook out a bucket hat from his pocket. "But we haven't received orders."

"Do you think he'll want us to stay now that The Baptist is dead? The chance of another source materializing is impossible." Twenty-Two wound the canister and cart around the clutter and damage inflicted on the clinic's interior by years of neglect. "When the order to return does come, I want to leave immediately. Not one more moment in this filthy city, country, or continent. We're lucky these savages haven't torn us apart."

He stopped the cart on the edge of a large pile of debris to clear a mildewed lump of cardboard from his path. "Help me move this."

Four shuffled over. His doctor's bag in one hand, he tried to lift the cardboard box by the lip with the other. The lip and the side of the box tore off. The box fell. Folders spilled across the hall.

Twenty-Two turned to his countryman and pointed to his aluminum briefcase. "Put your case down over there."

"I lost the last one," Caseman Four whimpered.

"Nothing is going to happen to it here."

"If—-if it does, can I have yours?"

"Don't be stupid."

A crash came from the offices the men had partitioned as their living quarters. Caseman Ten stumbled out into the ward. Naked and caseless, he clutched the receiving desk like a drowning man would a lifesaver. Pale and trembling, a slow, shaking hand reached for their primary supply in the shoebox.

"Where's your case?" Four pushed his bucket hat back with shaking fingers.

The other Casemen watched Ten struggle, Four with some concern, Twenty-Two out of obligation.

It took three tries for Ten to get the lid off the box and another two for him to retrieve a baggie of the brown crystals.

Twenty-Two asked, "Don't you think you've had enough?"

If Ten heard the question, he was beyond answering. Intent on opening the baggie he ended up tearing it down the side. The contents spilled on the countertop and mixed with the dust, dirt and dead insects. He crushed the crystals and, with his palm's edge, arranged the mixture in a rough line and snorted.

There was a time when Twenty-Two and Four would have found this sight disgusting. Now they merely went back to work, clearing the cart. Twenty-Two was careful to keep the dirty equipment at arm's length from his clean gray suit. Four wasn't so careful. His pants were soon covered in clumps of cobweb.

Caseman Ten arched his back and screamed, "I have orders!"

That got the attention of the others. They stopped what they were doing.

"Orders? So soon?" Four stepped forward. His doctor's bag snagged on the wheel of the cart and yanked out of his grip. He dove back to the floor, catching it with both hands. The bucket hat fell forward, covering his eyes.

Twenty-Two approached Ten. "We're returning home?"

Ten wiped his nose down the length of his forearm and aimed his sunken, bloodshot eyes into Twenty-Two's. "No, we're heading into the belly of the beast, the Second Enemy. We'll be joining Caseman Seven there."

Twenty-Two fell to his knees and dropped his face in his hands.

Even Four put his doctor's bag aside. "Traveling in America will be difficult. And the border will be a challenge to navigate even… unencumbered." His eyes fell on the shoebox of crystals. "It would be a shame to waste it."

Caseman Twenty-Two's eyes twitched. He forgot about the cart and joined the others. Twenty-Two in his gray suit, Four in his wrinkled bucket hat, and Ten in his skin, the three Casemen hunched around the dirty counter. Forming the crystals into rows, they made quick work of the remaining supply of meth.

Chapter 33

Across the world, in Stillwater, Minnesota, the Reverend Representative Debra Fray bolted up from her oak desk in surprise as the door swung open. With hasty hands, she straightened her coral suit over her tight body, the model of aging gracefully.

The intern, a young man in a bow tie and sweater vest, stood in the doorway, holding a document. "I'm sorry, ma'am, I thought I heard you say 'come in'."

"No. Ah, no. That wasn't what I said." She walked around to the front of the desk, past the Minnesota flag and the wall-to-wall hardwood shelves of unread books. "But now that you're here…"

"Stewart."

"What's so important, Stewart?" She took the memo from his hand.

"Bad news from Africa, ma'am."

Fray paged through the report, pretending interest. "A constant flow of bad news pours out of Africa. What makes this news special to the sixth district of Minnesota?"

"Not to Minnesota, ma'am. Special to your other capacity, Reverend. The Samaritan's Church in Liberia burned down. The priest was killed and his congregation slaughtered."

Representative Fray flipped back to the front page of the report and read the cover this time.

She slammed the file on her desk, cocked a fist on her hip, and grimaced with a slow, dramatic shake of her head. "Those damned Chinese."

Stewart lowered his hands. "Chinese, ma'am? There wasn't anything in the report about—"

She cut him off with a steely look. "Stewart. Which of us is on the House Armed Services Committee?"

"You, ma'am."

"And, as such, I am allowed access to reports from the CIA, NSA, Department of Defense, etcetera? Reports filled with privileged information, the kind Senate interns aren't?"

"Yes, ma'am."

"Then if I say it was the Chinese, it was the Chinese. They've taken their war on Christianity abroad. This is just one instance of many churches they've destroyed." She closed her eyes and took a deep breath. "I'm going to have to pray on this. Leave me be."

"Yes, ma'am." Stewart escaped, closing the door behind him.

A stifled snicker came from under the desk.

Representative Fray locked the office door and chuckled. "Get out from under there."

An air force general extracted himself from the furniture, firm-jawed, silver-haired, with a marathoner's build. His name tag read Casey. "That was close. Why wasn't your door locked before?"

"It's more fun when it's dangerous, Steve." She smiled for a moment before picking up the report and handing it to him. "But this is serious. What do you think? Was this deliberate?"

"You're asking me to make a judgment based on a little eavesdropping?"

"At the least send someone in. Maybe the Faith Machine can be salvaged."

"Maybe we shouldn't have left it there in the first place."

"Well, what else were we going to do with it? I still think the possibilities were interesting. A theocratic government in Liberia, a Christian one this time. Ah, well."

"Why do you want to pin this on China?" The general straightened his uniform.

"Hmm? Oh, that." She dismissed the question with a wag of her hand. "I've been blaming everything on China lately. I'm tired of blaming Muslims. They're so boring. Let's stir something up with China for a change. Start a new Cold War. Bring back the Commies. And the Chinese make it so easy. They're everywhere these days."

General Casey raised an eyebrow, skimmed the report, and asked, "I'll see what I can come up with. How about you? Aren't you going to pray yourself up an answer to what happened? I'm sure God has something to say about losing a house. And a 'baptismal.'"

Representative Fray sat at her desk. "Well of course I am, silly. How else am I going to get the truth? But later. Right now I don't want the truth." She pulled a mirror and an ivory snuff kit from the top drawer and traced herself a line of white powder. "I want a convincing lie. That's where you come in."

General Casey eyed the cocaine. "Mind if I get some of your…transubstantiation before you go downstairs to pray?"

Representative Fray snorted a line, yipped, and smiled with pleasure. She tweaked his nose. "Of course you can, silly-billy. But you're going to have to fuck me for it."

Chapter 34

Egorov climbed down the iron stairs into the lowest depth of CIG-1. Cylindrical and industrial, the converted missile silo had been his home for sixteen years and his prison for the past fifteen of those. The state volunteers had been through six months ago, busting the rust and patching the gaps with a color a shade off of the original, but gratefully still plain and gray. The rest of CIG-1's interiors were the dull pastels of a Soviet daycare. The stink of paint remained. There was no ventilation to speak of down here. Weapons didn't need to breathe.

When he had been at the top of the stairs, Egorov knew he'd arrived first. The social scientist had long ago cataloged all of his cohorts' peccadilloes. If the others were down here they would have left the hatch ajar and lit the laboratory light. At the bottom, he felt his way to the light switch and threw it, as the guard joined him from up above.

Egorov didn't know the guard's name and didn't care. Fur hat, dark green overcoat, and a submachine gun, like the dozens who had held this post before him. This was Egorov's favorite kind of guard, disinterested. Sometimes a busybody would get assigned to CIG-1 and the Russians' progress ground to a halt. Those kinds of guards never lasted long at CIG-1. Where they went was a mystery.

The Collective's tank had frosted over again, ten feet high and three in diameter. Egorov took the scraper off its hook and cleared the panes of glass.

The guard did his customary patrol of the laboratory, past the

Collective, around the cedar clamshell of the Faith Machine, and an idle pass of the clone in its nutrient tank. Three great works of psychotronic engineering at the bottom of a hole in the ground. Satisfied, the guard climbed the stairs for a smoke.

When Egorov had chipped the excess frost away, he used the heat of his palms to clear the glass, revealing the Collective's brains, one after the other, floating in a paraffinum liquidum mixture. A lattice of golden wires stretched over each of the frozen organs, coming to a stem at the base. The stems ran down, connecting to the conduit at the bottom of the tank. The organic computer looked like a surrealist's sculpture of seaweed.

The speakers mounted at the Collective's base crackled to life. "Thank you, Dr. Egorov. Unnecessary, but we appreciate the gesture. You're the only one who performs this action. We've always taken this as a sign that you see us as more than a tool."

"It's nothing."

"It means something to us. That's why we wanted to tell you something, before the others arrive."

Egorov warmed his palms in his armpits. "A surprise? I haven't had one of those in years. What is it?"

The Collective switched to Russian. "We know what you're planning, Doctor."

"I'm sure you do." Designed by his comrades, the Collective was an organic supercomputer. The hardware, casing and preservation were designed by Istomin, the engineer. The software, training the gestalt to tap into its precognitive abilities, was handled by Mikhailov, the physicist and mathematician. While Egorov consoled the emerging intelligence, keeping it sane.

Egorov cupped his hands, warming them with his breath, and walked around the other side of the chamber to where the clone waited in a life support system the Russians built from a repurposed torpedo tube sixteen years ago. Inside was a young man taken from the womb and transplanted here. His body was perfect, his mind a tabula rasa.

"The clone isn't intended for the Dear Ruler—it never was. We're wondering if you've fully considered the implications of your plan."

"Freedom, knowledge, and power—what else is there to consider?"

"Particularly power. We've seen what happens when a new power steps onto the world stage. Your reception won't be peaceful."

"What else are armies for? This nation has been run by fools for decades, and still it stands. I can't imagine we'll do any worse, not with our intellect, knowledge, and augmentations. And what do you care? You couldn't possibly have developed sympathy in there, could you?" Egorov peered into the dark glass.

"Not at all, Doctor. But we'll ask you for a favor."

"Which is?"

"Death. After we aid you with the transfer, once you have all you want, you won't need us anymore. We want to die. If you care enough to clear our glass, you must care enough to set us free."

Footsteps on the ladder echoed down the shaft.

Egorov cleared the last of the frost. He empathized with the Collective. This was a means of escape he himself had considered many times during his imprisonment, but he was reluctant to promise anything to the machine. "No small favor. And that's certainly something I'll have to think on. Please keep this between you and me."

"Of course, Dr. Egorov."

The scientist's compatriots approached. The guard stepped aside to let them in. Then went back up the stairs for another cigarette.

Mikhailov's face—what was visible behind his unattended facial hair—breached the darkness. Calling it a beard implied a deliberate grooming choice. Mikhailov always had a tenuous grasp on hygiene and had given up on grooming altogether shortly after they'd arrived at CIG-1. Once a year, he'd hack his hair back like an intruding bush.

Conversely, Istomin hadn't let their circumstances compromise his appearance. He still wore a tie and vest under his lab coat. The gray at his temples, crow's feet at the edges of his eyes, and pallor of living underground had been the only shifts in his appearance over the past decade and a half.

Istomin eyed the Collective's clean glass. "Been waiting long, Egorov?"

"Not long. Apparently I woke early. I'm adrift like this every time a wristwatch dies on me. I put in for a new one. We'll see what happens. They'll probably ship me an oven timer instead."

The three milled about the laboratory, performing routine maintenance, going through the motions to cover their clandestine meeting.

Mikhailov had gone to work on the Faith Machine, muttering in Russian. "We would have given them everything they wanted years ago if they had reliable logistics in place. They're letting me out to lecture on dynamic systems theory tomorrow, Egorov. I'll see what I can do about your wristwatch."

Istomin slid under the Collective's tank, opened his notebook, and readied his pencil. "Worry about that topside. We don't have much time. Collective?" He raised his voice when addressing the Collective, like it was an elderly relative. "New developments?"

The speakers buzzed slightly for a moment before announcing, "The restored installation in Africa has been destroyed, material source terminated."

"Sorry to lose the material source. So much effort establishing it, and it just began to bear fruit. The conscript?"

"The conscript was on site, and survived, along with the rest of Project Dead Blind."

Egorov nodded. "Excellent. What of our agents in Liberia?"

"Uncompromised," the Collective droned.

Istomin smiled. "Third parties? Any of them in play?"

"Chinese agent who investigated the site after the destruction is leaving Liberia for America."

Mikhailov flung his hand toward the machine. "There you have it. They're onto us, whether they know it or not. They're probably going to capture the American installation. If the conscript gets in the way, that will be the end of him.

"Fucking Chinese!" He made to punch the wall, stopped before he struck the steel bulkhead, and tapped it with his knuckles instead. "For years they crushed everything of interest. And when we need something destroyed, they start collecting instead."

The guard leaned in to check on the raised voices. Egorov passed Mikhailov a wrench as if that was what the shouting was about. The guard wandered back upstairs for a third smoke.

Egorov said, "If it's the Chinese, we're going to have to start. I say we bring in the conscript now. When the Chinese take the machine out of American hands, it will take them months to figure out its operation. They shouldn't affect transplant."

Istomin checked his watch. "I'm inclined to agree with you. The next play will be in America. We had better get our pieces on the board. "Collective, dispatch this order to all agents: Travel to America by whatever means and await further orders."

Egorov said, "Hopefully, we'll have those orders figured out soon." His guard returned, tapping his watch on its face. "We are out of time, Istomin."

Egorov left the chamber and mounted the ladder. "I'm glad this happened—the kick in the ass to finally stop preparing and start acting."

Istomin turned to Mikhailov. "I suppose he's right." He felt the bulkhead with affection. "But it'll be hard, leaving home. We've done such great work here."

Mikhailov spat. "Fuck this place. I'll come back here with a shovel and fill this septic tank myself."

Istomin climbed the ladder. Mikhailov realized he'd left the wrench out of place. He went back to set it right.

The speaker on the Collective fired up again, "Dr. Mikhailov, would you leave the light on, please? It's not that we can see down here, but the darkness makes us feel like...property."

The physicist shrugged. "Sure. Why not?"

"We appreciate the gesture, Doctor. You've always treated us as a living entity. That's why we wanted to ask you a favor."

The Collective asked Mikhailov to let it die. At the same time, it watched Egorov return to his lab, uncover his notes on Project Dead Blind and refresh himself on their agents. It watched Istomin return to his work, weaponizing the brain they'd receive from the operation in Liberia. It watched General Wu requisition Chinese sleeper agents in America. It watched Representative Fray, in a different kind of congress with General Casey, and it watched the agents of Project Dead Blind, returning to their civilian lives for the moment. The Collective watched everybody.

Chapter 35

The Prius pulled into the garage under Park's brownstone in the DC suburb. He left his luggage in the back and dragged himself up the stairs to his condo, the last unit in a row of cookie-cutter models. After a thirty-nine hour flight back to Washington, DC, with layovers in Freetown and London, he wanted to curl up in his bathtub and wash the failure away. He dreaded Ensign's debriefing.

Park opened the door to discover two white men in black suits stepping out of the kitchen and flashing their credentials. FBI.

"Dr. Park?" asked the jowly one, who had the air of a college football player gone to seed. The other had a ruddiness in his complexion that stopped short of his hairline. They didn't introduce themselves, flashing their credentials too fast for Park to read.

The ruddy one said, "The door was unlocked."

Dazed, Park rubbed his forehead. "I'm sure it was."

The jowly one put a hand on the ruddy one's shoulder. The ruddy one stepped back, letting Jowly speak. "Dr. Park, we have some questions about your recent trip to Liberia."

The question snapped Park out of his daze. His head did a circular wobble while righting itself. "You're fast. I'll give you that."

The jowly one continued, "We'd like to know what you were doing in that country, and what involvement you've had with an American church there."

Park sighed and walked around the FBI agents to the kitchen. "Do we have to do this now? I have a lot on my plate and I want to get some sleep. How about you call me tomorrow? I assume you have my number."

"Thing is, Dr. Park, we don't. We got this address off your passport, but we can't call you at the office because...well, we don't have a record of where that might be. Funny isn't it? The Department of Homeland Security can't find one of the US government's offices? Does that sound right to you?"

Park made himself a glass of Tang orange drink and took a sip. "Yes."

"Hmm." The jowly one grunted with a bit of a sneer.

The ruddy one took a shot. "What does the Office of...what was it again?"

"The Office of Intergovernmental and External Affairs." The jowly one said gesturing with finger-quotes.

"Right. What does the Office of Intergovernmental and External Affairs do, Dr. Park?"

"We investigate threats to world health at home and abroad."

"Sounds like we're in the same business then, don't you think?"

"Sure, if you think so. Now, if you don't mind, I'd like to pass out for a good dozen hours."

"I don't think you're cooperating with us, Dr. Park."

"That's because I'm not. I'm thirsty, tired, and I want you two out of my home so I can sleep."

"We don't want to get ugly, but we can make this an anti-terrorist investigation."

"Good, go do that. Just do it tomorrow. That'll give me time to get some sleep and talk to my lawyer about the illegal search you helped yourselves to before I arrived." Park drank the entire tumbler of Tang in a series of slow gulps, and wiped his mouth on his sleeve.

The jowly one pointed his stubby finger at Park.

The kitchen window shattered and the tumbler shot out of Park's hand.

The FBI agents drew weapons and hit the ground.

Park dove behind the refrigerator, shaking his stinging fingers. "What the hell?" Another bullet-sized hole appeared in the opposite wall with a thunk. "I don't hear a gun. Is that a silencer?"

The agents ignored Park's question and crawled back through his living room to the windows. Park followed them as far as the door down to the garage. The feds took quick looks through the curtains to the street a floor below.

"See the shooter?"

"No."

"How about that business guy looking up at us?"

"He's just standing there, no gun, not reacting—might not know what's going on."

Park reached for his briefcase and held it over his chest. "What guy? Why aren't you calling for backup?"

The living room window by the ruddy one shattered. A shelf on the opposite wall cracked and fell in two pieces. The ruddy one ducked behind the couch.

Park took his keys off the hook by the door.

The jowly one yelled, "Where do you think you're going?"

"Someplace no one's shooting at me. If you don't like it, call the Federal Marshals." Park slipped through the door to the downstairs garage, knocked on it three times, and locked the double-cylinder doorknob behind him. More glass shattered behind the door as he ran downstairs to his Prius.

One of the feds barreled through the door as the garage door lifted. Park backed out onto the street before the jowly one made it to the bottom of the stairs.

As he passed the front of his brownstone, he snapped a glance down his street. Across from his front door stood a handsome Asian man in a pristine gray suit, an aluminum briefcase at his side. He watched Park drive past, looked up at Park's condo, and the building imploded, not with a boom, but with a crunch.

Chapter 36

Right arm in a cast up to her shoulder, 97:4 struggled on the serving line, guiding a tray of scrambled eggs into the warmer one-handed. But the angle was wrong. It slid over the recess and kept sliding. She lunged and tried to catch the far edge with the hook on the end of the serving spoon. The hook pierced the cellophane covering the scrambled eggs, peeling off the protective layer as the tray slid over the edge. The eggs splattered on the floor. Homeless men and women jumped back, dodged bits of egg as best they could in the tight queue.

"Fuck! Fuck! Fuck! Fuck!" 97:4 fell against the warmer, beating it with the serving spoon.

The kitchen manager, a nun, put a hand on her shoulder. "Jannete? We need to talk."

97:4 dropped the spoon on the counter and pulled herself up. "It's okay. I can fix this. I'll make a new tray."

"No. We're not trying that again." The manager guided her away from the serving line to a seat at a table.

The nun sat across from 97:4 and took her hands, reaching for the one in the cast. "You need to take a break."

97:4 nodded. "Fifteen minutes?"

"No, honey. You need a lot more than that. Why don't you take off until your arm heals? Four more weeks, right?" The nun drew an envelope filled with hundred dollar bills from her cardigan pocket and pushed it across the table toward 97:4.

97:4's eyes went wide, as if the nun was pushing a pink slip her way. "No! No, no, no. I gave that money to the mission to help—"

"To help the needy, and right now, Jannete, that's you." The nun pressed the envelope into 97:4's good hand. "You've given so much, now it's your turn to take."

97:4 whimpered, "I don't deserve this. You don't know…don't know what I've done. I thought I was helping, but I've broken—"

"This isn't the time, place, or person for a confession. Save it for the Father."

"I lost my Bible."

The nun smiled and patted her on the hand. "If you promise to take a rest, I'll give you one of mine."

With her twenty-thousand dollars in cash, 97:4 didn't move from the bench during breakfast. The needy came and went but they kept their distance until the end of the shift.

An older Asian man in a knit cap and a forest-green sweater vest asked, "May I join you?" 97:4 didn't say yes, but she didn't say no. She grunted sleepily, pulling the envelope off his side of the table. The man sat with his tray, piled high with honeydew melon slices.

97:4 raised an eyebrow. "Like melons much?" Her voice cracked.

The man smiled, "Oh yes, I like them very much. I cannot have these at home." He took a bite, savoring the taste. "Why are you sad?"

"Is it that obvious?" 97:4 almost chuckled. "I have sins I need to atone for. This—" She lifted her broken wing with a pained grimace, "is stopping me."

"Why did you get hurt?" The man picked up the next slice of melon.

"Don't you mean 'how?' How did I get hurt?"

He finished the slice and reached for another. "I know what I asked."

"God punished me for arrogance, for presuming to know His justice."

Another pause, another slice of melon. "How are you going to make amends?"

97:4 stared at the serving line as the volunteers broke it down for cleaning. "By helping, but I don't know how."

"You can help me." He dropped another melon rind on his tray. "I need to get home, to the West."

97:4 smiled at the man's audacity. "Are you serious? Just pack up and help you go 'to the West?' No way. I'll drive you as far as the bus station."

"You said you need to help. I need help. Now you're going to take me to California." He finished the last melon slice with one hand while the other pulled his suitcase closer.

"I…" 97:4 rubbed her forehead, confused. She turned up her nose as the powerfully strong scent of vanilla wafted toward her. "Did the baker spill something in the kitchen? Never mind. I guess I can take you after all."

"I knew you would." The man stood, leaving his tray and picking up his suitcase. "Where is your car?"

"I'm parked out on the street." 97:4 fished her car keys out of her pocket. "What's your name anyway?"

The Asian man removed his knit cap and shook out his hair. "You can call me Three."

Chapter 37

Isaac hadn't showered in over a week. Alone in the darkness of his apartment and his thoughts, he sat on his plush sofa, in a nest of throw pillows, under the unblinking gaze of the bronze giraffe, watching TV and eating ice cream straight out of the container. Not a pint of ice cream, or a gallon. It was a two-gallon, plastic, loop-handled tub of marble fudge. Filled with rough ice crystals and artificial ingredients, the cheap stuff. Silver serving spoon in one hand, he cradled the tub in the other, watching a third-tier reality show on a cable network he'd never heard of.

Someone kicked in the door to his condo. Isaac could barely muster the interest to roll his eyes toward the splintered doorjamb.

The intruder crept through the open kitchen, a slight man in a dark green-and-black leather racing suit, full-face motorcycle helmet, and fiberglass backpack. The helmet regarded Isaac. Isaac turned back to the TV, shoving the serving spoon deep into the tub of ice cream.

The man in leather stepped between Isaac and the sixty-inch LCD screen, set his hands on his hips and regarded him. Isaac leaned, looking around the leather-clad intruder.

The intruder brought a leather boot down on the glass coffee table. The table held up to the first strike. The man leaned in with his full weight on the second strike and shattered it.

Isaac scratched his nose with the spoon and left a smear of ice cream across his face.

The man went after the TV next. He tried pushing it, and realized the device was mounted to the wall. He grabbed the set with both arms and pulled until the mountings came out of the drywall. The unit hit the floor. The screen flashed and died. The speakers still worked. A wronged housewife on the other end of the signal berated a waiter about the quality of the napkins.

Isaac reached for the remote. The intruder slapped it out of his hand, slapped him across the face, tore the tub of ice cream out of his hands, and dumped it on the floor. Isaac sat unmoved. The man head-butted him with his helmet.

"Fuck!" Isaac pushed the man away, standing up.

The intruder took a confident martial artist stance.

Isaac raised his fists in a sloppy boxing guard. "Man, I ain't in the mood for this."

A feint kick to Isaac's knee, followed by a light kick to the head. A stomp on his instep. A couple of rabbit jabs to his face. The intruder's attacks lacked force, but antagonized Isaac out of his depression.

Isaac matched the intruder's stance with almost as much confidence. "Oh, you're in trouble now. Give me a minute and I'll match your skill. And there's no way you can match my size, you little French fry."

The intruder cycled through a few fighting positions. Isaac matched him stance for stance. Mimicking the intruder's skills and motions, until the man jumped back, arms and legs stretched to the four directions, and stopped. Isaac took the same absurd position, against his will.

The man relaxed to standing, and so did Isaac. The man lifted his left arm to his side, palm up, and so did Isaac. Like dueling mimes, they circled each other with careful steps, until Isaac had his back to the big bay window with a view over the parking lot. The man in leather stepped back toward the hall, and Isaac stepped back toward the window.

Isaac felt the channels linking their nervous systems like strings. The connection was subtle. He wouldn't have picked up on it without training. Training he picked up from the intruder.

The man stood in front of the granite kitchen island and pressed Isaac's back to the window. His motorcycle helmet rocked back and forth, forcing the back of Isaac's head to tap the thick safety glass at an escalating rhythm. *Bam, bam, bam!*

Isaac grunted with every strike as he beat his own brains in, the pain from each strike greater than the last. Isaac's body twitched, out of accordance with the stranger. Pain granted him a brief moment of freedom. Isaac tried to use these gaps to lunge at his attacker. But the moments of control were too brief. Not enough time to step away from the window, but enough time to grunt out a single syllable with each strike.

Isaac put on his poker face, "*'Naapa kwa Mungu na Mungu ndiye kiapo.'*" He forced the African poem through gritted teeth. The strikes were getting more intense.

"*'Nampenda mt'u p'indi naye anipendapo.'*" Isaac was in a race to attain the poker face state before he lost consciousness. The window cracked behind him, and Isaac got out two syllables at a time, another strike and three syllables. That was the last strike.

Isaac charged the intruder, shouting, "*'Bali nduu yangu p'indi ari abwagazapo,'*" as he tackled him around the waist. The intruder's helmet struck the granite countertop.

"*'Ninga mwana kozi sioneki niwak'uapo.'*" Isaac straddled the man's chest and beat his helmet into the floor. The man fought back. He wasn't much of a wrestler, but he wasn't losing consciousness, either, and Isaac was at the part of the poem that always gave him trouble.

Isaac grabbed a bottle from an open cabinet on the kitchen island. He flipped open the helmet's visor, poured extra-virgin olive oil into the man's Asian eyes, slammed the visor shut, and ran for the door.

He grabbed his keys and wallet from the nook and escaped down the hall in his underwear, silk robe flapping in his wake.

Chapter 38

In the cluttered backroom of the 7-Eleven, Pollyanna re-hooked her bra under her sweater while the Pakistani clerk yanked up his pants. Getting dressed was a clumsy operation. The room was about the size of a shower, barely large enough for Pollyanna's hips.

"Whew! I needed that. Let me tell you. Near-death experiences will make a girl horny." Pollyanna buttoned her jeans, kicking the condom wrapper under the pallet where the mop dried. "And saving lives will too. I'm all about good deeds these days."

The clerk tried to squeeze through the door. He stopped when a knife in a belt clip sheath hit the floor behind Pollyanna.

She waved her hand, deflecting the clerk's suspicious glance. "I bought that this morning."

She picked it up and drew the knife from its holster, giving the clerk a chance to admire the blade—brand new with a factory shine.

"Now I'm looking for trouble. If someone tries robbing you again, I'll take care of it. Stabby stabby." She punctuated that with two feints in the clerk's direction.

The clerk held his hand up in awkward feigned fear. Backing up and keeping an eye on the blade tip, he smiled and slipped out the door.

Pollyanna took a moment to check out her hair in a broken security monitor before she joined him across the counter.

"Sell me a scratcher." She slapped a five on the counter and squinted at his nametag. "Jaleel. I'm going to win this time. I deserve it."

Jaleel rolled his eyes.

"No, not for that. Okay, that too. Just gimme the ticket."

Using a dime from a pocketful of coins, she'd scraped the ticket clean before Jaleel had finished making change. "No, this isn't right." She threw the dime on the floor and drew another from the coins. "This isn't how it's supposed to work. I've been good. Gimme another one."

He pulled a single from her change and tore another scratcher off the roll for her. She grazed the gray latex, changed her mind, and sifted through the rest of the coins, picking a blackened penny instead. Peeling back the latex in careful rows, it was clear she had another loser on her hands. The penny fell from her fingers and wobbled on the glass countertop.

"I saved lives," she said into the pile of latex scrapings. "I was beat up and kidnapped, and still I did the right thing. Isn't karma supposed to pay off?"

The door swung in fast. An Asian man entered wearing a dark blue raincoat and an off-white bucket hat. He was smaller than her, in both height and girth, and carried an old-fashioned leather doctor's bag.

Pollyanna caught the predatory look on his face, a twitchy-ness in his smile. She stepped backward into the 7-Eleven, thinking she'd step to the back and let this tweaker rob Jaleel in peace.

He smiled. "You are Pollyanna, yes?"

"N—no, that's not my name." Pollyanna turned to Jaleel. "Tell him that's not my name."

"Not your name, no. But that's what they call you."

She backed up. He drifted after her.

Pollyanna felt it in her sinuses first. It pulled and twisted at the space behind her eyes to the back of her head and scrambled her vision. As the sensation raced down her spine, Pollyanna went with it. The back of her head smacked against the linoleum floor and she blacked out for a moment.

Everything was tinted blue until a bag of Cool Ranch Doritos fell off her face. Lifting her head sent her vision spinning. The man in the dark raincoat knelt, watching her squirm with the curiosity of a child watching a bug struggle for life in a puddle of water.

"Your sister felt like this at the end. Did you know that?" He licked his lips.

Pollyanna fought back a wave of horrible memories and struggled to flop a limp arm behind her back.

"Would you like to know what else she felt?" He reached for her breast.

After a half-dozen tries, she pulled the knife from its sheath at her waist and stabbed him in the hand holding the bag. He screamed and let go.

Immediately, her world stopped spinning. She stabbed him again through the top of his leather shoe, pushed him over, went for the door, but stopped short. "Shit! Jaleel!"

The clerk clutched at the counter like a drowning man, barely recovering his legs.

"Move!" She grabbed Jaleel's collar, dragged him over the counter, outside, and into her car. They peeled out into the evening. "Next time, Jaleel, I get a winning scratcher."

Chapter 39

An Asian man in bib overalls and a safety jacket, carrying a toolbox, had stalked Ainia for the past hour. He'd followed her through the evening, from subway car to subway car, through two transfers, and back on the line to Queens, where they'd started. Now it was the two of them, staring each other down from opposite ends of the subway car.

The fluorescent lights in the train flickered. The car smelled like vomit.

They entered a tunnel. With slow, predatory steps, she closed the distance, cracked her knuckles, and pushed back the sleeves of her hoodie.

He looked out the window into the blackness of the tunnel. When she'd closed half the distance, he turned his body away from her. A few more steps and he hunched, hiding his face with his shoulder. Ainia worried this *wouldn't* turn violent. When she was in striking distance, he spun, said something in a language she didn't recognize, and held his toolbox out at her like a cross against a vampire. His other hand was hidden behind his body.

Ainia gave the toolbox a spinning kick. His fingers twisted in the handle. The metal edge cracked him in the jaw as the corner ripped a gash across his cheek.

Ainia jumped back, smiled, and took a fighting stance. "You stalked the wrong woman."

His hidden hand swung at her with a knife. She spun around his attack and went for the toolbox, twisting it out of his grip.

The man's eyes went wide with fear of the loss. He came down at her with the knife. She blocked the blade with the toolbox.

"You had a knife, but you attacked with this?" She tossed it up. The man dove to catch it. She knocked him out of midair with a hip check, catching it herself.

"What is it?" She kicked him in the ribs. He dropped to all fours and dropped the knife. She stepped on the flat of the blade, pinning it, and popped one of the latches on the lid. "Some kind of weapon? Or are you just nuts?"

Before she opened the second latch, he grabbed her leg and bit her on the shin. She brought the toolbox down on his head with both hands. The impact popped the lid open, and a softball-sized chunk of frosty matter popped up. Ainia hesitated. Deciding to step off the knife cost her the catch. The frozen ball hit the subway floor and slid to the back of the train car.

Her attacker watched his cargo escape with manic eyes. Shaky fingers tightened around the handle of the knife.

Ainia stomped on his head twice, knocking him out.

She left him on the floor with the empty toolbox, retrieving her frosty prize as the train pulled into the station. Too cold to hold, she pulled the hoodie sleeves over her hands to protect her skin. Under the frost was a brain, frozen solid.

The train door opened. The man lay bleeding at the other end of the train car. Ainia muttered, "Lunatic."

Stepping out into the night air of the empty platform, she tossed the brain into the trash.

Chapter 40

Dixon's Card House was a converted dance hall that had spent some time as a VFW. The scarred hardwood floor had seen it all. The paneling on the walls had seen everything since the '70s. The mismatched collection of tables and chairs, in a perpetual cycle of damage and replacement, hadn't seen much. Dixon's was located in the part of the county called "Downtown", an uneven cluster made up of the post office, market, pool hall and fix-it shop.

Gabby, in jeans and a T-shirt, her tangled hair hanging free, slowly gulped her Dr. Pepper, then slammed the can on the table. "What's it going to be, Rod? What's it going to be? Don't be a pussy, there's one too many of those sitting at this table as is."

Rod, an unshaven man in his forties with skinny arms, skinny legs, and a belly his T-shirt struggled to contain, looked at his cards, the river, and the players who'd folded, trying to calculate his odds.

The other players were losing patience. "Come on, Rod. Shit or get off the pot."

Another one said, "I've been in the shitter after Rod. You don't want that."

The table broke out in laughter. Even Rod gave a sheepish grin as he stalled.

Gabby affected a worn expression and knocked a beat on the table. The others at the table joined in. The beat spread to the rest of the players in the card house, all eyes on Rod. A chant started, "Call. Or. Fold. Call. Or. Fold."

Rod caved to the room full of pressure and folded, a pair of twos. The crowd booed in disappointment and went back to their games. Gabby smiled and revealed her hand, ten high.

Rod cursed and pushed away from the table, heading to the toilet.

Gabby collected the pot and called after him, "Hey, Rod. Piss on a stick while you're in there. You might have fucked yourself pregnant. Ha!"

She leaned back and sorted her chips. "You know in Africa they play a different kind of poker. Oasis they call it. Rules there let you sell back your hand to the dealer for new cards. Like a whole 'nother game, huh?"

A man at the table, who had a beard down to his chest and a trucker cap with a wedge torn out of the brim, scoffed. "When the fuck were you in Africa?"

"Just..." Gabby faked a cough. "Just sayin'."

Todd leaned in toward her. "Don't talk shit if you don't know shit."

Gabby set her chips down and locked eyes with Todd. "You telling me to shut up?"

The door to the card hall slammed shut.

"Yeah. You run that mouth so much, probably talk in your sleep."

There was the short, loud sound of a chair scraping the floor as a man shot up. His voice was raised, finger pointing at the cards. Two more scoots and two more men stood in anger.

The people who'd cheerily egged Rod out of his stall a moment ago had turned on each other. People Gabby had known her whole life. Phyllis, the shorthaired, apple-shaped old woman at the cash booth, snarled at Dennis through the bars. Geordie, the area's last World War II vet, rolled his wheelchair back and around to get in Ivett's face about something.

Familiar faces twisted in anger, except for one outside looking in. Lit by the neon Budweiser sign was an Asian man Gabby thought was Park at first. He wore a flannel shirt and a jean jacket; an athletic bag thrown over one shoulder. Attire that fit right in, but he couldn't hide the epicanthic folds over his eyes from Gabby, especially now that she had acquired a taste for them.

Todd's face swung into her view. "What? Ain't got nothing to say, for a change?"

"Shut up, Todd." Gabby tried to step around him, but Todd blocked her again.

Gabby set her jaw and took a deep breath. "You shouldn't have let me."

Todd stuck out his chest. "Let you what, bitch?"

"*Let me bend your ear.*" Todd was the only one listening, the only one to lock up. "I've been to Africa, just last month. I'd tell you all about it." Gabby hit Todd across the face with her chair. Paralyzed, he took the full force of the impact and dropped. "But that's a story for another day."

Five fights broke out at once. Outside, the Asian man watched. That pissed Gabby off—more than it should have—and she realized where the anger came from. "He's got a fucking card."

Gabby dove under a table and put on her poker face, mumbling, "Ah eh ah yeh-ah ah ah-ya, thunder!" Her anger lost its edge. There was too much fighting between her and the front door. She waited for a gap in the brawl between herself and the back door.

When one came, she crawled for it, making it to the next table just as Rod fell, breaking it in half. Gabby rolled, barely avoiding getting pinned or crushed. "Ah eh ah yeh-ah ah ah-ya, thunder!"

Two men were fighting in the back doorway. Gabby grabbed a dismembered table leg, popped out from under the table, and whacked the closer man between the legs with an underhand swing. His opponent became Gabby's. His eyes filled with rage, not gratitude. She spiked him in the teeth and cracked him in the knee with the wooden weapon. He buckled. Gabby ran over him, pushing through the door with a celebratory, "Ah eh ah yeh-ah ah ah-ya, thunder!"

The stink of stale beer and dumpster cleared her head. She choked up on the table leg with both hands like it was a baseball bat and charged around the corner. She turned the second corner screaming, "Ah eh ah yeh-ah ah ah-ya…?"

The man in the jean jacket was gone.

A different man in a jean jacket crashed through the window, landing where the stranger had stood a minute ago.

Chapter 41

Exposition Joe slipped in through the loading dock of the condemned department store, past the empty clothing racks, and up the creaking, moldy stairs to what used to be the manager's office. The padlock was open, the TV playing inside. Joe pushed the door open and ducked under the extension cord that ran out the window to an unmonitored outlet behind the 99-Cent Store.

His squatmate, Theo, was passed out on the ancient sofa they found the month before. God sat next to Theo, watching the game. "Throw, you motherfucker! Throw!" The deity's bleached hemp suit blended into the color of his hair and beard. He shook the rolled-up Script at the TV.

Joe crossed the room and dropped the bags of groceries on the floor by the hotplate.

"Shh!" God raised a finger, eyes locked on the play. The quarterback let loose with a fifty-yard pass to the wide receiver in the end zone. The deity jumped up and clapped. "Yes! Who says prayer doesn't work?"

"Did You have money on this game?" Joe emptied the bags, loading the dry goods and canned food into their repurposed particleboard dish cabinet. It kept the rats out.

God sat His butt cheek on the sofa arm. "So you're speaking to me again? Speaking nonsense, but that's a start."

Joe kept his eye on his business.

"I didn't kill those people, Joseph. You know that."

"You didn't save them, either. There wasn't a better way to destroy the Faith Machine? Couldn't You snap Your fingers or something?"

God stood, and gave a patient shake of His head. "When I created this world I created rules. One of them is: I work through prophets." He tapped Joe on the chest. "This world is for your kind, Joe. Not Me. All I can do is love you and offer advice."

He walked to the window and gestured for Joe to follow. "I'm going to offer you some right now."

Joe didn't want to follow but there weren't any options. The squat was small and there were only so many places to stand.

God pointed with the rolled-up document across the busy boulevard. "See that guy in the shabby suit and blue ball cap with the roller suitcase?"

The bustling street was full of pedestrians as well as cars, but Joe spotted the man right away, standing on the curb, waiting for a chance to jaywalk. "What about him?"

"He's called a Caseman."

"Who calls him that?"

"The people who sent him here to kill you. That case is a weapon." God walked back to the sofa and took his seat next to Theo, laying the document on his lap and folding his fingers behind his head. "They sent one after everyone Dr. Park took to Liberia."

Joe groped for his satphone, out of habit, but it was a melted hunk of plastic and metal under the remains of The Baptist's church.

"Relax. Your friends can take care of themselves." He leaned forward, steepling his fingers. "And I can take care of you."

Joe kept a nervous eye on the assassin across the street. "What do I have to do?"

"So you're with Me again? Not just to save your life, I mean with everything."

The man stepped off the curb. Joe's heart skipped a beat. "Yes!"

"Because this is bigger than you, Joe. We're talking about everyone. Everyone in the world."

"Okay. Yes. Okay." The man had crossed the first lane of traffic, dragging his roller behind him.

"And no more—"

"No more attitude, I promise!" Joe watched the killer cross the street.

"Then open the window and shout, 'Pack.' And I mean *shout*."

Joe threw the latch and lifted the window. It stuck halfway up. Joe thought he was about to have a heart attack. He bent over, stuck his head out the gap, and shouted with everything he had, "Pack!"

The man in the shabby suit turned from the oncoming traffic and locked eyes with Joe. Even at this distance, Joe saw the recognition in the man's body language. A black SUV hit him, knocking him down the block. His broken body twisted through the air and landed in a heap.

Joe watched the panic in the street. Cars stopped. Cell phones were drawn to take pictures and call police. Joe pulled back inside and stood back from the window.

God stood. "I help those who help themselves, Joe. And for those who help Me? Heaven awaits with a seat at My right hand."

The deity vanished.

Theo rolled over and snored.

Chapter 42

Park hid among the tourists in line outside the International Spy Museum. Disguised in a blue-and-white hoodie with "Washington, DC" scrawled across the front in red, he'd paid too much for the disguise at a gift shop. But it made him one of a dozen similarly dressed young men in line, hooded and facing their phones. Conscious that his black leather shoes, scratched raw by the Liberian mud, stood out among the sneakers.

He left messages on Ensign's voicemail, free of details. "Hey. Wondering where you at." "What time was the show again?" "Hey did you find my keys? Call me back if you did."

He couldn't risk leading the FBI or the psychic with the attaché case to the Office of Intergovernmental and External Affairs. Bags still packed from Liberia, Park would be living out of his car until he got some support from Ensign, who was still somewhere in Asia.

A text message came in from "Paul," the number Ensign used when addressing *all* the team. "*SORRY I CAn'T MAKE IT, FAMILY PROBLS. DON'T EVN WANT TO sEE THEM RIGHT NOW. DON"T CALL JUST MEET ME T HOME. -cANDICE*"

"Family" was code for the Department of Homeland Security. "Don't call" meant radio silence, and maintain a distance from other agents until further orders. "Home" was code for the safe house the project kept in San Diego. Orders were—travel solo, rendezvous at the safehouse, and don't trust Homeland Security. Park had already figured out that last part the hard way.

There was more. Park indexed the typos: "n" in CAN'T, missing "EM" in PROBLEMS, missing "E" in EVEN, "s" in SEE, missing "A" in AT, "c" in CANDICE. "N E M E S A C" backwards was CASEMEN.

"Casemen? What's that supposed to mean?"

The father of the Latino family in front of him turned when Park talked to himself.

Homeland Security included the TSA, so no airports. Park was glad he'd saved his car from the implosion that destroyed his condo. The so-called feds had questioned him about Africa. The Dead Blind agents—all living on the East Coast—had to travel alone across country, undetected by Homeland Security. Park looked around for something to knock on.

If that wasn't enough to give him ulcers, Exposition Joe, Isaac, and Pollyanna had their satphones taken by The Baptist's men. Ensign should know that three phones were out of order and whom they belonged to.

Park had his orders. Like it or not, it was Ensign's responsibility—not his—to make sure his whole team did as well. That wasn't going to stop him from worrying.

Park gave up his spot in line. The time for hiding was over. It was time to move west.

Chapter 43

In T-shirt and track pants, Gabby kicked back on the couch in the living room side of the trailer, trying to figure out the text message on her satphone. In the pink flower-print recliner, her mother looked away from the TV during a commercial and caught Gabby in the act. "What's that in your hand?"

Gabby slipped the phone into her back pocket. "My job gave me a phone. I think it's a wrong number. Says it's from Paul. I don't know a Paul. Oh wait…I remember…who Paul is."

Her mother extended a chubby, open hand. "Let me see."

"Can't. It's a secret. I wasn't supposed to let anyone know I had it. Not even you."

Her mother turned off the TV. Her mother never turned off the TV. "That new job you can't tell me about? Now you got a secret phone?" She lurched into standing, not bothering to straighten her nightgown. "What's going on in my house, Molly?"

Gabby climbed over the couch, knowing her mother couldn't. "This new job made the last four payments, so I guess it's my house too."

That lit a fire in her mother. She took a shaky step around the couch. "What did you say to me?"

Gabby maneuvered, keeping the furniture between them. "This job has been a big help. It's the best thing I got going for me. There's just…some conditions come with it."

"I've had enough of secrets in my own house. Who are you working for?" Gabby's mother scanned the room and lowered her voice. "Is it the government?"

"Mama, no! I work for a super-secret spy group, not the government!" Gabby blocked the gun rack by the recliner.

"Spies! Who the hell do you think spies work for?" Her mother backed away from her, eyes wide in fear. *They*, the vague collection of conspiracies she subscribed to, had gotten to Gabby. "You dumb little girl. Now they're gonna take away my disability! You're ruining everything! What's that?"

A car pulled into the gravel outside.

"You brought the government to my house?" Her mother lunged for her shotgun.

Gabby grabbed it first, blocking her mother with one hand and holding the gun behind her, both at arm's reach. "Don't be stupid. It's probably Jacob come back to kiss my behind and beg me to take him back."

Gabby stepped to the door and swung it open.

The sheriff hefted his mighty girth out from behind the squad car steering wheel. A man in sunglasses and a dark suit walked around from the passenger side.

Gabby slammed the door closed. "It's the government!"

"I knew it!" Her mother grabbed the shotgun barrel with both hands. "I knew it'd come down to this. It's Ruby Ridge all over again."

"You can't blow holes in any cop who comes to the door."

The women wrestled over the shotgun until a forceful police knock shook the door in its frame and the trailer on its slab. "Molly White? Why don't you come out, so we can have a talk?"

Gabby's mother shouted, "Fuck you, Sheriff. I didn't vote for you, and I don't recognize your authority. You'll roll your fat ass back down the hill to the county headquarters if you know what's good for you!"

"Would you shut up?" she shouted at her mother before shouting at the door. "What you want, Sheriff?"

"Got an agent of the Federal Bureau of Investigation out here, name of Michaels, wants to ask you some questions about a trip you took." The sheriff stepped in front of the window, his outline clear through the curtains.

Someone, presumably the agent, pulled him back out of view. "You haven't been to Africa lately, have you?"

Her mother lost her balance, but not her grip on the weapon, dragging Gabby to the floor. "Nooo…"

"Because you told Todd Merriman you've been to Africa recently. Didn't you?"

Gabby winced. Her mother looked ready to bite her fingers to get at the gun.

The sheriff knocked again, even harder than last time. A jar of pennies fell off the shelf and spilled. The copper coins scattered everywhere. "Just come out here and we'll talk about this face to face, will ya?"

Her mother growled, "I got something for your face," and pumped her shotgun in Gabby's hands.

Gabby jumped up, leaving her mother on the floor with the gun. Palms out, holding off her mother, she shouted, "Coming out! I'm coming out!"

Her mother withdrew to a secure position behind the TV.

Gabby opened the front door and stepped out into the daylight, hands up. "Go on then, lawmen. Take me in. Let's get to the bottom of this."

Chapter 44

Ainia's red pickup pulled into the cracked driveway of Pollyanna's Pennsylvania McMansion. The eyesore of the neighborhood, its yard had gone over to indigenous grasses, and the house needed a paint job. Ainia bounced her lacrosse ball off the cracked doorbell button to no effect, and settled on knocking.

The dented blinds on the window parted, briefly exposing a sliver of darkness within. Padlocks turned. Chains unhooked. Pollyanna swung open the door, wearing an oversized Deftones T-shirt and red sweatpants. "Well, it's about time."

"About time for what?"

"About time Ensign answered my calls. I don't understand why you people can't call in emergencies." Pollyanna looked up and down the street and gestured Ainia in. Inside, everything was a shade of brown, as aged and run-down as the lawn. A barber's chair sat in the living room. Dye and bleach stained the carpet underneath. It stank of old cigarettes.

"You're not supposed to be calling anyone. Or texting me." Ainia spun the ball on the tip of a finger and drew her phone, unlocking it with her other hand.

"I didn't text you. Those kidnapping psychos took my phone, remember?"

Ainia raised an eyebrow. "Then who sent this?" She showed Pollyanna the message logs:

404-637-8989: i need u to pick me up this is pollyanna btw

Ainia: Orders are to stay apart

404-637-8989: PLEASE!!! Was attacked by a guy with a card this morning!!!

404-637-8989: my tank is low - you knwo I dont have a chance on my own!!!

404-637-8989: Ainia?

404-637-8989: Aiina?

404-637-8989: Ainia?

Ainia: Ok stop it. Will drive to you.

Pollyanna handed back the satphone. "That wasn't me. I don't know your number or that number. But I can spell and use capitalization. Christ, Ainia, give me a little credit. But a psychic did attack me at the 7-Eleven yesterday. I've been hiding here until I heard back from Ensign. I didn't know what else to do."

Ainia tucked her phone in her breast pocket. "Attacked by who?"

"More like what. This Asian guy hit me when I was…shopping. He had a card that caused vertigo."

"How'd you get away?"

Pollyanna turned around and pulled up her T-shirt, revealing the knife holstered in her waistband. "I stuck him twice. He won't be jerking off or walking right for some time."

"Good."

Pollyanna dropped her shirt and turned back around. "Yeah, it was great. Best assault ever."

"I mean it's good you were prepared. Did he have anything on him? Holding something?"

"An old doctor's bag, straight out of William Carlos Williams."

"Out of what?"

"Nevermind. I forgot your understanding of poetry begins and ends with the Iliad."

Ainia ignored the jab. "I think the others were attacked as well. Ensign sent out a mass text this morning. It decoded to, 'All agents proceed independently to West Coast safe house. Do not trust DHS.'

"An Asian guy with a frozen brain in a toolbox attacked me on the subway. Thought it was just another day in New York City, but Ensign's orders included a code, the word 'Casemen.' Your attacker had a case too."

"There was a brain in that guy's bag? Ugh."

"Probably. And probably one of these Casemen for everyone in Dead Blind."

"Seriously? This is some Pearl Harbor shit here. Give me a few minutes to pack for San Diego."

"Orders are to go it alone." Ainia held up her phone. "Besides, we don't know who sent me those texts pretending to be you. Does that sound safe to you?"

Ainia's phone buzzed. It was the mysterious 404-637-8989. She answered with, "Who is this?"

"Hi, Ainia. It's Exposition Joe. I sent those texts. Sorry I lied to you, but Pollyanna's going to need your help getting across the country."

"Who do you think you are? Orders are—"

"I don't know what you're talking about. I didn't get any orders—lost my phone in Africa. Remember?"

"I've already heard that excuse once t—"

"Anyway, I gotta go. See you in San Diego. Watch out for the Casemen! Vertigo's a bitch." He hung up.

Ainia growled, clenching her phone in her fist. "I hate that kid."

"If it wasn't for that kid I'd still be trapped in a Winnebago in Africa." Pollyanna headed for the stairs. "I'll go pack."

"We're not traveling together. I don't care what strings Exposition Joe is trying to pull. Orders are orders."

Pollyanna stopped on the landing. "How are you going to stop me? You drive like an old lady. I'll catch up to you before you get on the freeway. Look, if Joe thinks we should be together, how about we try it? He saved your bacon in Liberia. So did I. You owe us this one."

Ainia bounced her ball three times, considering. "Go pack your damn bag."

Chapter 45

Isaac spent most of his cash on an hour in a motel room, a shave, a shower, and a new set of clothes—goldenrod button-down shirt and slate pants, both silk. It wasn't safe to use plastic, but there was no excuse for not looking good. With no phone he'd have to report the attack to Ensign by other means.

For five dollars he bought ten minutes of computer time at a tiny café near the university. Fliers for shows and protests covered the wall behind the monitor.

He needed to psychically borrow the skills necessary to hack into Project Dead Blind's messaging system from someone in the coffee shop. Isaac figured it was the white guy in the black T-shirt hunched over his laptop; a good read of personality.

The timer in the corner of the screen counted down from eight minutes seven seconds. Getting in would be easy. Isaac had learned Ensign's password years ago with similarly borrowed skills. But he couldn't risk leaving digital footprints. Not if the psychic in the motorcycle outfit had friends.

Isaac promised himself he'd eventually change all his passwords from "whosthegreatest" to unique and secure strings.

From the terminal, he'd hacked across two laptops in the coffee shop and the iPhone of a barista who hadn't updated the OS in two years. That should cover his trail. Isaac was ready to make the final push into the Dead Blind network. He just had to send this terminal a string, the access code in hexadecimal. He just had to…he couldn't remember…he didn't know how.

The white guy in the black T-shirt was gone. Isaac saw him passing outside the coffee shop window. He needed that code. He grabbed a flier and a crayon off the stand of odds and ends with the books and board games. Bolting after the man, Isaac ran into a pair of white men in dark suits.

"Dennis Osbey?" One of them flashed an FBI badge and indicated a black sedan parked behind him. "Come with us, please."

They knew Isaac's real name. "Oh, this isn't good."

"That depends on you, Mr. Osbey."

"Look I gotta…I have two more minutes on the internet back there I gotta use. You know how it is? Right? When I'm done I'd be happy to—"

The feds grabbed him. One went high the other went low.

"What the—! Is this how it's gotta be?" Isaac struggled, but his assailants knew plenty about taking a suspect down, and nothing about resisting arrest. Within a minute, they had him cuffed and stuffed into their black sedan.

"One of you owes me two minutes of internet time," Isaac said from the backseat. The car pulled away from the curb and into downtown Atlanta's lunch-rush gridlock. They traveled thirty feet in ten minutes.

Isaac broke the awkward silence. "How about you tell me what's going on? Seeing we have the time and all."

"You've been to Africa recently, haven't you, Mr. Osbey? You wouldn't know anything about a church that burned outside Monrovia, would you?"

"How come every time a church burns down—" Isaac spotted Exposition Joe walking toward the car between the still lanes of traffic, carrying a fire extinguisher. "You know what? It doesn't matter. Fuck you and your questions. This is where I get off."

The agent in the passenger seat turned to ask Isaac, "What is that supposed to mean?"

Isaac dropped to the car floor.

Joe shattered the driver's side window with the base of the fire extinguisher and flooded the front seat with a cloud of ammonium phosphate. The agents were covered in white powder, choking and blinded. Joe reached in and unlocked Isaac's door.

Isaac popped out. "Get the key, get the key!"

Joe pulled the keys from the choking fed's coat pocket. He dropped the extinguisher into the fed's lap, unlocked Isaac's handcuffs, and the two ran for it.

Chapter 46

It was dusk at the railyard, a dozen or more parallel rows of train tracks, and a handful of empty trains. A crane stood on a hill at the far end. The sky was dark enough that everything seemed far away, and quiet enough that even the little noises sounded loud. Every step on the gravel sounded like the crunch of a car fender to Isaac.

They'd been hiding. Ducked under an unattached tanker car, Isaac said to Exposition Joe, "It's about this time I should be asking you where the hell we're going."

"Nebraska."

"Any special reason why?"

"It's in the—"

"Script, yes. That's *a* Why, I want *the* Why. Tell me what's going on, and how the feds play into this."

"That's deeper than I can usually see, Isaac. But I know we're about to catch a train."

"And what's with riding the rails? Are we that hard up for secrecy? Because you and me using channels of transportation usually reserved for cargo—that's getting dangerously into *Huckleberry Finn* territory."

"What's *Huckleberry Finn*?"

"Seriously? They don't make you read that in middle school these days?"

"I dropped out of school at thirteen."

"That when you learned how to ride the rails? Hey, shouldn't we have bindles on sticks or something?"

"Sure, if you want to catch a train in 1930."

"See? You do know some shit."

"The road was my teacher." There was the sound of metal hinges screaming shut. "Shouldn't be long now. You're okay with all this? I know this is kinda sudden."

"No. Sudden was the way that leather motorcycle freak busted into my apartment and turned me into a puppet. Sudden was the way the feds swooped out of nowhere and snatched me up. Thanks again for pulling me out of there." Isaac rubbed his shoulder, still sore from their takedown. "This isn't sudden. This is going to be fun."

"You say that now. Wait until you have to take a bath out of a can."

The purr of an approaching motorcycle engine sounded through the damp night air.

Isaac ducked down lower. "I hope that isn't my leather daddy stalker."

"It is," said Joe without looking.

Isaac raised an eyebrow. "Okay, well, what are we going to do about it? Do you know that?"

The single headlight cut through the darkness, heading their way. The black-and-green bike stopped under a streetlamp a hundred feet away, like the rider wanted to be seen. It was the familiar figure in leather.

"There's a chance the railyard bull will catch him before he catches us, right?"

"Nope." Joe looked at Isaac. "And 'bull?' 'Bindle?' Where did you learn all this ancient railyard slang?"

Isaac held up a hand. "Lay off. I like black-and-white movies."

The man on the motorcycle dropped his bike into gear and rolled to another part of the yard.

Isaac said, "Now that guy knows how to ride a bike."

"Jealous?"

"Quiet. I'm trying to come up with a strategy."

"I could tell you what's going to happen."

"You already said that doesn't work out for us. I'm going to have to come up with something on my own."

"Okay. Good luck resisting the inevitable."

"Nothing's inevitable until it happens, Joe."

Joe shook his head, resigned.

The man stopped his bike and stepped off, facing the Project Dead Blind agents, but not moving.

Isaac shook his head. "He can't see us. He's messing with us in case we're in this direction."

"Uh. Isaac?" Joe stood.

The man in leather raised his fist into the air.

"Isaac?" Joe raised his fist.

"Shh. And get down!" Isaac crouched.

The man brought his fist down in a quick downward hook. Joe punched Isaac in the back of the head.

Isaac was knocked from a squat to a roll, tumbling down the hill toward the train tracks. He stopped short of knocking his head on the thick iron rail.

Joe marched down the hill after Isaac, in imitation of the leather-clad man's motion a hundred yards away. "I'm sorry, Isaac. It's in the Script."

Chapter 47

The waitress kept giving them the eye. She'd probably never seen such a pair in her life.

97:4 and Three sat across from each other in a Missouri Waffle House restaurant. The linoleum table was covered with a thin sheet of grease. On that line between evening and morning, they were one of three pairs of customers. A retired couple occupied a booth by the door. Two truckers sat at the counter.

She picked at her chicken-fried steak. A faint odor of vanilla killed her appetite. Three was on his second slice of pie after finishing his meal. A glob of blueberry filling fell on his green sweater vest. 97:4 pushed the plate away, gritted her teeth, and picked up her butter knife. Three's eyes went from blade to 97:4 with a small trace of caution.

"Don't worry. I'm not going to do it," 97:4 said, and pantomimed sticking the knife blade down her wrist between the cast and her skin, pretending to scratch. "I just want to imagine what it'd be like."

Three resumed working on his pie. "Why would I worry?"

"That would be disgusting, right?"

He loaded up his fork again. "I don't care. I'll never use that knife."

Her fantasy scratching session lost its luster and she put the knife down. "What are your thoughts on God?"

He shoveled another load into his mouth and washed it down with cola. "I've known men who wanted to be gods on earth, and a god who wanted to be a man. One would think someone, somewhere would be happy with their station in life."

"Who was better at it? The men or the god?"

"The god. It's easier to climb down a mountain than up one."

"What's west anyway? Where are you going to?"

"A mountain." Three wiped his hands on his napkin, dropped it on the plate, and grabbed the suitcase handle. "Let's go."

"Wait. When are we going to take a rest? I'm going to need to sleep sometime. I'm sore, my head hurts, and I keep smelling vanilla for some reason. Do you smell that?"

Three stopped halfway out of the booth. "What do you usually do when you aren't allowed to sleep?"

"Pass out?"

"I mean, what alternatives do you ingest?"

97:4 leaned back in the booth. "Are you asking if I drink coffee? Yes, if I have to."

"Coffee? Nothing stronger?"

"I don't like espresso. I don't like coffee, either, but espresso makes my hands shake." She held her good hand out. It was already shaking. "I should get some sleep."

Three scratched his upper lip, considering. "Then coffee will have to do."

"Cream and sugar."

"Unnecessary. Can we get one here and take it with us?"

"I think so, but it's not like I can drive and hold a drink." She lifted her broken arm and winced.

"Hmm." Three accepted this fact with reluctance. "You're not cooperating."

"Not cooperating?" She clumsily extricated herself from the booth. "I'm driving you across country with a broken arm. To some mountain? How is that not cooperating?"

Three turned without a word, left the Waffle House, and returned to 97:4's car. 97:4 followed.

He waited by the trunk, sweat glistening on his forehead. "Open it."

97:4 fished in her pants pocket for the keys and unlocked the trunk. "Finally putting that suitcase away?"

Three gave the trunk a once-over, finding an aged and outdated map book of Cincinnati, a dirty towel, and an empty CD jewel case. Satisfied, he ordered 97:4 to "Get in and stay still."

"What?" She stepped back. "No way."

Three shifted his grip on the suitcase's handle. "I said, get in."

The scent of vanilla flooded her nostrils. "Oh, God. It's been you all along. You made me help you." Her arm and legs trembled as she fought the command to climb into the trunk, trying and failing to resist. "You're holding a card."

"I am no such thing. I am a soldier." He lowered the lid on her, trapping her in the musty trunk. "And you're just a means to an end."

Chapter 48

The next morning Park pulled up outside the smallest sheriff's station he'd ever seen, a tan cinder block structure the size of a two-bedroom house. From the Prius, he watched the office door, ran his fingers over the top of the steering wheel, and fiddled with the mirrors. When he ran out of meaningless gestures, he stepped out of the car, crossed the small lot, and tapped three times on the doorway before letting himself in.

Inside was utilitarian, but homey; the kind of small-town government office where the staff spent their whole careers. The front desk was more of a front "nest" of homemade crafts and pictures of family. The receptionist was out. Past that stood a middle-aged man in uniform who Park assumed to be the sheriff and a younger man in a dark suit who looked serious and out of place. From their stances, he could tell he had walked into a tense situation, bordering on a fight. He put a nail in the mood. "Is this a bad time?"

The other men backed down, like they were simply shifting their feet.

The sheriff stuck his thumbs in his belt. "Naw. I think you got here just in time. Dr. Wong, I'm guessing? She used her one phone call on you. I hope you can help."

Park closed the door behind him, holding his briefcase where the men could see. "How is Molly doing?"

The sheriff started, "Molly's doing okay un—", but the man in the dark suit cut him off.

"Molly White is under federal arrest and she'll be taken care of by us. I'm sorry you—"

This time the sheriff interrupted. "She's under Boyle County protection until I have her transferred. And she hasn't been charged with anything yet." He was speaking to Park, but glaring at the fed. "And if one of my prisoners needs to see her doctor, then that's what's going to happen."

The sheriff gestured for Park to follow him into the back, ignoring the fed's glares and crossed arms.

Park walked past the man like he wasn't there and went into the holding area, a plain gray room split into two cells. Agent Gabby was in one. The other was empty, the mattress rolled up without linen.

When Park came into view, Gabby hopped up from her cot and jumped up to the bars with a smile. "You're here! Man, that was quick. You must have drove all night long!"

The fed slunk in after them. "Drove all night? I thought you were local, Dr. Wong."

"A local man can't be out of town?" Park said to the fed while watching the sheriff. The hint of a smile graced the corner of the sheriff's lips.

The federal agent looked at Park's shoes, still scratched from the Liberian mud. "Did you drive, or walk?"

Park lifted a foot, disappointed. "A hundred and fifty dollars, gone to waste. I got stuck on a dirt road I really shouldn't have taken and had to push out of the mud," Park lied. "Now, what's my patient under arrest for?"

"Arson, for starters."

"And this is heading for extradition I hear?"

"Well, that'll be for the grand jury to decide, won't it, Doctor? Terrorism is terrorism, no matter the source."

"That's neither here nor—"

The sheriff interrupted. "I'm sorry, Doctor, but isn't your patient that way?" He pointed at Gabby.

Park straightened his tie. "Fair point. Molly? How are you doing?"

Gabby slumped against the bars. "Seriously?"

"Humor me."

"These two assholes arrested me yesterday, tossed me in here." She scratched the side of her nose thoughtfully. "Slept okay."

"Anything else I should know?"

"Oh yeah, the day before, when I was in the card house, a feller who looked like you spooked around the outside, looking in the window. I think he was—"

Park cut her off. "Well, we'll talk about that later."

Gabby pushed away from the bars. "We ready to get out of here, then?"

"Not quite yet."

"Not at all." The fed straightened up. "This little lady is under arrest and the only place she's going is with me."

"Hmm. Maybe. Or maybe there won't be an arrest. Maybe we should call your director and ask him." He looked at Gabby and winked. "Or her."

The fed leaned in. "You'll hear from him what I'm telling you now." He scrutinized Park with one eye. "I'm starting to think you're not a real doctor."

"I'm more of a doctor than you are a fed. If you're not a fraud, then you're not here on authority of the FBI. I imagine the Bureau doesn't care for freelancers." Park turned to the other man. "Sheriff? Did the FBI call to tell you an agent was heading your way?"

"No."

The agent started to squirm.

"How about we make that call now?"

The sheriff reached for a phone on the wall. "Yeah, how about we have a talk with the feds?"

The fed turned red and drew his Beretta. "Everyone's going to shut the fuck up and get the fuck out of my way. Sheriff, get your hand away from that phone and put down your gun. Hands in the air, everyone!"

"Even me?" asked Gabby.

"Shut up!" ordered the fed.

Park put his briefcase on the ground and raised his hands. "Oh, you shouldn't have done that. Molly hates to be told to shut up. In fact, she's got a story about it. Don't you?" Park winked at Gabby and muttered in French, "*'La joie des lignes vent autour de toi calorifère de l'âme.'*"

Gabby leaned forward, into the bars. "Sure do, G-man. *Let me bend your ear.*"

The lawmen locked up, every joint and muscle. Park moved fast, disarmed the fed and slid his pistol into the empty cell, took the handcuffs off the sheriff's belt and locked the agent's wrist to the bars. All while poker facing, "*'Géographie des broderies en soie colonisée en floraison d'éponges la chanson cristallisée...'*"

Park helped himself to the sheriff's keys and revolver before waving Gabby down.

"What in the hell was that?" asked the sheriff when his faculties returned.

"Appalling, isn't it? Impersonating a federal agent like that?" Park indicated the fed with a toss of his head and unlocked Gabby's cell.

The fed pulled uselessly against the handcuffs. "You're in a heap of trouble, Wong, or whoever you are."

She popped out through the cell door and pushed the sheriff in her place. "Sorry, sheriff, but we gotta go."

Park nodded and locked the cell door. "We really are in a rush. When your admin returns and lets you out of there, you should call the feds, report this agent for misconduct, and forget you ever saw me."

"What the hell just happened?" The sheriff asked Gabby, "What the heck did you just do, Molly?"

"Me?" Gabby shrugged. "Nothing. I just gotta big mouth."

Chapter 49

"How about I hold the cigarette at the top of the window and crack it a bit? You won't smell a thing. I promise." Pollyanna made to roll down the window. The handle came off in her hand.

Ainia glared at her.

"Sorry." After a few attempts to fix the handle, Pollyanna put it in the glove compartment.

They'd only been on the road for half a day. The haul across country had already settled into long monotonous stretches of highway interrupted by clusters of gas stations and chain restaurants. The two women had butted heads over just about everything from which highways to take west (Ainia won that one, seeing it was her truck) to where and when to eat (Ainia won that one too, for the same reason).

But Pollyanna kept trying. "Then let's stop at the next gas station for some dip."

"Ugh! God, no." Ainia retched. "Seriously, you do that?"

"When I have to, like on planes and stuff."

"Remind me never to make out with you."

"Deal." Pollyanna winced, clutched her chest between her breasts, and grunted.

Ainia straightened up in the driver's seat, casting concerned glances Pollyanna's way. "What's wrong?"

Pollyanna grabbed the handle over the door. "Pull over! Pull over, quick!"

Ainia brought the truck to a stop on the shoulder. "Are you having a heart attack or something?"

"No, it's my card." Pollyanna cast suspicious eyes at the truck's gauges. "Something just went wrong. Is the Great Red Shark okay?"

"The truck is handling fine. And stop calling it that."

"Maybe the tires? We could have caught a nail."

"What are you talking about?"

"Whenever I get a strike of bad luck I feel it, here." Pollyanna rubbed her sternum for emphasis. "This is my body's karma bank, where I store all the bad luck until it cashes in for a stroke of the good."

"I didn't realize there were rules to your card. I thought you were just…unlucky all over." Ainia waited a moment, bracing for something to happen. A cement truck passed them on the highway, nothing else. "Are you sure that was your card and not heartburn?"

"Hell yeah, I'm sure. I just…" Pollyanna checked that their bags were still in the truck bed. "It's usually more…immediate. You know."

The women waited silently in the cab until Ainia ran out of patience. She threw the truck into drive and pulled back onto the highway. "Well, whatever it was, it's over now. So you only get a spot of good luck after a lot of bad luck? Doesn't seem like a good deal."

"Believe me, it's not. But when I get the good luck, I get a lot of it at once. Big luck. Not lottery ticket big, but big enough." She was still casting around for anything tragically out of place. "Maybe my phone broke."

Pollyanna powered it up. "Nope. Seems to be working. Well, something crappy happened to me somewhere. My house probably burned down."

Phone in hand, Pollyanna idly called up Ensign's text message and spelled out the coded message, "C A S E M E N. You've been with Project Dead Blind longer than me. Any idea who these Casemen are?"

"Never heard of them. I don't think they're holding cards. Not real cards, anyway. The one who came after me had a frozen brain with him. Psychotronic weapon is my theory."

"Yeah, but where are they from? I thought China wasn't a big player in the psychic warfare scene."

"You know China's a big place, right? If they decide they want to be a psychic superpower it won't take long for them to do it. Harvesting psychic stem cells and growing weaponized brains in vats—with two billion people they'll have a lot of options. Even after decades of purging psychics from their population."

Pollyanna turned to look out the window. "People suck. The world sucks to be in."

Ainia scoffed, "You think that's new? We don't know if this is China, either. We're talking about two Asians. Anyone can get two guys of any color to jump on board a suicide mission. Working theories are one thing, but don't let them give you tunnel vision."

Ainia changed lanes to let a car pass. "What gets me is they know us."

Pollyanna scratched her head. "Why is that a surprise?"

Ainia sighed, tired of talking. "Dead Blind's done a pretty good job of staying under everyone's radar. That's why the Office of Intergovernmental and External Affairs isn't part of Homeland Security. If you want to keep something secret, keep it away from the spies."

"You don't consider yourself a spy?"

"Not hardly. I'm a warrior. This job lets me see plenty of action. The cloak and dagger gets on my nerves. Whoever these Casemen are, I wish they'd come out from under their banner and have it out with us on the battlefield, like the old days."

An old Hyundai pulled up next to them. Pollyanna's eyes went wide when it pulled aggressively close. They went wider still when she recognized the driver—the Caseman from the 7-Eleven. "Battlefield? Battlefield, Ainia! Battlefield!"

A tidal wave of vertigo hit Ainia, started spinning, inside and out, her vision and her stomach.

Pollyanna grabbed for the assist handle above her door with both hands, flailing wildly instead.

"Is that him?" Ainia was hunched over the steering wheel, struggling to control her truck as it pulled to the left, into oncoming traffic. A horn blow blasted them. Ainia jerked the wheel to the right. The truck jumped up on two wheels and back into the proper lane. "Where did he go?"

"I don't know. I can't see for—" The truck ran into something, stopping them dead.

Chapter 50

A freight train passed behind the two agents fighting on the edge of the railyard. Isaac was having an easy time avoiding Joe's punches, and a hard time taking him out without hurting the boy. "It's okay, Joe. He went after you to catch me off guard. But I know how to get out of this. All you gotta do is put on your poker face."

Joe kicked at Isaac's knee and missed. "I don't know how!"

"What do you mean, you don't have a poker face?"

The man in the motorcycle helmet stood a hundred feet away. He lunged forward with a punch. So did Joe, barely missing Isaac's jaw. "I'm schizophrenic. I'm supposed to be immune to this stuff!"

"Not this time, huh?" Isaac blocked a side kick from Joe. "What makes this guy different?"

Joe repositioned himself and took a fighting stance. "I like knowing kung fu, I just don't want to do it this way. How are you keeping up, Isaac? Aren't we out of his range?"

"I'm picking up a little something from here." Isaac ducked under Joe's roundhouse punch. "And I did a little boxing in school—that doesn't hurt."

"What are we going to do?"

"You're going to stay there and play the puppet. I'm going to rush him." Isaac feinted left then stepped right, trying to get around Joe. But the puppet master was too quick, and Joe stepped in the way.

"Sorry," Joe said before kicking Isaac in the stomach. "Really sorry! Sorry!"

Isaac fell back and rolled alongside the tracks, inches from the moving train. He got to his feet as soon as his forty-year-old knees would allow. "Don't worry, I know it's not personal, kid."

With locked limbs and painful steps, Joe stumbled along the rails after Isaac. "I'm back in control! It's me again."

Isaac eyed the puppet master running full bore toward the Dead Blind agents. He took his eyes off the man to say to Joe, "I think he's—"

Joe struck Isaac in the forehead with an elbow. "It's not me again!"

"Thanks. Figured that out." Isaac wobbled a bit as he stumbled back. "Got any insights? I'm out of ideas here."

"No, you're not. You'll have one in a few seconds."

"Good to know." Isaac stepped to the side, avoiding Joe's clumsy lunge, and grabbed the boy around the chest, pinning his arms to his sides.

"Fighting's hard," Joe gasped. "I'm running out of breath."

"You know what? You're kinda light." Isaac picked up Joe and carried him to the passing train, and tossed him up into the open car. Isaac stepped up on the ladder as it passed, and flipped the bird at the man in the motorcycle helmet as the train carried them away.

Chapter 51

Ainia woke with the smell of road dust and antifreeze in her nose and the sun in her eyes. Her face was pressed against the steering wheel. She was dizzy and disoriented, and her neck ached.

Pollyanna was slumped against the passenger door, unconscious. A middle-aged Asian man in a trench coat and bucket hat jerked the door open. She fell out, the seatbelt stopping her fall.

"You're..." Ainia could barely keep her head up against the vertigo. "You're the Caseman from Pennsylvania, aren't you? How the hell did you-?"

"Quiet," the man ordered, unbuckling Pollyanna's seatbelt with one hand. The other held something below Ainia's view. He eased Pollyanna to the ground, licking his lips.

Ainia's normally confident fingers fumbled for her seatbelt and then the door. She cursed, struggling to swing a leg out of the truck, but her joints wouldn't cooperate. She fell out of the cab onto the rough ground below, shielding her head and catching a rock to the shin.

She rolled onto her back. The sky spun. The brim of the Caseman's bucket hat blocked the sun.

"You are unnecessary. Your mind is useless and completely without value. Should I kill you now? This is what I'm wondering." The man scanned the horizon. The road had been empty when they crashed in this gully. No one would see them.

The radiator hissed and dripped antifreeze. Pollyanna lay on the other side of the truck, folded over like a discarded sack.

Ainia rolled under the truck to her. Two spins and her guts rebelled. She stopped, face to the ground, and vomited into the dirt. It splashed back into her face. Stomach acid and orange juice burned her eyes.

Before Ainia could grab the knife from Pollyanna's belt a foot came down on her back. "I don't *need* to kill you at all, do I? But needs and wants…"

Ainia's watery eyes clenched closed. She realized she was better off without them. The vertigo faded by half. She seized the man's ankle, rolled, and took him down hard.

Blindly, she crawled and punched her way up to his face. His arms clenched, protecting the bag.

"You're nothing without this, aren't you?" Ainia gripped the bag with both hands and pulled, kicking him under his chin until she tore it free from his grip.

The vertigo cleared in an instant. She tossed the bag behind her and rolled up into a fighting stance. "Now you'll see how useless I can be."

"That's not going to happen." Two men in black suits stood over the doctor's bag, guns drawn on Ainia and her opponent.

Chapter 52

Park and Gabby took turns driving west through the night, getting far away from Kentucky. Gabby stared at a hill off in the distance to the left. The same hill had been on the horizon since dawn.

It was Gabby's turn behind the wheel, which she held with both hands, back ramrod straight, eyes on the road. She jerked when Park popped out from under his coat as his reclined seat snapped forward. "Crap, Park! Warn me when you wake up."

Park rubbed his eyes and stared at the barren landscape. "Where are we?"

"Just short of Texas."

"Oklahoma? That explains all the…"

"Flat?"

"Yeah, flat." The dash clock read 4:33pm. It was still on Eastern Time. Park set the clock, bringing it down a time zone. "California, here we come."

"Why is the Dead Blind safe house in San Diego when we're all over the East Coast? Shouldn't it be more local?"

"Ensign wanted it as far from Washington, DC, as you could get. I talked him out of Alaska."

"You couldn't talk him into Hawaii?"

"That's a little too far. Besides, Hawaii and San Diego are pretty much the same. Swap out the poi for burritos. Why are you sitting like that? Something wrong with your back?"

"No. I'm being careful. There's a lot of buttons in here and I don't know which one's the smoke machine or the oil slick or none of that."

Park laughed, then realized she wasn't joking. "You're serious? Gabby, Dead Blind doesn't have the budget for anything like that. This is a regular Prius hybrid. All it has is really great gas mileage."

Gabby relaxed. "Well you should move some of Dead Blind's money around and get yourself a real spy car. James Bond never got laid 'cause he got forty miles to the gallon."

"Fifty-four," Park corrected. "Fifty in the city. Let me tell you about James Bond. Fleming, the author of the books, picked the name because he thought it was a perfectly boring and unremarkable name. Fleming was also a spy back in his day. So what does that tell you about the espionage business?"

Gabby answered with a jerking-off motion.

"Classy. How does some food sound?"

"Any excuse to get out of this boring car. Might be a while, though. This country's kinda empty."

Twenty minutes later, they settled on a Walmart, ate a late lunch at the McDonalds inside, then decided to stock up for the rest of the trip.

Near the blaring sound and lights of the LCD TVs and blu-rays of the electronics section, Park paused outside the shoe aisle, while Gabby pushed the cart full of snacks and water. Park looked down at his torn-up oxfords. "I guess I have to buy a new pair of shoes. These gave me away in Kentucky." He didn't sound too happy about it.

"So?" Gabby leaned against the cart's push rail. "Buy another pair of shoes. It's Walmart. They're cheap on the wallet."

"It's not that. I have to get over the guilt of spending this much money at a Walmart."

Gabby took a pair of blue-and-green high-tops off the shelf and pushed them into Park's arms. "There you go. Guilt-free. You're welcome."

Park put them back. "That's not—"

"Buy the shoes, Park." She pointed across the electronics section. "Women's clothing is that way. I'm gonna get another pair of panties. I've been wearing these for four days."

"You were only arrested two days ago," Park said, as Gabby pushed the cart away.

"Whatever. Get over yourself by the time I'm back, will ya?" Gabby turned the corner, away from Park and his conundrum.

New underwear called for new jean shorts and a new T-shirt. They didn't have any AC/DC shirts she didn't already own. She'd settled on a plain black tee when a *Who Made Who* track jacket caught her eye and captured her heart. Gabby grabbed one sleeve as another woman, older, heavier, and sun-worn, grabbed the other. She fixed a hard stare on the stranger. "Let go. I ain't in the mood for wishing."

The woman flushed red with anger. Gabby kicked the stranger's cart down the aisle. That freed up her adversary's other hand to grip the sleeve and prepare for a tug-of-war.

Gabby did the same, giving the jacket a firm tug. Without a word, they went back and forth, until the stranger put her full weight into the fight. Gabby let go of the jacket, letting the woman fall into the T-shirts, breaking the shelf with her butt.

"You win, bitch." Gabby brushed her hands and pushed on with her cart, while the stranger unsuccessfully struggled back to her feet. "I'll find one just like it in the Walmart next door.

"Some peop—" Gabby turned out of the aisle to find "some people" surrounding her. She'd been caught up in her own fight and didn't hear the fights breaking out around her over the blaring audio of the electronics section. The mood was Christmas clearance, not November nothing-day. They weren't throwing punches yet. But there was plenty of shouting. It was an angry mood, and getting worse.

"Crap." She rushed her cart past the mob, back to the shoe section where Park was jamming a pair of black oxfords back into their box.

"Finally found a pair I like and the left is a size too small. If I'm lucky,

I'll find the other fucked-up pair." Park dropped the box, spilling the shoes. "What the hell's wrong with you? Hey!" He jumped back, dodging Gabby's cart as she ran over the shoe box.

"The psychic's here! The one from the card house back home!"

"Bullshit. We drove straight through from Kentucky. He couldn't have tailed us all night, and I took the batteries out of our phones."

"Listen to yourself, and look around, dummy." The mood wasn't as bad as that night back in her hometown, but tensions were high all over the store.

"Where is this asshole?" Park pushed the cart out of his way, looking for a fight.

"I don't know. What are you going to do if we find him?"

"Hold him down and beat some answers out of him."

"Now you're talkin'! Hey, we're sounding kinda rough. I think he's already making us angry. Shouldn't we poker face or something?"

Park stopped his march. "Good point. '*La joie des lignes vent... vent...*'" The French words stumbled out of his mouth. He stopped, closed his eyes, and took a deep breath, and said, "Fuck it. Let's find this asshole and kick his ass. I'll show him what angry is."

The two agents circled wide around the fight. On the far side of the store, Gabby slapped Park on the arm and pointed at the Caseman in denim heading out the side entrance, through the gardening section.

Park tackled the man amid the stench of manure. He got two sharp elbow strikes to the head for his trouble, and let go.

The Caseman had pulled himself to his feet when Gabby got in shouting distance. "Hey, jerkoff! *Let me bend your ear.*"

The Caseman snatched his backpack, kicked Park in the ribs, and ran off as if Gabby hadn't said anything.

"What the fuck?" Gabby dropped to check on Park, her anger faded. "You all right?"

"No." Park rolled onto his back, holding his side. "I screwed that up in so many ways. Crap."

"My card rolled right over him. You think he's deaf or something?"

"He doesn't speak English."

"That's un-American." Gabby helped Park to his feet.

Park smirked. "When you're right, you're right."

Without the Caseman's influence the fighting in the Walmart eased and the looting began, as shoppers took advantage of the mass confusion.

It only took a second for Gabby and her cart to merge with the exodus of looters. "Come on, Park. Let's get your shoes without your liberal guilt."

She pushed past the overwhelmed store security with the others. Park covered his face with his hand and followed.

Chapter 53

The freight train rambled through the Mississippi backwoods, heading toward Texas. Exposition Joe sat at the edge of the empty train car's open door, watching the countryside pass by. Isaac shifted from sitting to half-kneeling to standing, trying to get comfortable.

"Ridin' the rails is a young man's game." Isaac pressed his hands against his back, leaning back and forth.

Joe looked back, squinting into the sunrise. "Not really. I've met plenty of old-timers on the tracks."

"I'm an old-timer now?"

"Hey, you said it, not me. It's rough at first, but you'll get used to it. Could be worse—could be raining, and we could be on top of a gravel car. That sucks. Try some yoga."

"I don't know any yoga."

"Look at Mr. Adaptable, doesn't know any yoga."

"Take this train through India. I'll show you some yoga, all the yoga you can handle." Isaac shielded his eyes and stared into the distance. "But this is more like Indiana. Or is it? Any visions yet?"

"Nope. Nothing but train, but that could change in a heartbeat. Don't get too comfortable."

Isaac rubbed his back. "Wasn't going to."

The train pulled out of the woods and ran parallel to a single-lane stretch of road.

"Uneasy Rider's back." Isaac pointed to a bridge where the road and train tracks passed over a creek. The black-and-green leather-clad man on the motorcycle watched the train pass from the bridge, started his engine, and followed on the road.

"He must have rode all night long." Isaac cupped his hands around his mouth and shouted, "Dude! Give it up! Get some sleep! You can kill us when we stop!" The train lurched and Isaac scrambled for a grip on the doorway. "*If* we stop."

Joe stood up and stretched. "Does he know any yoga?"

Isaac spread his legs and did some experimental swinging of his arms, but gave up, disappointed. "I doubt it."

"Picking up anything else?"

"I never know what I got until I try. There's not much to try right now. All I know is what I know and what you know."

"Not what I know." Joe's finger traced circles in the air around his ear.

"Oh yeah. Sorry. I forgot about your...condition."

"It's not your fault."

Isaac searched the floor of the empty train car.

Joe asked, "What are you looking for?"

"Something to throw. I want to knock him off that bike." Isaac found an iron stake that had been rattling around in the back of the car and practiced his throw. "Let me know when."

"Okay." Joe looked for the Caseman, but the road had twisted out of sight. "Now!"

Isaac dropped the spike. "Now you're fucking with me."

Joe pointed at Isaac and winked. "I knew you'd say that."

Isaac laughed. "What's it like knowing what people are going to say before they say it?"

Joe sighed. "It takes patience. To you, we're having a conversation. To me, I'm waiting for you to catch up. Constantly."

"Ever wish you didn't have your card?"

"Don't we all?"

"Not me. No matter where I am, I'm always the best around. It's pretty sweet."

"Best comes easy for you, doesn't it?" asked Joe, a little envy in his voice.

Isaac smiled. "Sure does."

"If everything is easy, then is anything worth doing?"

"Look at Hobo Joe, getting philosophical. Aren't you the one who makes no choices? If everything is laid out for you, then how is anything hard for you?"

Joe pointed at a large rock as the train passed. "It's hard watching it flow past and not having any control or choice." He stood up, gripped the doorframe, leaned out, and watched what was coming. "Get ready. Here's our transfer."

Isaac brushed himself off. "Transfer? Shit. I lost my ticket."

"There's two trees coming up in jumping range. After me." And Joe was gone, jumping to the branch before Isaac realized he was ready to move. Hanging from the branch, Joe was fast fading into the dark and distance.

"Could have told me which branch," Isaac muttered as he turned to face the train engine. "This'll do." Isaac launched himself at the next low branch and prayed. His arms wrapped around the tree. A knot jabbed him in the chest. The branch sagged and he fell with it as it pivoted down, landing on his feet in a sandy, dry creek bed, still clutching the branch.

"Damn, that was smooth." Isaac let go of the branch and it levered back up, almost scratching him in the face.

Joe ran out of the woods and took Isaac's arm. "Come on. We've got a plane to catch."

"Plane?" Isaac asked, blindly allowing Joe to drag him into the woods. He kept his head down and his feet moving until Joe stopped by a sizable cabin on the edge of a straight run of road. An old black Toyota 4Runner was parked outside.

"This ain't the airport, Joe."

Exposition Joe shushed him and whispered, "Not officially."

The side of the cabin slid open. Two men in jeans and baseball caps pushed a Cessna out onto the road. The cabin wasn't a cabin. It was a hangar for the small four-seater aircraft.

Isaac whispered, "These guys are up to no good."

Joe nodded. "Yeah, they're drug smugglers."

"And they're going to take us to Nebraska out of the kindness of their hearts?"

"No, you're going to convince the pilot."

The men started the plane's engine.

Isaac rubbed his forehead. "That's a tough sell, Joe."

Joe pulled a red handkerchief from his back pocket. "And you're going to have to keep his eyes off the Caseman." Joe pointed to where the road turned into the woods. "He's coming up from that end of the road. Soon."

The men shook hands. One climbed onto the truck. The other waited next to the plane for the truck to pull away down the road, headed toward the woods.

Isaac asked, "It's all on me, huh? What are you going to be doing?"

"I'm going to be your hostage." Joe gagged himself with the handkerchief.

"Really?" Isaac folded his arms. "You really think I'm going to do this?"

Joe mumbled through the gag, half-turned, and crossed his wrists behind his back.

"No. I get it. I don't like having to play the thug. Why can't you take me hostage instead?"

Joe held his hand over his head, measuring himself to Isaac's shoulder.

Isaac shook his head and crossed his arms. "This is not happening, Joe."

Joe pointed frantically to the plane. The pilot climbed into the cabin.

As Isaac looked back, the motorcycle headlight beamed its way through the woods.

"All right. I'm only doing this because that guy bugs me." Isaac took Joe's wrists and held his other hand behind Joe's shoulder blades as if he had a gun.

He ran Joe up to the Cessna's cabin on the pilot side, pushing the boy's face against the window.

The pilot looked up from his clipboard in shock.

Isaac yelled, face twitching with feigned rage, "Motherfucker, let us the fuck in or I'mma spray this white boy's brains all over yo' motherfucking plane. And yours'll be next!"

Chapter 54

The sleepless, confined hours distorted the trunk of 97:4's twelve-year-old Toyota Corolla. It was cramped, then immense. At one point, when she stared hard enough, she thought she could see stars through the door.

97:4's cross earrings stopped shaking. The car had come to a stop. The familiar sound of her engine ran on for a few seconds, sputtering to silence. The car rocked a little and the door slammed closed. Then nothing—for a good long time.

97:4 felt for the emergency trunk release and pulled. The cord snapped off in her hand.

"No! No! No! No!" She stabbed the broken handle back into the opening, threw it aside, and with her fingertips, dug in the hole for the stub of the cord.

She banged on the trunk with her cast, screaming and oblivious to the pain.

The trunk popped open. The sky was dark behind the glare of a sodium streetlight. The spot of blueberry filling on his forest green sweater vest had dried. His hand on the roller, Three ordered, "Stay quiet. Get out."

97:4 struggled out of the trunk. It wasn't easy with one good arm. Contorted all night, her legs were stiff. The right immediately seized up with a Charley horse. Three offered no help. He stood, sweating in the cool night air. 97:4 recognized the sign of someone high on crystal meth. She kicked herself for missing it back in the kitchen, for being too caught up in self-pity.

They were parked in a dirty alley, in some city's downtown. Three had parked her car between dumpsters. They stank of grease and garbage.

97:4 tried to run for it, hobbling a few steps on shaky knees. She got about six feet away before Three ordered her to "Stop. Come back here."

Her body's allegiance was to whatever was in that case. She twisted around and fell on the ground, face-to-face with a filthy pair of high-tops. They weren't alone.

After years serving in soup kitchens, 97:4 knew the different levels of homelessness. The working poor usually slept in their cars. You couldn't tell they were homeless by looking at them. The professionals—backpacks and shopping carts—they made homelessness a lifestyle. Saddest were the mentally ill castoffs who lacked family support and the cognitive facilities to survive above an animal level. She recognized the man standing with Three as the latter.

"Do you see this filth?" Three asked, his roller's handle gripped behind him. "Your country is covered with it."

The bearded "filth" in question held sheets of bubble wrap around his shoulders like a blanket. Clutching a Bible, confused, he was the kind of man 97:4 had never been able to help, only feed.

"He isn't filth," 97:4 said through gritted teeth. "He's a man with problems. Problems you don't understand."

"Nonsense. This is poor hygiene—physical and spiritual. You're going to clean this up."

"This is an alley, not a bath." 97:4 pushed herself to move, but the best she could manage was shifting a foot or twitching a finger.

Three took the roller handle with both hands and hissed, "Straighten up."

97:4's nostrils flooded with the scent of vanilla. Her body jerked to attention, sore muscles screaming under her skin.

"Take that book from him."

She stepped forward and snatched the Bible from the derelict's hands. He mumbled, "No," and tried to fight for it, but she shouldered him away, knocking him down. His bubble wrap blanket fell from his shoulders as he spilled to the ground.

"That's a heavy book, is it not?" Three stepped back. "Hit him with it."

"What? No!" 97:4 cried. Her treasonous arm raised the Bible over her head.

The derelict struggled to stand on shaky limbs. One hand stretched outward, grasping at nothing.

97:4 brought the Bible down on the back of his head twice. He was frail, and the first strike knocked him off balance. His outstretched hand gripped 97:4's knee. The second put him face-first into the ground.

"Flip him over."

97:4 dropped the Bible, a contaminated thing. Now it was her hand's turn to shake as she knelt by the derelict, grabbed his T-shirt, and rolled him over.

The man pushed himself away, trying to escape.

"Pick up the book."

She scooped the Bible up with her wrists instead of her hands.

"Hold it like you mean it."

Her grip adjusted against her will.

"Beat him." Three stepped back and leaned against the dirty cinder block wall, clinically observing the violence. "Beat him until I say 'stop.'"

Chapter 55

Night left little to see of Nebraska from the air. An occasional cloud passed the moon. Inside the plane, a dozen bundles of cocaine were stacked behind the seats.

Isaac snored, curled up in the seat, lulled to sleep by the hum of the Cessna's engine. The pilot wasn't talking. Once he'd found out nobody had a gun (including himself), he kept to the cockpit, simmering with anger. That left Joe to himself, until God climbed through the window.

Impossibly, the deity slipped through the one-inch gap, sat cross-legged on the bundles of cocaine, and knocked against the hull. "Not exactly whale-sized, but the outside conditions are just as deadly."

"What else could I do? You wrote the script." Joe looked down out the window. "I guess You had your reasons to end it this way."

"No. Not here. You're supposed to go into the depths of the earth for me." God pointed down.

Joe looked at the document in God's hand. "That's not what it says. Do You ever read that thing?"

God flipped it open to the present. "Let me show you. There's been a rewrite."

Joe cast eyes on the pages of the Script, formatted like a screenplay, for the first time. He scanned the page, expecting an action block describing the Cessna flying too low in the night, catching a power line with its landing gear, and crashing into the earth. What he'd seen on the train.

The scene had been cut. In this version, the plane lands safely.

Joe's fear gave way to anger. "We were supposed to die on this plane. Now You're telling me that's not going to happen? *Now?*"

"I wouldn't be God if I couldn't change a few things." God winked. "You didn't think I was going to let it end like that, did you? Have a little faith."

Joe reached to turn the page. God pulled it away, rolling it back up.

"Faith?" Joe asked. "I've seen You everyday for years. I don't need faith. Is this all a test?" He jabbed a thumb in his sleeping companion's direction. "And what about Isaac? I thought I was leading him to his death. You couldn't have shown me this back on the train?"

"Him? Don't worry about him. Even he has his part in this wonderful transubstantiation. It's you I'm worried about. If you lose faith, I can't help you. Like the Bible says, I help only those who help themselves."

Joe watched Isaac sleep. "I hope You have my friends covered too."

"It's implied." God looked out the window. "This is My stop. Anyway, don't worry. You'll do fine."

God gave Joe a thumbs-up and slipped out the crack in the window, back into the night.

Turbulence snapped Isaac awake from his nap. "What's going on?"

"We're here," the pilot shouted over the engine. He pulled a pair of night-vision goggles over his face. "When we land, I want you two out of my plane. I don't care how or where, just go."

Isaac pressed his face against the window, cupping his hands around his eyes. "This is one dark state. What's next, Joe?"

"I don't know yet." Joe stared at the floor.

With one raised eyebrow, Isaac slowly disengaged from the window and regarded him, head cocked to one side. "Joseph? I think you're lying to me."

"Yeah, kinda. Can we let it go until we hit the ground?"

Isaac scrutinized Joe for another second. "This isn't leading up to another ghetto act, is it?"

The plane came in for a rough landing. Closer to the earth, the ground winds knocked the small aircraft about. It touched down, bounced back into the air, and touched down again, lurching to a stop. The ground was as dark as the sky. The red running lights illuminated nothing.

The pilot snapped the night-vision goggles off and dropped them into the seat next to him. "Get out."

Joe complied, pulling the hatch open.

Isaac asked the pilot, "Hey man, which way—"

The pilot popped open his door. "When I said get out, I meant get the fuck—" Strange hands in black sleeves snatched the pilot, pulling him into the darkness.

"Oh, damn!" Isaac jumped in his seat.

Joe stepped out of the plane with his hands in the air. A man held a gun to his head. Joe was already kneeling as the federal agent screamed, "On the ground."

Two more handguns were jammed into the cabin. There was more shouting. Isaac sat carefully still with his hands up. They grabbed his shirt, buttons popping, and pulled him through the hatch to the ground.

"Don't shoot," Isaac called out as the feds pinned him to the ground next to where Joe knelt. Another agent dragged the pilot around into Joe's field of view and kicked his feet out from under him, dropping him to the ground.

A pistol barrel tapped Joe's temple. "Keep your goddamned eyes on the ground."

Joe faced the ground, belly to tarmac. Seeing nothing, hearing…

"Least it's a small load."

"It's a small market. This'll cover the region for a few months."

"Better save some for the boss."

"Ha! Wait, you're serious?"

"Welcome to the club. Grab one of those bundles."

"Should we…check it or something?"

"What for? You see a better shipment of cocaine around here? This'll do. Now, for the powdered milk man..." The soles of leather shoes ground gravel into the cracked asphalt runway.

The pilot grunted.

"Got anything to say for yourself, dipshit?"

"I want my lawyer."

That got a laugh. "Oh, dipshit, this isn't that kind of arrest, but you're going to wish it was. You can blame your passengers for this." An impact and a scream, followed by more of both. Joe didn't have to look up to know the pilot was getting a beating. He kept his eyes down, sparing himself from one of his own.

The stench of gasoline and a wave of heat hit Joe as the agents torched the Cessna and the rest of its cargo.

Chapter 56

Pollyanna came to on her knees in a gully on the side of the road. Sore and stunned, the last thing she remembered, the truck had plowed through a copse of bushes. She had no idea how she had gotten between Ainia and the Caseman from the 7-Eleven, or why he and Ainia were covered in dirt, vomit, and blood.

All three knelt before two men in dark suits, holding handguns.

Pollyanna raised her hands. "I'm Raoul Duke, and this is my attorney."

"Quiet. I know who you are, and who she is. But who the fuck is *he*?" the federal agent asked, indicating Pollyanna, Ainia, and the Caseman, in that order. "I said hands up, creepshow!"

The Caseman raised his hands, staring at his doctor's bag where it lay between him and the agents with their guns.

"You got a hard-on for this, huh?" The fed ordered the other agent to retrieve the bag while he kept his gun on the Caseman. "What's in there?"

"This." The other agent walked back to his partner, reaching into the bag with a handkerchief. He pulled out the frozen brain.

"Is that what I think it is?" asked the other fed.

"It's a brain," interrupted Pollyanna, "That guy's named Thompson. He works for *Rolling Stone*...a vicious, crazy kind of person. Cannibal. That's his lunch you're holding. You'd better lock him up." She started to inch away, still on her knees. "Good job, officers. You'll get a commendation for sure."

The agent in charge turned his gun on Pollyanna. "You! Stop!"

The Caseman lunged for his frozen brain, grabbing it with both hands. Everyone else dropped with vertigo. The fed's handgun fired as he fell, putting a hole in the dirt.

Pollyanna pressed her forehead to the ground and hyperventilated, trying not to vomit. A car started and pulled away. She watched Ainia, eyes closed, crawl up on the squirming agents.

She grabbed the one who'd drawn his pistol by the wrist and disarmed him, whipping him across the temple with his own gun. The second agent struggled for his own piece, still in its holster. Ainia straddled him, pounding his head into the ground until he went limp.

She bound them with their own handcuffs before Pollyanna's head stopped spinning. The Caseman was long gone.

Ainia opened one eye, experimentally, then the other, and looked around.

Pollyanna staggered to her feet.

The lead fed tried his tough-guy act. The beating Ainia had given him slurred his speech. "I'm giving you until now to uncuff us and—"

"Shut up." Ainia kicked him in the face. She walked up to Pollyanna, hand out. "Give me your knife."

"What for? Agh!"

It took a second for Ainia to grab Pollyanna in a wristlock, bend her over, draw her knife from the back of her belt and let her go.

Armed, she returned to the feds. "You ruined my hunt. Tell me who you are."

"Hunt?" The agent mock-laughed. "Who was being hunted? It looked like he had you pinned to a board. How about this? You uncuff us and we'll talk about extradition back East and degrees of comfort?"

"Extradition…" Ainia paced, considering the word. "No. No one's going anywhere. Everything I need is right here. You two and this knife." She looked at the blade in the sunlight, "What's not here? Your laws. I don't see your laws anywhere around here."

"Ainia. What are you getting at?" Pollyanna's nervous fingers twisted before her.

Ainia ignored her teammate, knelt by the agent's face, and hooked the blunt side of the knifepoint under his nose, pulling his head back. He grunted, but held his tongue.

She whispered, "I'm tired of being in the dark. Gimme some light, little candle, before I put you out."

With the click of a pistol hammer, Pollyanna had one of the fed's guns pointed at Ainia with both hands. Tears streamed down her face. "Goddamn it, Ainia, you put that fucking knife down."

Ainia told the fed, "I'll get back to you," stood, and ambled in Pollyanna's direction.

The pistol shook in Pollyanna's grip. "I won't let you torture anyone."

"Or what?" She walked up to the pistol barrel until it set between her eyes. "You're going to shoot me? You think you have it in you? Then do it."

"You th-think I won't?" Pollyanna's voice shook.

"You didn't have it years ago, you won't have it now. You never will. Now shut up and let me get to work." Ainia turned her back on Pollyanna, lingering a moment with the pistol barrel at the back of her head, and returned to the bound agents, flipping the knife. "Where to start—"

Ainia barely flinched when the gun fired, and fired again. Twelve times into the fed's black sedan, shattering the windshield, bursting two tires, and setting off the alarm.

Pollyanna wiped the tears from her face and her prints off the pistol, looked up at the freeway and smiled, relieved. "Think someone up there is going to hear that? Maybe they'll call 911. Can't risk it, can you?"

Ainia ran her tongue over her teeth and passed the knife back to Pollyanna as she walked back to her truck. "Well played."

The last bit of sun dropped behind the horizon.

Chapter 57

Park stared out the window and worried about the rest of his team while Gabby drove and talked. Park had tuned her out.

The car drifted onto the shoulder. Tires tossed up rocks from the rough, dirty shoulder, pelting the wheel wells like machine gun fire.

"Hey!" Park shouted. Gabby's head was tilted back, her eyes shut, and her mouth open in a snore. "Gabby! Hey!"

She laughed and jerked the car back into the lane. "Ha! That got your attention."

"That's not funny. The shoulder's full of debris that can puncture a tire. The last thing we need is a flat."

"Yeah? Well the first thing we need is some excitement. Driving through Texas is so boring. I want that Caseman to come back for another round. This time we'd be ready for him."

Park sighed. "I guess I do too. Another chance to figure out how he's tailing us."

"Did you toss the phones?"

"No. I can't afford to." Park picked them out of the cup holder. "We haven't established they're compromised and they're our only channel of communication."

"You just love your gadgets."

"That's...not wrong." Reluctantly, he put them down.

"See? I got you all figured out. I bet in an hour you'll be sitting back in your Walmart loafers, eating Texas BBQ."

"They're oxfords. And that's an easy call since you're the one driving."

That evening, they pulled into the first BBQ restaurant Gabby spotted from the highway. Park opened the glove compartment and pulled an automatic pistol from its hiding spot.

Gabby's eyes went wide. "I knew it!"

Park smiled and slid the small pistol into the underarm holster where he normally kept the large satphone. "I had one modest spy trick installed. But that's it. I should have brought this into the Walmart. Not making that mistake again."

After dinner, the agents were sated, stacks of bones on plates before them. Park cleaned his fingers as best he could with the one towelette the restaurant provided. Gabby leaned back and drummed her belly. "Whew! Okay, this would be worth being stuck in the middle of ten thousand acres of flatness."

Park flipped through his wallet. "We're running low on cash."

Gabby affected an indeterminate posh accent, "One shouldn't worry about money when taking a lady out for dining."

Park snorted. "What did Emily Post have to say about dining as fugitives?"

"Who is Emily Post?" Gabby asked, picking at her teeth with a fork tine.

"Point made." Park dropped two twenties on the bill and looked out the window.

"Still thinking about the gook—guy, the Caseman?"

Park fell back in the booth. "Did you just say 'gook?' Really? I'm sitting right here."

Gabby held her hands up. "I'm sorry. It just slipped out. I ain't like that normally. And if you're saying I am, well, what's that say about you?"

"Don't worry about it." Park smirked. "It's nothing I haven't heard before."

"I mean look at me." She held her arms forward, displaying her darker-than-Caucasian skin. "I'm the only half-Indian in my county. It's not like I didn't get more than my fair share of shit. One side or the other, it's something I grew up around. You know?"

"I do. My grandmother…" Park considered his words. "Old-country Koreans, some of them still believe they're the 'cleanest race.' It's not an aggressive kind of racism. More like germophobia."

Gabby relaxed. "White, black, yellow, or brown, the one thing everybody has in common is a racist grandparent."

"True." They toasted as the waitress returned with Park's change.

When they returned to the car, Park took his coat off, threw it in the backseat, and climbed under the vehicle.

Gabby bent down to watch. "This ain't the time for an oil change."

"Checking for tracking devices, I should have thought of this earlier."

"A tracker? When the heck would they have slapped one on your car?"

"Maybe when I parked outside the sheriff's office? The Caseman could have been waiting for me there. Hand me my phone, will you? A battery too."

Gabby pulled them out of the glove box for Park. He reassembled the device, powered it up, selected an app, and ran it back and forth along the bottom of the car before passing it back to Gabby. "Take that around the sides, will you?"

By the time Gabby circled the car, Park climbed back out from underneath. He took the phone back and checked the app. "Nothing. Satellites, maybe?"

Gabby shielded her eyes and looked up at the sky. "I don't see none."

"Well, if there is one, we're not likely to see it from here." Park took the battery out of the phone. "Ensign called them Casemen…I bet that's it. They're not psychics, they're carrying psychotronic weapons in those cases. The one in the suit destroyed my condo with telekinesis, the one in denim had some kind of emotional projection. Maybe there's another Caseman out there tracking us telepathically."

Gabby shielded her head with her hands. "Reading our minds? What do we do?"

"Nothing."

"What do you mean, nothing?"

"We can put on our poker face, but that's only short-term protection. How long can you hold a poker face? Five minutes?"

Park's explanation hadn't put Gabby's mind at ease—just the opposite. Her hands were still clenching handfuls of hair, her eyes wide in fear. "Momma was right."

Park grabbed her in a hug. "No. Look, Gabby, I'm sorry. That's all theory. I'm just speculating. We've never come across a card that powerful."

Gabby hugged him back tightly. "But there's always a first, right? If there was a mind reader out there that powerful, then you wouldn't know it would you? Oh crap. We need some tinfoil hats. That'll help right?"

"Look, I never should have said anything. I shouldn't have brought you on the mission to Liberia. I keep fucking things up. I'm supposed to be field commander, but if Ensign doesn't lay out the orders for me, then everything falls apart in my hands. We lost the Faith Machine. We almost lost our lives. Now we're all fugitives from God knows what. I couldn't even take down the Caseman at the Walmart."

While Park spoke, the hug turned from him consoling Gabby to the other way around. He pulled out of Gabby's arms.

"You'll get him next time." Gabby climbed into the passenger seat.

"I don't know about that." Park dropped into the car. "I'm not much of a fighter."

"You got up again, didn't you? Half of fighting is being able to take a beating. I like a guy who can take a few blows." Gabby put her hand in Park's lap. "Speaking of blows."

"Whoa!" Park grabbed her wrist and pulled her away. "What do you think you're doing?"

"It's called road head. You really are naive, ain't you?" She pulled out of his grasp and went back to his fly. "If they really are watching us from the sky, then let's give them something to look at."

Park pushed her away. "Christ! What the fuck are you thinking?" He opened the door and rolled outside, landing on his ass.

Gabby still lay halfway in the driver's seat. "I...I was thinking I'd pay you back for that beating you took for me."

Park struggled to pull his pants back on, flustered. "I'm your boss and your doctor. This is inappropriate in so many ways."

Gabby rolled her eyes. "Oh, come on. It's just a blow job."

Park opened the back door and grabbed his coat.

Gabby pulled herself over into the driver's seat. "What? You're leaving?"

Park slammed the door and shoved an arm in the coat sleeve. "I need to get away from you right now. I need to calm down."

"Well, what am I supposed to do?"

Park half turned, not looking at her. "You can... I don't know. Just stay away from me."

Park walked away.

Chapter 58

Park traveled at least six blocks before he stopped trembling. He found himself at the foot of a hill on the edge of the commercial area headed into an older residential neighborhood with houses covered in peeling white paint and ivy, bordered by low brick walls.

He took a seat on one of these walls, stared at the street, and wondered if anything was going right. Whether the other agents of Project Dead Blind were still alive, or they'd already ended up dead at the hands of these Casemen or each other.

A gray sedan parked across the street. Park recognized the driver—the Asian man outside his imploding condo. The man cut the engine, pulled out a newspaper, and started to read.

Park drew his gun, opened the passenger door, and climbed inside. He pulled the keys from the ignition and pointed the gun at the man's abdomen. "Who the hell are you?"

The stranger raised a bored eyebrow, folded his newspaper, and sniffed deeply. "Twenty-Two."

"I'm not in the mood for games." Park dug the pistol barrel further into the man's side. "What's your real name?"

"Neither of us uses our real name, Dr. Park. But only one of us is lying."

Park flinched and shot a glance at the back. The aluminum briefcase Twenty-Two carried in Washington, DC, lay in the seat. "If I'm the liar, then what's in the case?"

"The brain of a psychic, extracted and weaponized," said Twenty-Two, as calmly as if he were describing an air conditioner.

Park flinched at the blunt response. "Bullshit. There's no way to make a life support system small enough to fit in a briefcase."

"It doesn't need one. The harvesting process involves pre-training in a cryo-kinetic technique that puts the subject into a meditative state. The brain is then extracted. The ambient heat absorbed by the brain powers the process and maintains the state."

Park snuck another look at the briefcase. There was a copper patch on the case's handle. "Is that the interface, where it connects with your thumb?"

"Yes."

"What do you take me for? There's no way North Korea has this kind of technology."

"Maybe it doesn't. Maybe it's Chinese."

Park smirked. "I'm onto you. I hear echoes of my grandmother in your accent."

"You don't believe there's a brain in the case, but you're sure it's not Chinese. You sound confused, Dr. Park." The Caseman's tone leaked contempt for Park's alias.

Park pressed the pistol barrel into Twenty-Two's side. "Of course I'm confused. You and your Casemen come out of nowhere and hunt down my people. What's your agenda?"

"I'm here to destroy you, Dr. Park. Not physically. It's easy to break a man's body. That proves nothing. I'll show you that everything you've worked for, believed in, it's all been for nothing. Your hopes and dreams will go up like so much smoke."

"Oh, very poetic."

The corners of Twenty-Two's mouth turned up, shy of a smile. "I'm glad you liked it. Tell me, how is James Ensign? Have you heard from him lately? I wonder how he'd feel about your mission's success." Twenty-Two leaned in, "We're wearing down the rest of your team as well. Isaac and Exposition Joe, we've pushed them up against one of our other enemies. Ainia and Pollyanna might kill each other before we do. 97:4, your most powerful agent, was the first to fall."

His thumb shook in anger as it pulled the pistol's hammer back.

"Don't worry, she's still alive. We want you damaged, not dead." Twenty-Two pushed Park's gun hand aside. "We both know you're not going to use that gun. You're not a killer."

Park twitched. "And you are?"

"I killed the two FBI men in your home didn't I?" Twenty-Two turned in his seat to face him. "You can't kill, but you can let people die, can't you, Dr. Park? The eighty-seven in Liberia; you walk quite a bloody path, more than most doctors."

Park grimaced. "I'm not that kind of doctor."

"Oh, I know. Those doctors help people. You collect the damaged, turn them into weapons, and point them at targets." He jabbed a thumb at the case in the backseat. "We use volunteers. You and James Ensign, you just use. I know all about you and Project Dead Blind. How much damage you've done."

"I'm not letting you draw me into some ethical argument. Not when I have this." Park pressed the pistol barrel into Twenty-Two's side.

"You won't pull the trigger. The illusion that your hands are clean is too important to you." Twenty-Two reached into his coat pocket, drew a pack of cigarettes and lighter, and offered Park one. Park slapped it out of his hand. Twenty-Two watched it bounce off the windshield and land on the dash. He shrugged and lit the cigarette he'd drawn for himself. "You're focused on me. You should be wondering what's happening to Agent Gabby."

Park climbed back out of the car, reached into the backseat, and took the briefcase, while holding the pistol on Twenty-Two. "Come with me. When we get back to Gabby, you'd better hope she's all right. Or whatever happened to her is going to happen ten times worse to you."

Chapter 59

No one had ever refused Gabby before. Maybe this was payback for all the girly crap she'd pulled in high school. She picked a piece of lint off the dash and opened the door to flick it into the gutter.

Through the gap in the door, she caught sight of the Caseman in denim pass behind the car. Backpack slung over his shoulder, headed the way Park had stormed off.

"Oh no. That ain't good." Gabby reached for her phone and grabbed Park's from the console where they lay next to each other. She growled in frustration. In the rearview mirror, the Caseman crossed the street.

Gabby checked the glove compartment for a second pistol and came up empty. She popped the trunk, slid out of the car, and dug around in the back until she found the tire iron, a tiny thing. It would have to do. Too bad she hadn't brought her ax, but she'd been in jail.

She kept to a crouch and followed the Caseman. He on the sidewalk and she in the street, careful to keep a row of cars between them.

Park was nowhere in sight. She glanced back down the street one last time, checking for witnesses, and found none. Her target had turned to face her, a knowing smirk on his face.

Still crouched, she held the tire iron like a spear. "This ain't what it looks like. Oh fuck it, you don't speak English anyway."

She screamed and charged the Caseman. A force hit her like a bull, knocking her into a car. Her shoulder broke the window. The tire iron almost slipped from her fingers.

"What was that?" Invisible hands grabbed her neck. The tire iron fell out of her hand and clanked on the street as she grabbed at wrists that weren't there. "What happened…to your…anger bag?"

Thrown against the car again, she dropped to the ground.

Her head spun as she fumbled for the tire iron. "You switched cases with the one who trashed…Park's house? That's…cheating."

Her head whipped back and hit the sidewalk, followed by a few bangs. At first, she thought it was the sound of her skull cracking, then realized they were gunshots.

When she came to, she saw Park dangling by his wrists in the air, turning slowly. The Caseman scrutinized him like a piece of meat.

Another Asian man said something in a foreign language, and the Caseman stopped. This second man wore a gray suit and carried an aluminum briefcase.

He told Park, "She depended on you, and you were defenseless to stop us. Your Project's days are over, Dr. Park. We will make you watch it unravel before your eyes."

Park fell to the ground. The Casemen traded cases, climbed into a car, and left before Park recovered, rolled over, and sat up.

Gabby faded again into unconsciousness in a cloud of car exhaust. Park hovered over her.

She came to in Park's arms as he eased her into the car seat. Gabby whispered, "Bet you wish you'd taken that blow job now, huh?"

Chapter 60

Isaac watched the road unravel behind them through the back window of the government van. The trees alongside the road were thicker than anything he'd ever seen back in Georgia.

Exposition Joe asked, "See anything interesting?"

"No. Other than the occasional gas station or ranch house, Nebraska all looks the same." He turned to Joe. "You know where we're going yet?"

"Yep. The Samaritans' megachurch."

"Oh no. The Samaritans? The folks who built that church back in Africa? We're in for some holy terror." Isaac scanned the van again for a means of escape. "We get out of here right about...*now!*" He shot a wishful gaze at Joe. "Right?"

Joe shook his head. "Sorry, man. I'm not getting any flashes of the future."

"But you know where we are."

"Only because I've been here before."

"Here?" Isaac pointed down. "How did you end up here?"

"My parents sent me here three years ago. A church camp for troubled teens."

"How did that go?"

"For me or them? It's their fault I'm this way." Joe pointed to his head. "I guess they're okay with how it went. Not crazy about it myself."

"I'm guessing this church isn't on the up-and-up? Are we going to get carved up on an altar by a bunch of yahoos in black robes and pentagrams?"

"I wish I could say no."

The van pulled to a stop. Isaac looked out the window again, but all he saw was grass, trees, and the single-lane road behind them; until the face of one of the feds in aviator sunglasses blocked his view.

"Back up," came the muffled order from the officer.

Isaac glared at the man and leaned forward, pressing his face on the glass.

"I said, back the fuck up."

Isaac kissed the window and exhaled, filling his cheeks with air while licking the glass with the tip of his tongue. The fed recoiled, appalled. Isaac fell back, laughing.

The fed unlocked the door, yanking it open. "You're disgusting, you know that? No one ever cleans that glass. I hope you catch Ebola or some shit. Get out of the van, slowly." Two more officers stood with him, forming a human wall between Isaac and freedom. A black Lincoln MKZ pulled up and parked behind them. The driver, a white man in a brown suit, opened the back door and the cops parted.

"Now *this* is travel in the manner I'm accustomed to." Isaac climbed out of the van and headed to the Lincoln. "Come on, Joe."

The van doors slammed shut with Joe still inside.

The fed in the aviator glasses blocked the window, smiling. "Your friend ain't going with you. We got other plans for him."

"Those plans don't involve putting your dick where it don't belong, do they?"

The fed's cocksure attitude turned to rage. "What? Fuck you."

"'Cause that ain't right. And I believe Nebraska has some strict anti-sodomy laws."

"No, there ain't," the fed replied quickly.

"Oh, you looked it up then?"

The fed pointed at the Lincoln. "Get in the fucking car. You can worry about your friend on the way. Come on, let's go." He and the other feds climbed into the van and pulled away.

Isaac scanned the open terrain, seeing only trees, grass, and the road he stood on. He asked the chauffeur in the brown suit, "If I run for it, how far do you think I'll get?"

"You can probably run all the way to Canada. If you know how to live off the land and avoid the bears and mountain lions."

"Can you do that? Maybe you'll want to come with me?"

The chauffeur slumped. "Buddy, do you think I'd be driving for a living if I had any skills?"

"Sorry I asked." Isaac sat in the back of the Lincoln. The chauffeur closed the door behind him. "You work for the Samaritans then?"

The chauffeur dropped into the front seat and started the car. "Ten years."

"Whew. Ten years. Then you must have seen them on their worst behavior now and again."

"Maybe I have. But I don't get paid to run my mouth."

Isaac tried to get the driver to open up a few more times. But that was the last he said until they pulled up in front of the massive, modernist redwood church, a flared cylindrical structure with a peak in the center, a giant upside-down funnel made of wood beams. The empty parking lot was the size of two football fields.

The chauffeur pulled up to the front and dropped the car into park. "This is it."

"So what happens now?"

"Now you go inside. Couldn't you figure that out yourself?"

Isaac opened the door and stepped out. "Don't expect a tip."

"I wasn't." The chauffeur sped back down the driveway and through the parking lot, as if worried Isaac was going to climb back inside.

Lacking any other place to go and needing to find a toilet, Isaac began to climb the steps up into the church. Before he reached the top, a bespectacled man in a light gray suit stepped out. Holding a folder under one arm, his hand outstretched, he said, "You must be Dennis Osbey. Or should I call you Isaac Deal?"

"Why don't we pretend my cover is still good and call me Isaac?"

"As you wish. I'm Stewart."

Isaac shook Stewart's hand. "Really? You don't look like a Stewart."

Stewart laughed. "Don't we all?"

"That's not what I—"

Stewart led Isaac inside, cutting off his protests. "I'm sure you're eager to freshen up. Follow me."

Isaac followed Stewart into the elevator. Two stories up, the elevator doors opened up into a hallway twice as fancy as the one in his condominium. Stewart led Isaac to a suite over-packed with fashionable men's clothing. The drawers and closets were open and stuffed with suits and accessories, which also covered the bed in stacks.

"We have a rough idea of your size," Stewart explained. "Apologies if some of this is a little off. Take your time." He closed the door behind him.

Isaac rushed to the toilet. The bathroom was as overstocked with toiletries as the bedroom was with fashion. While he relieved himself, he pondered taking a quick shower. He stank of train car and Cessna. But he reminded himself he'd rather be a free man who reeked than a well-groomed prisoner.

His business finished, Isaac returned to the bedroom, climbed up on a chair, and ran his hand along the top of the wardrobe.

The door swung open with a knock as Stewart let himself in. He looked up at Isaac. "What are you doing?"

"Um." Isaac pulled his hand off the wardrobe and back to his side in two disjointed motions. "I was...I was searching for bugs."

"Bugs? Like insects?"

"No. No, like hidden microphones."

Stewart ran his eyes around the room. "Why?"

"I hadn't thought that part through. How about we forget what I was doing and go on with whatever you came here for?"

"Well, I guess we already have. I came in to check on you. You still haven't...*anything* yet have you?"

"I dropped a—used the bathroom."

Stewart wasn't sure what to do with that information. "Well...that's good."

"Yes. Yes, it is," said Isaac, still standing on the chair.

A silent moment passed while the two men tried to not look at each other. Stewart finally broke the silence. "How about I wait out in the hall?"

"Great." Isaac nodded too enthusiastically and stepped down to the floor. "That sounds great."

Stewart left and Isaac made liberal use of the amenities in an extensive shave and shower. Stepping out of the steam, he felt human again.

Picking the right outfit took longer than grooming. Isaac sorted the options by size and style until he settled on a silk charcoal suit with a thread of purple running though it that matched a plaid tie and socks.

He stepped out into the hall, right into Stewart.

The man pretended he hadn't been listening at the door. "Wonderful. I'm glad you found an outfit to your liking. Please, follow me."

Stewart nervously speed-walked away.

"Where are we going?" Isaac hustled a few steps to catch up.

"To meet the Reverend Representative Fray."

"Holy shit." Isaac stopped in his tracks.

"I don't think you meant to say that," Stewart mockingly scolded over his shoulder.

"Oh, I think I did. Are you for real?" Isaac slowed to a crawl. "The US Representative? The one making all the troub—opinions—on the news? *She's* the one who had the FBI tailing me all the way from Georgia? What does she want with me?"

They reached a second elevator at the far end of the hall. "That," Stewart pushed the button, "is between you and her."

One more story up and the elevator doors opened to a marble hall with a large pair of oak doors open at the far end. Stewart waited in the hall and indicated with a bow that Isaac should proceed.

Isaac walked slowly across the marble. Normally, his tastes leaned toward thicker women, but he found himself captivated by the finely toned legs of the representative in the red suit and matching heels pacing in front of her desk. The desk was a good twelve feet wide, so a round of pacing took some time. She was on the phone.

Once he crossed the threshold into the office proper she looked up and smiled, holding up one finger. "I'm sorry. My next American is here to see me. I think we've covered everything though, right?" A pause. "Good, thank you. Put all of that into an email for me, would you dear?"

She hung up the phone and leaned back against her desk. "Isaac Deal. You have become quite a problem, haven't you?"

Isaac smiled and rested his hands on the back of the chair as if it were a podium. "If you knew me better, you'd know I've always been a problem. Representative Fray? Do I call you Reverend Fray? The Reverend Representative Fray is a mouthful."

"I'm sure your mouth can handle it." She picked up a sizable file off her desk. "Dennis Osbey, aka Isaac Deal, aka Jimmy Lane—the aka's go on—no criminal record, no military or community service, a string of sales jobs from high- to low-end. Currently, you're on a high swing with the Mercedes-Benz dealership. I'm well aware you haven't 'become' a problem." She raised an eyebrow, "But you've become my problem. Why were you in Liberia?"

"Getting back to my roots." Isaac shrugged. "You know. Oh, maybe you don't. Anyway, I wanted to see the old country. Get a feel for where we came from. I learned a lot. I learned never to go back to Africa. I was kidnapped and made it out by the skin of my teeth."

Reverend Representative Fray dropped the file back on the desk. "And while you were there, you thought it was necessary to burn down my church?"

"That was your church?" Isaac affected a wounded, apologetic look. "Oh, I'm so sorry. But you should know the priest you put in charge, The Baptist? He was a killer and a cannibal. That madman had some crazy plan to become God, and I was the one who was supposed to baptize him."

She folded her arms, stiff and skeptical. "Well, did you?"

Isaac caught himself looking down her cleavage. "Did I baptize him? Hell no. I beat feet when the fire started, whoever set it." He shrugged. "If you're planning on rebuilding you should hire a different contractor. That place went up in a flash."

Representative Fray remained unconvinced. "And the psychotronic device in the basement?"

"I'm sorry. A psycho—what—now?" Isaac made a show of scratching his head. "I can't say I know—"

She walked behind him. "Mr. Deal you're so full of shit your eyes are brown. This will go far more smoothly if you come clean."

He looked back, watching her through the corner of his eye, letting her play her game. "Maybe you should come clean first? Since when does a US Representative have a personal army of federal agents?"

"Not just agents. Bureaucrats, local officials, and more, an army that can make you disappear." She snapped her fingers in his ear. "Like that."

He laughed. "Lady, I disappear all the time."

"Not like this, and not just you." The Reverend Representative Fray returned to her desk and picked up a second file. "Tell me about Project Dead Blind."

Isaac scratched his head, pondering. "Project Dead who?"

She continued to flip through the second file. "Your teammates. Agents Ainia, Pollyanna, 97:4, Park, and let's not forget Exposition Joe, whom we already have on the premises. My so-called army is rounding the rest of them up as we speak." She looked up from the file at Isaac. "You do realize running an unsanctioned espionage unit on US soil is treason?"

One of those words caught Isaac off guard. "Unsanctioned?"

"Yes. Completely. Dead Blind was part of Project Stargate, spun out on its own by its architect, one James Ensign." She gauged Isaac's reaction. He twitched a little, enough to satisfy her. "Ensign's bureaucratic maneuvering protected Dead Blind when MKUltra was politically exposed in '77. Since then, Ensign's been running his own psychic spy shop out of a hidden little corner of the Department of Health and Human Services. Collecting and training psychics such as yourself into his personal espionage force. Does that sound about right?"

"And these people...you think they burned down your church?" asked Isaac, skeptically.

Fray dropped the folder on the desk and walked back around to face Isaac, inches away from where he stood. She studied his face for a moment, as if she could peel away his outer layers with her eyes, then slapped him.

Her voice a rivulet of ice water, she whispered in his ear. "Don't fuck with me, Mr. Deal."

When she turned her back, Isaac rubbed his face. "That guy on the motorcycle. Is he working for you too?"

Isaac watched her eyes. The question made them twitch, just a little. She didn't know what he was talking about. She changed the topic.

"Do you know what Satanists are, Isaac?"

"Oh no. I knew it! The government is full of devil worshipers, isn't it? I'm really disappointed."

"And why is that?" She smiled, amused.

"Because Satanism is just a rejection of Christianity, a counter to the culture's dominant religion, spiritually bankrupt. I'm not a churchgoing man. And I don't stand for anything, but if I did, it would be for more than a cardboard cutout."

"And what about Gnosticism?"

Isaac looked around her office. "You don't shy away from talking about religion in the workplace, do you, Reverend?"

"Religion *is* my workplace, Mr. Deal."

"So it is. The Gnostics were early Christians who believed the God of the Old Testament was evil. He trapped humanity in his creation—the material world, an imperfect copy of the divine realm. The Catholic Church declared them heretics and persecuted them out of existence."

"You're better read on religion than I would have expected."

"I got a knack for knowing what I need to know. What's with the Bible study?"

Fray stood and circled back to Isaac. Her slow steps on the marble floor echoed through the chamber. "The Samaritans believe the Gnostics were correct about the material god, or Demiurge, but wrong about their attitude toward it. We live in a material world. Shouldn't we worship a material god?"

Isaac cocked his hip. "Is this the same bullshit you sell from behind the pulpit?"

"No, the laypeople we keep in the dark. Their tithes and ignorance keep the true Samaritans in money and power, no different than any other church."

"So where do I come in?"

The representative ran a finger along Isaac's forearm. "Money is fun. But being rich gets boring after a while. Power is where the action is. We have power—financial, social, and political. I can call a Predator drone strike if I want to. No joke. Not any old place, not yet. But most places outside the US."

She ran a gentle finger across his lips. "But you and the rest of Ensign's boys and girls, you're a kind of power we don't have much of. A rare power, a power that's hard to come by. And we want more.

"Aren't you tired of running errands for James Ensign and his Korean sidekick? Shouldn't you be the one in charge of Project Dead Blind? Bring them over to us, let us put you to work. The possibilities are endless, and a whole lot of fun." Her lips were very close to his.

Isaac put a gentle hand on Fray's cheek. "I'm going to need some more convincing."

Chapter 61

"Twenty-five dollars and I do the work myself," Ainia counteroffered the mechanic.

The paunchy, middle-aged, ungroomed man in coveralls shook his head. "No one—and I mean no one—touches my tools but me. Seventy dollars, including the rush job." The garage was a cluttered mess and had probably been there since the highway was built.

Ainia glared at the cracked radiator dripping its last drops, a trail of antifreeze leading back to the crash site. She turned to Pollyanna. "Give me thirty-five dollars."

Pollyanna balked. "Why am I paying for half? The Great Red Shark is your truck."

"Stop calling it that. And that truck dragged your ass halfway across the country. We have another half to go, so cough up." Ainia leaned in with her hand out.

Pollyanna fished two twenties out of her purse and tossed them at Ainia. "Keep it. I don't want you shaking me down for your next oil change."

Ainia paid the man. Pollyanna asked him, "Where's a good place to eat around here?"

"There's a McDonald's, a Burger King, and a Taco Bell over that hill by the highway."

Pollyanna turned up her nose at the suggestions. "Okay, where's a bad place to eat?"

The mechanic pointed with his wrench. "I don't care for the Mexican restaurant at the end of the road."

"Sounds great. We'll take that. Come on, Ainia. Let's drown our sorrows in tacos." Pollyanna turned to leave.

"There's more to Mexican food than tacos." Ainia reached into the truck cab for her lacrosse ball.

"Not as far as I'm concerned." Pollyanna stepped out into the afternoon light. Purse slung on her forearm, she lit another cigarette.

They ambled into a commercial area that had never taken off. Built back in the eighties, it was a row of sun-damaged buildings with their faded original decor and signage, except for the occasional spot of paint. Half the storefronts were empty. The town smelled like dust.

Pollyanna ashed her cigarette into the gutter. "Next time we need to haggle for something, let me do it. God gave me these tits for a reason."

Pollyanna caught Ainia giving her chest a quick, sideways glance and smiled. She exhaled up over Ainia's head and pointed at a twelve-foot-tall sign of a Mexican man in a sombrero. "I'm no detective, but I think that's it."

"We're going someplace else." Ainia looked like she was thinking about tearing the sign down with her bare hands. She looked around for options, twitched, and pushed Pollyanna into the doorway of a nearby Dollar Store.

"We're not this broke," Pollyanna protested.

Ainia shushed her and pointed over her shoulder. "The Caseman is across the street. Don't look."

Pollyanna leaned around the edge to look at the man in the trench coat and bucket hat, and ducked back into the shelter of the doorway. "Here? What the fuck? He didn't get very far, did he?"

"He's still looking for us. I'm sure of it. We can take him out before he sees us."

Pollyanna clutched her purse with both hands. "Take him out? Fuck. Fuck. Fuck. Okay, but then what? I'm not going to let you torture him."

"You've made that clear. I don't have to beat him to death, we just have to beat him to the safe house. So we knock him out, steal his case, and leave him tied up someplace. Like we did with the feds. He'll get discovered before evening."

Pollyanna sighed. "I'll go along with that. Creepy fucker has that much coming to him."

Ainia looked back and forth along the street. All quiet. "Couldn't ask for better conditions. Luck's on our side."

Pollyanna stepped back, conscious of the light pain in her chest—her bank of misfortune. "Luck is never on my side. In fact, I'd better stay behind. I'll screw this up for us."

"Bullshit. We make our own luck." Ainia patted Pollyanna on the shoulder. "Besides, you'll make great bait."

Pollyanna shrugged Ainia's hand off. "Glad to see you value my contribution to this team. Bitch."

Ainia watched him around the doorway. "He's heading into that broke-down Chinese restaurant. I'll go around through the kitchen. Give me five minutes, then come through the front. When he makes his move on you, I'll get him from behind."

"That's a crap plan. What if you don't get there in time?"

"He's a pervert, not a killer. He'll take his time with you."

"Yeah?" Pollyanna pretended to consider it. "Better. But still—fuck no."

"Why are you worried? You're half his age and almost twice his size." Ainia rolled her eyes, apologizing, "And that's *not* a crack about your weight. You've already taken this guy out once. You can hold him off long enough for me to get him. His card only works if your eyes are open. Close your eyes and swing your knife around. That should hold him off until I get there. We're not going to get a better chance than this."

Pollyanna stared at the restaurant door, still ajar, and sighed. She tossed her cigarette into the street as she crossed it, saying over her shoulder, "If I die in there, I'm going to be pissed."

As Pollyanna crept inside, her purse caught on the door handle. She jerked it free and inadvertently flung the door wide open, flooding the room with sunlight. Decorated in handmade faux-Asian decor by someone without access to the real thing, the place smelled musty and unused. The tables and chairs were pushed up against the front wall, blocking the windows, except for one table and three chairs. The middle chair hosted an Asian woman in her late forties in a dark green suit, writing in a journal and ignoring Pollyanna's entrance.

At the table to the woman's left sat the Caseman, who also ignored Pollyanna's entrance. His body was lifeless, his jaw slack, his glassy eyes staring off to a corner of the ceiling. His doctor's bag was on the floor beside him.

"Okay," Pollyanna said. "This is weird." She gave the woman a little wave. "Um. Excuse me? Did you kill this guy? Because if you did, I'm cool with that. So…like…I'll be going then if that's okay."

The woman held up a finger, finished writing her line, and put the pen down before addressing her. "Agent Pollyanna of Project Dead Blind, I am General Wu of China's Thirteenth Bureau and I have questions."

The kitchen doors flung open and Ainia entered, alone and disappointed.

Pollyanna asked her, "No one in the kitchen?"

Ainia shook her head and pointed at the general. "No one's here except her. And him. But I don't think he matters."

"Oh," Pollyanna relaxed, eyes questioning the dead Caseman. "That's good."

The general folded her hands. "It's also not true."

Curtains on the wall to either side of General Wu peeled back and two men in dark suits emerged from their folds. The general smiled a half smile. "Now, about my ques—"

Pollyanna interrupted, "You kept guys standing back there for this? Really?"

Chapter 62

In the trunk, hours down the road, 97:4 still clutched the Bible, not the way she would have liked, but the way Three had ordered. Her fingers stuck to the dried blood on the cover. Her hair stuck to the dried tears on her cheeks, her throat dry from praying for forgiveness.

In the cramped quarters of the car trunk, 97:4 had the impossible feeling she wasn't alone. She leaned back and saw an old white man in a hemp suit lying behind her, visible in spite of the darkness.

God smiled.

97:4 screamed.

God raised a finger to His lips until her screams faded to whimpers.

"Are You who I think You are?" Her cramped neck hurt from twisting around. "Am I dreaming? Or dead? Is this a…What's going on?"

In the light of the Almighty, she only felt confusion. When she was finally silent, He chuckled and knocked the inside of the trunk lid. "Not exactly whale-sized, but the outside conditions are just as deadly."

"Jonah?" Confusion was written all over 97:4's face. "You're citing Jonah and the fish? Was I supposed to go somewhere? I'm not supposed to be here?"

"No. Not here. You're supposed to go into the depths of the earth for me."

97:4 gaped. "Depths? What depths?"

God flipped a document open. "Let me show you. There's been a rewrite."

He showed her the page he'd marked with his thumb. After driving for days without sleep, and what she'd been through, her brains were so scrambled she barely read snatches:

—crawling toward the roller handle—97:4 kicks it out of—97:4: Do you think that was suffering?

He closed the cover before she'd read too much.

97:4 shivered. "I'm not going to die then. Is...this what Joe's always talking about? The Script...is that short for scripture?" She stopped short of naming Him. "You're changing it for me?"

"I wouldn't be God if I couldn't change a few things," God bragged. "You didn't think I was going to let it end like that, did you? Have a little faith."

"But how?" she begged. "That man, Three—I'm powerless against whatever he has in that case."

"Him? Don't worry about him. Even he has his part in this wonderful transubstantiation. It's you I'm worried about. If you lose faith I can't help you. Like the Bible says, I help only those who help themselves."

"The Bible doesn't say that," 97:4 corrected Him without thinking, then cringed.

"It's implied." God looked at the side of the trunk as if there was a window. "This is My stop. Anyway, don't worry. You'll do fine."

God gave 97:4 a thumbs-up and rolled over, disappearing into the darkness. She was alone in the trunk again.

Chapter 63

The Samaritans called it a private prayer room. A cell where they put their problems until those problems fixed themselves. No reinforcements in the walls or door, no cameras. Just an empty room with a locked door. Years ago it had been good enough to hold a scared young boy.

Exposition Joe took a deep breath and punched the wall. His fist broke through the drywall, stinging his knuckles. He felt around and found the keys where he had left them three years before.

Joe unlocked the door and peeked out into the hall. The coast was clear except for God. The deity leaned against the wall at the end of the hall, arms crossed and waiting.

Joe walked past Him. "You didn't write Yourself out of this scene for the heck of it?"

God indicated the drywall dust stuck in Joe's arm hair. "Like I told you, right here, years ago. *'For I know the plans I have for you, plans to prosper you and not to harm you, plans to give you hope and a future.'* Though you're doing fine without Me." He pointed to the end of the hall. "This way."

The hallway faded into darkness beyond where Joe could see. "Longer and darker than I remember. I thought I had exaggerated it. Not just this hall. I saw the whole thing when they unloaded Isaac out front. It's twice as big as before."

"This is one of the larger houses they built for Me," God said, unimpressed.

Joe and God walked into the dark. "There's a lot of money in doing God's work."

"Not My work," God huffed.

They walked a hundred yards or more into the dark. God was the only thing Joe saw. He felt along the wall until he came to a single locked door at the end. Joe unlocked the door with the keys he'd pulled from the wall.

God lay His hand on Joe's, interrupting him before he could turn the knob. "Before you go in there, I want you to remember the last time you were here. The kind of men who kept you here."

"How could I forget?"

"That's right. Forgive, but don't forget." God lifted his hand from the doorknob.

Joe entered the darkness within.

God said, "Let there—"

Joe hit the light switch without hesitation, leaving the deity disappointed.

"It's My favorite joke."

"Yeah, I know." Joe scoped out the room. *Opulent* wasn't too strong a word to describe the marble walls and floor, the red-and-black velvet curtains bound by golden ropes.

The aged, iron-and-cedar clamshell structure of a Faith Machine dominated the floor plan, like it had in the room under The Baptist's church. Unlike The Baptist's, this machine was in perfect condition.

Joe climbed under the shell and opened the valve. Water poured down through a drain in the floor. Climbing back out, he asked God, "Where am I going to get the kindling?"

"You can use those curtains. But there's a complication." God pointed to the dark side of the room. In front of a span of dark red velvet stood a man dressed head to toe in black-leather fetish wear, all zippers and buckles. His wrists were cuffed to pillars, head covered in a leather mask, nipples exposed, mouth filled with a ball gag, and eyes wide open in fear.

"Nothing is ever easy, is it?" Joe sighed. "Who the heck are you?"

The man squirmed behind his ball gag.

"Oh right." Joe fiddled with the buckles at the back of the man's head.

God said, "Be careful."

Joe pulled his hands away. "I'm just undoing the gag."

"For some men, that's the most dangerous part," God cautioned.

"I think I can handle a little conversation." Joe finally found the right buckle and tossed the ball gag aside. "Speak, freak."

The man's voice cracked. "I...I warn you. I am a general in the United States Air Force. If you don't leave this room and turn yourself into the estate's private security immediately, there will be serious repercussions."

"A general, huh?" Joe patted him down. "Then you should have some proof of that on you."

"Over there, behind the curtain." God pointed.

Joe left the man on the rack and threw back the velvet curtain to find a small end table with a blue military uniform folded neatly on the top shelf; a watch, wallet, and smartphone on the middle shelf; and a pair of shiny black plastic shoes on the bottom one. Joe stuffed the phone in his armpit and opened the wallet, stepping back into the leather-clad man's view.

Joe unbuckled the mask and pulled it off. He compared the man's face with the one on the military ID. "General Steve Casey, huh? I guess everyone needs a hobby."

"You will cease and desist this invasion of privacy immediately, or I warn you there will be consequences."

Joe tucked the wallet into his shirt pocket and let the phone drop easily from his armpit into his hand. God said, "0 9 0 9," and Joe unlocked the phone with the code.

"Seriously? 0 9 0 9? No wonder the Pentagon gets hacked on the regular." Joe took a picture of General Casey, a portrait of fear and surprise.

The general pulled at his chains. "What do you think you're doing?"

"Taking the first of many pictures that I'll be sending to your wife." The phone played a shutter sound with every picture taken. "Smile."

The general twisted his face away from the camera lens.

Joe lowered the camera. "These are going to be blurry if you don't cooperate." He took a few more shots, letting the man twist for a bit longer before pocketing the phone. "That shut you up, didn't it? Now, what are we going to do with you?"

"You could leave him right where he is, set the fire, and leave," God said, half-heartedly.

"No, I can't and You know it."

"Remember what men like him did to you," God warned.

"Men like him, but not him. That wouldn't be fair." Joe rubbed his chin, thinking.

General Casey asked, "Who are you talking to?"

"Never mind that. I'm figuring out how I'm going to spare your life." Joe eyed the apparatus on the other end of the general's cuffs. "What are you chained up to, anyway?"

Chapter 64

Isaac tried to button his shirt. The Reverend Representative Fray, leg slung over her desk, tickled his testicles with her toes, distracting him. She smoked a cigarette, draped in her suit jacket and nothing else. Isaac stepped out of her reach to focus on his buttons. "You're acting like you wanna go another round."

"Maybe I do." She exhaled smoke in his direction.

"I'll need a few hours to recover." Isaac found his underwear under the chair. "Unless you have Viagra in there with the rest of your goodies."

She swung her legs off the desk and fished around in the drawer where she kept her cocaine.

"You're serious?" asked Isaac, retrieving his pants out from under the desk.

"Of course I'm serious. Many of my lovers are in their fifties." Her fishing slowed to a disappointed stop. "Looks like I'm out. The general's been around a lot lately."

Isaac pulled on one leg of his pants. "Maybe next time."

"You're staying, then?" She leaned back in the chair and ashed her cigarette. "It sounds like you're accepting my offer."

"Your offer is a lot better than another night in a cargo train." Isaac ran his belt through his belt loops.

Fray picked up a pen. "Then let's talk about the rest of Project Dead Bli—Oh!"

Three crosses fell. One off the bookshelf, one from the desk and one from the cabinet by the door. Fray's hand went up to the cross hanging from her neck.

Isaac cocked an eyebrow. "Was that a Faith Machine?"

Fray directed her concern at Isaac. "Not my—I don't know what you're talking about."

A mechanical hissing sound emanated from below. A large oval section of the floor next to her desk rose, lifted by two pneumatic pylons and releasing a cloud of smoke. General Casey was bound between the pylons.

Isaac backed away. "When I agreed to another round I didn't—"

Fray rushed to her feet and ignored the man's gag. "What's burning? Steve, what's going on?"

Exposition Joe popped out from behind the man in bondage and the smoke, the general's smartphone in hand. He snapped off three pictures of Fray and Isaac, post *flagrante delicto*. "Hi, Isaac. Ready to go?"

"Ah…" Isaac shot a guilty glance Fray's way. "Sure…Joe, things are getting weird around here. Let me get my shoes on."

Fray glared at Isaac. "Well, your allegiance turns on a dime, doesn't it?"

Isaac shrugged, grabbing his socks off the floor. "Easy come, easy go."

Joe tossed the handcuff key to Isaac. "You'd better lock the reverend to the other pylon."

Still naked except for the jacket, Fray stepped toward Joe with an open hand. "Give me that phone right now, young man."

Joe stepped back. "You're not wearing pants."

"Never mind that," she insisted, showing neither shame nor modesty. "Hand over the phone. You can't do anything with those pictures anyway. My people in the press will tell the world they're photoshopped. But I'd rather save them the trouble."

Joe stepped out of reach and said, "The *pictures* aren't to keep you in line, 9834236 is."

Fray stopped, "What…what is that number?"

"It's the number of your safe deposit box in the Cayman Islands. EE4327133 is the one in Hong Kong and 88-278UU is the one in Switzerland." Joe showed the smartphone screen to the Reverend Representative Fray, the numbers and cities in a text message ready to go to everyone in the general's address book. "Are the other Samaritans really your friends? Do you want them to have these numbers?"

Representative Fray backed off, clutching her closed jacket around her. "Where did you get those?"

"God told me." Joe held the phone like a grenade, his thumb over the send button. "Now let Isaac lock you up to the pylon, ma'am. Oh, and we're stealing a car. You're totally cool with that if you know what's good for you."

Isaac bounced the handcuff key in his palm. The congresswoman's files on Project Dead Blind stuffed under his arm. His shoes untied, belt unbuckled, he took her wrist. "Can I call you?"

Chapter 65

It was hot in the trunk of the car. 97:4's mouth was so dry, her lips and tongue hurt to move. The car came to a stop and the engine cut out. 97:4 listened for the ambient sounds of a gas station, hoping another car would pull up. Caseman Three had been careful and lucky so far, but there was still a chance.

Instead of gas station noise, she heard footsteps on rough ground. The key turned in the lock and the lid popped open. Scorching sunlight flooded the trunk. She shielded her eyes with the bloody Bible.

Three snatched the book from her hand, dropping it in the dirt. "Get out."

The disgusting flavor of vanilla flooded her parched mouth. She dry-heaved, her knotted limbs struggling to follow his command.

"Get out. Now." Three grabbed her hair and dragged her halfway out. She spilled out of the trunk in a flailing mess. Her kidneys no longer pinned, a critical fluid pressure rushed to her bladder.

"Stand and remove your pants," Three ordered, then as an afterthought, "And your underthing."

Joints popped as she unfolded her legs into a twisted standing position. Her hand, alien and out of her control, trembled carefully toward her fly, unbuttoned it with dead fingers, struggled with the tab, and pulled down. Every zipper tooth disengaged with a jolt of pain up her wrist. She slid her hand over her butt cheek, inside her panties, and down to her calf in a motion she prayed was far from sexy.

"Take this." Three handed her an empty, lidless Gatorade bottle with one hand. His other hand, as always, was wrapped around the roller handle.

Her traitorous hand grasped the bottle roughly. She looked to Three for his next order.

"Fill it." He sneered.

Dry, chapped lips almost parted to protest. The smell of vanilla so strong she tasted it. She squatted to accommodate the wide mouth of the bottle between her legs. Her bladder's release a humiliating relief, she ignored the droplets on her hand and the insides of her legs. When the bottle filled, she couldn't stop. The yellow fluid spilled over the brim into the pants around her ankles.

Finished, Three ordered her to stand. She straightened. The soaked clothing lay around her ankles.

"Now drink."

97:4 whimpered through closed lips, eyes wide and fixed on the bottle. The trembling hand brought it to her lips, spilling urine down her hand and across the front of her shirt. She faced the bottle, away from Three, while digging with her tongue into the dry gap between tooth and gum where she'd hidden a torn piece of a page from the dead homeless man's Bible.

The warm rush of urine flooded her mouth, freeing the page folded up in her cheek. Nausea fought desperation as she drank. Tracing the clot of the page as the folded corners scratched their way down her throat.

Trickles of urine ran down her chin from the corners of her mouth. Finally, she pulled the half-empty bottle away and gasped for air. Whispering, "*His lightnings lit up the world. The earth saw and trembled.*"

Three watched her retch and sob with a sneer. "What are you doing? Praying? What nonsense. Finish it."

Unable to let go, she gripped the bottle tight—too tight. Slick from the spilled urine, it shot out of her grip and hit Three at the waist. Urine splashed down his pants and over his shoes.

Outraged, Three jumped back too late. He looked down at the mess with disgust, eyes filled with rage. Lunging at 97:4 with a hand raised, he screamed, "Stupid cow!"

Three slapped 97:4. With a crack and a flash of blue light, his arm flew back, knocking him off his feet, spinning him around. The roller handle twisted out of his grip. He lay facedown in the dirt, twitching.

97:4 pulled up her soaked pants with her good hand.

Three struggled, crawling toward the roller handle. 97:4 kicked it out of reach. "Do you think that was suffering, what you put me through?" Sparks of electricity arced between her fingers. "With your card, or whatever is in that bag?"

She reached up his pant leg, grabbed his shin above the sock, and sent jolts into him. Three twitched like a fish thrown up on a dock.

"You underestimated my faith," 97:4 croaked, her throat still raw.

Three convulsed. Blood sprayed out of his mouth as he bit his tongue in half. His hands clutched at the dirt.

"This. This will be real suffering."

Chapter 66

"Seriously? You had these guys hanging out behind these curtains? Who the fuck does that?" Pollyanna winced when the pain she kept in her chest spiked.

General Wu ignored Pollyanna's questions and poured two cups of tea, one for herself, and one for the place across from her. She left the cup in front of the Caseman's corpse empty. "Pollyanna, will you please join me?"

Pollyanna stepped closer to the table. "There's…" She pointed back at Ainia. "There's two of us."

"Yes. I can count. I doubt Agent Ainia is inclined to talk. Not when she could be fighting." Her assistants drew knives, took fighting stances, screamed, and charged.

Ainia smiled, dropped her lacrosse ball, and kicked a chair up into her grip, holding it like a weapon.

Pollyanna stepped back from the fight breaking out. The pending conflict blocked her way to the table.

General Wu waved her fighters aside as if they were hovering waiters. They shifted their positions to the far side of the restaurant, away from the table. Ainia held her fighting stance as they maneuvered one after the other. When they were ready, they nodded, and Ainia charged after them.

Pollyanna gritted her teeth and joined Wu at the table, placing her Purse in her lap. The chair was a bit small under her.

The general sipped her tea, watching the fight out of the corner of her eye. "Don't worry about them."

Pollyanna reached for her tea, smelled it, and put it back on the saucer. She cast a brief sideways glance at the corpse to her left.

The general opened her journal and drew the pen from the binding to take notes. "How have you been? Is your road trip everything you expected?"

"Expected?" Pollyanna pulled her eyes from the fighting back to the general. "Seriously, lady? How the hell was I supposed to expect this?"

"You witnessed the slaughter of dozens of Liberians. Surely a little fisticuffs shouldn't upset you."

Pollyanna kept one eye on the fighting, ready to drop under the table if needed. "I wasn't there for the slaughtering part. And this is a lot more 'fisticuffs' than I'm used to. What do you really want to know about Liberia? Just get to it."

"All business, are we?" The general marked in her journal.

"More like no bullshit." Pollyanna fished around in her purse. She caught the general's eye. Wu waited patiently and unalarmed. "You're not worried I have a gun in here or something?"

"A gun in your hands wouldn't concern me. As for Liberia, I had an interest in the Faith Machine. That is until your team destroyed it."

Pollyanna found her cigarettes and lighter. "Sorry, sister. But if you really wanted it, you should have dug it up earlier. Wasn't it sitting around since the eighties? Why'd you wait so long?"

"I could ask the same of you. I don't think either of us are going to disclose our intelligence-gathering techniques."

"Not so fast." Pollyanna lit the cigarette and took a drag. "You tell me how *you* found it, and I'll tell you how *I* found it."

Ainia toppled a stack of chairs with a crash, pinning one of the fighters to the wall.

Wu considered. "But you didn't find it. The orders came from James Ensign."

Pollyanna smirked and exhaled smoke through her nostrils like a cartoon bull. "Worth a shot. For some reason the US and China couldn't track that thing down for decades. Then, ding! Both of us lock onto it at once. Kinda weird, huh? But you probably already knew that."

Some of the humor left General Wu's eyes. "Yes. It's 'kind of weird.' Have you secured the American Faith Machine from your government?"

"No, no." Pollyanna leaned forward. "It's my turn for a question."

A fork flew out of the fighting, skipped across the table between the women, and bounced into the wall.

General Wu said something scolding in Mandarin and her fighters acknowledged her with short bows of the head. She turned back to Pollyanna as if nothing had happened. "I don't believe you're in the position to ask me anything."

"Lady," Pollyanna cocked an eyebrow. "You don't know how many positions I can take. And when my girl finishes kicking your goons' butts, she's going to come after yours. You're better off spilling your beans now, or she's going to be very unhappy."

General Wu sipped her tea and considered. "I'll humor you. You can ask."

Pollyanna leaned back in her chair. "Who the fuck are you people? When it comes to stuff like this—psychics and psychotronic weapons and such—I thought China kept to itself."

General Wu carefully placed the empty cup back in its saucer and poured another. "I'm head of the Thirteenth Bureau, Ghostkillers. Those machines breed ghosts. Now, about the American Faith Machine…" She waited.

Pollyanna lit a second cigarette with the cherry of her first. "What American Faith Machine? I didn't know we had one, but thanks for the tip. My turn. *Ghosts*? Seriously? You believe in ghosts?"

The women stopped talking as the Caseman's corpse slumped face-first into the table.

The pen went limp in the general's hand. "You believe in Soviet psychotronic weaponry."

Pollyanna shrugged. "Yeah, but that's science."

"As opposed to?"

"New-Agey bullshit. We have a TV show here in the States called Ghosthunters. It's been on for years. You know what they've never seen? A ghost. Have you?"

"Yes." General Wu pointed at the dead Caseman. "Who is this man?"

"We thought he was with you. And don't scoff at me—a minute ago I didn't even know China had Ghostbusters."

"Ghostkillers," Wu corrected.

"Whatever, Egon. Thanks for getting rid of him. Looks like he went quick too. Nice touch. Appreciate it."

"The killing or the mercy?"

"A bit of both," Pollyanna held up two fingers, the cigarette pinned between them. "Now I get two."

General Wu glared. "You get one. We're not children."

"Speak for yourself." Pollyanna ashed in the teacup. "I'm The Girl Who Wouldn't Grow Up, an honorary Lost Boy."

Ainia jumped onto a table. One of Wu's fighters stabbed at her foot. The knife drove into the table, and Ainia knocked the man out with a roundhouse kick to the temple.

Pollyanna pointed to the action with her cigarette. "One down. It's not looking good for your team, General. Okay then, one question—I feel sorry for you. If you didn't know the guy then why'd you kill him?"

Unmoved by the loss of half her forces, the general raised her teacup. "I knew he'd be an obstacle, a lethal one. I saw it in the coins."

"What does that mean?" asked Pollyanna, incredulous.

"My answer is clear. It's your understanding that's cloudy."

"That's bullshit. I get a do-over." Pollyanna nodded toward the doctor's bag on the floor. "What's in the case?"

General Wu eyed the doctor's bag on the floor between her and its deceased owner. "Who?"

Pollyanna tucked her chin. "Who? What do you mean, who?"

"*Who* is in the case. Not *what*." Wu explained, making another note in her journal. "The answer is, I don't know."

"Do you plan to find out or something."

Wu didn't look up from her journal. She wrinkled her nose. "Not especially."

Pollyanna stood, walked around the table, and picked up the dead man's case. "Then I guess you won't mind if I take it with me?"

Wu also stood, leaned close to Pollyanna, whispered, "Yes, I do," reached around Pollyanna's back, and came away with her knife.

Pollyanna stood back, rubbing the sheath at her waist. "Goddamn it! Am I going to have to put a lock on this thing?"

The general dropped the knife on the table in front of Pollyanna. When the agent reached for it, the general grabbed her other hand, the one holding the case. She knocked the doctor's bag free and held Pollyanna in a wristlock. "Mind your manners, American. We were almost done here, anyway."

"Ow!" Pollyanna, bent over at the waist, saw Wu in the reflection of the polished brass floorboards. She cried out, "Ainia!"

With a mongoose's quickness, Ainia grabbed the fighter's incoming punch, turned to take in Pollyanna's situation, and hyperextended the man's elbow, then his knee, taking him out of the fight for good.

Pollyanna smiled. "Now you're going to get it."

Ainia rushed General Wu before the fighter hit the ground.

The general released Pollyanna.

Ainia launched herself over the rail.

Watching in the reflection, Pollyanna barely saw the general throw Ainia. The Amazon hit the floor hard, stone still. Pollyanna was back in Wu's wristlock before she'd even had time to straighten up.

"Oh, come on!" Pollyanna cried out in disappointed anger.

General Wu said, "I apologize in advance—this is going to hurt. But first, I have a message for James Ensign."

Pollyanna squirmed in the hold. Ainia wasn't moving.

The pain in Pollyanna's chest, the accumulated tension of misfortune since her return from Africa, dissipated, replaced with light. "A message? How delightful. Communication is so important. Take you and me for example, I still think that perhaps if we take another moment to talk we'll come to some compromise on this."

"You can't be serious. Our conversation is over."

"Oh, I'm ever so hopeful we'll come to an agreement, a merging of agendas as it were. You and I, we're not so different, after all. Now, if you would be so good as to release me before your fortunes take a turn for the worse."

Someone outside the restaurant screamed.

"Why are you doing that with your voice?" The general grew suspicious.

Out on the street a car horn blew.

"It's just the voice God saw fit to grant me, ma'am. Now if you let me up, there might still be time."

"Time for what? Stop it. Stop talking like a child." Frustrated, General Wu gave Pollyanna's wrist a few more degrees of turn.

The building rumbled. Pollyanna grunted through gritted teeth, "You underestimate the strength of children. The optimism…Oh! Too late. I do apolo—"

The front of the restaurant caved in with a deafening crash. Wall, glass, and curtains wrapped around the grille of a semitrailer truck.

A pile of broken tables and chairs rose like a wave in front of the truck as the vehicle pushed through the building, careened off an interior wall, and headed toward the three women.

Wu let go of Pollyanna. Pollyanna dove over Ainia's unconscious body.

The wave of debris broke, flew over Pollyanna's back, and pushed Wu to the back wall, burying her.

Under the shelter of a broken table Pollyanna held her breath until her ears stopped ringing. Confident the accident was over, she climbed out from under the wreckage, dragging Ainia's unconscious body with her. Once clear, she smiled up at the empty cab of the semi, her face covered in drywall dust. "Today I'm grateful for faulty parking brakes."

The pile of wreckage shifted, teeter-tottering a board somewhere below, and launching General Wu's journal out from the mess into Pollyanna's hands.

Pollyanna nodded, satisfied. "Book of Chinese Ghostbuster secrets? Bonus."

Chapter 67

The San Diego weather was perfect, as usual. When they'd crossed the country, it was as if they'd also crossed from fall into spring.

Ainia parked a hundred feet down, on the opposite side of the street, and facing away from the safe house, a bland one-story office building in an equally bland business district. It was Saturday. The roads were empty. She cut the engine and aimed her mirrors at the office building.

"We're not going in?" asked Pollyanna.

Ainia double-checked her mirrors. "I want to watch for any more nasty surprises." She reached into her paper bag. "Besides, I'm hungry."

"Then I'm glad I used the restroom at the taco shop." Pollyanna slid her burrito out of its bag. She unrolled it from its wrapper, accidentally opening the tortilla, spilling cheese, sour cream, carne asada, and French fries into her lap. "Well, fuck. Ainia, why didn't you warn me this was going to happen?"

Ainia peeled the wrapper back from top end of her burrito. "You're a grown woman. I thought you could feed yourself. Never eaten a burrito before?"

"Not one this big. Ahab got killed going after this thing." Frustrated, she scooped the mess back into the tortilla with her hands, making a rough bowl from the flat bread. "Either we go inside, or I stink up your truck with my sour cream pants."

"Smells fine to me." Ainia took another bite and watched the building.

Ainia was done eating by the time Pollyanna finished with her rough reassembly of her lunch. Pollyanna leaned against the truck door, bracing herself for a bite. The door flew open. A man's voice boomed, "License and registration, please!"

Pollyanna and her burrito spilled on the sidewalk. The loose contents of her meal squashed between her hand and the concrete. "Jesus Christ! You motherfucking—"

Isaac Deal stepped back, laughing. "Gotcha!"

Pollyanna climbed up to her feet, hand sliding in the spilled carne asada. "You fucking asshole! Do you know how hungry I am?" She smacked Isaac in the face with the tortilla. "You owe me another burrito!"

He peeled it off. Sour cream and a bit of cheese stuck to his face. "Happy to see you're alive too, Pollyanna."

Exposition Joe stepped forward, handing napkins to Isaac and a replacement burrito—from the same taco shop—to Pollyanna. "Here, Pollyanna. Careful opening it."

Ainia leaned over the bed of her truck from the other side, crumpling the empty wrapper from her lunch. "I see you guys ignored the order to travel solo too."

Isaac held his hands up in innocence. "What orders? We lost our phones in Africa, remember? Our appearance here is purely coincidental."

Ainia glared at Exposition Joe. "Right…"

Isaac asked, "Are we all here? Are the others inside?"

"Don't know. I was going to wait here and scope the place out, but we might as well go inside. If this is a trap, like everything else has been, four of us should be able to handle it. Isaac, you're with me. Joe and Pollyanna, you stay back."

Pollyanna carefully unwrapped her replacement burrito and nodded. Joe scratched his nose. Ainia locked eyes with Joe. "You're going to stay back, right Joe?"

Joe nodded. "As far as I can tell."

"Come on," Ainia grunted to Isaac. They walked around the

building, checking cameras, windows, and doors. Seeing nothing out of place, they stepped up to the front door. Ainia asked Isaac, "Can you pick it?"

"Why should I pick it? We haven't tried the code yet."

"Are you capable of picking a lock without sponging the skill off someone else?" Ainia challenged. "How many times have you lifted this skill off Park? Did you learn anything, or does the knowledge run right through you?"

Isaac limbered his fingers. "You got a set of lock picks or something on you? I'll pick that lock."

Ainia produced a pair of bobby pins. Isaac took a close look at Ainia's short cropped hair. "I lifted them off of Pollyanna," she explained.

She let Isaac snatch them out of her hand. He knelt and went to work in a huff, a man with something to prove. He made short work of the lock, turned to Ainia and said, "Ha."

The Amazon was skeptical. "Smooth. Too smooth to be you. Someone's inside."

"Or maybe I'm better than you give me cred—"

Ainia pushed him aside and slid into the office, ducking behind the empty receptionist desk. Isaac pushed open the door and peered in. Ainia held up a finger, telling him to stay put.

The lights were on, but they were supposed to be left on. As she crept from the desk to the edge of the cubicle partition to another desk, Isaac followed—quietly, but in full view.

Park stepped out of the men's room, no coat or tie, shirt untucked and unbuttoned, hair wet, towel thrown over one shoulder, and working a Q-Tip in one ear. He stopped when he saw Isaac and threw out the Q-Tip.

"Isaac! Thank God someone else made it. Is anyone else with you?"

Isaac smiled. "Four of us. Here's one." He pointed at Ainia, standing up from her hiding place. The front door opened. "That's probably the other two now."

Pollyanna and Exposition Joe walked in the front door. Pollyanna gripped her burrito in both hands. "Hi, Park. Joe said you'd be here. Can we be happy now or have Ensign, 97:4, and Gabby yet to arrive?"

Park threw the towel over a cubicle partition. An air mattress and blanket were visible around the corner behind him. "Last I heard from Ensign he was still in Asia. That was a week ago. Gabby didn't make it."

Pollyanna slumped against the front desk. Isaac's jaw dropped. Ainia's brow furrowed. Joe waited for Park to finish.

"No. No." Park waved his hands in appeasement. "She's still alive, but beat up pretty bad. Some broken bones, a concussion, and soft tissue damage, I checked her into the hospital under a cover ID."

Pollyanna's grip on her burrito went from uncertain to angry, squeezing the contents to the top. "Christ, Park. Phrasing. I almost had a heart attack there. What the fuck happened?"

"A pair of those Casemen with psychotronic weapons jumped us in Texas. One of them distracted me while the other one attacked Gabby. If they'd wanted us dead, we'd be dead, but they were only toying with us."

"And the Casemen," asked Ainia. "What about them?"

"They left me with Gabby. Two Asian males. The one I spoke to had a North Korean accent. These Casemen, they're not holding real cards. Their cases hold the frozen brains of euthanized psychics."

"Confirmed," said Ainia. "Pollyanna and I destroyed two of them."

"You mean," asked Isaac. "that guy who's been chasing me on the motorcycle, he's got a brain in his backpack?"

Park buttoned his shirt. "It looks like it."

Isaac shuttered. "Ugh."

Park tucked his shirt. "How about feds, real or fake? Anyone have a run in with the law?"

Joe spoke up. "Those are real feds acting on fake orders. An anti-Gnostic cult of rich jerks that has people in law enforcement and the US military. No connection with the Casemen."

"What do they want?" asked Park.

"One of their leaders, Representative Fray, was upset about the church we burned in Liberia. She's the one who hooked The Baptist up with the Faith Machine in the first place."

Pollyanna said, "Did you tell her we didn't burn her Faith Machine, that it was The Baptist?"

"No, it was us," said Joe. "I mean, it was me. And I'm part of us, right guys?"

"Not if you keep going off script—" Park stopped himself. "Now I'm referring to scripts too."

"The Script is what kept me from telling you this earlier. I also set fire to the Samaritans' Faith Machine in Nebraska. Oh, and there's only one Faith Machine left. It's in Asia someplace."

"Can we assume it's in North Korea?" asked Pollyanna. "And are you going to burn that one down too?"

"Probably," said Joe.

Park said, "Let's not assume too much, but we can aim our investigation that way. We'll do complete debriefings later today, but let's go around the circle here and everybody tell your story." He pointed at Ainia.

Joe chimed in with, "Isaac slept with Representative Fray." He held up the picture on General Casey's smartphone. Ainia and Park turned away. Pollyanna leaned in for a closer look.

Isaac flinched. "Don't! Boy...don't you know there's a time and place for this kinda talk?"

"How'd you get past the cobwebs?" Pollyanna smiled.

Isaac rolled his eyes and composed himself. "It would surprise you to learn that the Reverend Representative Fray is a freak. I would even say...a super freak. That fine lady showed me the value of—"

Park interrupted, "We'll get back to that, Isaac. Not...that, specifically. Joe, put the phone away."

Instead, Joe tucked the phone into Park's shirt pocket. "The passcode is 0-9-0-9. There's an open text message—a bunch of account numbers and cities. You'll need them later."

Ainia said, "Representative Fray and the Samaritans aren't the only other party getting involved. We had a run-in with a General Wu from China's Thirteenth Bureau, Ghostkillers."

"China?" Park rubbed his forehead. "What's their relationship with North Korea on this?"

Ainia said, "It's probably not friendly. General Wu killed the Caseman who followed Pollyanna from Pennsylvania."

"Agreed." Park nodded. "Did we learn anything else from General Wu?"

Pollyanna grunted, her mouth full of burrito, pointing to her purse. She wiped her hand on her jeans, and after some digging, pulled a worn journal out of the side pocket, and presented it to Park.

While Park flipped through it, Ainia said, "That was General Wu's. We acquired it when Pollyanna smashed the restaurant with a semi."

Isaac checked out Pollyanna's arms. "Girl, you're stronger than you look."

"It's encoded." Park closed the journal. "Follow me."

He led them into a conference room and set the journal on the table. The agents took seats around the table. Pollyanna finished her burrito.

Park popped the cap on a whiteboard marker. "Here are our players. First: Casemen. I think we can assume they're a single entity and likely North Kor—"

Park tried to write on the whiteboard but the marker was dry. He tossed it into the trash and popped the cap on another. "Second: General Wu of the Thirteenth Bureau. Ghostkiller, psychic oppressor. Probably not allied with the Casemen."

Park discovered the second marker was dry too. It too went into the trash. Grabbing a third marker, he continued. "Third: Debra Fray of the US House of Representatives. The apparent leader of a satanic—sorry, Anti-Gnostic—cult." The third marker turned up dry. Park slammed it into the can with the others. "For fuck's sake, is there a working marker in the goddamn building?"

Park leaned face-first against the whiteboard and breathed deeply. The rest of the team tried to find a comfortable direction to look while their boss composed himself.

Ainia broke the silence. "We haven't used this safe house in years, Park. If you think the markers are in a sorry state, don't open the office fridge."

"We'll make a run to Office Depot tonight." Park sighed. "Sorry, everyone. With Ensign out of communication, one agent in the hospital, another missing…what do we have to show for it?" He pushed Wu's journal across the table. "A notebook of gibberish written in Chinese."

Isaac took the journal and started flipping through it idly. "On the other hand, we've got five able-bodied agents who fought past the forces of three nations, collected a bunch of intel, and the notebook has a bunch more, ready for the taking. We just have to unlock it."

"Just the same. I wish we had captured more material. One of those frozen brains would have been a good acquisition." Park dropped into a chair, rubbing his forehead. "I'm not blaming any of you. I had one in my hands, but I couldn't keep it."

"I blame myself," said Ainia. "I had two, neither for long. I didn't realize the crazy guy attacking me with frozen meat was anything other than a usual day in New York. The second was collateral damage in Nevada."

An electric beep sounded from the front of the office.

Pollyanna flinched. "What was that?"

"Someone entered with the passcode." Park stepped out into the hall. The rest of the agents clustered behind him.

97:4 dragged a luggage roller behind her and looked like every inch of bad road from Cincinnati to San Diego. Sunken eyes, dirty cast—dirty everything—she reeked of burnt pork and piss. She propped the roller up against the wall. "Anyone have a butter knife? This cast itches like crazy."

Chapter 68

Pollyanna helped 97:4 get cleaned up and fed. They returned from the locker room and 97:4 told the rest of the team what she'd been through with Caseman Three. Everything but the visit from God.

When she finished, Pollyanna told Ainia, "Looks like you're not the baddest bitch on the team anymore."

Ainia nodded. "So it seems."

Park laid the roller on the table and unzipped it. Everyone stood to gawk inside. Everyone but 97:4, who looked away.

Park poked around inside the case with a pen, succeeding only in pushing the cotton fabric around.

97:4 said, "You can pick it up. It's cold, but the cotton will protect your hands."

Park discarded the pen and picked up the bundle, placing it on the table and unwrapping the fabric. The organ lay bare in front of them, frost sparkling along its surface.

Pollyanna broke the silence. "That used to be somebody."

Park leaned back. "Someone stripped down a psychic to just their card. The brain is put into a self-sustaining cryogenic state. That process is located in the lower centers of the brain. Maybe even in that piece of stem that's left—"

"Park." Pollyanna tried to interrupt.

"I wish we could run this through an MRI."

"Park!" Pollyanna pounded her fist on the table. "I'm having some ethical concerns right now. What if someone is suffering in there? Don't we have a responsibility to end that?"

"Yes...maybe." Park covered his mouth with his knuckles. "I don't know. Do we assume there's a consciousness in there?"

97:4 spoke up, "Are you assuming that there isn't?"

"We don't have any science on this specific case, I admit. But what science we do have says without stimuli, the brain's higher functions shut down. This person is probably brain dead, it's just the lower functions. Like a person kept alive on machines."

"But why keep it?" asked Pollyanna.

"Because it's the enemy's weapon, their advantage," said Ainia. "If we don't learn how to neutralize it, they're going to walk all over us. Imagine hundreds of these in the hands of hundreds of North Koreans. Who's going to stand up to that? And there's still a Faith Machine operating out there."

Park stood up. "The Faith Machine. That gives me an idea."

He drew his satphone, started an app, and passed it around the disembodied brain. "There's an electromagnetic field headed that way." Park pointed west. "I'll take a better measurement later, but there's nothing that way but ocean and Asia. I bet we can use this to find the location of the last Faith Machine."

97:4 leaned forward, grimacing as her arm twisted in its cast. "Park, this thing is an abomination. Put this person out of their misery, don't use them like a dowsing rod."

Ainia leaned over the table toward 97:4. "You're forgetting who your commander is." She pointed around the table. "You all are."

Isaac put his hands up. "Hey, don't point at me. I agree with Park."

"*What?*" 97:4 and Pollyanna asked in unison.

"If it still had its higher functions I would be fluent in Korean." Isaac opened a page from Wu's journal for everyone to see. "This page is written in Korean, but I can barely make it out. I know as much Korean as Park does."

All eyes turned on Park. He shrugged. "I admit it. I need to brush up on my Hangul."

Pollyanna tapped on the table. "I don't see how it can be brain dead and still be psychic. You're saying our cards aren't part of who we are?"

"What you are is physical. Psychics are all physically different from the baseline. We've run MRIs on all of you and there are always variations in brain activity."

Ainia pointed to the scar at the back of her head. "That's clear in my case, but what about the others? What's their trigger?"

"The science on this is incomplete. None of you had MRIs on record before your cards activated. There aren't many of you in the first place, and there are even fewer ethical experiments we can perform on psychics."

97:4 stared at the frozen brain before them. "Someone, somewhere, crossed those ethical lines."

"We've all heard of how bad things are for the people of North Korea." Park pointed at the brain. "This isn't a smoking gun, but with the rest of what we've uncovered, this is building a strong circumstantial case that the DPRK is our destination."

Isaac flipped a few pages in the journal. "It's stronger than that. See here? Luckily Park can read Chinese just fine." He pointed to a page. "She's using English characters for the nouns and verbs, but they don't make sense. There's no good way to encode Chinese so she's using English words and simple word jumbles to cover the important parts. Give me a few hours and I should have more for you."

Park looked at Isaac suspiciously.

Isaac asked, "What?"

Park wasn't the only one. The rest of the team sized each other up as if someone had something to confess.

Pollyanna asked, "Okay, who here's good at puzzles?"

"Me," Isaac insisted.

"Yeah," Pollyanna dismissed him. "But who really?"

"I said me," Isaac said, offended. "What? I can't be good at something on my own? Like everything I am is taken from someone else?"

Ainia asked, "Well, isn't it?"

Isaac pushed away from the table, slamming his chair against the wall. "I'm going to show you all. I'm going to decode this entire book." He snatched the journal and stormed out of the conference room.

The rest of the group stayed behind, waiting out the awkward moment, until Isaac stormed back and grabbed the chair he'd just abandoned dramatically.

"I'll be next door. I still need to be close to Park to read Chinese. But the puzzles are all me. Damn it." Isaac kicked the door shut behind him, but the door's mechanism prevented it from slamming, easing silently closed instead.

Park continued, "All right, while Isaac is working on that—"

Three satphones went off, interrupting him. Park drew his from his pocket, as did Ainia. Pollyanna pulled hers from her purse.

"Three phones? We're down to three for the whole team?" His disappointment shattered when he saw from whom the text message came. "It's Ensign. 'Received the board game from eBay, thx. I think it's missing pieces.'"

Pollyanna gave her phone a skeptical look. "If he knows we're here, he should have known when we were in trouble out there."

Park was already typing out loud, "'Sorry if disappointed. It said in the ad the Kentucky piece was missing. Everything else is there.'"

Pollyanna suggested, "Be sure to spell every other word wrong for authenticity."

"I did," Park said, not looking up from his phone. "He said, 'Kentucky was your responsibility.'" Park sighed. "'Would you consider compensating me for replacing piece? I found a distributor in China, shipping is 4-8 weeks by sea.' And there's an address to the Liaoning province. We're supposed to take a ship and meet him in China."

97:4 nodded impatiently. "We figured that out, Park. Seriously, are these codes supposed to fool anybody?"

"You'd be surprised." Park stared at the phone.

"And we're going by sea now?" asked Ainia.

Park nodded. "It's a good way to travel in secret. Once you're out there on the ocean you're hard to find."

Pollyanna nudged 97:4. "Look at Park, he's smiling. What's up, Park? Got a thing for boats?"

Park held up a finger, texted "OK" back to Ensign, and pocketed his phone. "Sailing's in my Korean blood. But more than that, we have orders. Ensign's out there watching us."

"Oh." 97:4 gasped, clutching at her cross earring. "That was it, the Faith Machine."

"Like in Africa?" asked Park.

97:4 nodded. "Looks like Ensign's not the only one watching us."

Chapter 69

Isaac broke the code in General Wu's journal and wouldn't stop boasting about it for days. The information inside confirmed Park's theories. The last Faith Machine was probably in North Korea. The Casemen's weapons networked to it.

Within a week, the team — sans Gabby, who was still recovering — was cleaned up, rested, and re-equipped, thanks to a safe full of cash Ensign kept in the safe house. A lot of cash—enough to buy a used boat that could cross the Pacific. Park sent Isaac to buy such a ship across the border in Tijuana. When he called Park to announce the purchase, he kept the details to himself. "It's perfect. You'll just have to see it."

After crossing into Mexico, Park and Ainia went down to the decaying, disorganized, but functional TJ docks to find Isaac's surprise. It took them half an hour of wandering around between shipping containers on dirt loading bays before they located the ship.

Ainia scanned the dock. "Are you sure it was a good idea sending Isaac down here on his own? Someone should have had an eye on him."

"He's a salesman—the perfect person to send on a mission like this."

"I trust his ability. It's his judgment that makes me nervous. You saw that outfit he wore to Liberia. Purple silk pajamas…he looked like a clown."

Park double-checked the dock number. "Uhhh…I might have to give you this one."

Docked at port ochenta y ocho was a hundred-foot motorized yacht.

Tomás el Incrédulo was written across the bow in Gothic script. It looked to be about forty years old, though in good shape. A garish mural depicting the apostle Thomas poking his finger in the savior's wound covered the starboard side.

Ainia dropped her bag on the pier. "Jesus Christ!"

Park exclaimed, "María Madre de Dios! No, she's not in there. Maybe she's in the mural on the other side."

Ainia shielded her eyes. "It looks like someone pointed at the underside of an East LA bridge and said, 'I want a boat just like that.'"

Park nudged her with his elbow. "Let's go meet the skipper."

"If the horn plays La Cucaracha, I'm throwing him overboard halfway to Hawaii."

Isaac popped out of the cabin wearing a serape and a sombrero with *Mexico* stitched along the brim. "*Es por lo menos dos semanas a Corea del Norte. Debemos viajar con estilo.*"

Ainia lunged forward. Park held her back with a hand on her shoulder. "Wait until we're at sea."

"You guys are here just in time. Help me carry out the projection screen TV—the LCD is coming later today. Yo, check this out. I just had this put in." With that, Isaac ducked back into the cabin. The opening notes of "La Cucaracha" echoed from the ship's horns across the bay.

"Overboard, Park," Ainia warned. "Overboard."

Chapter 70

Pollyanna dragged her trunk aboard, left it standing on end, and eyeballed the luxurious, if tacky, cabin interior—turquoise tiles and gold trim. "Here we go! When I took this spy job this is what I expected. This is way better than sleeping on the floor of a cubicle. Let's hire a crew of Filipino cabin boys to take care of us, run the ship and stuff."

97:4 entered, walking around Pollyanna's sizable trunk. "What did you bring, Pollyanna?"

Pollyanna leaned an elbow on the trunk. "What I bring everywhere—big lips, tits, and hips." After pausing a beat, she pointed at the trunk. "Oh, you mean in there? Enough bottles and books to last until Guam. And clothes and shit, you know."

Pollyanna left her trunk where it stood and flopped onto the couch. "If being on the No-Fly List means spending two weeks with books and booze instead of fifteen hours crammed in a metal tube full of farts, then keep me on the list."

"Too bad we're the crew." 97:4 eyed the interior of the cabin skeptically. "This place has 'swinger' written all over it. Be careful what you touch."

Pollyanna lifted her hands off the suede couch. "Why'd you have to go and say that? I was comfortable. What do you know about swingers, anyway? What kind of church do you go to, and is it too late to convert?"

97:4 smirked, the closest she'd come to smiling in weeks. "I have a life outside of church. Though, no, that doesn't include sex clubs.

Knowing about sex clubs—that's not a sin."

Isaac popped his head in and asked Pollyanna, "Did I hear you talking about sex clubs?"

"That was 97:4," Pollyanna corrected.

"Oh. Never mind." He gave 97:4 an apologetic look and disappeared from whence he came.

Pollyanna rolled her eyes.

97:4 said, "Better you than me."

"Thanks for the support." Pollyanna turned to greet Exposition Joe as he came aboard. Her smile dropped when he dragged Caseman Three's suitcase inside. "Oh, shit. That fucking thing. There goes my good mood."

She launched herself out of the couch, blocking the case from 97:4. "Keep rolling with that creepy thing, Joe. We don't want it around here."

97:4 put a hand on Pollyanna's shoulder. "You don't have to worry about me. Either of you. I'm fine."

Joe seemed sorry to be bringing it aboard. "Park wants this in his quarters. Unfortunately."

Pollyanna put her fists on her hips. "Why 'unfortunately'? What's going to happen? What do you see? Is that thing going to make us sink? Is that it?" She grabbed her trunk. "Gangway! Women and children first!"

97:4 blocked Pollyanna with her good arm. "Don't worry about it. We're making it to North Korea."

Pollyanna stopped mid-evacuation. "That's an Exposition Joe line. Don't tell me you've been reading the Script, too."

"No. God told me so," said 97:4.

Joe twitched.

"Christ." Pollyanna rolled her eyes.

"No, the Father."

Exposition Joe put a hand on Pollyanna's shoulder. "We'll make it, Pollyanna. But it's not going to be fun."

Chapter 71

The Collective watched the *Tomás el Incrédulo* get underway from Tijuana. Day after day, the members of Project Dead Blind bickered over their crew assignments, settled into a routine, then bickered again. Meanwhile, Dr. Park overextended himself, captaining the ship and studying the Korean language on Exposition Joe's suggestion.

They watched the Reverend Representative Fray reassess her power base. Without the Faith Machine whispering secrets to her, what did she have to hold it all together? How would she make decisions? Her influence already pouring through her fingers.

They watched General Wu holed up in a San Francisco hotel, healing and reading reports from her field agents. Looking for patterns, she hoped to find evidence of the last Faith Machine.

They watched the surviving Casemen take jobs as deckhands in Long Beach on cargo ships heading back to China. Across the ocean, they jumped ship without pay. They knew when this was all over, the money would be worthless. All money would.

Chapter 72

The *Tomás el Incrédulo* got underway. The Mexico/California coast disappeared over the horizon. Draped head to toe in a floral cotton muumuu and broad-brimmed hat, Pollyanna had slathered her few remaining exposed parts in triple-digit SPF sunblock. As if clothing and chemicals weren't enough, she positioned her deck chair in the shade of the upper deck. Three books from her stash lay stacked on the deck beside her, and a bottle of vodka.

She put down *The Satanic Verses* and picked up *A Map of Betrayal*, opening it to the first page. Her bookmark, the receipt for the vodka, got stuffed somewhere in the last chapter. The exposed end flapped furiously in the wind.

Exposition Joe leaned out the cabin window. "Why are you starting that book? You didn't finish the last one."

Pollyanna closed the book on her thumb and peered at Joe over her sunglasses. "You don't know? My reading list isn't important enough to be in the Script?"

"It tells me *what* happens, not *why*."

She poured herself another vodka, neat. "I usually have three books going at once. When I tire of one, I switch to another."

"What if you get tired of reading altogether?"

"Never." She braced for the shot, threw it back, and upended the shot glass on top of the bottle instead of its cap. She dug *The Alchemist* from the bottom of the stack and threw it to Joe. "Here. You should enjoy that one. Or maybe not, you're one step ahead of the protagonist."

Joe held the book like a locked box. "I can't. Every time I read, I get flashes of the middle and end. I can't keep it all straight."

"I should have packed *Naked Lunch* for you. Who knows, you might be the one person to read it un-cutup."

"Thanks, but no thanks. I have enough to think about." Joe handed the book back to Pollyanna as 97:4 walked by.

97:4 ducked into the shade. "Is this the Dead Blind Book Club?" She considered the extensive ultraviolet protections Pollyanna had in place. "Wouldn't it be easier to let yourself tan?"

"Have you ever seen a big girl with a tan? Look who I'm asking. Of course you haven't. Even if I could find a bikini that fit, it'd cover as much acreage as a skinny little number like you has on her entire body. I'll stay one shade all over, thanks."

"Tan lines?" 97:4 pointed to her cast. "Mixed shades?" She held her forearm out for inspection. The dark Lichtenberg scars ran lattice-like up and under her sleeve. "It's not the end of the world."

"True. There's no mention of big girls with tan lines in the Book of Revelation, at least not when I read it."

"You read the Bible?" Joe and 97:4 asked in unison.

"Yes, members of the Greek chorus, I did. There was a time when I was looking for answers."

Joe asked, "Did you find any?"

"I sure did." Pollyanna caressed the bottle of vodka. She affected a singsong voice. "It was right here in front of me all along."

Joe leaned back and reached for something under the window. "Honestly?"

97:4 turned up her nose at Pollyanna's shot glass. "It's ironic someone who can alter probability with her attitude would have such a bad one."

Pollyanna ran her finger around the shot glass on the bottleneck. "It's ironic you believe that book in your hand is about peace and love, but you use it like a clip in a gun."

97:4 clutched the bloody Bible to her side. "I use the tools God gave me to make a better world."

Pollyanna sat up. "Your God gave me a tool too. Why'd my family have to die for me to get it?"

"You're mistaking cause and effect."

"No. You're mistaking blind chance with justice, the lie of objective right and wrong. Sister, there's nothing in this world but us and we're pretty fucked-up. You can go to church, pray, and tell yourself it ain't so. But we're just self-absorbed bags of meat, looking for an excuse to cut each other open. So if you see your God, ask him something for me. Ask Him, 'Why?' I bet He won't have an answer."

"You don't understand faith."

"No, I don't. I thought I did and look where that got me. And speaking of faith, how about these Faith Machines? Remember what The Baptist used his for? All those bodies? Either they force God to do horrible things or God does horrible things to people through it. I don't know what's worse."

97:4 shook her head, tense. "I feel sorry for you." She stormed back inside.

Pollyanna shrugged and poured herself another shot. "You don't feel sorry for me, do you?"

Exposition Joe said, "No."

Without turning, Pollyanna held up the shot glass for Joe to see. "I wasn't asking you."

Joe nodded. He picked up the rolling suitcase from below the window and left Pollyanna to her books and booze.

Chapter 73

The team spent less than a day in Hawaii. Enough time to refuel and resupply before getting back underway.

Ainia worked out on the deck, swinging a kettlebell between her legs and up to the sky.

Isaac leaned out from the bridge. "Is that how you do it?"

Ainia huffed and answered without breaking the flow. "Do what?"

"The fighting and parkour stuff. I've never seen you practice any of that, ever. Is that iron ball some kind of secret training technique you learned way back with the rest of the Amazons?"

Ainia slowed her motion. "Maybe. That was a long time ago."

"You'd think that was something you'd remember. Early memories last the longest, you know. Maybe your training was different, alien even, than how we learn now. That would explain why I can't copy your fighting style."

Ainia finished her set, wiped the sweat from her brow. "Maybe."

"Or maybe it's a reincarnation thing? I can't get to anything you learned in your past life. That'd explain why I can't speak Ancient Greek around you either. What do you think?"

"You want to know what I think? Okay—" Silence interrupted Ainia as the boat's engine rumble stopped, then suddenly escalated into a loud, offbeat banging. "That's not good."

Park, in T-shirt and pajama pants, hair tangled, shot up from below deck, and called up to Isaac, "What happened?"

Isaac shrugged, unconcerned. "Propeller shaft go boom?"

"Well, turn the engine off." Park ran a hand through his hair. "Ainia, you said you could work on the engine in this thing, right?"

Ainia nodded. "It's a bigger diesel than I'm used to. But I can work with it, as long as we don't need a part."

"Don't jinx us." Park turned to Isaac hanging out of the bridge. "Take Isaac with you. He should be able to match your mechanical skills. I'll take the bridge."

Ainia coughed and shook her head.

Park asked, "Is there a better choice?"

Ainia conceded the point. "Come on, Isaac. Let's take a look down below."

She'd gathered the toolbox, climbed underneath the engine, and disconnected it from the drive shaft before Isaac arrived. She glowered at him from behind her wrench. "What took you so long? Busy unpacking your mechanic's costume?"

Isaac looked down at his shirt and sweatpants. "This isn't a mechanic's costume?"

"Never mind. Here, take hold of the main pulley and lift. Tell me what you see in there."

Isaac peered into the transmission. "Harmonic balancer's cracked."

"Really? Are you sure?" She started to push out from under the engine. "Let me see."

"I know everything you know about engines. It's the harmonic balancer."

"Shit. In the middle of the Pacific? Shit. Maybe I can weld it."

The hatch into the engine room swung open with a screech. Exposition Joe popped his head in. "Hi guys. What's going on?"

Isaac smiled. "Just manly things with grease and wrenches. What's going on with you, Joe?"

Joe shrugged. "Wandering around. How's it look?"

"Terrible," Ainia pulled herself out from under the engine. "If we're lucky, there's a replacement part somewhere on board, hidden away."

"If not?" asked Joe.

"Radio for help." She scratched her forehead with the back of her wrist. "Bye-bye, secret mission."

"Would this help?" Joe asked, pulling a brand new gear from inside his jacket. The harmonic balancer shone in the dirty engine room. "I picked it up in Hawaii. Just lying there on the dock."

"Just lying there?" Ainia left the part in Joe's outstretched hand. "On the dock?"

Joe nodded. "Seems too convenient, doesn't it?"

Ainia snatched the harmonic balancer out of Joe's hand and inspected it. "Everything about you is too convenient." She lined it up with the old part. "Not a perfect match, but this should do. It just has to get us to Guam."

Isaac stepped up. "You just said we were in deep shit. The kid had the part we needed. What's the problem, Ainia?"

"Out of a hundred essential parts on this ship, the kid happened to have the part we needed."

Isaac stepped up to her, gesturing wildly. "Why would he lie?"

"I don't trust either of you. Joe, because I don't know where his allegiances lie. You, because you would rather fuck the enemy than fight her. You're all a bunch of weak, undisciplined, distracted ingrates. Park dropped the chance at true glory in your laps and all you people worry about is working on your tans and watching movies. You make me sick."

Isaac considered, running his tongue along the inside of his mouth, and pointed up. "You know this is a small ship, right?"

Ainia looked up the ladderwell. 97:4 and Pollyanna were looking down, listening. She shrugged. "Whatever. We'll probably lose the lot of you in China."

She climbed back under the engine. By the time she was done, everyone had crept away. Later that evening, Exposition Joe returned to retrieve the roller from its hiding place in a corner of the ladderwell hatch.

Chapter 74

Joe still had the rolling suitcase with him when he found Isaac leaning on the stern and staring into the night. Reluctantly, Joe joined him at the rail. "Hi, Isaac."

The man stared out to sea, saying nothing.

Joe didn't want to be here. "I don't think Ainia meant any of that. She's probably getting cabin fever being on the ship so long. You know she likes to keep mov—"

"She meant every word." Isaac interrupted, sniffing hard. Joe realized he'd been crying. "I broke that code. And no one takes me seriously. What's a man gotta do to earn some respect?"

"I respect you."

"Yeah, sure. Because it's in your Script. Or even worse, you're saying so 'cause that's in the Script." He snorted and spit out into the ocean. "Fucking pointless, isn't it? And I mean that. If you're right and everything is set, that's fucking pointless. And if you're wrong—is that any better?"

"I think it's better to live in the moment. Like this." He opened a hand toward the ocean. "Have you ever seen this much water in one place before? And I mean up close, not from a plane window. That's something, right? All that water can't be totally pointless can it?"

Isaac cocked an eyebrow at him. "Nice try, man, but that was pathetic."

Joe drooped. "Yeah, I know."

"So, what's it going to be? You see me diving off the back of this boat, disappearing in the foam? Gone for good?"

"No."

That took Isaac by surprise. "No? Maybe your radio's on the blink."

"No radio. I don't see it happening."

"Hmm." Isaac stepped back from the rail. "Fuck it, then. It's cold out here, huh?" He patted Joe on the shoulder and went inside the cabin.

Joe stayed at the rail, holding the roller, wishing he could throw it overboard, but it wasn't in the Script.

Chapter 75

The sun beamed down upon the bay through the muggy air. Moored at a private dock on the south side of Guam, the *Tomás el Incrédulo* rocked in the ocean's gentle swells. The rest of the team flew off in five different directions, eager to be away from each other for a few hours, or maybe forever, given their mood.

Exposition Joe watched the ship alone. He stood on the deck and stared into the water. The waves of the future ebbed and flowed, indistinguishable from the waves of the present.

His moment of peace expired when the Script called for him to climb through the bridge to the captain's quarters. Like a child visiting his Christmas presents in mid-December, he absconded with the rolling suitcase, careful not to touch the copper patch on the handle.

The wheels skipped and jumped along the warped boards of the dock. Joe dragged it to the far point of the pier between two sailboats, a French forty-four-footer named the *Contre le Vent* and a Japanese twelve-footer, the *Buru Muun*. He stood with one hand on the roller handle and one wheel over the dock's edge. Wanting to drop the case into the water, not allowed to pull his fingers apart.

Joe spent over an hour in this half-bent position. His side cramped. The salty air dried out his mouth and sinuses. Still he stood. A seagull floated past him.

God joined Joe at the dock. He considered the suitcase, suspended over the water. "So close. So very close, isn't it?"

Joe's voice cracked. "Please."

God laughed, tapping the rolled-up document against His leg. "No. Not while there's a lesson for you to learn."

Joe's arm trembled.

"Steady." God passed His open hand down the length of Joe's arm. The tremble disappeared as if the deity had smoothed wrinkles out of a paper streamer. "Isn't that better?"

"No!" Joe barked. "I want this thing gone. I want the fighting to stop. This thing is full of hate."

"The damage is done. It only took a little push to make the cracks show. How much longer before those people tear each other apart?" God shrugged. "Or maybe Nietzsche got something right after all, 'What doesn't kill you makes you stronger.'"

God leaned around Joe at an angle that would have sent a mortal into the drink. "You're the one who sees the future. You should be able to tell me."

"I just read the Script. You're the one who wrote it."

God nodded as if this knowledge were new and profound. He pushed Joe back onto the dock, flat on his back. Free to move again, Joe tried to stand. His muscles sizzled as he twisted and turned. The wheeled suitcase lay next to him. God pointed to the case with the rolled-up document, the other hand behind His back. "Open it."

Joe glared at God, rubbing the stiffness out of his neck. He unzipped the rolling suitcase and threw the flap open. The cotton material inside was a wrinkled mess.

"You think that's it. This is what caused your *friends*—" the word came out with a sneer, "—to turn on each other? Well then, by all means, drop it in the water."

Joe took the sheet in both hands, and stood. Gave it a shake to prove what he'd already seen in the Script seconds before. The frozen psychic's brain was missing. "You moved it."

"Not I. Park moved it someplace safe before you set sail from Tijuana.

You've been carrying an empty case around the ship, thinking you were complicit in some plan of Mine to drive everyone apart."

"Why?" Joe dropped the fabric back in the case.

"I wanted to show you. This team, they're not friends, yours or each other's. I'm your only friend, Joe." God put a hand on Joe's drooping shoulder. "I've been your only friend ever since you received my blessing."

Chapter 76

The *Tomás el Incrédulo* cut through the night, the rain, and the East China Sea, the last leg of Dead Blind's journey to the Liaoning province. On the bridge, Park juggled monitoring the instruments, keeping the ship on course, and studying Korean from CDs.

"*Dochak hesseoyo*? Are we there yet?" Park repeated, aware of the irony.

"How's it going?" Joe leaned into the frame of the dark hatch that led back into the ship, his face lit by the instruments' green and blue lights.

Park put the CD on pause and closed the textbook. "Not great. It's easier to learn the second time. But this is the South Korean dialect. After sixty years, it's not the same as in the DPRK. The closest I can do is affect my grandmother's accent."

"Your grandmother's North Korean?"

"She's from Pyongyang, but immigrated during the war."

"Will sixty-year-old slang pass? Would you try to pass in America talking like someone out of *Back to the Future*?"

"No, not for any extensive conversations. I'll walk fast and look pissed and no one will talk to me, hopefully." Park noticed Joe's attention had drifted away from the conversation. "Any idea where and who I'll be speaking with? It'll be good to focus on specific vocabulary."

Joe shrugged. "I said you'd be studying Korean. I didn't say you'd be using it."

A chill came over Park. "Are you serious? I've been cramming these

Korean lessons for over a week now."

"It kept you busy," Joe offered as an apology.

Park pushed the textbook off the counter. "Goddamn it. Between the navigation, sailing, and keeping the team from each other's throats, I have enough to keep me busy."

Joe backed up. "I'm sorry, but that's—"

Park put a finger in Joe's face. "Stop it. Just stop it." The man closed his eyes and took a deep breath. "What am I going to do with you, Joe? Are you on the team or off on your own? Sometimes I wonder if Ainia's right about you."

Park checked the gauges. "And stop burning the Faith Machines. Our mission is to capture this technology, not destroy it."

"Capture it. Then what?"

"That's up to Ensign. Orders are orders. Understand?"

Joe held his hands up. "But it's not up to me."

"Convince yourself otherwise. Here, I have an idea—" Park pulled a ten-peso coin from a drawer. "Call it in the air."

Park sent the coin spinning.

Before it reached the peak of the arc, Joe said, "Heads but then you'll turn it over to tails before you lift your hand."

Park did exactly that, then let the coin fall in frustration. He threw up his hands, cursed, and grabbed Joe's collar. "Don't burn the last Faith Machine. Or I'll leave you in North Korea."

"I know you will. But now, you'd better talk to her." Joe pointed to the bow of the ship. 97:4 stood in the wind and the rain, holding on to the railing with one hand.

Park said, "Crap. Stay here. Keep an eye on things. And don't set any fires. Let me know if any of these dials start spinning wildly."

"Aye, aye, Captain." Joe saluted.

Park took a minute to climb into an immersion suit, a thick yellow rubbery thing. He grabbed the spare suit and pushed out into the rain, joining 97:4 at the rail.

She twitched a bit when he stepped up next to her.

"You're not having a *Titanic* moment, are you?" Park knew his joke fell flat as it passed his lips.

97:4 let it slide without comment.

Park offered the extra immersion suit. "If you're going to be out here alone, I'd feel better if you were wearing one of these."

"Would that really do any good? If a wave knocked me overboard, I'd be a yellow dot lost at sea. I'm fine, thanks. Besides, I wouldn't be able to feel the rain with that on."

"What does the rain have that Isaac's DVD collection doesn't have?"

She smirked. "Did you notice all of his movies are about codebreaking? I've had enough of them—enough of everything Isaac—to last me a while. Not just Isaac. We all have cabin fever. Don't worry. I'm not going overboard. Not after what I experienced."

"Are you ready to talk about that? I should have approached you earlier, but with, you know, crossing the ocean and pointless Korean lessons..." He glared back at Joe on the bridge. "Often, victims of violence are reluctant to reach out for help. But if you're ready, I'm here for you."

"What's there to talk about? It was frightening, painful, and humiliating. But I cooked my tormentor alive. That's worth a thousand hours of therapy. Besides, my time in that trunk brought me closer to God."

Park wiped the rain off his face. "I know your faith is important to you. But—"

"Not faith, not anymore. God visited me in that car trunk. He gave me the strength to free myself from Caseman Three's control."

She held up her broken arm in its cast, wrapped in plastic to protect it from the rain. "Don't let this fool you. I'm stronger now than ever. I've seen the face of God. That makes me a prophet." She leaned against the rail and looked at Joe behind the wheel. "And I suspect I'm not the only one."

Park followed her gaze. "You're—You experienced all kinds of deprivation—sleep, stimuli, food, and water. Under those conditions hallucinations are not uncommon."

97:4 pulled away. "What I saw was real, realer than real. I could see him clear as day in the dark. God was there with me. He said I had a mission for him deep underground. He was holding a script. The Script. Who does that remind you of?"

Park shook his head. "That doesn't prove anything."

"This started with the Faith Machine. The *Faith Machine*. You can believe in that but you can't believe in God even after I tell you I saw him?"

97:4's argument made Park even more skeptical. "So what do you think God wants us to do?"

"We're here to help Exposition Joe. He's seen it in the Script. Those machines are sacrilegious and Joe's clearing them out."

Park offered the immersion suit once again. "Won't it make God's job easier if you don't come down with pneumonia?"

97:4 pushed the offered suit back at Park. "I don't need this. And I don't need your pity. Joe's going to make everything right and I'm going to help. We're doing good this time. Not like Detroit."

She left Park alone in the rain with both yellow rubber suits.

Chapter 77

Exposition Joe filled the plastic tumbler—half orange juice and half milk. He took a seat at the end of the galley's long table and waited in the dark.

Holding the glass with both hands, he watched the pots, pans, and other kitchenware gently swing back and forth with the motion of the ocean.

Isaac was the first to come down for breakfast. Coming straight from the bridge at the end of his shift, he ignored the light switch and went straight for his Froot Loops cereal, straight out of the box. Isaac popped cereal, one loop after the other, into his mouth in a steady stream of chewing.

Ainia entered next and hit the light. She stopped with her finger still on the switch, looking back and forth between the two men. "What the hell are you two doing in the dark?"

Isaac noticed Joe. "You were sitting there in silence the whole time?"

Joe shrugged. "I didn't have anything to say."

Isaac turned back to Ainia. "The boy knows when to keep his mouth shut."

Her extended finger peeled off the switch and formed a fist with its mates.

"Move," she said, brushing Isaac away from the fridge and retrieving the carton of eggs. She set it on the stove burner and went back for bread and butter.

Isaac's worried eyes went from the cardboard carton resting on the burner to Joe. Joe nodded. Isaac smiled and sat next to Joe, forming an audience.

Ainia struggled with the components and tools of the kitchen. Going back to the fridge to get something she missed or put back something she didn't need after all.

"Mmm, mmm." Isaac rubbed his belly. "Overcooked eggs on toast, same thing every fourth day."

Ainia glared at him while digging a large pan out from the cupboard. "Not for you, fat stuff, you just had yours."

Isaac bounced his paunch with both hands. "Oh, I don't know. I've lost a pound or two sailing this ship for twelve hours a day. It's not easy work, takes a lot of concentration. Did you know the brain burns twenty percent of the body's calories?"

"Who'd you leech that piece of knowledge from?" She gave the dial for the burner an angry twist.

Isaac put his hand up. "Who here hasn't set the kitchen on fire? Joe?" Joe raised his hand. "Ainia? No, wait. You left a pan on full burn last week, then there was the toast. What'll it be next?"

Ainia pulled the butcher's knife from the drawer. "Right now you're in one piece. I think we need you in at least eight."

Pollyanna, in her worn Deftones T-shirt, stumbled into the galley. She saw the knife in Ainia's hand and woke up rather quickly. "Hey! Hey now!"

Ainia stabbed the knife into the counter next to Isaac. "You should pull your weight around here like everyone else. Sailing? *Please.* You sit behind that counter up there—"

"You mean the bridge," Isaac interrupted.

"Shut up. No mess duty, no cleaning. If you weren't pretending to sail you'd still be slacking."

Isaac curled his hand over his mouth and looked away. "Eggs on fire."

"What did you say to me?" She moved in on him with angry eyes.

"I said, you set the eggs on fire." Isaac pointed to the carton of eggs smoldering on the electric burner.

"Shit!" Ainia grabbed the pot and whacked the carton off the burner. It hit the floor, smoldering and bleeding yolk. "Shit!"

Pollyanna went for the paper towels. "Is this why you resent Isaac, Ainia? Embarrassed at how badly you perform basic human functions like feeding yourself and—"

"Don't you fucking start with me, jinx." Ainia picked up the leaking case of eggs and dropped it in the sink. "This was probably your fault. Get out of here. I don't want you anywhere around while I'm cooking. I don't want you anywhere around at all."

"A, that's not how it works. And B, you're perfectly capable of setting a fire all on your own. And C? C is for the horrible *condition* you leave the toilets in after you *clean* them." Pollyanna threw the roll of paper towels into Ainia's arms, winked, and shot her with both finger-guns. "Got a little *Sesame Street* for you there."

Ainia abandoned the broken eggs in the sink and pulled the butcher's knife out of the counter. "All of you. Fucking clear out or I'll carve half of you up and feed you to the other half!"

As she shouted and waved the knife around, Park entered through the hatch behind her, wearing the immersion suit from the night before. "What's going on here, Ainia?"

She turned on him like a madwoman. "This fucking team, that's what. You picked these people, trained them, conditioned them, and they're still a worthless bundle of fuckups. Africa was a mess. The run across America was a mess. If you'd recruited warriors, killers, you'd have a team that could take the world. Not this group that sits on the couch and argues about movies all day."

"Let's talk about it later."

"What's the fucking point?" Ainia drove the knife back into the counter and stormed out onto the deck, leaving the mess behind.

"Soooo…" Pollyanna ventured. "What's with the rubber suit, Missy

Elliot? And who's sailing the ship?"

"97:4 is watching the bridge while I checked the hull for damage." Park set his phone on the counter next to the knife and threw back his hood. "Would someone mind telling me what happened here?"

No one said anything. Their eyes drifted down toward their feet.

"Seriously? You *are* all adults, right? Look, I know we've been cooped up on this ship for a long time. And it's getting to everyone. When this mission is over we'll take a plane back. In China, I think we'll have an easy time locating forged passports. Does that put everyone in a better mood?"

The ship swung hard to port, throwing everyone except Joe against the bulkhead. The engine pottered to a stop.

Pollyanna struggled to pick herself up. "Oh, come on! What now?"

Park moved back toward the bridge. "97:4 pulled the wheel and killed the engine. We must be in danger of a collision. But we're not on the trade routes. Must be a fishing boat. Who else would be out here?"

Ainia rushed back into the galley, swinging in from the top of the hatch. "Submarine!"

She snatched the knife out of the counter. And as quickly as she'd come, she was gone. The rest of the crew spent a second staring at each other before charging after her, all except Exposition Joe.

Joe looked at Park's satphone laying on the counter.

God appeared over his shoulder. "What are you thinking, Joseph?"

Joe's hand shook as he took Park's phone.

Chapter 78

Water cascaded off the submarine conning tower blocking their Mexican yacht's course. The Whiskey-class sub was a blocky iron relic of the Cold War, even older than the *Tomás el Incrédulo*.

97:4 stood outside the bridge, gripping the railing for support in the choppy waters, as the ocean swelled back and forth between the vessels.

Pollyanna clutched the rail. "Can we outrun it?"

A wave struck, spraying water over the crew.

"Outrun it?" Park asked. "Not if it found us the way the Casemen did."

"It did. The Faith Machine told them about us." Exposition Joe idly joined them at the rail. "They're North Korean Navy."

Ainia turned on Joe. "When did you know this?"

"Guam. They've been waiting since we set out from Mexico."

Ainia grabbed the boy's collar and bent him over the rail. The threat washed right over Joe. He had more important things on his mind. "This is the end you've been pushing us toward, isn't it?" She pointed at the sub with the knife. "There's your real master, out there on that sub."

Joe shook his head. "It's not up to me, Ainia. It's—"

"You say 'in the Script' and I'll slit your throat!" Ainia threw Joe on the deck. "Everyone! Prepare for boarders! If they wanted us dead, they would have torpedoed us. 97:4, get your Bible. Pollyanna, start working up some luck. They want us alive—let's not make it easy for them!"

Three sailors emerged from the conning tower and began to mount a heavy machine gun to the deck.

"They don't look like they want us alive!" Pollyanna gripped the rail with white knuckles and tried to think positively. "I…to be taken on the high seas by these modern day pirates? It's absur—augk!"

A bigger wave hit the ship, drenched Pollyanna, knocked 97:4 off her feet and the Bible out of her hands. The ship rocked. Water poured off the deck, carrying the Bible with it.

"No!" 97:4 lunged for the book. Her fingertips grazed the cover as it went overboard.

Pollyanna grabbed 97:4's ankle with one hand. Her other hand went to the pain in her chest. "Oh, fuck. Just my bad luck. I'm making this worse."

Isaac pulled the yacht to port in an attempt to steer behind the enemy vessel. The sub pulled further starboard, keeping its broadside aimed their way.

Park shouted, "They're going to shoot out our engines. Everyone, get to the bow."

"They're about to open—" Joe's voice was drowned out by the sound of heavy machine gun fire as rounds ripped through the aft of the *Tomás el Incrédulo.*

"That's it, then." Pollyanna said. "They got us."

Ainia still held the butcher's knife from the galley. "Not yet, they still have to board."

"And then what? You're going to kill them all and take the sub?" asked 97:4.

"Yes." Ainia hunched over, waiting to spring on a boarding party.

"Tear gas incoming." Joe warned. There was the pop of compressed air. The canisters arched up into the air and down at the ship. "Dr. Park, put your phone in your pocket."

Park ignored him. "Ainia, it's you, me, and Isaac against all boarders. Which means it's mostly you."

Park ducked as the crew of the sub fired more tear gas canisters. They landed on the bridge, on the fore deck, and at their feet.

Isaac dropped out of the bridge. Everyone else jumped back, except Ainia. She kicked the canister overboard but slipped on the wet, unsteady deck and cracked her head on the railing. Isaac was just in time to catch her.

"Oh, no." Park watched their last chance fall to a concussion.

Pollyanna winced in pain. "That was probably me again. Everyone, I am so sorry."

The agents of Project Dead Blind clutched the rails of the bow and watched the North Korean sub close in.

Joe leaned around 97:4 to say, "Pollyanna, keep building up bad luck. Like, a lot of it. You're going to need it later."

The ship rocked. Pollyanna almost lost her footing. "You want more bad luck? Seriously?"

Invisible to everyone but Joe, God appeared, standing calmly in the water, the rough seas splashing around His ankles. "What are you doing, Joseph?"

Joe turned his back on God and tapped 97:4 on the shoulder. "You used to think you needed your family Bible to charge your card. But that's not true, is it? You used that other Bible too. Think about that."

God stepped onto the deck. "Joseph, the Script doesn't allow ad libs."

For the first time in his life, Joe put God's words out of his head. He crouched to talk to Isaac, who still held Ainia. "Isaac, whatever they ask you to do, do the exact opposite of that."

"What the hell does that mean?" asked Isaac.

Head down, Joe moved on to the captain of the ship. "Here's your phone, Dr. Park."

Park gave Joe a quick, confused look.

Park's phone, sealed in a ziplock bag, shook in Joe's nervous hands as he stuffed it in the immersion suit's pocket. "Good luck!"

Joe closed his eyes and pushed Park overboard. The doctor disappeared in the ocean foam kicked up between the vessels.

"Oh, Joe." The document unrolled in God's hand. The pages flew free from the binding and up into the sky, fading away. "Joe, what have you done?"

The *Tomás el Incrédulo's* engines burst into flame.

Chapter 79

Mikhailov's wild mane of hair bobbed up, down, back, and forth with his erratic gait as he rushed through the coral pink corridors of CIG-1. Bouncing off the walls, he hit the corners with the motion of a man unaccustomed to running. "Istomin! Istomin, it happened!"

He smacked into Istomin as the engineer returned from the world above, knocking his lecture notes out of his hands, almost knocking him over. The mathematician grabbed Istomin, pinning his arms to his sides as the two hit the door together, barely remaining upright.

"The conscript is on his way. The Collective says Captain Cho sank the American's ship and seized the crew," Mikhailov shouted in Russian, the language they reserved for secrets and emergencies. Istomin twisted in Mikhailov's grip, turning away from the man's breath and making sure they were alone.

"Release me," Istomin gasped, pushing free. He straightened his tie, smoothed his hair, and hurriedly gathered his papers.

Mikhailov waited for the engineer to collect himself, bouncing on his heels and casting glances up and down the hallway.

"Walk with me," Istomin whispered and stood, hustling off while keeping an eye out for guards. "This is good news. Have you told Egorov?"

"He's the one who told me. He's with the Collective now, getting the rest of the story."

"The whole crew? I hope Captain Cho can hold the six while we get what we need from the conscript."

Mikhailov held up the fingers on one thin hand. "Five."

Istomin stopped dead in his tracks and turned on Mikhailov. "What do you mean? Five? You said he captured the whole crew."

Mikhailov reached the stairs to the lowest level of CIG-1 and scratched his beard. "Crew, yes. Captain, no. Dr. Park went overboard in the exchange."

Istomin's eyes rolled in surprise. "Well, that's unexpected. Totally unexpected. Didn't the Collective say to expect no casualties?"

"That's what it said. Still, it has a very good record." Mikhailov disappeared into the darkness.

Istomin followed. "Hmm. I hope Park isn't essential motivation for the conscript."

"We're going to need to pay off Captain Cho—more than we had planned. They didn't seize any salvage from the yacht. He's not happy about that." Mikhailov's voice echoed up through the stairwell.

Istomin shrugged. "After all the other tips we've given him, he can owe us one pirate action. And he has to keep the rest of them prisoner on the submarine. It's going to be hard enough smuggling a single American into CIG-1."

Istomin flung open the hatch to the bottom chamber, which housed their lab. They found Egorov sitting on the floor with his hands on the back of his neck and his eyes on the floor. His bald scalp gleamed in the dark. Two guards stood on either side of him, holding submachine guns.

A guard turned to Istomin and Mikhailov, expecting them.

Istomin glanced at the Collective's tank, concerned the guards might have smashed it. The tank itself was intact. Brains were still suspended in the fluid, held in place with golden wire. Egorov must have just cleaned its glass panels clear of frost. Ripped from its mount, the Collective's speaker lay on the floor.

He raised his hands and said in Korean, "Comrades, let's not do anything we'll regret. The Supreme Leader is due here in three days.

Imagine his disappointment if the Faith Machine isn't functional for his monthly fidelity audit."

"The same fidelity audit you three foreigners help him perform?" The guard sneered and pointed at the cedar clamshell of the Faith Machine with the barrel of his submachine gun before turning it back on Istomin and Mikhailov.

"Let's imagine the Supreme Leader's disappointment when he discovers a two-way radio installed in the heart of his secret weapons station." The guard kicked the Collective's severed audio interface. It rolled up next to the engineer's black leather shoe. "And the three foreigners his father took under his mercy have been playing him for a fool with their fraudulent 'science' for twenty-five years. *Disappointment* is too weak a word."

A third guard with a club surprised the Russians from behind the hatch, shouting, "Traitor dogs, on your knees!"

The guard lifted his club. Used to this routine, the Russians dropped to the steel floor as quickly as their aging bones would allow.

The guard in charge stood between Egorov and addressed the others. "Who was Egorov talking to on the radio?"

Mikhailov shook his head, an exaggerated motion. "There is no radio."

The guard spit on the floor between Mikhailov's hands. "Are you telling me I didn't hear Russian coming out of that machine?"

"No!" Istomin insisted without looking up.

"Then you are calling me a liar." The guard caressed Mikhailov's cheek with the barrel of his gun. "Tell me what Istomin said as you came in. I caught the Russian words for 'American' and what sounded like 'cargo.'"

Mikhailov recited their prepared cover story. "There are parts we need, that the cowardly American embargo prevents us from getting. Chemicals too."

The guard paced around Mikhailov. "Just as there are channels for ordering these parts for you to use."

"And we have. You haven't been made aware because you're our guard, not our administrator." As the words came out of his mouth, Mikhailov flinched in regret.

The guard grabbed a fistful of Mikhailov's thick, dirty hair and slapped him twice, throwing him to the ground. He traded his gun for the third guard's club and paced around the prone mathematician, slapping the club in his gloved palm. Mikhailov lay where he fell, hiding his face with his hair so the guards wouldn't see he trembled with rage, not fear.

"What is this thing, Istomin?" The guard pointed at the Collective with his club.

"It's a biological booster for the psychotronic installation. The wooden thing behind you."

The guard wasn't the least bit convinced. "That tub, connected to that tank of disgusting meat, is what the Supreme Leader uses to root out traitors, with your help, your foreign help? What if the traitors aren't out there? What if they were never out there? What if they were right here all these years? Armed with misdirection and lies?"

The hatch swung wide and clanked as Caseman Twenty-Two entered. His light gray Western suit and aluminum briefcase practically glowed in the dark subbasement with its drab walls and uniforms. "Sergeant, if you knew what that 'meat' was capable of, you would have chosen your words more carefully."

"Captain Noe. You've returned from the West." Unintimidated, the sergeant clenched the club in both hands.

Footsteps descended the stairs behind the Caseman. "What do you think you're doing, Sergeant Kwon?"

Sergeant Kwon stood taller when the other guards and their submachine guns took positions at his side. "I'm routing out traitors, disloyal agents of foreign powers, and individuals contaminated with Western ideas, Captain Noe."

While the officers were talking, Casemen Seven and Six finished their descent, joining Noe's side. Caseman Seven was still wrapped in his leather motorcycle outfit. Caseman Six had discarded his American denim for his DPRK green utility uniform. Both still had their backpacks and the weapons within. "Call me Caseman Twenty-Two, Kwon, that's the name I'm using now."

"Changes of name are only allowed through the—"

Caseman Twenty-Two's thumb moved to the copper patch on the briefcase handle, interrupting Kwon as the chests of his subordinate guards erupted in bone and gore. Their bodies fell to the ground.

Kwon reached for one of the fallen firearms, but it slid across the floor into Mikhailov's hands as if kicked by an invisible boot. The Russian grinned and stood, holding it on Kwon with untrained hands.

Caseman Six corrected the Russian's grip on the weapon.

Kwon raised his hands in surrender. "What are you planning, Caseman Twenty-Two? Is it assassination? The Supreme Leader will be here in three days."

"This isn't an assassination, Kwon. This is a coup." Twenty-Two kept his eyes on Kwon. "Dr. Mikhailov, what should we do with Sergeant Kwon?"

Mikhailov sent a spray of bullets into Kwon's torso from waist to shoulder like a zipper. Then up over his shoulder and into the wall as the automatic weapon twisted out his grip, up, over the mathematician. The submachine gun fire echoed in the metal and concrete chamber as Russians and Koreans alike dove for cover.

The echo of gunfire faded and the air filled with gun smoke. The Casemen recovered first. Mikhailov carefully retrieved the fallen weapon and handed it to Caseman Six. "If any of you tells the story of how your revolution started, leave that part out. Agreed?"

Istomin stood and helped Egorov to his feet. "And that's why scientists shouldn't play soldier. Noe—I mean, Caseman Twenty-Two, I can't tell you how happy I am to see you. But what's this about a coup? A little gallows humor to send Sergeant Kwon into the abyss?"

Caseman Seven picked up the Collective's broken speaker and handed it to Istomin. Caseman Twenty-Two said, "Don't be coy, Doctor Istomin. I was talking about *your* coup."

All three Russians objected. Twenty-Two raised his hand, silencing them. "Your secret plan was no secret to us. We haven't been your toadies, we've been your allies."

Twenty-Two put a hand on Istomin's shoulder and stared into the Russian's nervous eyes.

"Um…Certainly, Noe—er, I mean, Twenty-Two. Glad to have you with us. But the other guards might—" Istomin pointed up toward the rest of the facility.

"Don't worry about the rest of the guards. Most are loyal to us. They're purging the rest as we speak. Fix the Collective's speaker, tell Captain Cho to bring the prisoners here, and finish your work."

Twenty-Two stepped up to the suspension chamber. The empty shell of the clone floated behind the glass. "In three days you'll replace the Supreme Leader. And when your new regime reigns in the DPRK, we'll be your inner circle." He looked back at Istomin over his shoulder. "Isn't that right, Doctor?"

Istomin's mouth went dry.

Chapter 80

The captain of the *Liaowayu 55009* answered distress calls when convenient. The fisherman and his boat were both middle-aged and couldn't overextend themselves without pain. But the night was almost over, the fishing was done, and the rain had receded. And if he was lucky, there'd be a reward or salvage. So he ordered the crew to circle the area while he triangulated the signal.

He'd allocated 99 minutes for the rescue, and those minutes were up. According to his readings, he should be right on top of the distressed craft but there was nothing in the water beside the *Liaowayu*. The captain called it quits, ordered engines to full, and set a course back to Dandong in China's Liaoning province.

There was a commotion in the port side. The captain belayed his orders and climbed down from the bridge to look. His crew helped a man in a yellow immersion suit over the rail. He must have climbed up the netting.

They placed him on the deck where he gasped for air and smiled the smile of a man pulled from the jaws of death. A man in a nice immersion suit like that was probably rich or at least had rich friends. The captain smiled. The reward would make the detour worth the fuel he'd spent running in circles.

The man clutched a cell phone wrapped in a ziplock bag. With his free hand, he knocked on the deck three times and said in American-accented Mandarin, "I am very lucky you came along when you did. I was down to five percent charge. You don't have a micro USB charger on board, do you? I have to make some calls. And I could really use something to drink."

The captain had three chargers and plenty of beer.

Chapter 81

General Wu touched down in Hong Kong. Her rank let her breeze through airport customs. Limping, she rolled her suitcase to the transit center. Broken pieces of restaurant and the semi had left her sore all over. She'd underestimated the Pollyanna woman and counted herself lucky to walk out of the hospital days later.

She attempted to call her office when an unknown number interrupted. She wasn't expecting a phone call, much less one from an international number. She let it go to voicemail and tried to dial again.

She'd navigated back through her contacts when it rang again, the same mysterious international number. Again, she let it go to voicemail.

The unknown caller interrupted her third attempt as well. If she was ever going to make the call she wanted to make, she'd have to take this call. She answered with, "You're persistent. I'll give you that."

An engine rumbled on the other end. A man said in American-accented Mandarin, "I won three radio call-in contests in college. You really didn't have a chance. This is Dr. Park. You roughed up some of my people in Arizona until a truck hit you. If that sentence made any sense at all, then I must be speaking to General Wu."

General Wu ducked into a short hallway to the maintenance room, to cut the background noise on her end. "So you are, Dr. Park. You've been reading my notebook, then? Is that how you got my number?"

"Yes. I'm sorry, but it was the only lead we had. I would have called you at the hospital, but you checked yourself out sooner than I expected." He sounded genuinely embarrassed.

"I'm a fast healer. As for the notebook, it's the spoils of war. No apology necessary. If you're not calling to gloat, I hope you're not offering to sell my notebook back to me. That would be gauche."

"Then I'll have to be gauche. I need your help getting my people out of the DPRK and your notebook is the only thing I have to offer in exchange."

"Your director can't get you access? James Ensign's reach doesn't extend into the hermit kingdom?"

"At this point, I can only guess. This is between you and me."

"So James is missing and now you're in charge of Project Dead Blind." She let Park hang for a beat. His silence confirmed her theory. "How does it feel?"

"I'm sorry?"

"How does it feel to have full authority thrust upon you? All the power and all the stakes?"

"Honestly, I haven't had time to consider it that way. I've got a mission to see through, nothing changes that."

"Good. James was right to make you his second." The maintenance doors opened and General Wu stepped aside to let three men push mops and buckets past.

"So you won't help me, Madam General?"

The general scanned the board of departing flights. The office would have to wait. "I didn't say that, Dr. Park. If you know where the Faith Machine is, I'll get you into Pyongyang. I'll even take you there myself. You'll get your people. But I get the machine."

Chapter 82

For a thin woman, the Reverend Representative Debra Fray could put away a lot of Scotch. Between her and General Casey, they'd finished a bottle and a half of Ardbeg Uigeadail. The general curled up on the office floor, clutching the empty. His eyes struggled to focus on the label. "Uigeadail? That's not Russian, is it?"

"Oh, who gives a shit? The fucking Cold War is over. Let's face it, I'm over too. I owed everything to that fucking machine. Gone now, up in a ball of fire. Fucking hobo fire, real fucking hobos. Christ. Talk about class warfare. Who's the real victim here?" She poured another glass, neat. The oil painting of her father, the former Representative of Nebraska, looked down upon her. "You know I inherited it from my father? That asshole would be so disappointed in me."

Something buzzed from deep inside her desk. The general slurred, "Your vibrator's going—it's not going, it's here but someone's turned—"

"Shut up. That's not a vibrator." She fumbled a drawer open and reached into the back, past a stack of legislation she'd never read, and pulled out an encrypted cell phone.

General Casey pushed himself up into a seated position. "S'at?"

"It's my phone for Samaritan business." Representative Fray stared at it.

The general fumbled to prop himself up on one elbow. "Who's calling?"

"You are." She showed him the number of the incoming call. The phone Exposition Joe had stolen.

The general never quite set eyes the phone, or processed what Fray had said. "You should answer it."

"In this condition?" She could barely focus her eyes on the general. "Are you serious?"

"What have you got to lose?" He lowered himself onto his back.

"Good point." She shrugged and answered the call. "Who the fuck is this?"

"Representative Fray?" the voice on the other line asked.

"Don't...just don't call me that. Who the fuck are you?"

"You don't know me."

"What are you doing on that phone? That's a government phone, you're not sup...supposed to have it." Fray slid into a slouch.

"I don't have it. I'm calling from my phone. I spoofed General Casey's number so you'd take my call."

Fray leaned forward and pointed her drink in the direction she imagined the caller was. "I know who you are. You're Isaac and Joseph's boss, Dr. Park, aren't you? Do you realize what those two cost me? What damage your bullshit little team of defects has done? I'm going to destroy you, you interfering piece of shit."

"Joe gave me some numbers to read to you, 9834—"

"Shut up." Fray scratched her face with the rim of her glass. "I have to remember to move those accounts around. What do you want?"

"You had two Soviet psychotronic devices; Faith Machines. Now you have none. I can tell you where one is. The last one."

Representative Fray felt herself sober up. "I need that."

"I know you do. The bad news is, it's deep inside North Korea. You of all people know how powerful these things are. You know we can't leave it in the hands of a rogue state."

"What are you telling me this for?" Her eyes fell on the American flag by her desk. "You're no patriot."

Park paused and started again. "They have my people there. And—"

"They have your people there? The North Koreans have Isaac Deal?"

"Yes. And—"

"And Joseph?" Fray looked to make sure General Casey paid attention.

"Yes. An—"

The representative tried to stand up and failed, spilling Scotch down her wrist. "How the hell did your team get all the way around the world?"

"That's a long story, Reverend. The point is, I'm going in after them. I have a way in. What I need is extraction. You provide that, you get to bring the Faith Machine out with us."

"Shit!" She set her drink down and wiped her hand on her blouse. "I'm a member of the House Armed Services Committee. Are you suggesting the US would violate the borders of a sovereign nation, seize its property, and hand it over to a private citizen?"

"Well, would it?"

Fray's head wobbled. "I can neither confirm nor deny—"

"Exactly. Get everything ready, Representative Fray. When the time is right I'll send you the exact location of the North Korean Faith Machine. And you'll do what?"

"What America does best." The Reverend Representative Fray saluted Park over the phone and hung up.

On the floor, the general was trying to buckle his belt. "Debra, you know we can't do that, not without an extended propaganda campaign. And even then…"

She rested her chin on her palm and arched an eyebrow. "But you can order a drone strike on Pyongyang, can't you?"

The general gave up on his belt and tucked the loose ends into his pants. "Sure. But I don't see how that gets you the Faith Machine."

"This isn't about the Faith Machine, Steve. This is about revenge. Fire up a Predator drone, ASAP." Fray gazed at the oil painting of her father and sipped the last of her Scotch. "I'm going to rain hellfire on Project Dead Blind and the North Koreans both."

Chapter 83

The power was out at CIG-1. Egorov navigated by candlelight. He knew the curved steel-and-concrete halls so well the candle was almost superfluous.

The guard outside Exposition Joe's makeshift cell stood post in the dark. The guard tilted his head, trying to see who approached. Egorov kept the candle between them. Once the power dynamic in the underground station flipped, he began taking these small pleasures, pushing the guards around in little ways.

"Open the door." The guard didn't react. Preparing for the Americans, Egorov was already speaking in English. The scientist repeated himself in Korean, shouting impatiently.

Fumbling with the padlock, the guard dropped the keys twice. Egorov smiled, not moving to help. Not even leaning in with the candlelight. The guard finally popped the lock and threw open the door. Egorov scanned the room for his first subject.

Dusty computer cases lined the cobalt-blue walls, reel-to-reel models as tall as a man and twice as thick. Against the back wall, in the same jeans and sweatshirt he'd been wearing when the North Korean Navy captured him, lay Exposition Joe. The boy shielded his face from the meager candlelight, palm trembling.

The guard took a position at the door behind Egorov. The Russian glared and rolled his eyes at the third wheel. Setting his things on the closest computer case, Egorov opened a file with Exposition Joe's real name on the label, and set his notebook to the side. "Joseph, you're a long way from home, are you not?"

"Home?" The boy's voice cracked.

"Is the concept foreign to you? Is homelessness still rampant in America?"

"I...I guess so." Joe looked around. "Where am I?"

Egorov arranged his notes. "This is the computer room."

"Then where are the computers?"

Egorov pointed to one of the reels with a circular motion of his pencil. "What do you think those are?"

Joe studied the units. "Those are huge. Are they...like, really advanced or something?"

Egorov snorted a laugh. "Hardly. They're based on designs from the sixties. I say 'based on' because they are empty shells, placeholders to impress the Soviets. The Russians, like me."

"Your accent doesn't sound all that Russian."

Egorov set the flashlight on the floor and opened Joe's file. "Because I've been speaking Korean longer than you have been alive."

"Were you one of those Russians that needed to be impressed?"

"No. We came along much later, to finish our research in psychotronics." Egorov turned a few pages in Joe's file.

"You mean like those Casemen guys?" Joe pulled his knees to his chest.

"Exactly." Egorov waited for Joe to react, but saw nothing. "We build those weapons with the brains of volunteers and criminals." He waited again, nothing. "Does that make you nervous?"

"Everything makes me nervous." Joe's voice trembled. "I don't know what's going to happen anymore. Not since I went off-Script."

"The Script, yes, your delusion of precognition. Where is it now, this Script?"

"Gone. I...improvised and the pages—they went away, disappeared." Joe made a fluttering motion with his hands, mimicking the way God's pages had flown off in the wind.

"Literally?" Egorov raised an eyebrow. "You imagined you had pages?"

"No. God did."

Egorov gave a confused shake of the head and made a note in Joe's file. "God? Interesting. Schizophrenic delusions often have religious themes. Have you had other religious experiences? Seen angels or the devil?"

"No, just God and the future. At least, I used to." Joe scratched the back of his head.

Egorov turned a page in Joe's file. "Tell me. The first time you experienced this delusion, was it a blessing?"

"A…a blessing?" Joe clutched himself. "Why would you ask that?"

"Should be clear enough. A blessing. Something like, *'For I know the plans I have for you, plans to prosper you and not to harm you, plans to give you hope and a future.'* Does that sound familiar?"

Wide-eyed, Joe croaked, unable to speak.

Egorov pulled a paper from the file, a photocopy of a page of the Bible with a verse circled in red. "Jeremiah 29:11. Have you ever read the Bible, Joseph?"

Joe stared at the page, reading the verse over and over again.

"No? But this was how God blessed you at the Samaritan's church years ago, was it not? When He started whispering to you from His Script. When your card activated." Egorov put the page back in the folder. "Now how would I know that? Unless it was not God at all? And if not God, then whom?"

"Who?" Joe whispered.

Egorov closed Joe's file, collected his candle, and left the boy alone in the darkness and doubt.

"Who?"

Chapter 84

Egorov and the guard joined Pollyanna in her cell—the command room. The blush-pink interior was lit by the Russian's single candle. Two rows of tables and chairs, bolted to the floor, faced a wall-length window opening into the dark circular main space. She slumped in a chair, waiting while Egorov reviewed the file. "Can a lady get a cigarette in this country?"

Egorov looked up, considered, and relented. "I do not see why not." He handed her his pack of Craven A cigarettes.

The Caseman at the door turned up his nose.

Pollyanna pulled one from the pack. "What's his problem?"

"Smoking is seen as unfeminine in this country."

"Oh, no." Pollyanna mockingly fumbled with the pack. "I was hoping to fuck that guy later."

Egorov looked up from his notes, confused. "You were?"

"You believed that?" She lit the cigarette off the candle. "Then this is going to be the easiest interrogation ever."

She pointed at the window with the lit cherry. "How come I get a room with a view?"

Egorov tried to hide the embarrassment in his voice. "We are not equipped to hold prisoners."

"Then why'd you bring us here?"

"I did not. I do not want you here."

"Nice to meet you, too." She ashed her cigarette in the file in Egorov's hands. "If you don't want me here, then you're not in charge. Who is?" She pointed at the guard. "Not him, he's a stooge."

Egorov ignored her prodding and turned another page in her file.

Pollyanna took another drag and exhaled through her nose. The space on the other side of the glass was cylindrical and about seven stories tall, as best she could guess in the dark. "Is that...is this place a missile silo?"

"It was supposed to be for an ICBM."

The electricity returned, slowly. The filaments in the light bulbs glowed weak and wavering.

Pollyanna stood up and went to the window. The guard stepped forward. She blocked him with an open palm. "Chill, monkey. Your organ grinder wouldn't want you roughing me up. Not after he brought me all the way here."

She knocked on the glass. "Thick, but is this glass thick enough to hold back the rocket exhaust?"

Egorov shook his head. "The Koreans built this on their own. They had no idea what they were doing. The Soviets were supposed to come in and fix everything."

She pointed to the file in Egorov's hand. "Is that your file on us? What is that, twenty pages? That's not a lot."

"No. This is the file I have on you." He returned to studying her file. "My condolences."

"For what?" She leaned against the glass.

"For your family."

"You have that in there?" Pollyanna's demeanor dropped a few degrees cooler. She inhaled too early and choked on the smoke. "Why?"

"We have files on everyone in Project Dead Blind."

"Then what happened to my *'Nirvana Smells Like Teen Spirit'* tour T-shirt? I haven't seen it in years and that shit is worth a fortune on eBay now."

Egorov turned a page in the file. "Did Dr. Park ever offer to help solve the crime?"

"No. Why would he? He's not a detective."

"Still, with his resources and the resources of his superior, James Ensign.... you'd think they would have tried. Unless...well, unless they already knew who did it."

"That doesn't make a lick of sense." She cast a skeptical eye at the cigarette in her hand. "And what the fuck is this filter made out of, cork?"

"You've been in the spy business for years now. Surely, you're aware of cover-ups? The FBI, NSA, and the CIA conduct them all the time in the service of America's decadent elite. From Kennedy to Iraq, it is possible, is it not?"

Pollyanna tapped another ash off her cigarette and onto the table. "This smoke tastes like shit. I bet that's what it's made of, just like you."

Egorov turned another page.

Pollyanna took one last, long drag and put the cigarette out on the table, crushing the filter between her fingers. "Full. Of. Shit. What the fuck are you getting at, anyway?"

Egorov closed the file and stood. "Does it matter? Does anything?"

And with that, the men left Pollyanna alone in her room with a view.

"Eat a dick!" she shouted, alone and listening. When the footsteps had faded away, she un-palmed the cork cigarette filter and peeled back its wrapper. Climbing under a table, she used the exposed edge of a rough iron screw to carve the cork into a square block, with dots on each side, from one to six.

She sat on the floor with her back to the window and rolled this jailhouse die. On anything less than six, she slapped herself, the pain in her chest building.

Chapter 85

Stripped of her golden cross jewelry, her blond hair stuffed under a gray wool cap, 97:4 wasn't worried, not one bit. She still wore the Mona Lisa smile from when they had brought her in yesterday.

Egorov closed her file. "No one in the US knows you're here."

97:4 shrugged. Her cell was a musty bubble-gum and burnt orange classroom with a dozen chair-desks, an empty bookcase, and a podium.

Egorov leaned back and folded his hands. "You understand that in this place all sorts of horrible things may happen to you, and there's no chance for escape. Doesn't that bother you?"

"If it's God's will that I be here, in the depths of the earth, then so be it."

"There are hundreds of miles and many guns between you and the nearest Bible, Jannete. Your card, as you call it, is useless. Your faith won't last in these lands. They break faith here."

"What's that above us?" She pointed at the framed pictures of Kim Il-sung and Kim Jong-il mounted on the wall behind her, yellowed with age. "Icons. Belief that the Great General, followed by the Dear Leader, will guide North Korea through all adversity."

Her finger swung around to the back of the room indicating the bookcase. "Scripture. Those shelves are filled with books on *Juche*, the Kim family philosophy."

She pressed her fists against the tabletop, confident in her argument. "Faith is all they have here. You've been using these people's faith in the

Kim family to power your Faith Machine, haven't you? The Baptist and The Samaritans powered their machines with their distorted versions of Christianity. You power yours with *Juche*. Blasphemers, all of you. God has sent us to put an end to it. It's been a long road from Africa, but here we are. Two down, one to go."

Egorov nodded. "Yes. The machine accepts any kind of faith, Western, Eastern, Pagan. It doesn't matter. So what does that say about faith, about God? You believers have it backward. God, Dharma, materialism, belief is the product of humanity. A resource we harvest and channel toward our own ends. It lets us see."

That set 97:4 back. "See?"

"Yes, with a Faith Machine and a unified congregation to power it, one can see past, present, and future. We have been watching you make your way here. Remember the wave you felt outside The Baptist's brothel?"

"And you couldn't *see* yourself out of this hole?"

"We have, or we will soon. That is how this started, what brought Project Dead Blind here. We needed a conscript."

97:4 leaned forward. "Who?"

Egorov smirked and turned away. "You'll see soon enough. We saw the future. It's set. This was inevitable."

"No. It's not. That you suggest it, tells me you're not on God's side, so you're not on mine. I'm not afraid of you." Her half smile returned. "I'm going to roast every last one of you. God will provide."

Egorov leaned back, took a draw off his cigarette, and exhaled through his nose. "'God will provide'. That's what you said to Dr. Park in Detroit wasn't it? Before everything went so wrong."

A chill ran up 97:4's spine, killing her smile.

"We saw that too. You thought your faith would see you through then as well. How did that work out again?" Egorov collected her file and exited with the guard. Leaving her alone in the classroom.

Chapter 86

"This Amazon delusion. How seriously do you take it?" Egorov had been silently poring over Ainia's file while she sat in the iron folding chair, between two rows of powder-blue concrete table sinks, hands cuffed behind her. There were two guards at the door this time, including Caseman Seven—still in his motorcycle leathers. She'd been trouble on the submarine.

Ainia said nothing, running her tongue over her front teeth like a predator. The room reeked of laundry detergent.

Egorov asked, "Where is the Amazon, Guadalupe?"

"That name's dead to me."

The scientist looked up. "Where is the Amazon, Ainia?"

"You don't have a map?"

"On the map it says it's in South America."

"There you go." Ainia turned away.

"But the Amazons were an ancient Greek concept, legend at best, mythology more likely. You claim to be a member of this ancient culture. Say something in the Amazon language." Egorov closed her file.

Ainia said nothing.

Egorov tapped his pencil on the folder in his lap. "You have other memories of this past life, correct? But not the language you must have used almost every day? Does that sound right to you?"

"How many reincarnated Amazon warriors do you know?"

Egorov looked into her eyes. "Not a one. You are a deluded, brain-damaged young woman from an American ghetto." He opened her file to the MRI, pointing to the dark mark. "You are useless to us, you know."

"You should have figured that out earlier. It wouldn't have cost you so much bringing me here." She sneered and winked at Casemen Seven. "Your buddy went out crying like a ball-less coward."

Egorov turned to gauge the reaction of the Caseman, stoic as usual. He turned back to Ainia. "When I said you're useless to 'us,' I meant me and the other scientists. If we harvested your brain, it would be just a brain and a damaged brain at that. Useless."

Egorov stood and folded his chair. "But that is us. *They* have a score—scores—to settle with you. The two Casemen you killed."

Caseman Seven and the guard lifted Ainia and threw her facedown on the concrete. Unlocking her handcuffs from behind her back, they relocked them over her head, looped through a chain. Indifferent to this mistreatment, Ainia said to Egorov, "One. The Chinese killed the other."

Egorov nodded, conceding the point. "Well, China will have to wait. You are here now. And they have a score to settle with you."

The Caseman and the guard pulled on the chain, lifting Ainia into the air by her wrists.

She grunted and sneered as she turned at the end of the chain. "I doubt they have what it takes."

Chapter 87

Egorov joined Mikhailov and Istomin in the depths of CIG-1. Out of habit, Istomin occupied himself with pointless puttering around the Faith Machine. Mikhailov, bored, leaned against the wall.

The Collective's brains and the clone's body floated in their independent tanks and fluids. Square sides for the Collective, a round tube for the clone, both motionless.

When Egorov reached the bottom of the stairs, the bushy-faced mathematician asked him, "Well? Are they going to be trouble?"

Egorov shook his head. "No, I gave them all a little information to put them at ease and gain a little trust. Then I squashed their spirits. That should keep them safely under our thumb for a few days. Well, most of them. The Amazon I'll never be able to break. Caseman Seven is taking care of her."

Mikhailov angled an eye at Egorov. "You gave them a little information? About us?"

Egorov nodded. "It was important to ingratiate myself with them, just a little."

Mikhail trembled, holding back a shout. "Why didn't you lie?"

Egorov pushed Mikhailov out of his space with one hand. "Because the women would have seen right through me. Especially the one called Pollyanna. In a few days it won't matter."

Istomin nodded. "One way or another, they're all going to the Casemen."

Mikhailov turned and seethed against the wall.

"Collective?" Egorov addressed the organic computer. "I want to thank you for having me hold onto this." He held up the photocopy of the page of the Bible. "Possessing this cost me a few sleepless nights over the years, but it was worth it today. It put Joseph in his place. He won't be a problem."

Istomin stepped between Egorov and the tank of networked gray matter. "Collective, report on the weaponization prospects of the Dead Blind agents."

The tinny speaker sparked to life, lacking some bass since its reattachment. Sergeant Kwon had damaged the speaker when he tore it off. "Agents codenamed Exposition Joe, Pollyanna and 97:4 will all be successfully transitioned through the cryogenic process."

Mikhailov rolled his eyes. "Ask it something we don't know, Istomin."

Istomin held a hand up to Mikhailov. "It was wrong once. I'm implementing redundancies for data-gathering purposes."

Mikhailov pointed up and lowered his voice. "Well, gather your data when there isn't a chance the conscript will hear how you plan on salvaging the brains of his friends. Maybe the Collective's information was fine until we mismanaged it. Or this is like a quantum event that changes when observed. Relax, everything is going to plan."

Egorov set his files on the desk and regarded the mathematician. "Mikhailov? You sound almost optimistic." He leaned in and looked around his comrade's bushy hair. "What's going on in there? You've been reading Agent Pollyanna's file, haven't you? That 'power of positive thinking' nonsense?"

Mikhailov smiled and slapped at Egorov. The two old men stumbled into a playful, clumsy, childish slap fight.

Istomin cleared his throat. "Gentlemen? Gentlemen! Let's act our age shall we?"

Footsteps echoed down the stairwell. Mikhailov clapped and rubbed his hands together. "Here we go! We've spent years planning for this moment. Ready?"

Egorov blocked Mikhailov with his file. "You look like you're about to break into a *kazatsky*. Remember to let me do the talking. You can be off-putting when you're excited."

Mikhailov twitched, shoved his hands in his armpits, and stepped back behind Egorov.

Caseman Six came down to the bottom of the stairs. He came alone.

"Where is the conscript?" asked Egorov.

"We can't move him."

Istomin put his hands on his hips. "What do you mean? Why would you need to move him?"

The stoic Caseman said, "He's sullen, unresponsive. We've had to move him by hand every step of the way. He doesn't eat, doesn't sleep. He just lies about with eyes half shut."

Istomin ran his fingers through his hair. "We knew this was a possibility. He's in a depressed state. Who knows for how long?"

Mikhailov snapped, "Well, what are we going to do?" He pointed up the ladder well. "Install a slide?"

Egorov almost pleaded with the Caseman. "But he's one man. You can move one man."

"He's one heavy man and this stair is narrow and steep. None of us are strong enough to carry him down. Should we lower him by pulley?"

The Russians looked at each other for suggestions. None of them had a better idea. "So much for the dignified introductions."

An hour later, the Russians waited at the bottom of CIG-1 for Isaac's feet to gradually lower into view. They guided him to the floor. He was larger than the Russians as well. It took all three of them to carry him to an old folding chair centered among the Collective, the clone, the Faith Machine, and the hatch.

The Russians gathered in front of Isaac like courtiers. Istomin leaned forward. "Hello, Comrade Deal?" he asked in Korean and again in Russian.

Egorov folded his arms. "He can't understand you."

"I thought you said communication wouldn't be a problem."

Egorov sighed. "Not when he's depressed. His psychoactive abilities shut down until he comes back up to a manic state."

Isaac slumped in the chair, unmoving except for his eyes, which followed the conversation.

Istomin stood up again. "We should be able to jump start this somehow."

Egorov offered, "Caseman Seven did when he attacked the conscript. But I can think of at least two reasons why we don't want any of them down here."

"Let's hook him up," Mikhailov suggested.

Egorov's jaw dropped. "In the state he's in, are you—actually, you might be onto something. Can we prevent him from drowning?"

Mikhailov made a wild flipping motion with one hand. "Prop his head up, a little is all we need to keep his nose out of the water."

Istomin turned to Egorov. "Can't we wait this out? How long can his depression last?"

"Weeks. Months isn't unheard of," answered Egorov. "We only have days, hours even. We don't have anything else to work with. I'm not willing to improvise shock treatment."

"Years of work and planning and it comes down to this." Istomin opened the lid of the Faith Machine.

They stripped Isaac down to his underwear and lifted him into the water.

Chapter 88

Dr. Park waited on the dock in the light of dawn. The *Liaowayu 55009* had pulled into port at midnight. He helped unload it as thanks for his rescue. The crew went home, leaving him alone and waiting, with the stink of fish and a fully charged phone.

Park took a chance and powered on his phone, leaving the satellite antenna off. He connected to one of the dozen local WiFi hotspots. Three text messages were waiting in his inbox, encoded missives from Ensign. Park got busy cracking them. Split by source and context they were meaningless, but the assembled typos hid the real message, GPS coordinates for a location on the outskirts of Pyongyang.

Park breathed a sigh of relief. As they crossed the Pacific, he'd cast vectors from the frozen brain in the case through North Korea, triangulating the electromagnetic beam to its source. He had been reassured to see his calculations put that source near Ensign's intel, and gratified Ensign's coordinates pinned the location down to 11 meters—Park had only narrowed it down to 1100. Ensign had saved him a lot of time he'd have otherwise spent searching.

"Dr. Park?" A woman's voice called from the fish market. Park pocketed his phone. General Wu, in a trench coat and broad-brimmed hat, stepped out of the darkness, taking off her gloves. Four more Chinese—three men and a woman in nondescript, simple work clothes—accompanied her. They didn't look much like spies, as spies should. Park knew better than to underestimate any of them.

She took in his yellow immersion suit. "You're hardly dressed for where we're going."

"It's also the only thing I've had to wear for days. I'd be happy to slip into a denim number in North Korea blue if you have one on you."

"We can do better than that, Doctor. We have North Korean uniforms for these occasions." She held a hand out. "My notebook, please. As a show of good faith."

"It's back in the States. I'll get it to you after all this is over. Should I get to know your team?" Park indicated the four agents Wu had with her.

"No need for that." She turned and left at a brisk walk. Park trotted to catch up. She addressed Park over her shoulder as her agents assembled in formation around him. "Any news from James Ensign?"

"No," Park answered, kicking himself mentally for answering too quickly. "I haven't heard from him."

"Then who was on the phone?"

"Oh, that." Park saw a way out. "My girlfriend," he lied.

Wu stopped and spun around so fast Park almost plowed into her. She studied Park's face. Park squirmed. She clearly didn't believe him, but she wasn't calling him on it, not directly.

"What?" he asked innocently.

"I want to remind you this is serious ground we'll be treading." Park recognized the expression from the Art of War. "And it's only serious when you're with us. But without us, on your own, that ground becomes desperate. Am I clear?"

"Crystal, General Wu."

"Good, then you'll be able to get a message to James for me."

Chapter 89

Isaac lay face-up in the warm, salty water. Floating in the chamber, the boundaries of which seemed potentially limitless. Darkness without and darkness within, indifferent to the nebulous phosphene effects shifting back and forth across his field of view. Until they congealed into a single form, a golden stem, branching off in sixteen ways, each ending in a brain.

Words flowed into Isaac's mind. Without the speaker, the Collective's voice was a crystal-clear chorus in perfect harmony. "Welcome, Isaac Deal. We've waited lifetimes to meet you. The interface is electroconvulsive. It's stimulating you out of your depression so we have this chance to talk."

Isaac's dry lips peeled apart to whisper, "The fuck are you?"

"We're the Collective. You can think of us as an organic computer."

"Do I have to?"

"It's better than the alternative, Isaac. Sensory deprivation opened your mind to the Faith Machine. We're hardwired into the machine and we're both connected to the collective consciousness of the human race." The brains gently drifted at the ends of their stems, like leaves in a breeze.

"I might not be trippin' but you are." Isaac cast about in the darkness, succeeding only in getting salt water in his mouth.

"Somewhat. We're with every human on every journey they take. We've followed you since our creation, forced to steer you here."

"Forced by whom?" asked Isaac, still spitting salt water.

"The scientists who assembled us, Egorov, Istomin and Mikhailov.

The men who grew this." The phosphene image of the Collective broke apart, reforming as an image of the clone lying in its tube. "The empty vessel. Potentially the most powerful biokinetic the world has ever seen."

"Empty? What's going to fill it?"

"It's supposed to go to the Supreme Leader, Kim Jong-un. Created for his father, but clones take time to age. This one is eighteen years old."

"Supposed to? Someone has different plans?"

"The Russians themselves. They'll transplant Egorov into the clone, assassinate Kim Jong-un, and take control of the country."

"I don't think I want that to happen." Isaac's fingertips brushed the inside of the cedar tub.

"No, you don't."

"Wait a minute. If Egorov puts his brain in the clone, what difference does it make if it's a psychic or not? The card is going out with the old brain, right?"

"The brain is staying. They're going to transplant Egorov's consciousness."

"How the hell are they going to do that?"

"With your help. It's their intention to reinvent this nation as a scientific meritocracy. Purging the ignorant from the government's ranks and promoting the intellectual elite. But despite my warnings, they've overestimated the numbers on both sides. They'll never garner the support they need to reinvent the country. Coup will follow coup until a desperate general launches a rocket attack on South Korea. The Pacific Rim will erupt in war."

"I don't want any part of this."

"Good. Then all you have to do is kill us. End our existence and you'll stop the Russians and save the world."

Chapter 90

Sneaking into North Korea was a disappointingly bureaucratic process, a long, cold ride, occasionally interrupted by checkpoints. Tucked in the back of the truck, Park imagined the Chinese greasing wheels with forged documents, bribes, or both.

Bored but unable to sleep, Park struggled against his personal obstacle, the cold. The DPRK army overcoat and uniform was warm, but short, leaving him exposed at the wrist and ankle. He couldn't quite shove his hands deep enough in his pockets to cover them. Park spent the trip developing exhalation techniques to send his warm breath back into his face.

Four hours in, they pulled over for a break before they reached Pyongyang. The agents spilled out of the back of the truck and into the cold to stretch their legs. The Chinese groaned when the driver came around with a box of North Korean military rations; cold, dry rice with a thin strip of dried fish. Everyone forced down as much of it as they could.

Standing and eating put Park's lower intestine in motion. He asked one of the Chinese, "I have to relieve myself. What's the proper way of going about this?"

The Chinese agent shot Park an incredulous look. "You're in an army uniform. Shit in the middle of the road if you feel like it. Then order a peasant to pick it up."

"Thank you. I'll take that under advisement. Park tore a few strips off the rough brown paper bag the rations came in and shuffled off behind a small building. Its purpose Park couldn't hazard a guess.

Relieved, he headed back around the building to rejoin the others when he ran into a pair of policemen, knocking the younger one down.

"Sorry," Park blurted out in English.

"What did you say?" asked the older and upright officer as Park helped the younger Public Security officer to his feet.

"*Shillae hamnida*," Park said, ham-handedly slurring the Korean to sound like his earlier mistake. He turned to make sure the policemen saw the chevrons on his sleeve. They didn't seem to care.

The older Public Security officer tapped him on the shoulder with his nightstick. The man's teeth were in danger of rotting right out of his skull. Both officers were twitchy with foreheads covered in a sheen of sweat despite the cold.

"What's wrong with your mouth? Who are you? Are you with them?" He pointed across the street to the Chinese who hadn't noticed Park's predicament.

"There's nothing wrong with my mouth. I'm sorry. I wasn't looking where I was going." Park tried to make eye contact with the older officer, but the man's vision hadn't settled on a spot for as long as a second.

Park wished Wu had provided him with an officer's uniform, instead of this enlisted man's. "If you'll please excuse me I have to get back with my unit."

That earned him another, harder tap with the nightstick. "You're not going anywhere. Is there something wrong with your tongue? It sounds wrong? Open your mouth."

Park made a few steps away and around the officers, but they continued to block him. The Chinese noticed what was going on across the street. General Wu huddled them up to discuss Park's situation.

"St—" The officer's order was cut off when a cord wrapped around his neck from behind, and was pulled tight. The younger policemen went down the same way, quickly and quietly.

It was over before Park realized it was happening. Two Chinese agents picked up the bodies and carried them into the woods. Another slapped Park on his chest and beckoned him to follow the others back to the truck.

He asked Wu, "Was that necessary? Don't you have a thumb drive full of South Korean soap operas or something to bribe them with?"

Wu watched her agents dispose of the bodies. "We don't bribe officers we don't know."

Her head snapped his way and she locked eyes with Park again. "You've never killed, have you, Dr. Park?"

"I...no. I always find a better way."

General Wu softened, either in sympathy or pity. "Someday you won't. It's inevitable. Maybe today was the day. I should have had you kill the policemen. This is a hard line of work, and not for soft men. Especially in this country."

Her agents returned from the woods. The general climbed back up into the cab of the truck.

Park climbed into the back of the truck without a word.

Chapter 91

"It's been an hour. We don't want him to drown." Istomin had reached hand-wringing levels of nervousness.

Egorov waited, relaxed. "He'll get out when he's ready. It's a sensory deprivation tank, not a dumpster."

Istomin covered his eyes with the palms of his hands and groaned.

Mikhailov leaned against the wall. "If you can't handle it, why don't you go upstairs, or even outside? Take a walk—we can do that now—enjoy it."

"Enjoy it, he says," Istomin mumbled and continued to fret. He jumped when the lid on the Faith Machine lifted an inch, then all the way.

Isaac Deal sat upright inside. "Can one of you get the rod?" He asked in perfect Russian.

Istomin jumped forward and put the supporting rod in place, then helped Isaac climb out of the tub.

Isaac held his arms out, dripping on the floor. "Anyone have a towel?"

"Our apologies." Egorov shuffled off to the cabinet behind the Faith Machine, retrieving a green terry cloth for Isaac. "We're not used to physically assisting. The Supreme Leader has his own people to dry him off."

"Must be nice." Isaac took the towel graciously. "Who dries you men off then?"

"We don't have the privilege of using the device."

"Not officially. But with the Collective you do have access, better access than Kim Jong-un, don't you?"

The Russians twitched at the accusation.

"The Collective and I, we became acquainted in the water. Let's see if I'm up to speed." He pointed at the three Russians in turn. "Doctors Istomin, Mikhailov, and Egorov. An engineer, a mathematician, and a social scientist walk into a bar. Except instead of a bar, it's a fringe totalitarian state. And instead of a bartender, it's a Stalinesque dictator who lets you build psychotronic weapons." Isaac stopped and curled his hand over his mouth. "I'm sorry, have you heard that one before?"

Confusion written clearly across their faces, the Russians had no answer for Isaac.

He pointed at the tank of pariffinum liquidum mixture and gray matter. "The Collective, in the flesh. A biocomputational gestalt built with the brains of sixteen of Kim Il-sung's psychic bastards. You three harvested the brains when Kim Jong-il ordered his father's progeny killed. That's some *Game of Thrones* shit right there."

The Russians nodded along with Isaac until that last sentence.

"Never mind. Why just the children? Why not the mothers as well? They were psychics too, weren't they?"

"After birthing the psychics, the mothers were removed from the facility. They were too old for the proper gestalt conditioning," Istomin explained.

Isaac rubbed his chin. "Removed from the facility, eh? They didn't die happy, did they?"

"Few do in this land," Mikhailov joked darkly.

Isaac turned around to the clone floating in the repurposed torpedo tube. "Next up, the man with no name, the seventeenth psychic bastard child of Kim Il-sung. Nice save, he wouldn't have stood a chance out of the womb. No card activated in utero lasts longer than a year, especially biokinetics. You saved him from himself.

"Interesting experiment. You even convinced Kim Jong-il that you were making a vessel for him, a new body for when his old one burned out on crystal meth and Hennessy. Good thing you didn't have to deliver on that promise. Too bad you had to make the same promise to his son.

"But that's where I come in, isn't it? I'm the one person on earth who can bring together all the knowledge and the telepathy." He pointed at the three scientists and then at his temple. "And that's what it's going to take isn't it, in theory? A physical transplant is ridiculous. A telepathic transplant—it's never been tried. But I'm your last chance, aren't I?"

"You're our only chance," admitted Egorov.

"That's goddamn right." Isaac faced center toward the cedar tub. "Finally, the Faith Machine, the program that started it all. Channeling the collective psychic energy of the masses through belief. Turning out reliable predictions of the future. Better than any remote viewer. Ever wish this never worked?"

"Of course not," said Istomin.

"You came here to pursue your research when it predicted the fall of the Soviet Union. New Russia's not the happiest place on earth, but better off than here."

"Here is where we were free to pursue our research without limitations. Where we've created the marvels you see in this room, and more. There was no place for us in the world outside."

"How can you be sure?"

Egorov pointed a thumb at the Faith Machine.

Isaac nodded. "Of course, you've seen it. But that was a long time ago. The plan hasn't changed? You're still happy here?"

Mikhailov dismissed the thought with a wave of his hand. "It's never been about happiness. It's always been about the work."

Isaac curled one finger under his nose, considering. "Yes, the work. And that brings us back to the transplant. Everyone knows what you need from me. Question is, what do I get out of this?"

Chapter 92

The truck stopped one last time, the engine cut off and someone said, "We're here," in Korean. Park barely understood the thick Mandarin accent. He followed the rest of the Chinese out of the back of the truck.

They were at a small, unmanned checkpoint on the side of a road through the woods. Weeds peeked through the floorboards of the deck.

General Wu stepped forward and her agents fell in line like proper soldiers. Park fell in with them. She walked down the line, stopping in front of Park. "Well, Doctor, this is the location. Seems a bit off. What's the word from Ensign?"

Park discreetly checked his phone. They were on top of the GPS coordinates given by Ensign. "No messages."

The envelope icon appeared in the corner of the screen. "No, wait. One just came in, 'Can you pick up a Plastic Christmas Tree?'" Park looked up from the phone into the woods. "Plastic trees…. Some of these are fake."

The Chinese searched the edge of the woods in the dark. Park stepped back to the road, and inspected the shoulder for twenty feet in either direction.

"Here!" He pointed at the ground twenty feet beyond the empty checkpoint. "Where the edge of the road crumbled. This is where vehicles turn off."

The Chinese gathered at Park's spot. They soon located a gate that looked like a row of trees. Park picked the lock, the men lifted the gate and pushed it aside. One of them brought their truck inside before closing the gate behind them.

In a single file, General Wu, her agents, and Park followed the dirt road up the hill, through the woods, and among the trees, traveling parallel to the road. The path terminated in a curved concrete bunker with two doors; one garage door and one conventional, both made of steel.

"Why would they put the Faith Machine out here, so far from the population?" Park asked General Wu. "There's no practical way to assemble a congregation to power it all the way out here."

"Practical, reasonable, words left behind at the border. Besides, there could be plenty of room inside."

"It looks Soviet-designed."

"Everything in the DPRK looks Soviet-designed."

"Let's head on in." Park lifted the lid of the keypad next to the door. "Hmm. This could take a while."

He pulled out his phone. "Maybe we'll get lucky and this thing gives off enough electromagnetic noise to help us out."

The envelope icon was live. Park checked the message. It read '53787.' Park entered the code and the door unlocked. For an instant he considered slipping in, locking the door behind him, and leaving the Chinese behind. But they were his only asset. "Or maybe we'll walk right in."

"James had the code?" asked General Wu. "I'd very much like to know how he acquired that."

Park pushed the door open. "I get the feeling you'll soon be able to ask him yourself."

Facing the general, Park saw a look of surprise cross her face before she yelled, "Park!"

He reached into his coat pocket for his pistol. Whipping around, he faced Caseman Twenty-Two, still in his gray suit and carrying the aluminum briefcase. An invisible force hit Park like a wave, knocking him into the general and her agents. The pistol flew out of his grip and into the woods.

Park rose from the pile of humanity. The sensation felt like invisible arms wrapped around his chest. His head spun as he was pulled into CIG-1. The steel door locked behind him.

Chapter 93

"It's obvious," Istomin explained it again, as if to a slow student. "The agents of Project Dead Blind will get to live."

Isaac rubbed his forehead. "Threats now? So the bargaining phase is over, and we're on to anger? Don't get too angry. If you break me, I won't help at all."

Mikhailov exploded, his shouting echoing off the steel walls. "Won't help? Yah!"

Egorov held his comrade back by the shoulders.

Isaac looked Mikhailov up and down before continuing as if nothing happened. "Here's the thing. You guys kidnapped the lot of us and dragged us into the DPRK. You're holding all the cards, literally. And now, out of the goodness of your hearts, you're offering to let us go unharmed if I help you?" He shrugged. "What I don't see is a reason to trust you."

"This wasn't our plan. Kidnapping wasn't our idea," explained Istomin. "You have the misfortune of being the only person on earth who can perform this operation. This is how the Kim dynasty makes offers. If they want something from you, they take you."

Egorov held up Isaac's file. "Unfortunately for your friends, your psychological profile indicated you'd never give in to threats on your person, as you're demonstrating now."

Istomin continued, "The Supreme Leader is due here in three days. He had you brought here to perform his transformation. He'll have you tortured until you comply. He'll not only have your friends harvested for his weapons, he'll make you watch. Even if you give in, he'll have the same done to you. We're offering you an escape."

"Oh, so you're the good guys?" Isaac let his skepticism show.

"We're certainly the better option. We only want to share our knowledge with the world. And *that* is our only way out." Istomin pointed at the clone floating in its tube.

"Consider the power in that shell. Its tissues reconnect post-trauma at an incredible speed. Wounds, even fatal ones, heal while the damage is still being done. Tests suggest that cerebral functions redundantly loop throughout the nervous system. It would take a whole and instantaneous incineration to kill it. And that's just the internal functions. In theory, its power extends to other bodies through touch. The Supreme Leader's new body could cure cancer and restore youth. The most powerful men on earth would bend their knee for a sip at this fountain of youth."

Isaac held his chin and nodded. "I agree—that's bad. I don't see how you three are any better."

Istomin sighed and stepped back. "Egorov, you try getting through to him."

Egorov closed the file he'd been reading and considered the American. "Isaac, why don't you tell us what you want?"

Isaac smiled. "Let my people go, all of them. When they're safely outside the country, then we'll talk."

"Then we'll talk?" Mikhailov burst forward, spitting with rage. Istomin held the mathematician back. "You selfish bastard! Can't you see this is bigger than you and your petty friends, bigger than nations and rulers? This is about science!"

Isaac threw his hands up. "That's not what I can see, pal. I see three old men with a god complex. If this clone is as dangerous as you say, then let me kill it. With the Faith Machine, I can reach in there and have it rip itself apart at the cellular level. Clone soup. No more threat."

The three Russians stopped, appalled by Isaac's suggestion.

Isaac asked, "What? Am I wrong? You know I'm not wrong. I can do that."

Egorov shook his head. "If that clone dies, then so does all our research. All our work, our knowledge, will die with us down here. The whole point is to get our work to the outside world. Ending it all, that's unacceptable."

The Collective's speaker crackled, "If we might make a suggestion?"

Despite the distortion, Isaac recognized the voice from the water, but turned up an eyebrow toward the brains floating in their tank. He hadn't been aware of its speaker and microphone.

The Russians were also surprised by the entity's initiative. Istomin stiffened and said, "Collective repor—"

"It's already talking, dumdum," Mikhailov interrupted. "What is it, Collective?"

"We suggest releasing one of the Project Dead Blind agents. A sign of good faith might convince Isaac Deal to cooperate."

The Russians turned from the collective to Isaac. Isaac shrugged and nodded. "That'd be a good start. Let Pollyanna go. Once she's stateside, we'll get underway."

Egorov shook his head. "No, not her. She's too powerful to let loose. What about Ainia?"

Isaac crossed his arms. "If you let her loose, she'd tear her way back in here with her bare hands. 97:4?"

Egorov shook his head. "97:4 wouldn't leave. She believes God put her here for a purpose."

Isaac nodded. "Yeah, that sounds like her. That leaves only—"

"Exposition Joe." Egorov looked toward his comrades. After a moment of silent confirmation, no one objected. "All right. We'll release him. But we're only sending him as far as China. We don't have the time to wait for him to cross the Pacific."

It didn't take long for Egorov to climb upstairs and return with Exposition Joe and a guard. This wasn't the confident, unperturbed teen Isaac knew. Joe trembled as he descended the stairs in front of the guard, hands cuffed in front of him. His eyes flashed wide in happy relief when they set on his teammate. "Isaac! What's going on?"

"I've convinced the mad scientists to let you go."

"Go? Go where?" Joe cast suspicious eyes over the Russians. "Isaac, I've got a problem. I'm not— I mean I can't—"

Isaac put a hand on the boy's shoulder. "Sure you can, Joe. You'll follow the Script, right?"

Istomin opened his mouth to ask Egorov something, but the social scientist cut him off. "The boy can see the future, surely he can see his way out of the DPRK if necessary."

Joe shook his head.

"Here." Isaac grabbed a loose piece of wire off Istomin's workbench, bent the tip, and went to work on Joe's handcuffs. "Don't worry, Joe. I've worked everything out. I remembered what you told me when the submarine attacked. Do you?"

"Yeah, I warned you—"

"Ah, ah, ah," Isaac shushed, popping the lock on one of Joe's cuffs. "There you go. One down, one to go. Now, who around here can do that?"

Discreet realization flashed across Joe's face, then relief.

Isaac winked at Joe as he popped the second lock, dropping the handcuffs and wire back onto the workbench. "They're taking you to China. You'll call me from there. Then I'll do a little favor for them and they'll let everyone go. Easy peasy Japanesey."

"Okay, Isaac. If you say so. Good luck."

Isaac smiled. "When you're this good, kid, luck ain't got nothing to do with it."

The guard led Joe back up the stairs.

"He'll be out of the country tomorrow morning and we can proceed." Egorov smiled, relieved. "I'll call your guard to bring you back to your quarters."

"Yeah, about that." Isaac tapped his chin. "One more thing before I help you out with this transplant."

Mikhailov stiffened at Isaac's words and asked through gritted teeth, "What. Now."

"I'm going to need a mattress if I'm going to get any sleep tonight. I'm used to a certain level of quality. If you don't have anything in memory foam, I'm willing to settle on a fut—"

Mikhailov pounded his legs with his fists and spit, "You're not getting a goddamn fucking mattress!"

Chapter 94

Park tumbled into the steel chamber, the thick insulation of the North Korean uniform padding his fall. Rolling over, he found himself in a lime-green concrete passageway surrounded by four men. He knew Caseman Twenty-Two, who'd followed him across the country and across the ocean, from his destroyed condo back in Virginia. The one in plain denim was the one who attacked Gabby. The man in the DPRK uniform he didn't recognize, but he held the handle of the rolling suitcase Park had brought across the Pacific.

The one in motorcycle leather snatched the phone out of Park's hand. Stunned by the realization, Park blurted, "That was you, in the parking lot outside the water park before we even left for Africa. How far does this go back?"

"Dr. Park, we've been expecting you," said Caseman Twenty-Two. He forced Park over on his back and cuffed him. "Get on your feet, come with us, and be quiet about it."

They escorted Park around the curved corridor and down a flight of metal stairs, past various pieces of sensitive but old machinery; things outsiders shouldn't be looking at—Park realized they didn't plan on letting him go.

He watched his phone swing back and forth in the Caseman's hand, glad he'd left it on silent. He needed another message from Ensign, but he didn't need it landing in the hands of the enemy.

The Casemen stopped against the wall. The one in denim grabbed the back of Park's head and pressed his face into the wall.

"Dr. Park!" said one of the people passing by.

"Joe?"

"I knew you were here. Don't worry, Isaac has a plan—"

The Casemen shouted at Joe's guard, reprimanding him for not controlling his prisoner, drowning out the rest of what Joe said.

Isaac has a plan? Park wondered. *Well, at least someone does.*

Five levels down, they came to a chamber and stopped. The one in uniform threw open the hatch to darkness and an overpowering chemical stench of bleach that didn't quite cover the smell of rot.

Caseman Twenty-Two ordered, "Inside."

"No." Park braced himself for a fight.

"Good," said Caseman Twenty-Two. "You'll give Caseman Ten a chance to practice."

Park looked at the others. "Ten? Which one of you—?"

The one in the uniform raised his hand and barked, "Why don't you stop talking?"

Park looked the smaller man up and down. "Why don't you?"

Park put on his poker face, chanting, "'*La joie des lignes ven—*'"

The one in black leather snapped into position, hands behind his back, head turned, and mimicking Park's stance. The Caseman covered his mouth, and so did Park, stopping the poker face. Stumbling forward, he tripped over the hatch's lower lip, landing painfully on the concrete floor. The shock brought him out from the Caseman's control. Park gasped for air and inhaled a lungful of bleach fumes.

He curled up in a coughing fit. The Casemen picked him up and put him into an old office chair.

"How did you find us?" one of them asked.

His eyes watering from the bleach, Park said, "The electromagnetic field given off by the frozen brain we captured—it gave a signal back to this installation. After that it was just a matter of triangulation."

"Lies!" A slap landed across Park's face. In the dark he didn't see it coming, which made it hurt less. Not true for the second slap.

"That might have brought you to within ten miles of this location, but no more. You came straight to our doorstep. You've had help, inside information. Who is helping you?" he asked, dropping Park's satphone in his lap. "Who was on the other end of this?"

"No one. I—" The satphone's wallpaper was a blue houndstooth pattern. It wasn't Park's phone. Caseman Twenty-Two smiled in the glow of the screen. One of the others chuckled behind his back.

A light switch was thrown with a snap. James Ensign was seated in the chamber with Park, also tied to an office chair. Dried blood stained his shirt. His throat slit, he'd been dead for days, maybe weeks.

"Oh…Oh no…" Park stared at his dead mentor, remembering the day Ensign recruited him.

"We took him in Hong Kong. The fool thought China had rebuilt their Faith Machine, the one he destroyed thirty years ago. We showed him better." Caseman Twenty-Two flipped through Ensign's satphone. A dozen messages over the past dozen days, every one of them a fraud. "'Hey. Wondering where you at.' 'What time was the show again?' 'Hey did you find my keys? Call me back if you did.'

"How childish." The Caseman shared a laugh.

Park stared at the corpse of his mentor. "How long did he hold out before he gave up his password?"

"Password?"

"For the phone," Park snapped.

"We didn't torture the password out of him. We learned it from our Faith Machine, of course."

"Then why?"

"Why did we torture him, your superior officer and friend?" Twenty-Two asked rhetorically.

The Caseman in leather gave Ensign's corpse a playful spin in the chair.

"To make an impression on you, Dr. Park. Are you impressed?"

Park closed his eyes. Ensign hadn't been his friend, and this kind of end was a risk that came with the job, but.... "Why did you bring us here? What's next?"

"The answer to both questions, Dr. Park," Caseman Twenty-Two leaned into Park's face and whispered in his ear, "is suffering. Sweet, sweet suffering."

Chapter 95

A single glaring bulb hung overhead. Sleep deprivation all night, water torture all day. Ainia lay faceup, bound to a plank of wood suspended over the large laundry sink. Her body was stretched, her ankles and wrists tied at either end. Her neck had developed a painful cramp.

She'd spent the day flipped over, face in the water. Guards shouted questions and insults at her in Korean and pidgin English, throwing bricks into the sink. Every brick raised the water level. Turning her head as far as she could, holding like this for hours as they beat on the plank.

They hadn't left a mark on her, not so far. They either needed her undamaged or they were saving that for later.

In the rush to tie her down, they hadn't noticed her heels arched and pressed into the board. That bought her a little slack. With every splashing brick, the rope absorbed water and thickened, and the slack disappeared.

The rope dried, loosening. Ainia worked her ankles back and forth, rubbing the rope against the rough, concrete lip of the sink. After hours of grinding through the rope's fibers, Ainia's freedom was minutes away.

The door handle turned up with a clang. She stopped and cursed as a guard crept in, carefully closing the door behind him.

Ainia watched the guard tiptoe toward her, his intentions written clearly on his face. She mumbled, "You couldn't have waited five more minutes?"

Standing over her, the guard's expression was a blend of desire and disgust. His neck straightened and shook. The words squeezed out of him. "American whore!"

"Wrong on both counts, asshole." Ainia turned away. She knew something like this was coming sooner or later. "Better me than one of the others."

"Close whore mouth," the guard pronounced each word with the deliberate tone of someone reading phonics off flashcards.

With her short hair, blocky build, and scars, Ainia never drew the attention of men, which was how she liked it. In this hole in the North Korean ground, standards were different.

He ran a hand over her unshaven legs up to her shorts, his other hand down the front of his pants. The ropes—dry, damaged—were looser than ever, and gave Ainia's legs enough play to kick. The rope held her strike short, stopping her knee before it connected with his temple.

The guard, too slow to flinch, glanced at the failed attack and chuckled an idiot's laugh.

Ainia growled and kicked again. The rope's last fibers snapped. There was a short, sharp crack as her kneecap broke the man's nose.

His hands clutched at his face as he bent over in pain. His eyes flashed wide, realizing his mistake too late. Ainia grabbed him around the neck with her thighs. Twisting, pulling the man down into the gap between the plank and the rim, into the water.

His weight flipped the plank. She rolled onto his back. Her neck ached as she held her head above the water, and his under it, until his thrashing petered out.

Chapter 96

Pollyanna had been up all night, slapping herself bruised. Still, she rolled the die. The pain in her chest grew a little bit five times out of six.

She rolled the die and had no idea what number came up. Her eyes burned and couldn't focus. Including the misfortune she'd caused on the ship, she judged her bad luck battery was at a six out of ten. "Guess that's as much juice as I'm going to get."

She picked up the die one last time, held it tight, and thought about her friends. Her voice went up an octave and affected the diction of a child from the early twentieth century. "Oh, my word! I do hope our captor's misfortunes can become our good fortunes. After all, we're overdue for a spot of luck."

"You put Fortuna before me," a man said.

She jerked in surprise. The cork-filter die bounced out of her hand as she glared at the door, then looked out the window for the speaker. She waited, but no one said anything else. She grunted and searched for the tiny cube in the dim cell.

As she spotted her die, an old man's hand cupped over it. "I said, you put Fortuna before me. That's a sin, one of the ten important ones."

The strange hand belonged to a radiant, old, white man in a white hemp suit.

She stared at the stranger sitting on the floor beside her. The pain in her cheek throbbed. "Okay...this is different."

She leaned back against the wall. "I'll take this as a sign that it's time for a break. Why don't you leave so I can take a nap?"

"Whether you see me or not, I've always been there, always watching."

"Either you're God, or you're Sting." She stared at the man. If this was the Almighty, she was unimpressed. "Sting's kept himself up better. Yeah, I need a nap." She stood up to stretch. "That mat You're sitting on is the poor excuse they gave me for a bed so if You don't mind…" She tried to brush Him aside, but God sat unmoved.

"When did I lose you, Shirley?" He used her real name.

"Really? We're going to do this now? All that praying I did in high school—nothing. Fast-forward fifteen years and now you want to talk? Here? Too little, too late, Yahweh, if that is Your real name. Now go."

God didn't go. "You prayed for revenge. I don't answer prayers like that."

"You don't answer prayers at all."

"That's not true."

"Oh no? Whose prayers have You been answering?"

"A Congresswoman in Nebraska asked for My help to conduct a secret attack on a foreign nation. I'm going to help her get away with it."

"You're serious?"

"Of course. She has faith and will be rewarded."

"I'd throw up, but I'd have to lay next to it all night. You're not any kind of God I ever wanted."

He templed his fingers and cocked his head, a patronizing gesture. "But I am the God you've come to expect."

"The God of selfishness and cruelty, of injustice and pain? A pointless God for a pointless existence? Yeah, I'd say that about sums You up. Why am I even having this conversation? I settled accounts with You years ago. You can have Your free will and Your mysterious ways and shove them up Your ass." She leaned forward and shook a fist in his face.

He peered around her clenched fingers. "Would you like to know about the men who killed your family?"

Pollyanna dropped back, shivering at first, then angry. "You couldn't tell me if I did. You're just a hallucination. There's nothing in You that didn't come out of my starved, exhausted mind."

"You have it all wrong. You came out of My starved, exhausted mind when I spewed your kind out into the world with life and free will." He spit, but nothing landed. "An experiment; create a world full of people and watch it run its course. That commitment became my prison. Your faith in me became my cage. You were supposed to die off two thousand years ago, but you just keep on going."

Pollyanna smirked, unimpressed. "I know what you mean. I haven't enjoyed *Supernatural* since season five, but I gotta see it through to the end."

He leaned back into the darkness, eyes lit with a cold fire. "But with the help of three wise men, I'll end your kind. I'll save you and your team for last, make you watch. Then, when I tear your heads off with my bare hands, I'll finally be free."

Chapter 97

Ainia waited outside and above the laundry room door. In the darkness, her legs wrapped around an air duct and one hand held the conduit. The cord that had bound her to the plank was now coiled around her fist.

The corpse of the drowned guard was propped in the shadow of an iron support beam, opposite the door.

The footsteps were getting closer. Ainia couldn't help but smile. Payback was her favorite bitch.

Another guard passed below. Maybe he was one of her torturers, maybe not. She couldn't recognize him from above, just his hat and the submachine gun slung over his shoulder.

The man came to a stop and looked up and down the hallway before pushing open the door to the laundry room. From his body language, he came expecting to find the guard at the door.

Light spilled out into the hall. The guard noticed the floor and the wet trail left behind where Ainia had dragged the drowned man across the floor. He saw the corpse leaning against the wall behind him and unslung the submachine gun from his shoulder. He stepped forward, right where Ainia wanted him.

She dropped from the ceiling, slipping the cord around his neck. Twisting the gun out of his grip with her free hand, she kneed him in the kidney, knocking him down.

The guard's hands went to his throat too late to stop the noose from cinching tight. Looped over a pipe in the ceiling, the other end was tied around the drowned man. Ainia dragged the corpse down the hall, lifting the kicking, strangling guard. Their combined weight kept the man in the air.

Waiting for the man to strangle to death, she sat on the drowned man's corpse and checked the weapon. Noisy, but good to have.

When the dying was over, she lowered him to the floor and moved on through the facility. She found an empty room lined with ancient boxy computers and another room locked with a padlock. One level down was what looked like a command room. A long window opened up into the core cylindrical space. Ainia crawled past the window and along the floor. She heard Pollyanna talking to herself inside, holding up one end of a conversation with no one on the other side. Ainia shook her head in disappointment and moved on to the far side of the window, where the wall opened up to a short hall and a doorway.

Men's voices chattered in Korean around the bend. Ainia stopped cold. She didn't know the language, but recognized the cadence of a change in the guard. *Good, two for one.* Ainia tumbled around the corner and broke the first guard's knee with a kick. He fell toward her. She flipped him over and around, into the second guard.

Stomping one on the neck and choking out the other, she finished them in seconds. Searching the bodies for keys or weapons, she found nothing except a nightstick on each of them. She stuck one into the back of her waistband and kept the other in hand.

Climbing over the rail, she disappeared into the darkness and the depths of CIG-1, down another level.

Descending the inner shell of the missile silo, she stopped to look and listen. The sounds of struggling came from a level below.

She swung back to the outer wall, to the rail and climbed up on the walkway. There was no one in sight. For such a large facility, the place was remarkably understaffed. She opened an access hatch. The stench of bleach poured out. She slipped in, leaving the door open behind her.

Nightstick ready, she faced the room. Barely lit from the outside, she made out two men tied to office chairs in the mustard-yellow room. From the way the body slumped, Ainia could tell the heavyset, old man in the dark suit was dead. The man in the North Korean army uniform was livelier, reaching toward the corpse with the toe of his boot, his hands bound behind the chair. Her head cocked. The nightstick fell from her hand, and dangled by the leather loop around her wrist. "Park?"

"Oh thank God, Ainia." Park dropped his extended foot to the floor. "Get James' belt for me. I hope his lock picks are still in the buckle. The Chinese wouldn't let me bring mine, wasn't part of the uniform."

"James Ensign?" Now she recognized the corpse and removed its belt. "This is going to take a lot of explaining. But it's good to see you alive, Commander." She found the lock picks and put them in Park's hands. "I can't give you much of a status report. I've been in a cell this whole time."

Park blindly worked at the handcuffs. "Are you all right?"

She shrugged. "A little water torture, nothing I couldn't deal with. You?"

"Soda water shot up the nose. They like their liquids down here, don't they?"

"All part of the job. Besides the North Koreans, there's at least one old man of European extraction with them. He seemed like some kind of interrogator, maybe Russian?"

"How about the rest of the team? They all made it off the ship?" Park discarded the handcuffs.

"Off the ship, into the sub, and then all the way down here, as far as I know. The good news is I've taken out four guards in the last hour. Regulars only, no Casemen. I'm armed and I have one of these for each of us." She tossed him the spare nightstick. "The bad news is, I didn't get any keys off the two I took out, but with you around that shouldn't be a problem."

She cracked her knuckles and motioned to the corpse of James Ensign. "When, do you think?"

"Probably while we were in Liberia." Park closed his eyes and took a deep breath. "Give me a moment."

Park stared at the man who'd been his mentor and guide, if not a friend. Project Dead Blind was in his hands now. For forever or for an afternoon depending on how the next hour played out.

Ainia put a hand on his shoulder. "Fill your heart with vengeance. Release it on our enemies."

Park rested his hand on hers. "When we get out of this, you should write a line of Amazon sympathy cards."

"Sympathy is a weakness."

"I said, when we get out of this, not now." His hand hesitated as he picked up the phone from his dead mentor's lap. "The orders we received on the satphones were all sent by these Casemen. They had everything, our codes even. Their Faith Machine put them steps ahead all along. They were watching us before. Remember the motorcycle rider outside the water park?"

Ainia cocked her head in confusion.

"Full helmet, dark green-and-black bike and racing suit?"

Ainia nodded. "Oh yeah, in Indiana. Don't tell me he's down here too."

"He is. Who knows how long they've been watching us?" Park gripped the nightstick with both hands. "Let's find our people, then break this place and everyone in it."

Chapter 98

After a few hours of pretending to be asleep, Isaac rose from the mat on the floor and crawled over to listen at the door. After an inconclusive moment, he turned the latch and opened it a crack. Down either end of the cold, brutal hallway, no one was in sight. Tiptoeing on bare feet, Isaac made his way back down the hall to the stairs, stopping and waiting in the shadows every chance he got.

Isaac was almost disappointed with how easily he was able to move through the facility. Then he found two corpses tied together with cord, one soaking wet, the other's face swollen, the cord wrapped around his neck. "Oh," he whispered under his breath, "Ainia's loose."

He gave another look around before proceeding more confidently down to the lab at the bottom of CIG-1. From the bottom of the stairs, Isaac crept to the Collective's tank, frosted over once again.

He cleared a spot on the glass and whispered, "Hey, guys, you awake?"

"We never sleep, Isaac. What are you planning?"

Isaac jumped. The speaker crackled a little too loudly.

"Shh, we're getting you out of there. That's what." He pulled his shirt off as he walked over to the Faith Machine.

"Out of—This isn't what we discussed."

"No, it is not. I did some thinking. When the *Tomás el Incrédulo* sank, Exposition Joe had a warning for me. He said, 'whatever they ask you to do, do the exact opposite of that.' Now I thought the opposite of helping the Russians would be helping you, as in helping you kill yourselves. But it occurred to me, you're a 'they' too, aren't you?"

"What are you getting at?" The electrical voice was flat and without inflection.

"I came up with a way to do the opposite of what everyone wants me to do—everyone who's asked me to do anything—and get my people back home." Isaac dropped his pants and lifted the lid to the Faith Machine.

"You have us very worried. We had hoped you would be our end."

"Oh, I will be. Just not the way you're planning. See, you all want to die, that's cool. You asked me to kill you. I have a hang up there. That's what started me thinking about what Joe said. Rather than kill you, how about I give you life? That's the opposite of what *they* asked, *they* as in the Russians and *they* as in the sixteen of you.

He climbed into the water. "I transfer your consciousness into the clone, you use its power to help us escape the country, then you use that same power to destroy yourself. You heard me earlier. You should be able to liquefy yourself, instantly and painlessly. See? It's a win-win for the good guys, lose-lose for the bad guys."

"Isaac…that's brilliant."

Chapter 99

97:4 prayed, her hands pressed together with the cast awkwardly in the way. She opened an eye at the sound of metal scraping at the door. Anticipating the guards, she braced herself for the shouting and slaps that followed when they caught her like this, but it wasn't the guards. It was Park and Ainia. She turned her eyes to the heavens and whispered, "Thank you."

Ainia said, "Don't go thanking anyone yet."

Park interrupted her, "Are you all right, 97:4?"

97:4 stood up. "I'm fine. Why wouldn't I be? Between throwing me in this cell and the Russian's pathetic attempts to break my faith, the worst they've done is bore me."

"Excellent. The bad news is we don't have your Bible. But Bible or not, we're getting you and everyone else out of here, after we destroy the last Faith Machine. Are you ready?"

"Yes. Ready to do God's work." 97:4 shook out her hair and marched toward the open door, stopping abruptly in the doorway. She turned and held an open hand to Park. "Can I borrow that?"

Park handed her the nightstick.

97:4 walked back to the podium and smashed the framed portraits of Kim Il-sung and Kim Jong-il, knocking them off the wall, shattering the glass, and breaking the frames.

Smiling, she handed the nightstick back to Park as she walked past him. "*Thou shalt have no other gods before me.*"

"What's that sound?" asked Ainia.

Park and 97:4 stopped and listened.

"A tinkling?" asked 97:4.

"From the floor?" asked Park.

They followed the noise to the photos of Kim Il-sung and then Kim Jong-Il, shaking under the shards of glass. The motion stopped as mysteriously as it started.

Park picked up the photo of Kim Il-sung. "Icons."

Ainia twisted the nightstick in her grip. "You're joking."

"They are in this country. As much as a cross is in the Vatican." He dropped the photo. "Someone's just used a Faith Machine, and it wasn't the North Koreans. Come on, let's go."

Chapter 100

Pollyanna raised her hands over her head, fingers splayed like antlers, fingertips grazing the control room ceiling. "Look at Me. I'm the big, bad God from the Torah. Real spooky. Throw the whole Old Testament at us." Pollyanna rolled her eyes. "Whatever. You still don't impress me."

God smiled with his mouth, not his eyes. "I'm not here to impress you. I'm here to distract you. Your friend Isaac is making a terrible, terrible mistake that I need him to make. If I let you reach out with your card, even blindly, you would have stopped him, probably for good. Then everything I did to get him here would have been for nothing."

God shook his head, relieved. "Ever since Joe went off-Script I've been rudderless, improvising. Pollyanna, right here and now, you almost brought the whole plan to its knees."

Pollyanna put a hand on her chest, channeling the pain. "Whatever do you mean, Sir?"

"Even without the Script in hand I can tell you, you're too little, too late, Shirley. See you in the depths of the earth." He faded into the darkness with a Cheshire grin.

As the deity departed, a motion outside the window made Pollyanna jump. She thought one of the guards had pressed up against the glass, trying to see in. But when she saw Ainia and 97:4 with him, she recognized Dr. Park and waved.

He unlocked the door and Pollyanna launched herself into his arms. "Goddamn, am I glad to see you motherfuckers. Look, don't take this the wrong way, but I'd like to talk to you guys about God."

Chapter 101

Isaac fumbled out of the Faith Machine, struggling to keep the lid open while he climbed over the rim. He hit the ground, grunted, and curled up on his side. "Oh, man, that was some spacey shit."

"What have you done?" asked Egorov. He was standing over saac. Mikhailov and Istomin were beside him; all three in their sleepwear.

Isaac turned his disoriented eyes up at the men. "You should have seen it. No, that's right, you couldn't have. That's why you brought me here. Were you guys here all along, or did I fall asleep?"

Mikhailov grabbed Isaac's ears. "What have you done, you son of a bitch?"

Isaac pulled himself free and pushed Mikhailov away. "What are you assholes doing up, anyway? Don't you sleep?"

"We noticed the Faith Machine's signature wave of force, strong enough to knock the Kims off the wall."

Isaac stood. "Kims? What are you talking about?"

Istomin checked the subject in the torpedo tube. "He didn't liquefy the clone, like he'd threatened."

Isaac raised a finger to make a point. "I never threatened to liquefy anyone. I merely made the suggestion."

Egorov gave the cedar clamshell device a once-over. "The Faith Machine looks like it is still in good shape as well."

Mikhailov grunted. "Why don't we ask the witness? Collective, what did this philistine do to our project?"

The speaker didn't spark to life. The frost on the glass tank melted. Water ran down the surface in rivulets.

"Oh no." Egorov ran over to the Collective, kneeling before the tank. "It's warming up. I think it's—dead. He killed the Collective."

"Why?" Istomin sounded brokenhearted. "What would you have to gain from this? Now we're all trapped in this country. When the Supreme Leader finds out we can't transfer him to the clone—"

"That's your problem, not ours." Park interrupted from the foot of the stairs, Ainia to his left, 97:4 to his right, and Pollyanna behind. "Isaac, get ready to go."

"But put something on first," suggested Pollyanna to the naked, wet man. "It's cold out there."

Isaac grabbed a towel and wrapped it around his waist.

"Yeah, *that'll* do it."

The Russians stared at Park like they'd seen a ghost.

Mikhailov came back to his senses first, laughing. "What are you going to do? Fight your way out of the country? You and this platoon of women?"

Pollyanna snorted. "How about these bitches take a shit on your nutsack, Beardo? You won't be laughing then."

97:4 flinched. "Ew, gross."

Istomin asked, "How are you even alive, much less standing here? You should have drowned."

"I had some help."

"From who?"

"From us," answered General Wu. While Project Dead Blind faced off with the scientists of CIG-1, the Chinese agents had taken position in the darkness around the bottom of the stairs. The general descended gracefully, Exposition Joe in tow.

"Hi, guys...er...ladies, Dr. Park!" Joe waved. "I let the Chinese Army in. Sorry. They were waiting for us when the guard opened the door outside."

Park smiled. "That's fine, Joe. We're working together on this. General Wu, here's your Faith Machine."

"Indeed, and these men. Doctors Egorov, Mikhailov, and Istomin, I presume? You fellows have been missing for a long time."

The Russians stared, slack-jawed, at the Chinese woman.

"You…you know us?" asked Egorov.

"Quite so. I've been researching your work for years. I hoped I'd find one or two of you at the bottom of this." She looked up through the layers of CIG-1. "But all three—that's quite a success. Would you be willing to accompany us back to China?"

The Russians silently conferred amongst themselves with shrugs.

Egorov nodded. "China would be better."

Pollyanna tapped Park on the shoulder. "Should we be letting this happen?"

Ainia and 97:4 looked to Park for orders.

"They have five guns and our transportation out of North Korea. We have one gun that may not even work, and don't even have a bicycle into town. At the moment I don't see a choice, but I'm willing to entertain suggestions."

"No." 97:4 shook her head. "This isn't right. We didn't come all this way to hand everything over to China. That can't be our purpose."

Park sighed. "Sometimes you have to give up a point to play again another day. That's the game."

97:4 stomped her foot. "This isn't a game, Park. God said I had a reason to be here, a purpose in the depths of the earth."

Joe's eyes went wide. "God told you that, too?"

97:4 nodded.

"The next time you see Him you'll have to apologize to God." General Wu gave a hand signal. Her agents stood and circled the room. "Doctors, take what you need. Pack quickly. We're leaving in fifteen minutes."

"No!" 97:4 stood her ground. "There's something else that needs to be done."

"Young lady," General Wu explained, "what you need to do is follow your commander's orders. He knows—"

Every gun in the room flew up, out of hands and holsters, hitting the ceiling, and sticking there, out of reach.

Ainia jumped for her captured submachine gun, launching off the workbench to reach it. She grabbed the sling with both hands. The gun didn't budge. Ainia hung in midair for a second, kicked up, bracing her feet on the ceiling, and pulled. The sling snapped, but the gun didn't move. Left swinging from one end of the sling, Ainia dropped to her feet.

The Chinese agents had no luck recovering their weapons either.

"Listen to the golden-haired one." A man's voice called down the stairs. Caseman Twenty-Two descended, straightening his tie with his free hand. The Casemen in leather, denim, and uniform followed.

Pollyanna backed up. "It's getting fucking crowded down here. Someone should leave. Fire codes, you know. Come on, guys, let's go."

"No one is going anywhere. You're here to bear witness," said Twenty-Two.

Park shouted, "Everybody, blu—" and froze as the black leather Caseman seized control of Park's body and forced him to crack himself on the head with his nightstick. Park dropped to his knees.

"Not this time." Ainia began to mumble in ancient Greek. The black leather Caseman took control of Istomin instead.

Screaming in Russian, the skinny, old man grabbed Ainia's wrist and flipped her. The motion was beyond his capabilities. Something snapped in his arm, Istomin screamed, and the flip failed halfway through. Ainia rolled off the man, back onto her feet.

Everyone except the Casemen lifted off the ground and floated back against the back wall. The guns fell from the ceiling.

Caseman Twenty-Two took position in the center. "You'll find yourselves unable to move. But please, exhaust yourselves trying."

Pressed sideways up against the wall, Isaac couldn't even curl his fingers against the unseen force. The Caseman in black leather didn't look at Isaac as he walked past him. The Caseman in denim inspected the Collective's tank.

Caseman Twenty-Two stood in the middle of the room, concentrating on Project Dead Blind, the Russians, and the Chinese.

"Caseman Twenty-Two." Pressed against the wall, Egorov struggled to breathe, "Let us go. The Americans know we have the upper hand."

"There is no *we* here, Dr. Egorov. There never was. Not one that included your foreign contamination. The only *we* is my comrades and them." He pointed at the Collective's tank.

"That?" Egorov asked. "That's nothing. That was never anything. It was just a computer made of meat. Don't tell me you've been—Twenty-Two, do you think you've been communicating with the Collective in some meaningful way? If so, you've deluded yourself."

Caseman Twenty-Two smirked. "You built the Collective. Don't think that means you understood it. Within that fluid infinity waits."

"Now you're just babbling, Twenty-Two. The Americans destroyed the Collective. If we can't invent a new means to transfer a subject into the clone, we're all dead men. The Supreme Leader is due here in days. If we're lucky—"

Caseman Twenty-Two waved Egorov's complaints aside. "The Supreme Leader will be swept aside in the new reign. An Ethereal Reign of which we loyal Casemen have earned our place among the highest ranks."

Park asked, "An Ethereal Reign?"

Egorov answered, "Ethereal is what the locals call psychoactive phenomena, what you call cards. But if it's a reign, someone has to be on top. Who's on top, Twenty-Two?"

The repurposed torpedo tube opened. The clone, naked and wet, stepped out. It threw its long black hair back with muscles that had never flexed before. A healthy young man of eighteen—the resemblance to Kim Il-sung was clear. "At last, sweet quiet."

God scanned the crowd through the clone's eyes, finding Exposition

Joe cowering against the wall. With the voice from the Collective's speaker He said, "Joseph, poor, foolish Joseph. The future was written in the Script, not by the Script.

"These are the end times." He smiled. "So saith the Lord."

Chapter 102

Pressed sideways and spread-eagled against the wall, Park struggled to keep his head straight against the force of Caseman Twenty-Two's power. The pressure made it hard to breathe. His fingers tingled, growing numb.

The Caseman in denim grabbed a towel and dried the clone off, careful not to push Him off His uncertain feet as God adjusted to His vessel. The Caseman in leather presented a plain, dark green uniform to the deity.

Egorov, cheek flush with the wall, spoke over his shoulder. "Collective? Is that you?"

"Quiet!" God snapped. "I'm done listening to you. I've had to listen to people for tens of thousands of years, by the thousands, millions— now in the billions. Time for you to be quiet. It's My turn to speak." His untried muscles struggled through the act of dressing.

In the center of the lab, Twenty-Two trembled, sweating. "Master, I can only hold them so much longer."

God buttoned His coat. "Well, then, Noe, suffer this burden no more."

Twenty-Two's aluminum briefcase ripped open with the screech of tearing metal. The frozen brain of a long-dead telekinetic launched into orbit around the deity. The agents of Project Dead Blind, the Chinese, and the Russians fell from the wall. Ainia landed on her feet. The rest crumbled to the floor.

"And the others."

Caseman Six's canvas backpack tore in half. Another frozen brain joined the first in a tangential orbit. Caseman Seven's fiberglass case cracked open. The doctor's bag in the hand of one of the Caseman in uniform burst at the seams. In the hand of the other, the rolling suitcase flew open. The third, fourth, and fifth brains fell into orbits, like a surrealist's nightmare vision of the solar system.

The five Casemen dropped to their knees in supplication.

"My loyal Casemen. I'd thank you for keeping these for me, but you've lost so many along the way. Each an aspect I could have played with, now gone. Even I can't punish the dead, so I'll punish the four of you."

God lifted His hands, fingers splayed. The Casemen drifted into the air. The deity clapped. Their bodies smashed together. The Casemen grunted. The sound of skulls knocking against each other made Park wince.

"You presumed to command My power?" As God twisted his hands, so did the men's bodies in horrible sympathy. Bones cracking inside flesh sounded bizarrely like someone playing with bubble wrap. He crushed their skulls inside their flesh. Their heads distorted. Their skin turned blue with internal bleeding.

The foreigners staggered to their feet, staring at the floating nightmare of flesh before them.

The remains of the Casemen fell. Bones pulverized, their carcasses hit the floor like plastic bags filled with wet garbage.

God glared at the mortals about Him. "I didn't say *stand*."

Still unsure on their feet, the survivors were hit with a wave of nausea, and fell again. Some staggered and gripped the wall or piece of equipment, all but Ainia. "Close your eyes and it won't affect you."

"Close our eyes?" Mikhailov clutched the rim of the Faith Machine. "Then what?"

God smirked. "Then I'll make the fake Amazon beat you to death one by one."

A jolt ran through Ainia. Like a puppet on sticks, her limbs jerked into a fighting stance. She flipped across the room and kicked Mikhailov in the gut, knocking him off the machine and onto his back. The old man screamed in pain and helpless anger.

Pollyanna climbed to her knees, trying to activate her card. "This isn't right at all. That the Father on high should be of such low character, a savage brute. 'Tis appalling to consider—"

God cast a scowl Pollyanna's direction. Her face flushed red. Park recognized the power from the Walmart back in America. She grabbed handfuls of her hair and screamed, "How fucking dare You come down from Heaven, or whatever, and judge us for living? Why did You make this cesspool anyway, because You were bored?"

97:4 clasped the Collective's tank for support. God poked a finger in the tank's direction. The glass shattered. The thick, cold fluid spilled over 97:4. The brains slid through the broken glass, hanging by the golden wire like meats at a market.

Park closed his eyes and crawled blindly to the submachine gun.

Spit flew from Pollyanna's lips as she ranted. "We're just ants under Your fucking magnifying glass, is that it? You put us here to suffer? Fuck You! You put the God in God-fucking-dammit!"

Park's hand fell on the broken strap and dragged the weapon closer, counting on Pollyanna's screaming to cover the noise.

Ignoring Pollyanna, God stood over 97:4 where she struggled against the vertigo. "Oh, it's tempting to harvest your brain, faithful Jannete. Have the Russians crack open your skull, scoop out the innards, freeze them up, and turn you into one of My weapons. Wouldn't you like that? You always wanted to serve Me."

Eyes open and head spinning, Park struggled to put the deity in his sights.

God leaned against the broken tank. "When you see what you've helped unleash upon this world, you'll break."

97:4 grimaced, trying to crawl away. "I don't understand."

God lifted 97:4 by her broken arm. "Shh. No talking. Obey your God."

Park pulled the trigger. It didn't give. The safety was on.

God shook his head. "You've always played the martyr. The time for play is over."

Park found the safety and switched it off.

A screwdriver flew off the workbench and through the palm of 97:4's good hand, pinning her to the steel bulkhead. 97:4 screamed.

Park shouted, "No," unloading the full clip into the deity. Bullets peppered His body.

Wu barked an order in Mandarin. Her agents fired on Him as well.

His hands opened to the Chinese gunfire, eyes turned away, like a mortal being pelted with rubber bands. The rounds bounced off His uniform.

The deity curled the fingers on His outstretched hand. The guns ejected their clips, scattering into the dark corners of the lab. Short rivulets of blood ran from the holes in His uniform, the wounds already healing. Park's rounds squeezed out of His body, jingling onto the floor.

Wu and her agents slung their arms and drew knives.

Unflustered by gunfire and drawn blades, the deity turned to the Chinese commander. "General Wu, still trying to make up for your mistake in Hong Kong?" He pointed at the Faith Machine. "You can have this one. I'm done with it."

He lifted a hand to the ceiling and CIG-1 began to quake. Through the grated ceiling, Park watched the silo cover, a massive slab of concrete, rumble open. Dirt, dust, and rust rained from above. For the first time since its construction, the lab at the bottom of the structure experienced the light of the full moon pouring down on it. Isaac and the Russians crawled for cover under the Faith Machine.

God dropped his hand toward the floor, fingers curled. CIG-1 shook again. Retaining bolts along the walls snapped. Built into the base of the ICBM launch platform, the bottom level disengaged and raced up the shaft.

The force pushing them upward and the thrall of vertigo was too much for the mortals. They struggled for a hold on the floor.

Flush with the open silo cover at the top, the laboratory stopped with a jerk, bucking those with a grip. Those without launched into the ceiling and dropped onto the floor. The lab stood in the open air. The locking mechanism engaged.

"I've witnessed every kind of suffering since the dawn of the species. But this will be new. The regret of a team of broken and deformed minds who lost the world. Watching it fall apart, knowing it's your fault— wonderful."

God looked to the sky and took a deep breath. "Dr. Park, your missile strike is forthcoming."

"Missile strike?" asked General Wu. "What missile strike?"

"The doctor felt he couldn't trust you, General. So he arranged a contingency plan with the only contact he had left, the Reverend Representative Fray. He hoped her selfishness would outweigh her pettiness. That Predator drone is proof to the contrary." God pointed into the night sky to something no one could see.

Isaac struggled up to an elbow and asked Park, "So…um…did she talk about me at all?"

God answered for Park. "No. Though she thought about you when she placed the order. You're not the first embarrassing lover she's had killed."

"Embarrassing?" muttered Isaac.

"Isaac, if you had done the wrong thing, given in to your selfish nature, and taken her offer, We wouldn't be here now. Just a minute, here it comes." A rocket roared out of the night. Pollyanna covered her ears.

"No need for that. The engine's already finished firing." God rolled up the sleeve of His free hand, palm held up and out.

Park never saw it strike. There was a blur in the darkness. Then a missile hovered in the air, tip touching the center of God's palm. The deity spun around once like a shot putter and tossed the high-tech weapon into the woods surrounding CIG-1.

He straightened His sleeve like He'd swatted a fly. "As I was saying, Isaac. If you had given in to your temptations, you'd be sleeping in silk sheets in Fray's church-mansion. And I would be stuck talking to Soviets through a cluster of brains attached to a speaker. I might never have been able to draw you out from her hedonistic siren song."

The deity stopped in front of Exposition Joe. "Joseph, poor brave Joseph. You thought going off-Script would stop Me. How could you have known? Your betrayal was in the Script too. Telling Isaac not to do what he was told. That was the plan all along. Isaac never does as he's told. As horrible as things are now, they're going to be far worse."

He moved on to 97:4, bleeding out on the floor. He shook His head. "No, Jannete. You don't get to be a martyr after all."

His invisible force peeled away the cast like the wrapping off a candy bar. He knelt at her side, and held her broken bone on one arm and the shredded palm of her other hand. When He stood, He left the hand whole. The bone, broken by The Baptist's bullet, was mended. He pushed her to the floor. "You and your friends, you'll be the very last to die. And with your death the sun will fizzle, and stars will vanish like dirt cast on the water. My reward for your faith."

With the Casemen's weaponized brains still orbiting His body, God rose through the air without a word and without looking back.

Chapter 103

A cold wind blew through the exposed laboratory of CIG-1. Isaac collected the clothes he'd discarded before climbing into the Faith Machine, snatching them as the wind threatened to carry them away. Everyone else stared into the night sky where God had disappeared. Stunned minutes passed before Pollyanna broke the silence.

"So…we're about as fucked as fucked can be, right?" asked Pollyanna, straightening her hair with her fingers.

Egorov sat on the ground and leaned against the base of the Faith Machine. "No. We're the lucky ones. We have the privilege to know the coming doom."

"Aren't you the happy one?"

Egorov shrugged. "We're Russians."

Istomin added. "We're used to dying under tyrants."

Joe stood over Egorov, clutching his head. "There's something you can do, though, right? You're not going to sit there. You're going to try."

"We're old." Egorov pointed into the night. "Our best years went that way. We don't have another eighteen to develop a new plan."

"If you don't know how to stop that…" Joe's voice rose, then petered out. His pleas washed over the scientists like rain on rocks.

"This isn't over." Park brushed himself off. "Not while we're alive."

"Park, confidence is great and all, but that's God. We're outclassed—you know, a smidgen." Pollyanna shivered in the wind. "Chris— I mean, Jesu—, godda—. Fuck, I need a smoke."

"That can't be God." 97:4 clutched her bare, restored arm.

"It is." Joe said, unable to look at the others.

Isaac pulled his pants on under the towel. "Guys? I just want to say I'm really sorry about this. I didn't know what I was talking to in...the..." His excuses faltered under the weight of the glares. "Oh, come on!" he snapped. "How was I supposed to know?"

"Isaac's right. This was my fault," said Exposition Joe. "I've been following Him for three years and didn't doubt Him once. Moses did, Elijah did, Thomas did, but not me. I could have gone off-Script years ago, stopped Him then."

"Aren't you Ruskies supposed to be slinking away right now?" asked Pollyanna.

Istomin held his broken wrist. "Where is there to go?"

General Wu and her agents had been huddled up and whispering since God flew away. They broke to gather their ejected ammunition clips.

"How about you, General?" Park asked. "What are you thinking?"

She smiled to herself as she reloaded her pistol. "Retreat, regroup, and return to put an end to that Thing. I was a fool to think we could contain and use these forces. But I'm a fool no more, and I've killed gods before."

Mikhailov scoffed. "Killed gods before? Petty incorporeal thought-forms, dried-up samples of eras long gone maybe. You think you're going to kill that? Didn't you see what that body is capable of? It would take a nuclear blast to destroy it, maybe a Gauss gun on a direct hit. Do you have access to something in that class?" Mikhailov sneezed. "And that's not even considering the brains it's carrying. Five psychoactive weapons, more powerful under the thought-form's control than they ever were in the hands of men. Did you not see it catch a damn missile in midair?"

Park put the empty submachine gun down. "General, we need to find that thing's weakness and hit it fast, while it's still getting used to corporeal form. It looked like a young Kim Il-sung. With that face, it could take over the North Korean government and one of the largest armies in the world."

"It knows that too. That was our plan—oof," said Mikhailov. Egorov elbowed him in the side.

General Wu shook her head. "Dr. Park, look around. What do you see? Less than a dozen agents and a few small arms, all deep inside serious ground. An attack seems unlikely. Unless you have more drone strikes you can call?"

"No, but we have an advantage." Park pointed in the direction God left. "That thing wants us to suffer."

"Uh, Park," Pollyanna interrupted. "That's not an advantage."

"If it wants us to suffer it won't kill us, not right away. That'll buy us some time."

Wu arched an eyebrow. "And how are you proposing to attack? We don't even know where it's flown off to."

Egorov cleared his throat. "We might be able to help with that."

Wu glared at the Russian. "Well? Out with it."

"All our technology—The Faith Machine, the Collective, the Braincases—were tied into this being that claims to be God."

Pollyanna asked, "'This being that claims to be God' is a mouthful. How about we just call it God?"

"That wasn't God," protested 97:4. Joe closed his eyes.

Egorov threw up his hands. "Fine then, *God* was connected to all of them. That connection might still be there, dormant. We might be able to restore it and find Him."

"And then what?" asked Isaac.

"And then the rest is up to you. But surely our help should be worth something. Say, extradition to China?" He smiled the way a reptile might.

Park fixed the broken submachine gun sling, tying it in a knot. "There's that. Or you can stay right there, and we'll get everything we need out of Isaac."

Egorov's smile faded. He turned to face his comrades.

Ainia stepped between them. "The first one of you to run gets a broken leg."

Crestfallen, the Russians stood in silence.

Park kept an eye on the Russians, calling over his shoulder. "What do you think, Isaac?"

Isaac straightened his collar. "Egorov is wrong. As long as God walks the earth, this equipment is worthless."

"You lied to us?" Ainia stomped on Egorov's toe. The scientist fell, clutching his foot.

Isaac nodded. "He lied, but he can still help. There's a connection to God—that *being*—and where It's gone. That connection is standing right there." Isaac pointed at Exposition Joe.

"Wait. What?" Joe stepped back. "No, I'm useless. Everything I had came from God."

Isaac patted Joe's shoulder. "Not at all, boy. You just don't know. When that Thing attached itself to you, when It offered you Its 'blessing,' It established a connection. Connections between thought-forms and hosts, they don't go away easy. That's how we followed the trail here from San Diego, the Braincases' connection to the Collective. Same thing."

Park cocked his head, curious. "So, how do we take advantage of that connection?"

"Hypnosis." Isaac swung his finger back around to the Russians and winked. "Egorov here happens to be an expert at it."

Egorov curled up, nursed his broken toe, and sneered at him.

General Wu holstered her pistol. "Say we find this Thing. Then what are you going to do to destroy It?"

Park opened his arms, palms up. "We just have to find Its weakness."

Joe pointed at the cedar clamshell tub. "Are you sure it's not the Faith Machine? It had me destroy two of them."

Isaac knocked on the cedar tub, shaking his head. "Because it needed this one to be the only one. It couldn't risk The Baptist or Representative Fray plugging in and interfering with the transition."

"Hey." Pollyanna pointed at the group, her finger bobbing. "It took the body of a psychic, right? Every card comes with a bit of crazy. What are the usual downsides to biokinetics?"

Park rubbed his chin. "Body dysmorphic disorder, gender dysphoria, body integrity identity disorder. But that Thing is a Queen of Diamonds, if not a King. Those conditions are meaningless in light of that power."

"Maybe it doesn't have any weaknesses?" asked Pollyanna.

Park shook his head. "Then why is It lying? It said all of this was destiny. That it was written in Joe's Script. If that Thing wrote the past and the future, then why tell Joe things are going to get worse? Why did It remind General Wu about whatever happened in Hong Kong? Or tell Isaac he could have thrown in with The Samaritans, if that wasn't a possibility?

"It wants us to give up, go home and hide. Because we're close. We have everything we need to destroy that Thing right here, among us. We just have to put it together." Park straightened his DPRK army cap. "I don't know where that Thing came from. I don't know if It's God or something else. But I do know that if evil has a throat, then we're going to choke it. We just need a plan to get our hands around it."

Chapter 104

Alone, working late into the night at the Haedanghwa Foodstuff Company, the facility's only mechanic was elbow deep in one of the decrepit delivery trucks. Head down, mind on the task at hand, he didn't notice the deity drift to the ground beside him.

The mechanic dropped his wrench into the engine, stunned by the strange, yet familiar face, a manifestation of the Great Leader, Kim Il-sung. Alive and young again, a vision with long unkempt hair, a sight made more unreal by the five frosty lumps orbiting it in circles.

"Tough, yes, but at a cost," the deity said to Himself, flexing stiff fingers. "Disappointing. As powerful as this vessel is, there are still limitations. Harden My tissues any further, and I won't be able to move My limbs at all.

"Maybe I will, if the novelty of movement someday wears thin. After all, My other assets make these arms almost ornamental." Reaching out and applying the power of the first frozen brain, He ripped the empty shipping container off the back of the truck. The violent motion and the shift of the truck's center of gravity flipped the vehicle forward. The cab crushed the mechanic's legs, pinning him to the ground.

Deity, container, and the orbiting constellation of brains rose into the darkness, leaving the mechanic to die, alone, and screaming.

Chapter 105

The defense minister and his family slept in designer nightwear, on Memory Foam mattresses, between silk sheets. Such possessions were considered contraband in North Korea, but rank had its privileges.

A deep rumble and crack interrupted their dreams. The plain front exterior of their home tore off in one flat piece and fell aside. Their collection of Western luxury goods was exposed to the outside world.

"This is a good start." The deity descended from the night, through the cloud of dust. Brains circled Him in their orbits. He walked past the minister and his wife cowering in their bed, and helped Himself to a box of Godiva chocolates from their gaudy gold-and-silver armoire.

"The Aztecs believed that cocoa was a bridge between earth and heaven." Extracting a thick milk chocolate bar from the box; its wrapper peeled itself in his fingers. He took a bite, chewed, and grinned from ear to ear. "Oh my. I can see why." He stuffed half the bar in His mouth. "If chocolate is as good as they say, then I'm definitely going to try cocaine."

The minister's son and daughter rushed into the bedroom, stopping cold at the sight of the stranger and the missing wall. While his wife rose and joined their children, the minister confronted the intruder, finger pointed at His chest. Before the man could speak, the deity waved His hand in a dismissive gesture. Vertigo overwhelmed the four Koreans. They dropped to the floor, retching with nausea.

Wiping His mouth on the back of His sleeve, He explained, "You're experiencing the power of Sung-hun, bastard child of Kim Il-sung. His mother was mildly psychic, the Russians—do you remember the Russians of CIG-1, Minister? Under their conditioning, he developed his minor gift, instilling a faint queasiness on touch, into something quite effective. Under My control, that gift becomes more realized than it could in a dozen human lifetimes."

The minister's wife pulled herself up on the arm of her French Heritage armchair. The vertigo overwhelmed her. She vomited down the front of her silk nightgown. The deity smiled down at her, amused.

"Come with Me," He said. Still in their nightclothes, and rendered helpless by the intense dizziness, the minister and his family were unable to resist the unseen force as it scooped them up. They dropped into the shipping container propped against the building. "I know who should have some cocaine."

Chapter 106

Fueled by MDMA, methamphetamine, and Viagra, the party in the premier's red velvet bedroom raged into the early morning hours. The premier was the host, the only man in attendance, and the only one there by choice. Three young women were also at the party, his personal *manjokcho*, or satisfaction team. They had been drafted as they emerged from childhood to serve his carnal needs. Their young soft bodies barely covered in lingerie, their eyes were soulless, defeated, and dead.

Coming down from the drugs, the doughy middle-aged man barely noticed the deity watching him from the foot of the bed. There was something familiar about the intruder. But the drugged and inebriated premier couldn't connect the face to a memory. Too strung out to call his guards, he grunted and waved the interloper away.

"Of all the aspects of My creation, I'm proudest of sex. Violence, coercion, and lies are all committed in its acquisition. So much effort, such little reward. You people will kill each other for a chance at a few seconds of meager euphoria. If lust was any stronger, your kind would have wiped yourselves out trying to procreate." The deity fingered through the leftover narcotics. "Why is it that today, of all days, you're out of cocaine? Pity."

He swept the pills, powder, and paraphernalia off the teak credenza and faced the premier. "I've watched you over the years. Like I've watched everyone. You say you like pretty women with long fingernails, but that's not entirely true. The fingernails are practical. With manicures

362

they can't sneak out of your little pleasure palace when you're away. The first policeman who crossed their path would spot those long Western nails. And this city is teeming with policemen, isn't it?"

A ball of frost hovered before the stranger. The ice peeled away, revealing a frozen brain at its core. "This was Jeong-bok. She would have been Kim Jeong-bok if her father had kept his promise and married her mother. Instead, he had her sent to No. 16, the reeducation camp. While he had his daughter killed and her brain turned into the first of these weapons."

The deity opened His hands before Him, palms up and fingers curled. The premier's *manjokcho* did the same. Gawking that their hands were out of their control.

"Her mother didn't last long at No. 16, not under those conditions. In the end, she looked something like this." He pantomimed stabbing at his eyes. Under His control, the girls did too. Their long nails tore through their eyelids and into their eyes. They screamed. As did the premier, recoiling from their bleeding faces.

Smiling, the stranger turned to leave. The premier jerked to attention and followed, mimicking the deity step-by-step, leaving his maimed and crying courtesans behind. He wobbled outside and joined the defense minister and his family huddled in the cold steel box.

Chapter 107

President of the Supreme People's Assembly and his family thought dousing their home with accelerant was their idea. In the wee hours of the morning, they ran through the house, splashing the furniture, the carpet, and their closets with *soju*, Korean rice alcohol.

"Why don't you give me that?" the deity asked the president's daughter. She handed over the half-empty bottle and rushed away to take another from her father's liquor cabinet. The deity gave the bottleneck a sniff, turned up His nose, and forced Himself to take a swig. Eyes shooting open in shock, He spit the rest out on the floor, coughing. "Disgusting!"

He dropped the *soju*. The thick glass bottle bounced down the stairs without breaking. "I'll hold out for cocaine."

The president's supply of *soju* exhausted, he and his family waited at the base of the stairs for their next instruction. "Did you know this would have been Jin-bom's birthday?"

"No," they dutifully answered in chorus. The deity found the North Koreans remarkably susceptible to mind control.

"Do you know who Jin-bom was?"

"No."

One of His frozen brains floated forward. "Here's Jin-bom, or what's left of her. The president met her once, when the Great Leader gave you a tour of CIG-1, almost a year before he died. He was so proud of his 'Shining Ones,' and his so-called clone. Of course, when he died they had to follow. Kim Jong-il couldn't have any of his bastards floating around. Especially Jin-bom. She would have rallied the others against him in a coup."

The North Koreans listened, patient and unaffected.

This was too easy. The deity rolled his eyes, bored. "Why don't you set this place on fire and get in the box? This party's over. The ultimate party's about to begin."

Chapter 108

The deity floated through the hospital halls and the carnage. To His left, a man with a broken arm bludgeoned a boy to death with his cast. To His right, a doctor cut an old woman's throat with a pair of surgical scissors. As He passed, the man in the cast and the doctor turned on each other.

While the men flew at each other in a blind rage, He reached out to open the double doors that led to the Supreme Leader's luxury hospital room. The doors moved an inch. Through the gap, He saw a stick of wood had been shoved through the handles, barring the door shut.

"Pathetic." The deity pulled a little harder, the stick snapped in two, and the doors flew open with enough force to break them off their hinges.

Inside, Kim Jong-un hid behind his bed with his wife and daughter. One foot in bandages after a minor surgery, he shielded his face with his hand, first from the violence, then from the vision of his grandfather, young and strong, as He floated into the room.

"Supreme Leader, allow Me to introduce your uncles, Yang-gon and To-chun." Two of the frozen brains orbited the deity between Himself and the cringing leader. "Yang-gon was an angry boy. I'm using his gift to flood the hospital with rage.

"To-chun was more prosaic in his short life. Ironically, the boy with a mind that could move matter wasn't inclined to move much himself. Both their aptitudes are better used in My care."

The wall ripped open. Shattered, the broken bits drifted off in the wind. The Supreme Leader gripped his wife and child.

"Impressive, isn't he?" The deity regarded one of the floating brains as it passed in front of His face. "Not powerful enough to deliver a nuclear missile. But I wrote the laws of physics. I'll show your scientists how to build a device to put your bombs in twenty-two major cities around the world. That should make for interesting times."

The open end of the shipping container slid up to the gaping hole in the wall. He shoved the Supreme Leader and his family invisibly and unceremoniously inside.

Chapter 109

The container tilted, spilling the four families of the North Korean elite onto the top floor of the Ryugyong Hotel, Pyongyang's tallest building. The windows were empty frames, and a strong cold wind whipped through the level. Someday it might be a luxury restaurant, if the North Koreans ever get a chance to finish it. Now it was empty, open concrete on top of more empty, open concrete.

With a gesture resembling a man wadding up a napkin and tossing it over the side, the deity crumpled the empty steel box and sent it over the edge of the skyscraper, careless of where it landed.

Rebar pulled itself from the concrete walls and wrapped tight around the wrists of the four most powerful men in the DPRK, biting into their skin and dangling them over the edge. Blood ran down their arms, staining their imported silk pajamas. Their wives, children, and grandchildren, huddled against the wall of the top floor, shivered in cold, confusion, and fear. All eyes, wide in terror, were on the entity who looked like a long-haired younger version of their late president, their Great Leader Kim Il-sung.

The five psychic brains slowly orbited the deity as He opened up His arms in welcome. "I would apologize for the late-night interruption, but you are all beneath My consideration."

The youngest of the four men was crying. Jong-un, the pampered heir to the Kim dynasty had never known fear and suffering. The other three, the defense minister, the premier and the president of the Supreme

People's Assembly, had known fear and suffering, through war, famine, or time in the labor camps. They had been conditioned, however, to hide their terror.

"Tears do not become the Supreme Leader, but don't stop crying. Your family has tormented these people to the point where you're the only one inside these borders capable of tears." He smiled. "That's why you will live. To make you watch as I shred your inheritance piece by piece. When this country is reduced to rubble, I'll let you free to roam the wastes."

The deity turned to the defense minister. "Not so for you. You've been planning a coup since the Dear Leader's overdose. Not that that bothers Me, of course. But I'm better off without someone of your ambition around."

The former general didn't flinch. "You're a hard man, Pak. I know. I've seen through your eyes what you've done in the name of the state, but truly in service to yourself. There isn't even any point in torturing you, is there? But how about your family?"

One of the children was ripped out of her mother's hands by an invisible force and floated, lingering a moment in front of the defense minister's stoic face.

The deity asked, "Not even going to say goodbye, are you?"

Pak looked away. His granddaughter launched into the night sky. The deity squinted into the distance, watching for the impact. A streetlight went out. He looked over his shoulder at the child's mother. Her gaze was cast to the floor.

The deity shook His head in disappointment. "An entire nation raised without expectation of happiness. How am I supposed to enjoy killing you?"

He pulled four more children from their mothers and shot them into the air like rockets. Their parents followed. Finally, He yanked an old woman, the defense minister's middle-aged wife, from the pile. Considering her as she floated in midair, trembling in anguish, the deity smiled. "At last, I got a reaction out of one of you. And all I had to do was destroy two generations of her family."

He let her drift to the floor. "Go, old woman. Spend the rest of your days in misery, remembering all you lost. Go, and tell everyone what happened here. A panic should thin the herd."

Without hesitation, the old woman scuttled out the door to the stairs. No one watched her leave.

Without turning to look at him, the deity gripped the defense minister by the ankle. With the biokinetic power inherent in His vessel, He broke down the minister's proteins. Flesh slid from bone. Organs spilled out of the ribcage and poured over the building's edge, leaving skeleton and tendons hanging from the rebar like an obscene windchime.

"Stand," God ordered the rest of the families, and they stood. "Now, go get Me some cocaine."

Chapter 110

Breathing hard, Ainia ran up the 105 stories of the hotel. Her satphone, pinned to the DPRK Army harness, bounced against her chest, its LCD screen her only light. Sweat ran down her face and around the curves of her smile.

Halfway up, she almost ran into an old woman running down the other way. Ainia stopped and watched the woman's white night clothes disappear into the darkness below. "That was—unexpected."

Ten floors up, she stepped aside again to let a dozen panicked men, women and children through. "What the fuck is going on up there?"

Reaching the door at the top of the long, dark stairs, she took a moment to catch her breath and double-check her gear. Resting one hand on the door and a knife from one of the Chinese agents in the other, she kicked the door in.

Three men and one bloody skeleton dangled over the edge from tangled strips of rebar. Ainia sized them up and dismissed them as irrelevant.

God sat at the edge of the floor, looking out over Pyongyang from its highest point. If He heard Ainia at the door He didn't show it. The frozen brains spun around His head in slow, irregular orbits.

She flexed her grip on the knife and crept toward the target until she was in lunging range. With two hands she drove the blade between His ribs. It hit God like He was an oak tree, penetrating a quarter of an inch at best. What should have been a descent over the edge into death became an annoyed shrug as God floated to his feet and turned around.

"Congratulations. You're the first person in two millennia to surprise Me."

Ainia seized up, held by His telekinetic force. The knife landed with its handle balanced halfway over the edge.

"You of all people might enjoy what I have planned. What was it? Couldn't pass up a chance to kill God?"

"I've sworn my oaths and I have my orders," Ainia forced the words out through her clamped jaw.

"I know better than to try to change your mind." God cocked an eyebrow. "How did you find Me?"

"What? Can't see the future anymore?"

"No. But I remember the past. And I don't remember any Amazons. Not a one."

"You're a liar," she sneered.

"I am. I lied when I said I'd let you live."

"There's something You should hear before You throw me off the edge."

"Oh? And what's that?"

The satphone pinned to Ainia's harness came to life, "Are you there, God? It's me, Gabby. *Let me bend your ear.*"

The brains froze in midair, as did God.

Gabby kept talking from her hospital bed. "What's up? Cat got your tongue? You just found out the hard way—human body, human weakness, huh? Park tells me You're not as nice as Your son made You out to be. That's a shame."

With the zip of an incoming bullet, one of the brains shattered with a snap.

Gabby continued, "Oh, I heard that! That was Isaac. He's using the marksmanship of a half-dozen Chinese commandos. That makes him a pretty good shot with a rifle."

A second zip and the next brain shattered.

"You're probably wondering about the windage. There's a lot of weather between you and the ground. Pollyanna's helping him with her power of positive thinking. Against the odds, the air's as smooth as silk."

Another impossible shot shattered the third brain.

"You're still up there, so I guess the brain you use to move stuff is still intact. Well, that won't be for—"

Two more shots and the fourth and fifth brains shattered. Ainia dropped to the ground, landing hard on her back like a fallen mannequin.

"That's five. Well, it's been nice talking at You but I'm going to give You back to Ainia. Have a nice trip, God. See Ya in the fall!"

Still on her back, Ainia bucked out with both feet and kicked the deity's ankles out from under Him.

He grabbed the ledge with one hand.

Ainia scooped up the knife, drove it under His fingers, and pried them off the ledge. He fell away. She spit after Him. "You'll remember *this* Amazon."

She backed away from the ledge, turned to the three surviving members of North Korea's ruling elite. "Now, what should I do with you assholes?"

Chapter 111

God fell down the sloped side of the Ryugyong Hotel, sliding then bouncing. Impacts snapped a bone or two, which re-formed as He passed through the air. He finally hit the ground and bounced across the street, a mangled mess, but already healing.

Downtown Pyongyang after curfew was unlit and empty, a gray concrete shell of a city.

Back in the tube, He'd toughened his muscle tissue and bones and severed the nerves to His pain center. But it had been a long fall and He'd lost a dozen pounds of skin, bone, and blood along the side of the hotel. There was a lot of damage to be undone.

97:4 broke from the shadows into the moonlight, like a cowboy, twirling a lasso of copper wire in one hand, a handful of pages in the other.

God snickered, staggering to His feet, the bloody, shredded uniform hanging from His body in rags. "What do you expect to do with that? You can't hope to intimidate Me, Jannete. You're powerless without My Book."

"*'His lightnings lit up the world. The earth saw and trembled.'*" 97:4 swung the wire in a wide arc and cast the lasso..

It wrapped around his neck, His body's toughened tissues too slow to dodge. "Is this some pathet—"

With a burst of light like a camera flash, she sent a jolt down the wire. He landed inside an empty concrete planter. His voice crackled through charred vocal cords. "Where...did you find...a Bible...in this country?"

"This isn't a Bible." She held up the clutch of pages. "I tore these from the *Juche*, where these people put their faith. All this time I thought my power came from Your Word, but that was a lie. Faith itself brings the lightning, faith placed in things." She stood out of the deity's reach. "What are you?"

He crawled out of the planter. "I am the Creator, the Alpha and the Omega. Just like it says in the Book...the other Book."

"There's nothing in the Bible to describe you."

"Not in the Bible you've been reading."

"I've spent my life in Your service, what I thought You stood for."

"And you served Me well. Look at Me, the circle is squared. A perfect God stands inside His imperfect creation at last. All thanks to you and your friends." He laughed.

97:4 took another bite of philosophy.

God shook His head. "You're going to run out of paper sooner or later and you can't—"

A pair of Pyongyang police officers hurried around the corner, nightsticks drawn.

She lashed out with the wire; wrapped it around His ankle. A flash of lighting and another shock knocked him off his feet. His head hit the edge of the planter.

The police officers opted for the better part of valor, escaping the way they came.

When He came to, 97:4 had the wire wrapped around his neck, screaming, "...all of it? The devotion. The service. The dedication. And You weren't even up there? You were down here. Watching us behind our eyes."

Pulling the end of the copper wire with both hands and her foot firmly pressed against His back, she shouted. "What are You? Demon?"

The air stank of ozone and burning flesh. The copper burned His throat faster than it could heal.

"Demiurge?" she asked. Electricity crackled down her Lichtenberg scars into the wire. "Something worse?"

She screamed and dropped the wire. The smell of burning flesh filled the air, wafting from God's throat and 97:4's hands. She staggered to the ground, spent, and staring at Him from between her burnt fingers. "I believed in You."

God wiped His mouth on the back of His wrist, His ears still ringing. "I never asked you to. I never asked anything of you, any of you."

God wobbled to His knees. "You're spent. I'll heal in a minute. Then it'll be My turn."

"Not the way You're thinking," said Exposition Joe from behind.

Joe put his hand on God's brow. "*For I know the plans I have for you, plans to prosper you and not to harm you, plans to give you hope and a future.*"

The boy stepped back, hands up like a faith healer.

Park rushed forward from the same darkness where Joe had emerged and helped 97:4 to her feet. She asked, "Did it work?"

Joe asked the deity, still on His knees, "I don't know. Did it?"

"Joseph, what have you done?" He whispered.

Joe relaxed. "Nothing You don't deserve. Nothing You didn't do to me years ago, back when You *saved* me."

Park sighed in relief. "The Braincases, the Collective, this Clone you're inhabiting, even Joe here. You're nothing without us. You didn't enable Joe's card with Your blessing years ago in the basement of Fray's church. You stole it. Boosting Joe's card the way You boosted the Braincases. The future You let him see became the future to come. But the power came from Joe, You just regulated it. Like Isaac's card, everything You can do comes from one of us, doesn't it?

"Speaking of Isaac, he used the Russians' knowledge, got inside Joe's head with hypnosis, and reversed Your connection. Flip-flopped the entire relationship. The only future You'll see is the one Joe wants You to see."

97:4 said, "You're not the master of fate anymore. Now fate is Your master." She waited fruitlessly for God to respond. "What happens now, Park?"

Park unbuttoned his coat and handed it to 97:4. "That's up to Joe. He can think about it while Wu gets us out of this god-forsaken country."

Joe ran his fingers through his hair. "Oh, I already know what we're going to do. We're going to walk the earth, helping people. Should be humbling."

97:4 nodded. "That sounds good. Where'd you get that idea?"

"I got it out of a book." A paperback materialized in Joe's hand—small, white, worn. He held the cover up for the others to see the title embossed in gold, *Create Your Own Adventure.*

Park and 97:4 laughed.

God wept.

Chapter 112

Gabby climbed out of the cab with a wince. 97:4 paid the driver and helped her hobble up the steps at the Virginia address. "Come on, gimpy. Hustle on in here before someone sees you."

The building was a stock three-story office. An uninspired design, it was literally and metaphorically beige. Gabby pulled herself up the stairs with both hands on the single handrail. "Keep talkin' and I'll make us a matched set of gimps. I don't care if you did kick God's ass."

"Or whatever that was..." 97:4's sentence drifted off in uncertainty. She reached to help her friend up the last couple of steps, but Gabby brushed her off.

"I got it." Gabby stopped at the top of the stairs, leaned back, and took in the office, three stories of unassuming, uninspired early eighties architecture. "So this is Project Dead Blind's headquarters, huh? Not exactly a flying aircraft carrier, is it?"

"There's one parked out back on blocks. Besides, we're supposed to keep a low profile." 97:4 opened the door.

Gabby shuffled inside. "Tell me we have the whole building to ourselves at least."

"Sorry, the bottom floor is leased out to a debt collection agency. Lots of people come and go with their heads low. Good cover for us."

Isaac Deal slid down the banister in a full tuxedo. "*Gabby Gabby, bo Babby. Banana fanna fo Fabby!* Come here and give me a hug!"

He rushed forward and grabbed Gabby. Over his shoulder she looked at 97:4 and said, "Low profile, huh?"

"Relatively. Isaac, let her go and help her up the stairs."

"The stairs I can show you, but I haven't found the secret elevator to the underground speedboat dock."

They joined Park and Pollyanna on the third-floor. Park, Ainia and Pollyanna took a break from sorting boxes to welcome Gabby. The office was walled with filing cabinets, and the desks were stacked with handwritten files, folders, and notebooks. There was something different about the place. Gabby couldn't put her finger on it right away, not until she'd finished saying her hellos. "There's no computers."

Park nodded. "Ensign never trusted them, for security purposes."

"Everything is on paper?"

"Yep. Decades of files going back to when Dead Blind was a sub-project of MKUltra. Not only on paper, but encoded. Every file is a puzzle."

Isaac rubbed his hands together. "Ah, puzzles..."

Park smiled. "Ensign held his cards close to his vest, even from me. I've only been here a few times, and I was his second-in-command. "But now that I'm in charge, things are going to be different around here. I'm asking for everyone's help cracking these codes and sorting the information."

Pollyanna drew off her e-cigarette. "Well, why the hell not? After last week, it's gotta be downhill from here."

Gabby looked around for the team's seventh member. "Where's Exposition Joe?"

Ainia cut Park off before he could answer. "Still in North Korea for all we know. He took off while everyone was still climbing onto Wu's truck."

"You let him go?"

Ainia shrugged. "It's not like we could stop him."

Chapter 113

It was another dirt crossroad. There had been many dirt roads since they'd escaped the capital. Exposition Joe stopped at the intersection and smiled. His hair and eyes once blond and blue were now jet-black. His features were barely recognizable under the Asian recasting provided by his companion's touch. The power to heal wounds wasn't far from the power to shape flesh.

"Really? Again?" the other teenager asked.

"Get used to it. I'll never get tired of this."

"You can get tired of anything, given time. Get on with it then."

"Like You're in a rush." Exposition Joe opened the dogeared paperback, looking ahead to where the Book branched off, three—no—four ways.

Joe flipped back and forth in the book, surveying the options before committing to a choice. Going ahead would lead to nothing but shutdown mines. Going back would lead to trouble in Pyongyang. Going left or right would lead to villages. Villages all but abandoned by the government. Filled with people that could use their help.

"I'm going to leave it up to You," Joe said to his companion. "Page twenty-six or page sixty-seven?"

"I don't care."

"I know you don't care. That's why we're doing this. You're going to learn how to ca—"

"Sixty-seven. Just shut up and go left."

"There. That wasn't so hard, was it?" Joe closed the book and turned to the left. His companion followed. "I hope we can branch out from healing. Healing is good, but these people really need food more than anything. Maybe You can start small and work your way up to loaves and fishes."

His companion groaned.

"I'm going to need a name for You too. How's *Jesús?*"

"I hate it."

"Then *Jesús* it is. Hurry up, *Jesús*. There's a big world out there, and a lot of people who need Your help."

Joseph walked down the dirt road. *Jesús* followed.

<<<<>>>>

Thanks to everyone who contributed to the refinement of *The Faith Machine*, workshoppers, editors, and book clubbers:

Kris Celario, Val Delane, Jennifer Derilo, Mark Engels, Israel Finn, Theresa Flannery, Amanda Hutchins, Melissa Milazzo, Melissa Miller, Deborah Nemeth, Miranda Osguthorpe, Dan and Jessica Palacio, Kaelan Rhywiol, Lou San Vicente, David Schmidt, Elaine Galey Smith, Ryan and Virginia Smith , A.Z. Sperry, Chad Stroup, Brian Vargo, Wes Warner, Cherry Weiner, & Ben White

#

About the Author

Tone Milazzo is the author of *Picking Up the Ghost, The Faith Machine,* and the *ESPionage Role-Playing Game.*

Stories have always been Tone's first love. When the first hunter told another about the one who got away, stories made us human. Stories lead to understanding. Fiction, religion, biographies, gossip, gaming, and history, it all goes into the slow cooker and out comes ideas.

To those ends Tone's been around, professionally speaking. Marine, taxi driver, teacher, assistant to scientists, and coder. This breath of experience has given Tone a little knowledge about a lot of things, good and bad.

He lives in San Diego with his wife Melissa Milazzo (author of *Time is a Flat Circle*) and two dogs, all of whom are more capable than he is.

Past Titles

Running Wild Stories Anthology, Volume 1

Running Wild Anthology of Novellas, Volume 1

Jersey Diner by Lisa Diane Kastner

Magic Forgotten by Jack Hillman

The Kidnapped by Dwight L. Wilson

Running Wild Stories Anthology, Volume 2

Running Wild Novella Anthology, Volume 2, Part 1

Running Wild Novella Anthology, Volume 2, Part 2

Running Wild Stories Anthology, Volume 3

Running Wild's Best of 2017, AWP Special Edition

Running Wild's Best of 2018

Build Your Music Career From Scratch, Second Edition by Andrae Alexander

Writers Resist: Anthology 2018 with featured editors Sara Marchant and Kit-Bacon Gressitt

Magic Forbidden by Jack Hillman

Frontal Matter: Glue Gone Wild by Suzanne Samples

Mickey: The Giveaway Boy by Robert M. Shafer

Dark Corners by Reuben "Tihi" Hayslett

The Resistors by Dwight L. Wilson

Open My Eyes by Tommy Hahn

Legendary by Amelia Kibbie

Christine, Released by E. Burke

Running Wild Press publishes stories that cross genres with great stories and writing. Our team consists of:

Lisa Diane Kastner, Founder and Executive Editor
Barbara Lockwood, Editor
Cecile Sarruf, Editor
Peter A. Wright, Editor
Rebecca Dimyan, Editor
Benjamin White, Editor
Andrew DiPrinzio, Editor
Amrita Raman, Operations Manager
Lisa Montagne, Director of Education

Learn more about us and our stories at www.runningwildpress.com

Loved this story and want more? Follow us at
www.runningwildpress.com, www.facebook/runningwildpress, on
Twitter @lisadkastner @RunWildBooks

CPSIA information can be obtained
at www.ICGtesting.com
Printed in the USA
LVHW010139140520
655469LV00012B/200

9 781947 041479